BURIED TRUST

Kingsley is back!
Fans will not be disappointed as she takes on an evil so sinister it could bring death to her family, and an unsuspecting farming community. Kudos to Hughes on this unique and compelling series.
—**P. D. Halt**, Killer Nashville Silver Falchion Award Best Suspense Novel Finalist

****

"Nancy Hughes is a voice to watch. In BURIED TRUST, she layers an authentic setting with a complex plot, beautiful prose, and touching, believable characters. Her Kingsley is a treasure."
—**Saralyn Richard**, award-winning author of the Detective Parrott mystery series.

DEDICATION

In memory of the Covid 19 victims,
their families, and friends.
In honor of the scientists who persevered to produce
the vaccine to crush this deadly pandemic.

OTHER BOOKS BY NANCY HUGHES

The Dying Hour

The Innocent Hour

A Matter of Trust

Redeeming Trust

Vanished: A Trust Mystery

Buried Trust

A Mystery Novel

by Nancy A. Hughes

A Black Opal Books Publication

Buried Warning
Prologue

Summer, 1849

She terrible sick," the young mother whispered to their children's father. She ministered to their little daughter with heart-felt anguish, having nothing but a wet rag to soothe her fevered brow. The mother dipped it in the tepid water again, which did little to lower her temperature. "What we gonna do?"

August heat and humidity pressed on their companions, huddled in the underground shelter. Black fabric covered the window wells, and a lone candle lit the cavernous space. They remained silent as statues, knowing that exposure might betray them to killers. They had followed the route by night, then would proceed tonight when the knock came.

"She can't travel." She followed her husband's gaze to their three other children, the youngest barely two, and made a decision. Setting the five-year-old in her father's arms, she headed toward the steps, shrouded in shadows cast by the solitary candle.

Mounting the cellar steps on all fours lest she stumble, she eased open the door. It made the tiniest squeak but nobody in the great house responded. Ahead, ambers glowed beneath a kettle hung in the kitchen's corner fireplace. The house, otherwise, seemed dark. Silently she proceeded, groping, hoping to find something—anything—to help her child.

As she rummaged in the kitchen, the homeowner appeared as quietly as a spirit. Swallowing her fear, the mother begged, "Missy, please help. My baby awful bad sick." From somewhere nearby a clock bonged twelve times.

Her hostess followed her into the vast darkened cellar. "There," she said, pointing to the little girl, cradled in her father's arms. Three distinctive knocks on the exterior wooden door that led to the woods echoed through the basement. Twenty-six men, women, and children jumped to their feet. The anguished mother sobbed, torn about the risk to her daughter.

"Leave her with me," their hostess said. "I'll nurse her, then send her with those who follow. What is her name?"

"Rebecca." The hidden cellar door to freedom opened and a scruffy mountain man beckoned to the travelers. Silent as shadows, each gathered their bundles and headed outside single file. "Go with your family," the homeowner insisted. "They need you," she added, nodding to the tiniest boy. "I'll hide and care for your little one until she's well enough to rejoin the travelers."

"God bless you, ma'am," she whispered, entrusting Rebecca to the lady. With a final kiss to her daughter's forehead, she herded her others into the line that disappeared into the inky, moonless night.

Mrs. Krick made a hasty nest for their newest guest in one of their grown children's old bedrooms while Mister closed the draperies. Ordinarily, their travelers stayed below briefly, but the dank cellar was no place for such a sick child. Gently she removed the drowsy child's rags and bathed her. The little angel was skin and bones with sores on her ebony skin.

She dressed her in a muslin nightshirt she'd dug from the old steamer trunk, cradled and rocked her while spooning small sips of water through her parched lips. Mentally, she inventoried the herbal remedies and tinctures she had on hand and what herbs to harvest from her kitchen garden. She'd gather garlic, bergamot, and calendula for teas and mullein's large velvety leaves to cover her poultices.

"Poor little thing. She needs the doctor."

"Can't risk it. You've heard him condemn Mr. Lincoln. He'd tell. And the bounty hunters would find us. Brew her a tonic; mix up some salve. Then it'll be in God's hands." The pair offered prayers on her behalf for His intervention.

Chapter 1

Present Day

Did you see those weird lights again last night?" Todd Henning called to his wife, Kingsley, through the break in the white pine fence row they were planting. He tossed the post hole digger aside to part the branches and hear her response.

"Just those three other times," she replied, angling to see him better. "It's strange. I thought the Amish farmer to our west was buying the land for his son who's getting married. It's their custom to buy a farm for the next generation, adjacent to theirs, if possible, to farm together. Those sixty acres to our east would have been right-sized for farming with horses or mules.

"If he bought it, why would he be prowling around at night with lanterns? They go to bed as soon as it's dark to get up at five for milking."

"I suppose we could check with the recorder of deeds. Or a realtor. Or the township, since you're so curious. In the meantime, pass me the metal measure and a screwdriver." They landed near her feet with a *thunk*. "Thanks." She anchored the tape's metal loop into the ground with the screwdriver, then dragged the retractable ruler to mark the exact distance, securing it with a rock to prevent it from retracting. "I'm surprised he didn't buy our land when it came on the market," she continued, momentarily neglecting her job to mark another pine's position.

"Way too expensive with that historic stone house. They'd have to retrofit it to make it *plain*. And the Historical Society would pitch a fit. Besides, our seven-acre property is too small for their kind of farming. No, much better to build a house and barn on undeveloped farmland like the property next door," he replied.

"That would have been ideal for us if the Amish bought it. We're so used to the previous owner renting it for crop farming. What if a developer has bought it and throws up hundreds of track houses? Or worse, what if zoning is changed from agricultural to commercial? We could end up living next to a rendering plant."

Silence caught the mother's attention. "Where's Billy!" She dropped the metal measure and frantically scanned the front yard. "He was right behind me a minute ago." Todd stopped what he was doing, and the pair jogged through the yard, calling frantic orders for their two-year-old son to show himself immediately.

"Could he have gone into the house?" Kingsley called, skidding to a stop, gasped, having circled the exterior of their home.

"He can't manage the door. Oh, dear God—the road." They plowed through the twelve-foot wild honeysuckle bushes, rhododendron, and mountain laurel that separated their front lawn from the rural two-lane. A quick look left, then right revealed no dark-haired toddler in a red hooded jacket.

"You go east; I'll go west," Todd said, pointing and sprinting toward the Amish farm while she ran toward the property of their recent discussion. No little boy.

Panting, Kingsley wailed to Todd. "Not again!" Burned in her subconscious, no matter how much therapy, yoga, and prayer, she could not stop the day-and-nightmare residual left from their then-infant son's being kidnapped. Kingsley rarely let Billy out of her sight unless he was secure with family or responsible adults. She knew that wretched things can and do happen to ordinary people.

Circling to the back lawn a second time where a play gym anchored the back-left corner, the frantic mother stopped. Billy, trotting from the farmer's field, was clutching the filthiest little dog Kingsley had ever seen. Not wanting to alarm her child and cause it to bite Billy, she summoned her most soothing voice. "Put the puppy down, Billy."

The child scowled and stuck out his lower lip. "Mine!"

"No, honey, that puppy belongs to somebody. And they're probably worried about him." Billy clutched the mutt to his chest, hugging its skinny body against his muddied red jacket, the little dog's feet reaching the child's knees, its mouth inches from Billy's cheek.

Not wanting to frighten the dog and cause him to snap, she tried another tactic. "Some little boy will be worried— Billy—stop! You're squeezing him. That might hurt." If the child released his grip just a little, maybe the pup would wriggle free and run home. Instead, the dog covered Billy's face with sloppy kisses. The cat-loving mother scrunched her face in disgust. *Oh, yuk!*

At that moment, Todd ran around the east corner of the house, braking hard. He grinned. "What have we got here?"

"Your son has found the grungiest little dog and won't give him up."

"Put him down for a minute, son. Let's have a look. Maybe he has a collar with some ID. Then we can locate his owner. By the looks of him, he's had a romp in the creek."

Rather than following his father's instructions, Billy clutched the dog tighter, swiveling his back to his parents. "No! Mine!"

"What are we going to do?" Kingsley mouthed to Todd.

"Billy, if we're going to find his family, we'll need to clean him up first. Do you think he'd like a bath in the laundry tub? You can help shampoo him."

Billy peered over the dog's head at his father as if he knew he was being played. "Maybe the puppy would like a treat?" Todd suggested. Billy's little brain appeared to be working the new angle. "Do you think he'd like Pandora's kitty treats or a cookie? Mommy, are there enough cookies for Billy and the pup?"

Billy smiled. "Cookies. The big ones. With the chips."

"We'll need to fashion a collar and leash, so he won't get lost in the house. Mommy, do you have something of Pandora's we can use?"

Cats do not have leashes, you fool, she telepathed, but instead verbalized a reasonable response. "I'll see what I can makeshift. In the meantime, why don't you see if you can keep Billy *safe*?" she hissed over her shoulder. At the front door, she glanced back at her filthy child who was beaming with delight at the pup who was licking his chin.

Shortly she returned with a skinny leather belt, a leftover from her pre-Billy size zero wardrobe. She handed Todd the belt and a leather punch she'd snagged from the basement workbench. He eyeballed the dog, gauging the size of his neck, and punched several holes near the buckle. Approaching cautiously, he slipped the loop over the animal's head and fastened it securely. "There. Do you think you can walk him to the door?"

"Todd! Persian runner?"

"Easy, Mom. I'll pick him up *if* we can get someone's cooperation."

If only. Kingsley knew she'd wish later that they'd grabbed a camera. Filthy dog and child, standing side by side on a crate in the basement, watching Todd half-fill the tub with warm water. Her precious boy looked for all the world like a miniature of her husband with his crystal blue eyes, curly dark hair, and dimples when he laughed. When Todd reached for liquid detergent, she reacted. "Eyes!" And leapt to remedy the situation by running upstairs for baby shampoo.

Todd lifted the dog into the water, letting Billy maneuver his plume of a tail. The dog tolerated his bath surprisingly well, bracing his front paws on the divider that separated the double tubs while licking his muzzle continually when Todd hosed off the shampoo. Blackened water cursed down the drain, revealing a beige dog with black tips on his ears. Todd laughed. "He's adorable!"

Oh, brother! Not you too. "Daddy," she hissed in her best executive-banker voice, "Do not get attached. We need to find his owner. He's merely clean enough to ride in the Explorer." Her husband looked up quizzically. "Well, he's not getting in my Lexus," she preempted.

"Dear—it may have sentimental value since your Grammy left it to you, but it's ancient."

"But it's my ancient clean. Boycar. Dog. Dad. SUV. You get it?"

"Yes'm."

దిలిలి

"That's Scruffy! At least that's what the kids call him," said Jacob, the Henning's next-door dairy farmer. He'd just hiked uphill from the barn, wiping his florid face with a red bandana. "We thought he was black!"

"So, he's yours?"

"Well, we've been feeding him. Took him to the vet. Got his shots. He sleeps in our summer kitchen then spends the day out and about. Sneaks in the coal bin to nap. One of these day's he's going to get hit on the road. He has the *wanderlust*." The Amish man gazed at the two-year-old, planted in the grass, his arm around the pup that was snuggled against him. The pair looked adoringly at each other.

"He must belong to someone," Kingsley said. "Any idea who? Is he chipped? Anyone reported him missing?"

"Vet said no. He's been around, ah, maybe six months. Someone put him out on the highway when he was a puppy and sped off." He frowned. "But I wouldn't worry about him. Won't be long now till he's just a splat on the highway."

Kingsley's temper flared. "That's a terrible thing to say!"

The farmer shrugged. "Tis true. Couple of our cats get hit every year, but we have no mice in the barn. Guess it's nature's way." The Amish man nodded toward the boy and dog. "Boy loves that dog."

"But. But. I'm a cat person."

"Yeah. Got a few dozen of them ourselves."

"But we're gone all day. Who's going to let him out?"

The farmer approached the dog, and with no objection from the pup, pried his mouth open to look at its teeth. "He's a young'un—I'd say, maybe a year? House train him and he'll be good for twelve hours. Dogs hate to soil. Wait here. I'll get you the name of the vet. She can tell you all about him."

Kingsley looked from Todd to Billy to Scruffy, shaking her head. "First off, that name's gotta go. It's undignified."

As they entered their home via the front door, Kingsley remembered Pandora, her long-haired tuxedo cat who'd arrived when Kingsley had no intention of adopting a pet. Her best friend, Barrie, had brought the kitten one stormy night, complete with her motorized litter box and plenty of food. Same ploy—the kitten was doomed to the kill shelter unless someone would take her. Kingsley had left her own adorable Pesto with her parents when she left for college, after which her mom refused to return her. Pandora and Pesto could have been twins, Barrie having seen Pesto's photo on Kingsley's desk. The cat lover was hooked.

The Hennings foursome stood on the same square yard in their foyer not sure what to do next. Pandora was nowhere in sight. "Go for it," Todd said, encouraging Kingsley to unbuckle the leash and let the puppy explore. Nose down, he sniffed in widening circles, finally picking the living room to his left. "Nose brains," Todd said. "They can go blind and deaf, but as long as they can smell, they can adapt."

What caught the pup's focus eventually was Todd's leather sofa, a remnant of his bachelor condo days, its back to the front wall and flanked by double-hung windows with deep window sills. As they stood watching—aghast—the dog lifted his leg and emptied himself. "Nooooo!" Kingsley howled at the dog, leaping to snatch him and rub his nose in it. She hustled him on her hip like a football toward the front door. "Very bad dog! Horrible beast! Bad! Bad! Bad!" She yanked open the door and planted the dog on the ground just beyond the brick entrance. Storming back into the house, she slammed the door.

In her absence, Todd had located an old dishcloth and mopped the couch, the pine floor, and the puddle. Thankfully the dog hadn't nailed the Persian rug under the old trunk that served as their coffee table. Billy stood transfixed, watching the drama unfold, his parents darting to and fro, calling directions. Out front, Todd found a sturdy stick, and tying the dishcloth to it, drove the stick into the ground. He returned to the foyer.

"Do you think he got the message?" Kingsley asked Todd, who had grown up with black labs. She was ashamed that her son had witnessed his mom's wrath in its extreme.

"He got the message!"

Sniff.

Kingsley glanced at her toddler. Anchored to the spot, a single tear rolled down his cherubic cheek. From outside the walnut door, a pitiful whimper broke the silence. Todd cracked the door and in slithered the most sorrowful looking creature Kingsley had ever beheld. He slinked on his belly through the foyer and down the hall, turning right into the kitchen. He scurried under the kitchen table, head down on his front paws, eyes rolling left and then right as if braced for whatever punishment came next.

Kingsley crouched to his eye level, overwhelmed with compassion for the dear little dog that couldn't weigh more than fifteen pounds. In grabbing him, she had noticed he was mere skin and bones under all that fluffy fur. She wouldn't have blamed him if he snapped at her as she offered her hand, palm down, to sniff. He gave her fingers a tentative lick, permitting her to stroke his head. As she smoothed his long silky ears, he closed his eyes in contentment.

"You must be hungry," she said, repurposing one of Pandora's heavy water bowls and adding leftover pot roast. She offered him a morsel under the table but didn't have to coax him toward the bowl. While he was scarfing his meal, she rescued Pandora's food and water dishes and moved them to the counter. She'd worry about territorial disputes later as she watched him drain a soup bowl of water.

Todd snapped their makeshift leash on an old collar Jacob had given him. Kingsley watched the three males troop down the hallway to the front door and head for *his spot* in the lawn. *Pandora, we girls are officially outnumbered,* she mused. Going to the foot of the staircase, she spotted Pandora, stock still on the landing, her yellow-green eyes riveted on the door below. "It's okay, baby," she cooed, as Pandora turned from the landing to mount the remaining six steps to the hall that led to their bedroom in the front quadrant. "We'll keep the interloper downstairs."

The little dog reclaimed his position under the kitchen table while the family ate dinner. Even though it was past Billy's bedtime, forgiving his bath was hardly an option. In spite of cleansing his face and hands before dinner and stripping his clothes, he was filthy. As the parents mounted the stairs, the little dog waited, as if needing an invitation to follow. It occurred to Kingsley that stairs might be a foreign concept in his short outdoor life, and the smooth wood was slippery. When he tested with one front paw, Kingsley froze mid-step, glared at the dog, and said, "No! Stop!" And he did, flopping instead at the foot of the staircase. After Billy's bath was finished, the dog hadn't moved.

Hand on the banister, Billy two-foot hopped downstairs to the dog. Sitting on the bottom step, the dog wriggled under his outstretched hand. "Where's the dog going to sleep?" Todd whispered to Kingsley.

"Not upstairs. Let's nip that idea in the bud."

"How do we keep him from sneaking upstairs?"

"Let's put him in the basement behind a baby gate. We don't have a dog bed, but I doubt a little highway dog would even know what to do with one," she said.

"Our neighbor said he curled up on an old rag rug in their summer kitchen. I'll look in the basement among the drop cloths and kneelers we used during the renovation. First, let's tuck Billy in, read him a story, say prayers, and then deal with your horrible beast."

With the baby monitor engaged and Billy's door shut, the parents hustled downstairs to consider the dog that was waiting patiently at the foot of the stairs. "Pandora!" Kingsley remembered the cat. "Aaaah! Her litter box is in the basement. Why don't you take you-know-who outside and I'll lure Pandora out from under our bed?"

"There goes the basement doggie den concept. Any other ideas?"

"I have an aunt with a willful, nasty schnauzer. He slept in a doggie bed in the kitchen attached to a very short leash that was clipped to his bed. Has since he was a pup, and doesn't expect to be anywhere else, although the leash is long gone. Maybe we could loop his leash over a doorknob above an old throw rug."

"Should work."

As Todd was bringing the pup back inside and Kingsley was descending the stairs with Pandora anchored on her hip, the animals spotted each other. Both froze. Before either adult could react, Pandora erupted from Kingsley's hold. Instead of fleeing, she hurtled the remaining stairs, hissing and spitting, her fur electrified from nose to tail tip. She yowled.

The dog, in a delighted spurt of energy, yanked free from Todd's grip on the leash and darted toward Pandora, skidding to a stop on the pine floor a foot from her face. In a flash, claws extended, Pandora swiped, raking his nose. Yelping, he slinked behind Todd. Head erect, Pandora stalked around the banister and trotted down the hall to use her potty and find her supper, ending the shortest turf war in their family's history.

"Is he bleeding?" Kingsley asked Todd, trying to get a better look at the dog's face." Together they parted his fur and inspected the damage. "Poor thing," she empathized with the wounded creature. "Let that be a lesson to you. Make friends, but never underestimate her."

"Sage advice for any male," Todd said, giving his wife a playful squeeze.

Chapter 2

Around midnight, Kingsley heard whimpering. She often joked that before leaving the delivery room every new mother was issued a second pair of ears. She was no exception. She, who could sleep through a thunderstorm, woke if her baby coughed once. She listened. Then heard it again. Todd, of course, was sound asleep.

Wriggling into her slippers and flannel robe, she padded down the hall to Billy's room. Like his dad, he was fast asleep. She sighed. It wouldn't be long before he outgrew the cherry spindle crib her father had crafted for his first grandchild. It was especially meaningful to her dad since she and Todd had been diagnosed as being unable to have children. Surprise! And then, when Billy—just eight weeks old—had been kidnapped…Saying her thousandth thank you to God for the safe return of her baby, she eased his door shut and headed downstairs.

The pup raised his head as she descended, hopping to his feet. He did a little dance, seeming to be begging at the door. "Outside?" she asked. He leapt up and down as high as the doorknob as if he had springs for legs. She disengaged the security system and, without turning on any lights, stepped onto the front stoop into a velvety black spring night. Instead of heading toward his spot, the dog alerted, stock-still, staring east into the darkness.

Then she heard and saw it too—an engine and a strange light simultaneously. The dog uttered a menacing growl deep in his chest. She stooped to him, smoothing his head while murmuring that it was okay, even as her own hackles rose. In the pitch-black Amish country, with all the Henning's lights extinguished and no nearby civilization, she trusted that they were invisible.

She strained toward the sound as a strange pair of lights pierced the darkness and seemed to be moving back and forth. Judging from her own property's dimensions, she figured the machine was several hundred feet back from the access road and a quarter-mile from their eastern border. The light and faint rumble continued back and forth, back and forth. A bulldozer? Had to be. But why late at night? Having seen lights on previous nights, she had made a point of glancing at the neighboring cornfield for a contractor's signage or advertisement for a coming business enterprise or housing development. But there had been nothing but the corn stubble remnants from the previous fall's harvest.

Kingsley almost forgot why she was standing there until the little dog tugged at his leash. "Go take care of yourself," she urged, and he dutifully trotted to the stake, squatted, and finished his business.

§

It was still dark when Todd and Kingsley, dressed in banker gray and sipping coffee, performed the breakfast ballet—he cooked their eggs and prepared toast while she handled beverages and packed Billy's lunch and snacks. "What about the D O G?" she whispered. *Thump, thump, thump.* Billy, having mastered the route to the floor from his crib and tall enough to manage the antique elbow latch, entered the kitchen in his footed pajamas, the dog's leash in his hand. The pup planted its rump beside the child, both looking extremely pleased with themselves.

"Todd—will you please empty the dog?"

"On it. Come on, boy." Dog and boy sprinted toward the front door. "Stay!" Todd commanded. Both did. "The eggs and toast, sweetheart? They're almost done. Dog, you're with me. Son, go help your mom."

Billy dragged a wooden kitchen chair close to the stove and scrambled up to help. Kingsley had heard enough war stories from little boys' mothers about these urchins climbing from stools to chairs to counters, cupboards, and beyond. She could kill Todd for letting him *help*. At least the next time the child attempted unsupervised egg cracking, they'd have a dog to lap up the mess. With the luxury of no audience, she glared at her son. "No Daddy, no climbing."

Billy was about to try tears when his mother had a better idea. "Until we find the dog's family, we should give him a name. If we call him that name when we feed him, he'll know we mean him. And hopefully, he'll come when he's called." The child immediately forgot the joy of being eye-level with the skillet.

"Omowwee!" He belly-slid from the chair, hurried from the kitchen, and scurried upstairs on all fours to his room. Shortly he two-foot hopped back downstairs, clutching the rail with one hand, and flapping a greeting card in the other. "Omowwee!" he repeated with delight. Kingsley took the card, immediately recognizing his favorite second birthday card from her parents, now shabby from love.

She read to him…"Guess who's wishing you a happy birthday?" She opened the card that showed a pair of fluffy beige dogs with black-tipped ears and identical happy expressions. "Two silly little dogs named O'Malley!" She got it. And it worked. Even though the little guy's new words were tumbling faster than his parents could keep up, his Ls and Rs were still a work in progress. Cute as his attempts sounded, they agreed not to reinforce them.

As Todd with pooch re-entered the house, Billy erupted from the kitchen, flapping his card. "Omowwee!" He lunged for his pet that permitted the child a rough hug. Todd threw back his head and laughed. "Of course!"

"Um—about today? And O'Malley?"

"Let's close him in the kitchen with the pocket doors. Leave him with food and water and his rug. Until we make sure he doesn't have accidents, chew fringe off the rugs, or be destructive, let's trust him a little at a time. He already understands that upstairs is off-limits."

For once both parents would keep the same schedule and share the ride to Keynote National Bank where they had officers' responsibilities. Before exiting their neighborhood, however, Todd slowed by the farmland east of their property and stopped. Just as Kingsley remembered, no signage existed. In fact, there was no evidence of any commercial enterprise except for a bulldozer parked a couple hundred feet from the road. Its presence could be explained by a fledgling agricultural or commercial enterprise underway. No one was around. Perhaps the workers were moonlighting nonunion employees making ends meet the old-fashioned American way.

"If you're really curious, K, why don't you check the Recorder of Deeds and see who bought the land? We know it sold recently—our Amish neighbor told us about losing out—so the new owner will be listed."

She sighed. "I am so sorry Jacob wasn't able to buy it for his son and daughter-in-law. Lancaster/Berks County soil is perfect for farming, but it's become scarce and very expensive by the acre. It's some of the best in the state—may be the country—and that should have ensured our being surrounded by farms and not overwhelmed by development. This deep limestone soil is tillable and fertile. Let developers build tract housing on land that's too hilly and rocky for farming."

He laughed. "That from my Philadelphia Mainline city girl."

☙❧

In a Grand Hyatt Hotel luxury suite in Midtown Manhattan, two businessmen scrutinized their latest venture in microscopic detail. "Our plan had to be failproof if we wanted your approval—and capital—to convince you," said Alan Deal, known only as Dealmaker to his clients.

The dealmaker said. "I reviewed every contingency from the land's suitability to zoning to privacy and myriad other intricacies from the culture to the weather. And we nailed it."

"What about personnel? And the workers?" the moneyman asked.

"Every on-site supervisor will be expert in his field without cross-contamination from other departments. They'll execute their function on a need-to-know basis without understanding the true nature of our business."

"Congratulations on closing the deal with that Holland grower, Liam Van Dijk, to try hydroponic farming in America. And what about buyers for his produce?"

"Van Dijk is very excited about expanding into the American market since global warming and rising sea levels might threaten his tulip business. He wants to diversify. As for the produce, these affluent New Yorkers will pay three bucks apiece for a perfect tomato. And a wholesaler in New York is on board to handle distribution, assuming there is any."

"What about the land behind the greenhouses? Is the plot plan consistent with such a dual operation?"

"Absolutely! The greenhouses will be built wide and shallow, parallel to the road, with a half-acre setback from a rural road. Seedlings will be started in the secondary greenhouse. A big-ass fence will hide our operation from nosey neighbors. The surrounding area—sides and back—will be planted in field corn, as it has been for years. That supposedly hides the greenhouses from competitors' eyes. The acres beyond the greenhouses can't be seen from the street, especially at night.

"Did you have any trouble buying the land?"

"Paid a bit more than we would have liked, thanks to a stubborn Amish farmer who wanted it for his kid. But we're well within budget. I'm telling you, we'll make a killing in the first year of operation. And, God forbid, if the greenhouse operation is unsuccessful, we've purchased insurance to cover our losses and still can resell the land for a shitload of money. Rumor has it that a developer would have liked to build 120 tract homes on half-acre lots."

"So why didn't he outbid you?"

"Didn't come to that. The rural community set up such a howl that the developer gave up and bought land in King of Prussia instead."

"Speaking of the timeframe, explain the narrow window of opportunity during which the sensitive work must be completed."

The dealmaker laughed at the entrepreneur. "You're such a city slicker. The corn will be planted as soon as the ground's workable. It will be 'knee-high by the fourth of July.' Depending upon growing conditions and the weather, it won't be harvested until October when the corn has dried down. Those three months, my friend, dictate the timeframe for our camouflage screen. Nothing out of the ordinary for crop farming."

The entrepreneur shook his head. "Too many extra

people. I say let's limit our operation to one business and forget that whole hydroponic thing. Stick to the corn and you won't have the cost of building the greenhouses."

"Can't. We've already signed the contract with Liam Van Dijk and he's making payments as scheduled."

He sighed. "Okay. But I'm still concerned about nosey neighbors. And the press. Just how much interest could hydroponic gardening generate on this scale?"

"We simply will not accept interviews. The press likes stories about local industry and people, and we are neither."

"And the neighbors?"

"Amish farmers go to bed early, their lives focused on their families and property, except for Sundays, when our operation will also be idle. The only other neighbors are a banker couple who work long hours in the city and wouldn't be out jogging between midnight and five."

"If you're satisfied that you've thought of everything, then I think we're good to go. Email me daily reports."

"What's next for you?" he asked the entrepreneur.

"Nothing exciting. Routine mergers and acquisitions." They shook, and the dealmaker escorted his investor to the elevator. "Want to share a cab to JFK?"

The dealmaker shook his head. "I've postponed my flight to troubleshoot some issues that concern the foreman, including payroll challenges."

"Not to worry. You do your part and sufficient funds will be deposited to the account as per our schedule."

The dealmaker watched as the big man's impeccable form glided down the escalator to the Grand Hyatt's revolving front doors. He remained diligent until a doorman closed the moneyman into a cab and thumped the trunk lid for it to take off. Grinning, he permitted himself a moment's celebration with one half of his dual operation's wheels greased. After the greenhouse business collapse, he'd resell the acreage to the Amish. What lay beneath—deal number three—would be buried too deep for tractors or mule-drawn plows to unearth.

He retreated to the suite's privacy and dialed the foreman. "We're good to go," he said, preempting the foreman's inappropriate pressure for details. Just how many offices, malls, and factories the foreman had built were of no consequence to the dealmaker, who regarded blue-collar types with disdain, regardless of their record and accumulated wealth. The foreman would do as he was told, without question, or nobody would ever hire him again. That, he had the power to do, and the foreman knew it.

Euphoria overwhelmed him as he mentally counted his money. His extraordinary brain could keep it all straight without three separate spreadsheets. Dear old dad never envisioned him becoming a farmer when he sent him to Harvard, but he would approve of him being filthy rich.

Chapter 3

The following Saturday, freed from weekday responsibilities, the parents sorted their options regarding the unplanned *guest* in their house. "Face it," Todd summarized the obvious. "Give a pet a name, and he's yours. Billy loves him, and the D O G seems to be accepting our house rules."

Billy looked up from his French toast, a bit of maple syrup dribbling down his chin. "D. O. G. Dat 'pells Omowwee!"

Two and a half? Kingsley dabbed his face with a napkin and turned back to her husband, rolling her eyes. "We need to teach *our guest* to come when he's called. He does great in the house because there's food or attention involved. But he has to learn to obey us. That we mean business."

"You're the sexiest alpha dog I've ever met."

"Hush—little ears!" Billy touched his own ears, his attention diverted by how syrupy fingers stuck to his hair, lifting it and not letting go. He giggled.

"Let's take O'Malley outside this morning, attach that new ten-foot leash to his collar, and reward him with praise for coming when he's called," Todd said. "If he bolts, we can step on the leash and stop him—if we're fast."

Kingsley chuckled. "Was it only two weeks ago that we were trying to get rid of him?"

As planned, the parents stood fifteen feet apart, taking turns positioning O'Malley at their feet. When the dog was focused elsewhere, Kingsley let the leash slip to her feet, pleased that the animal didn't notice. When Todd called his name, O'Malley scampered across the void. Each time either adult called his name, Billy joined in the footrace. They repeated the exercise, over and over, until Billy, reduced to being the *monkey in the middle*, wailed in frustration.

"Take the leash off altogether," Todd called. "Let's see how he does. Let him wander around the yard a bit farther."

"Fine. Then you can explain that lesson to our son when he bolts a half-mile to the highway and gets killed by a truck." Todd ignored her warning, unclipping the lead and letting their pet explore the backyard, nose down, in widening circles. When he wandered more than twenty feet, Todd called him. O'Malley's head shot up, he focused and ran gleefully toward him and the generous praise that was heaped upon him.

"I think he was starved for attention and craves it," she said. "That he'll do anything we ask if he knows what that is. If we never reward him with people's food, he won't beg during mealtime or be a nuisance when we entertain. Have you noticed?" she added. "He doesn't bark. I've never heard him—not once. Did someone or something traumatize him? Some watchdog he'll be!"

"Little dogs can be yappy. He must think he's big. If he accepts us as *his*, I think he would go for the jugular if anyone threatened us."

"I can't imagine that. He seems to love people unconditionally."

Late Sunday evening, the tall-case clock in the foyer bonged midnight. Kingsley sighed, wishing to linger just a little bit longer over her book, curled in her favorite library chair. She knew if she went to bed, the minute she closed her eyes the alarm would jolt her into another arduous day at the bank as if sleep hadn't happened. She couldn't complain—she loved heading the bank's commercial lending department which, still in her twenties, was a major coup that rewarded her education, determination, and grit. Still, she begrudged the time, now that she had a family.

The clock bonged the half-hour. As if on cue, O'Malley's head jerked to attention, turning questioning eyes in her direction. "Outside?" The little dog pranced toward the front door. Kingsley reached for his lead, then reconsidered. As she opened the front door, he looked at her face expectantly. "Go take care of yourself," she commanded, mimicking Todd's inflection, delighted when he trotted to his spot. She stooped to his level when he had finished. "You are a wonderful little beast, aren't you?" He ducked his head under her hand for an ear rub.

Suddenly, O'Malley alerted, staring east into the darkness as machinery began rumbling in the distance. Before Kingsley could react, he bolted in the direction of the sound, barking as furiously as any large breed she had ever encountered. She yelled his name to no avail; and by the time she'd reached the end of the brick sidewalk that connected to their gravel driveway, O'Malley was gone. Her instinct was to chase after him until she glanced at her slippered feet.

She tore through the house, pulled on her barn boots, shrugged into a hooded sweatshirt that hung on a hook, and sprinted out the back door, circling toward the lane. She knew exactly where he was headed, and tore cross country to the construction site, only slowing to squeeze through an opening she found in a new chain-link fence. Suddenly work lights exploded through the blackness, exposing excavation workers glaring at her.

Kingsley brushed past two men in coveralls who gaped

at the intruder. "O'Malley!" she shrieked, stumbling over toolboxes, rebar, Dewalt hand tools, and extension cords. A portable generator rumbled beyond the circle of light. "Have you seen a little dog? Beige with black ears? About fifteen pounds? We live down the road, and he's run away." The pair shook their heads.

Peering into the darkness beyond the light's circle, she spotted a hulking figure in jeans, a dirty tee-shirt, and yellow hard hat. He was turned sideways, but she could see he was gripping a shovel, choked up to the blade. "Hey mister, have you seen…" As he pivoted toward her voice, she could see O'Malley, anchored on his hip. The hulk was winding up, his right arm ready to connect with her dog's head.

Instinctively she rushed toward him, screaming. "Stop! You coward! Don't you dare hurt my little dog!" A weapon. She needed a weapon! By the drag on her jacket's right pocket, she recognized the feel of her garden clippers. But as she grappled to free them, they stuck on the fabric. Crazed, she lifted them through the pocket and pointed them like a gun. "Hurt my dog and I'll shoot you dead!"

The man froze. Lowering the shovel, eyes darting from her face to her hand, he dropped O'Malley on the ground. Kingsley pivoted, stepping backward to keep all three men in her line of vision. "That goes for all of you!" she yelled. She could feel the little dog velcroed to her legs, shaking, and scooped him up.

"Lady, keep your damn dog at home."

"Home? Home you say? You don't live here. We do. You are strangers who disturb our sleep night after night. I'm going to make it a point to get to the bottom of this—this—intrusion. Get out of my way. Let me pass."

Anger propelled her from the construction site, down the lane to her driveway, and through the back door. A quick examination revealed no apparent injuries—just caked mud and oil. "Let's give you a bath," she soothed O'Malley, flicking on the basement lights and heading for the washtubs. Still clutching him on her hip, she ran warm water and half-filled the tub. Then, as Todd had done, she hosed and shampooed him and toweled his fur. Luckily, she'd left the old hairdryer nearby and finished the job. "Young dog, another lesson—come when you're called."

At their first possible opportunity, they'd walk him around and around the front, side, and the back garden's edges to delineate his boundaries. As her blood pressure settled and her nerves calmed, she took mental inventory. It was her fault. She never should have let him outside off the leash. If he had vanished, or worse, been found dead and mutilated, how could they explain that to Billy? But she vowed to find out exactly what that construction was all about. Confession—she'd have to tell Todd about her adventure, but beyond their bright little son's imaginative mind.

Chapter 4

Todd's reaction was shocking and unexpected. Her sophisticated, highly educated, brilliant husband, who could keep hundreds of shareholders enthralled while explaining the minutia of the bank's increased profits and earnings, rarely raised his voice. Sometimes she wished he wasn't so sensible, the grownup, level-headed eldest child, who commanded respect regardless of circumstance. His mild-manner, she suspected, came naturally and was how he won the cooperation of influential people.

"What?" he bellowed.

"I, ah, had no choice but to go after him. I didn't think. I reacted. Maybe if we invested in Invisible Fence…"

"Not my point! Did that workman threaten *you*? Raise that shovel, as if to strike *you*? If he thought you really had a gun, he might have. And having witnesses to vouch for him, the cops might conclude that he had been justified. This could all have ended badly."

Kingsley opened her mouth to retort, but reconsidering, shut it. Her moment of contrition passed quickly, however. "We've got to find out what those guys are up to. I've written enough loans financing commercial enterprises to detect something's amiss. I'm going to find out who bought the land, what business they're in, if it's approved for nonagricultural use, what's in the agreements, who's financing it…"

"K, you can't use the bank's resources to satisfy your personal curiosity. But you can ask Margaret to check out the real estate transaction—who's the new owner of record, the financing, etc. That's public record. Even though she's in charge of residential real estate lending, she knows every realtor in multiple counties. Pete, her legal eagle husband, might have heard something about the business or its owners."

"Zoning. This land is zoned agricultural, not commercial. That I can check myself."

"And then," Todd said, his gaze far away into the depths of his mind, "I will have a little chat with the owner. 'Top-down.' Not 'bottom-up.' I see no benefit in confronting workmen who are following somebody's orders."

⁓ఎ⁓ఎ

Margaret Stiles, Kingsley's dear friend, a fellow officer at Keynote National Bank, and sometimes co-conspirator and amateur sleuth, rapped on Kingsley's private office door frame. Kingsley had been deep in conversation with an unqualified prospective client. She swiveled from her calming view of the lush vegetation on the hillside beyond her floor-to-ceiling windows. She motioned Margaret toward a visitor's chair, crossing her eyes at the phone while making a circular motion with her index finger. Margaret smothered a chuckle as Kingsley fabricated an excuse to hang up.

"Him again?" Margaret asked, referencing the caller who would not give up."

"I've told him—repeatedly—that he's undercapitalized. He and his bride exhausted their savings to buy 120 acres of farmland. He has a hefty home mortgage and wants an additional loan to renovate the house and barn, buy cows, and launch a dairy business. He was angry. Said 'you won't give us young folks a break.' I told him, 'By turning you down, I *am* giving you a break. You could lose everything with an ill-thought-out business plan.'"

"So, what was your advice?"

"Keep their day jobs. Rent the land for crop farming. Invest sweat equity in renovating their house. Listen to the Cooperative Extension Service. Meet other dairymen in their district and learn from their experience." She smiled at her friend whose stunning sapphire cashmere sweater set accentuated her startlingly blue eyes.

"Shall I shut the door?" Margaret asked.

"If that folder contains something incendiary, that might be prudent." Margaret took a moment to do so, after motioning to Kingsley's AA in the outer office that she'd just be a minute. She opened the folder, passing several documents across Kingsley's desk.

"Here's what I found. I'm afraid you'll be disappointed. A farmer, who leases part of the acreage for field corn, is continuing to do so. And there's a new business on part of the land in question called Hydroponic Products. While that's not about growing crops in the ground, like corn or wheat, it's still agriculture."

"As in growing lettuce in water tanks full of nutrients?"

"Precisely. But here's the interesting part. Rather than being owned by your local Pennsylvania Dutch farmers, the land appears to be owned by a corporation registered outside Pennsylvania. That, in turn, is owned by a shell corporation, registered outside the United States with an alphabet-soup name. The closest I got to speak with an officer of that entity was an overseas number and a woman with an eastern European accent that I couldn't understand."

"Todd's not going to like this. I suspect his plan was to

overwhelm the owner with veiled intimidation and Ivy League gibberish, without his ingratiating smile. Let them know that he's a force to contend with minus resorting to anything actionable."

"Are they really that much of a bother?"

Kingsley narrowed slit eyes to Margaret. "He was seconds from bludgeoning my dog." She shook her head and started to laugh. "Suppose I had managed to yank those clippers out of my pocket and threatened to shoot him with them?"

"I'd have bought a ticket to witness that scene." Margaret flipped a glance at her watch and rose. "Better get back; got a real estate client coming to initiate preapproval to buy a horse farm. I may need another bank to participate. It's a hot property because horses raced in Pennsylvania now must be born in the commonwealth. That's driving prices for suitable farms through the roof."

Kingsley motioned to the research that lay on her desk. "Many thanks for this. And good luck with the ponies."

∽∾∽∾

Todd left the bank as soon as he wrapped up the senior officer's meeting. As he strode to his vehicle, he breathed the intoxicating scent of spring's earliest daffodils and budding trees. What a wise choice he'd made, leaving big-city New England banking where he would always be a specialist cog where junior officers were chewed up and spit out. Even here, he thought he'd end his career as a small-bank executive vice president in charge of lending, technology, and branch administration. He never anticipated the president's departure under a cloud of suspicion and being offered his job, only to be followed by the chairman's pending retirement.

Tonight, out in their country home, he'd review all the

department heads' reports after tucking their little one into bed. He and Kingsley would talk shop, having ignored each other at today's meeting except when she reported on commercial lending. As the bank's president, he anchored the banquet-sized board table, and she sat as far away as possible. If any other senior officers resented their relationship, they'd gotten over it. Theirs had not been a company romance but a confluence of tragic circumstances by two single people who weathered it together.

As he drove, he switched from banker to personal mode. Billy had balked at leaving early and missing another tyke's birthday party. That jolted Todd, who had to accept that his toddler son had a life of his own, courtesy of Keynote's daycare center. The gregarious little guy loved his friends, his teachers, and age-appropriate activities, which sometimes made weekends challenging as Billy expected nonstop entertainment there too. O'Malley, Todd admitted, was a welcome playmate.

That business next door—later he would try the eight hundred number Margaret had found. Forty-five minutes later, he exited the highway and motored west on the rural two-lane, crossing the county line into picturesque farmland.

Within a short distance of their private driveway, he spotted new activity on the adjacent property. A bevy of vehicles paralleled the construction site, beak to tail. Judging from their position, a new F250 had arrived first, followed by an assortment of jeeps and older trucks. Bringing up the rear was a pristine black limo, which Todd noticed bore New York plates. The meeting must have just broken up, as a man in a thousand-dollar suit approached the limo's driver-side door.

Todd didn't have to think twice. Putting the SUV in reverse, he stopped double parking beside the black car and circled to face the driver. "This your business?" he asked in neutral tones but without extending his hand.

"What's it to you?"

"I have business with the owner. Might that be you?"

The man flicked a glance at Todd as if taking his measure. "That's none of your business."

"Actually, it is. I live right over there, stone house, at the end of the lane before it dead-ends at the dairy farm. Your operation, if it is yours, is keeping my family awake at night. You might want to reconsider your hours of operation before I ask the township to intervene."

"Don't threaten me. I have a perfect right to have my crew work when they're available. Besides, there's no ordinance against it."

"Did you check? There should be hours between which you can't exceed a certain decibel level. I intend to find out."

"Good luck with that! My hours are *grandfathered*."

"Which can be denied. Look—I don't want to get off on the wrong foot with a new neighbor, but this is a peaceful community that's zoned *agricultural*, not *commercial*."

The man jerked a thumb over his shoulder to the gathering group, half in work clothes, half in suits. "This *is* an agricultural enterprise. And if you do anything to impede its progress, I'll..."

"You'll what? Come after my family with shovels?"

That stopped him. Momentarily, the men glared at each other, neither backing down from the pissing contest. "Just keep them off my property."

"By the way—what is the name of your business? Its provenance is rather murky. Is it privately held? Or publicly traded on the stock exchange?"

The man raised a clenched fist, which caused the semicircle of men behind him to inch forward. One of the suits grabbed his forearm. "Enough," he barely whispered while easing the boss backward and opening his car door like a practiced security guard. He maneuvered the man into his seat.

If looks could kill, Todd would be dead. Undeterred, he called, "Never threaten my family again, or I will shut you down. Count on it."

"Well, keep 'em at home! I mean it. My land. My rules." Firing his engine, he shot a U-turn, blanketing Todd and his SUV with dust. A guy in a white foreman's hat motioned to the workers with a jerk of his head while punctuating a message by stabbing his palm. They dispersed to their tasks while the suits manned their cars and followed the boss. Todd climbed into his SUV and eased toward home on autopilot, stunned by how quickly the conversation turned confrontational and nearly got out of hand.

ↄↄↄↄ

Randall Shannon and Barrie Brown erupted through the back door, obviously bearing exceptional news. Kingsley motioned them to their familiar places at the old trestle kitchen table and, mid-greetings fired the Krups and assembled raspberry rugalachs on a pottery plate. Todd joined them directly, trailed by Billy and O'Malley.

Todd shook his life-long best friend's hand, exchanging claps on each other's backs. Barrie rose to accept his hug. "What are you up to this early on a Saturday? Been flying?

Barrie and Randal exchanged conspiratorial glances. "We've been scouting the perfect place for our wedding," he said.

"So. What's your next insane idea?"

"Wing-walking toward each other from opposite sides of the plane. However, the wedding planner dismissed us as crazies, my insurance agent was apoplectic, and I'd exhausted the pilots who owe me. And then there's the parents of our godson/ring bearer…"

"But we have a perfect plan," Barrie giggled, taking Randall's hand.

"Well?" Todd and Kingsley exclaimed in exasperation and exhaustion from hearing months of insane plans, one worse than its predecessor. Two crazy pilots—go figure. Why couldn't they be normal for a change?

"The details will have to wait on location and weather."

"So—is a plane still involved?"

They smiled conspiratorially at their best friends. "Wouldn't have it any other way."

Kingsley scowled at Barrie, a contradiction in every sense and Kingsley's complete opposite—a tiny, dizzy blonde who resembled a 1920s flapper, an incorrigible daredevil who could pick any lock. A legendary bank controller whose numbers never failed. She grinned at Kingsley, winking her nearly transparent pale eyes.

"And you're not going to share…"

"Nope. But to keep in your good graces, we do have a surprise for you. We scoped out your neighbor's business and took some aerial shots." Randall pulled his iPhone from his bomber jacket pocket and scrolled to *photos*. The foursome nearly clunked heads over the trestle table. "If you want a really good look at what they're up to, I'll email these videos to your computer."

Todd and Kingsley bolted for the library, trailed by their friends, a small boy, and a curious dog. Todd fired up his PC and opened Mail. "There," Randall pointed to four icons. "Open the third one. That should show the best detail." A double-click later an aerial view of the property opened for their inspection. As Randall had dipped the wings and Barrie continued to film, the worksite below was digitally captured. "Start from the beginning, Barrie, then freeze motion when I say…there! Freeze that."

"Looks like a big hole, covered with—what?"

"Watch." Randall clicked computer keys, sharpened the scene, and enlarged the portion in question. "There."

Todd scowled. "I don't see anything but a big hole, covered with some kind of netting."

"Precisely," Randall agreed. "Now ask yourself. Why would a hydroponic vegetable grower bring in heavy equipment and dig a hole to China?" Nobody spoke. "Suppose your neighbor has a contract with the Fed to dispose of ordinance that can't be shown on the books?"

"That's ridiculous," Todd said. "We'd have government types all over the project, checking—whatever."

"Unless they want no one to know. I was in the military; you weren't. It's not like what you see on TV."

"Is that why you resigned your commission in the Air Force?" Kingsley ventured. There was no better entrée to ask, and she'd always wondered. For once, jolly red-headed Randall, quick with a joke, looked subdued. "No." In spite of his outgoing, wise-cracking nature, he'd never spoken to her about those nine years, and Kingsley sensed the wisdom of not asking her husband.

Todd was intent on the frozen frame. "Can you enlarge that section right there?" he asked, pointing to the bottom right corner. "The hole looks like it's coated with something too shiny for concrete. Like metal. Or lead? And they've leveled the ground in front of the hole, but where are the footers?"

"A containment chamber?" Kingsley ventured.

"Tell you what," Randall responded with an idea. "Tomorrow is Sunday. No one should be around. Let's fly a drone over that hole. If we're lucky, we can send it right down its throat, take stills, and have a closer look."

"There's gotta be a law against that," Barrie said.

"Only if we get caught, baby. And hey—we were just showing the little guy the fun of flying a drone. Not our fault if it got off course."

Barrie snapped her fingers. "Why don't you simply ask the dude? Like 'Say, buddy, whatcha building over there?'"

Todd shook his head. "That might have worked a few confrontations ago, but we're way past that welcome-to-the-neighborhood part of our relationship."

"Wouldn't hurt to ask him," Barrie added. She and Randall telepathed an idea. "Invite him and his significant other for cocktails on the veranda. Then ask him."

"Huh?" Todd spared Kingsley the necessity of asking what they meant.

"It's a great story," Randall began. "This guy over in the valley bought a house on a few acres of farmland. During his first two years in residence, their snooty next-door neighbor ignored them, even if their cars passed each other on the lane. The neighbor, he learned, was a retired corporate CEO—big fish in a little puddle, who must have thought the new neighbors were beneath him. The chairman had this gorgeous property, designed and maintained by the same guy who managed the CEO's country club's golf course.

"The new guy had made a fortune in manufacturing, but still was a down-to-earth blue-collar guy. One day the new guy started building a cyclone-fence enclosure near the CEO's property line. Not encroaching, code perfect, but in plain view of his country estate and their street. Ten feet tall, thirty by thirty, or thereabouts."

"Randall—get to the point."

"Okay, you tell it better than I do, Barrie." She batted the air, then picked up without losing his place, her eyes dancing with merriment.

"Retired CEO was observed watching the construction in progress from one window or another. Still, he never ventured toward the property line to introduce himself or welcome the not-so-new neighbor. Then one day, after the construction was finished, they received an invitation on the wife's monogrammed Crane stationery. *Come on Sunday at four for cocktails on the veranda.*

"So, the guy digs his old wedding/ funeral suit out of mothballs and his wife put on the dress she wore to their son's rehearsal dinner, and they troop across their neighbor's blade-perfect lawn at four o'clock sharp. The CEO greets them warmly and invites them to sit. His wife floats seamlessly onto the veranda in a silk dress and updo, ala Donna Reed. He positions a small cocktail table near the guests. She places a little sterling tray on an embroidered linen cloth and hands her guests matching linen napkins. They sipped martinis while the owner makes small talk."

Randall interrupted, "Don't forget; he's a beer drinker. He'd never tasted a martini, which he said later tasted like turpentine. Go ahead, Barrie."

"At exactly four-thirty, their host rises as if to dismiss them, thanks them for coming, and shakes the man's hand, merely nodding to his wife. As they prepare to step onto the lawn, the CEO calls after them. 'Say. By the way— what are your plans for that structure?' Without missing a beat, the guy responds, 'Gonna run hogs in there.' Host's mouth dropped; wife holds her nose and bobbles the tray. Guests fled, lest they explode in laughter."

Kingsley asked, "So what were they going to do with the enclosure? I mean, surely not hogs. They'd stink."

"Seems the wife was a member of the horticulture society and a Master Gardner who owned a small floral shop. When they moved to the country, she decided to grow some of her own flowers, rather than buy everything from a wholesaler. The first two summers, her attempts were devoured by a herd of white-tail deer. She convinced her husband that deer fencing would be cheaper than a psychiatrist—or a divorce lawyer—if he didn't agree. Which he did."

Kingsley said, wiping her eyes. "Todd, can you whip us up a veranda?"

Chapter 5

Todd took the elevator to Keynote's executive area on the fifth floor, nodded to coworkers, and hung his raincoat on his grandfather's coat tree that once occupied a corner in the elder banker's Boston office. Todd's secretary followed him into his suite, notebook, and pink slips in hand. After noting the challenges de jour he said, "Please hold my calls for a few minutes. I need to attend to a personal matter." She left, closing his door.

Without opening his briefcase or checking his inbox for the latest crisis that screamed for attention, he punched 9 for an outside line and dialed his township manager's number from heart, adding his four-digit extension.

"Todd! How's the city boy adjusting to country life? And what are you planning for that old house this time that requires more of our permits?"

"We're fine. And we love it. Best decision I ever made besides asking Kingsley to marry me. I'm calling about another matter regarding the farm to our east that recently changed hands."

"Sorry you didn't buy it?"

"Had no idea it was on the market. Heard about it after the fact. Besides, our seven acres are all we can handle. I'm having a noise problem with the new owners and hope you can give me some background information. Does our township have noise restrictions, particularly at night?"

The township manager laughed. "That's never come up. Your neighbors are not known to party-hearty. You might object to tractors running at daybreak during planting or harvesting season, but that comes with the territory. Where you have restrictions is in the burbs, gated communities, or where homeowners' associations voted on them. That is, folks who enjoy having neighbors but value peace and quiet and respect each other's privacy."

"We're zoned *agricultural*, but it appears we're getting a commercial enterprise right next door. Construction is taking place between midnight and five a.m., heavy industrial equipment and lights, trucks coming and going five nights a week. It sounds like they've installed an industrial-size generator. Are you permitted to tell me what type of business they're in and if anyone's checking to make sure we're zoned for whatever they're building?"

"Humm. Let's have a look." Todd heard keys tapping and shortly his friend responded. "Huh. Looks like they're going to do exactly what the previous owner did—grow field corn and vegetables."

Todd felt his eyes narrow, a frown creasing his brow. "That doesn't make sense. You don't need a physical plant to do that."

"Maybe he's going to grow corn and soybeans for the grain. That would be dried in storage bins, which takes lots of electricity. Your local power lines couldn't handle the demand, hence the need for a large generator."

The manager tapped additional keys. "Now this is interesting. According to the plot plan, a small portion of the land facing the street will be used to grow hydroponic vegetables in the winter and to start bedding plants—flowers, herbs, vegetables—for the summer season."

"Isn't that a commercial business? We're not zoned for that. I checked before we bought our house. That could morph into gardening and hardware supplies, huge parking lots, and hordes of retail shoppers."

"Not if it's a wholesale agri-business. You might expect trucks hauling product to market, but by this description, you might be talking panel vans, not tractor-trailers."

"But what about buildings? Are they zoned for that?"

"Sure. Farms have homes, barns, equipment sheds, and sometimes multiple dwellings as parents build homes for their grown kids and families to expand the farming operation. And generators—even the Amish need generators if they operate a dairy. Milk has to be cooled in bulk tanks and maintained at a specific temperature if it's to be sold. Back in my grandparent's day, milk went from the cows to milk jugs, which were cooled in a stream. That's no longer permitted by the FDA."

Todd pictured a scene in his mind. "Kingsley and I found a Lancaster farm with a new two-story house, a barn, and a one-story business between the two. She noticed a quaint windmill and the lack of electric lines running into the house. Inside the shop, young Mennonite girls in matching calico dresses and white *capps* sold beautiful quilts. It was late, maybe five o'clock, cloudy, and getting dark in the building, which had minimal windows. Then we were startled by the strong scent of kerosene followed by a *whoosh*! One girl had thrown a switch while the other ran from one hanging light to another to light the lamps. The fuel smelled so strong by the time she finished, we were afraid there would be an explosion."

"Did you see a generator?"

"No. The farm was surrounded by field corn, so from what you're saying, there was no need. Come to think of it, the Amish neighbor to our west does have a line to his barn, but not to the house. I assumed their sect was progressive."

After exhausting Todd's list of potential violations for

which the supervisor had reasonable explanations, Todd ended the call with his thanks. *She's going to be disappointed.* Still, his gut told him that something was wrong, and he was going to find out what the paperwork wasn't telling.

❧❧❧

The township supervisor and his inspector rolled up to the construction site and coasted to a stop. As the foreman watched from a distance, the pair seemed to be consulting notes on clipboards, pointing to various areas on the site. After twenty minutes and much conversation and pointing, they emerged from the vehicle and began stepping off the distance from the road to the work in progress. Next, they measured from the right corner's recently-poured footers to the pin that marked the property line. Then they repeated the procedure from the left corner to the opposite line.

"Can I help you with something?" the foreman said, approaching the men with a hostile expression.

"We're from the township," the supervisor provided, thumbing the lanyard that displayed his credentials. "It's our job to verify that construction matches the specifications on file and that the project is *code*. We'll be stopping by from time to time—just ignore us. We'll be out of your hair in a few minutes."

"You should have let me know you were coming. I'm sure the boss won't appreciate surprise visits."

"He'll tell you what I am—that unannounced inspections are in your contract. Now, if you don't mind, we'll have a quick look around so that we can update our records." They didn't wait for the foreman to reply but continued traipsing the length and breadth of the disturbed earth, ignoring a startled worker who was driving stakes to delineate a twenty by twenty-foot area in the corn stubble.

"What's that going to be?" the inspector asked the worker while flipping several pages to the overview of the area.

"Don't know. Not paid to ask questions." He drove a fourth stake, then connected the four with white twine while the township men watched. Finishing the job, the worker gathered his toolbox and headed toward a battered pickup truck. Momentarily, he was gone as was the foreman.

❧❧❧

Randall Shannon grinned at his godson who was struggling into a tiny pair of barn boots. "Let me help you with those, buddy."

"No! I do mine own self."

"This may take a while," Todd said, smiling at his son. "Sometimes it would be so much more efficient to do things for him, but he wouldn't learn and it's not worth the tantrum. Got the drone?"

"You had doubts?" He retrieved a large cardboard box from his jeep and set it on the ground behind the barn. Billy alerted instantly when Randall extracted the drone. His godfather then produced a small plastic airplane and offered it to Billy who immediately forgot about the drone. With delight, the child dissolved into his imagination, zooming the plane in widening circles with surprisingly accurate noises.

"I don't want him anywhere near that hole," Todd said, scowling in the direction of the construction site.

"Not to worry. I'll fly with our little guy while you photograph the hole. Here—instead of using the drone, use my camera. It has an obscene number of pixels and great depth of field. Circle the hole and shoot all four sides, top to bottom. Oh! And get anything else you see lying around that looks interesting. We can play with the drone later."

"Why don't we park you-know-who with his mom and Auntie Barrie, and I'll explore what's disturbed for what they've left behind that might reveal what they're really doing."

"You're that sure they're up to no good?"

"In my business, I have to be a reasonably good judge of character. But that isn't personal. It's just about money. But after what we've been through…" He didn't have to reiterate their multiple bad-dealings with law enforcement. "I don't know who I hated more, the criminals, the press, or those detectives who blamed us for Billy's kidnapping. It poisoned me somehow; left me jaded. I assume the worst of my fellow humans until I learn otherwise, which is backward. Happily, for most people, that happens quickly."

"And now?"

"I'm having trouble tamping down my anger. Avoiding the triggers, which I admit border on paranoia. The foreman and that guy in that limo—their evil came off them in waves." He chuckled, sardonically. "Not a pleasant gift to have."

"Oh, I don't know. If you get tired of banking, maybe you should try law enforcement."

Todd shook his head. "Too much bureaucracy. At least in my line most people respect me or address me tactfully when I'm wrong."

"Hey, Billy!" The child looked up, beaming at his godfather. "Let's go see if your mom has any cookies." At the C-word, Billy seemed to miss that his father wasn't following them. Happily, he led his godfather toward the back door, clutching his new toy to his chest.

Todd wasted no time striding toward the multi-acre construction site where the central portion was disturbed. Had he been standing up on the lane instead of behind his own barn, he would have had an unobstructed view of old corn stubble and newly sprouted plants. The rectangle of hard-packed clay and the hole would be hidden. Closest to him, behind the hole, large amounts of earth had been pushed aside and leveled during excavation.

He approached the central area, searching the land and sky for unwanted eyes. There were none. He rolled back camouflage netting that covered the hole that hadn't been there when Barrie shot the pictures. He peered into the void. The hole, while not inordinately wide, had to be two stories deep. He photographed the target from multiple angles, then rolled the net back into position.

Satisfied that he had been thorough, he stepped off the disturbed worksite in a grid. With a stick, he also probed the contents of two burn barrels, hoping to find incriminating papers. He found nothing. What did catch his attention, however, was an unusual footprint in the dust. Just for fun, he took its picture beside one of his own size twelves. Must have been made by someone taller than him, he mused, being six feet two.

From this location, he paused to capture the view of his home. A late afternoon sun, edging over Jacob's farm, snaked shadows of branches from the towering black walnuts that bordered their mutual properties. Todd repositioned himself and shot multiple angles to capture a rare glimpse of their home. He flipped his wrist to check the time. How long had he lingered?

As he was stepping through the debris, his eye fell on a faded scrap of paper that was trapped under a piece of construction-grade two by four. He guessed it was leftover from forming the footers that delineated the rectangle of hard-packed clay where something was going to be built. He tugged, but it wouldn't budge until he raised the wood with his boot. He squinted at a drawing that meant nothing to him.

The sound of an approaching engine drifted down from the road. The Amish family didn't drive, and the Hennings weren't expecting visitors. He pulled the paper free, folded and stuffed it into his hip pocket, then trotted downhill. A few dozen feet beyond the hole, he angled west toward their barn. Once behind it, he squinted to scan the construction site. Near the road, he could make out the front of the new Ford F250 he'd noticed during the latest confrontation.

℘℘℘

"You're not going to like this," the foreman broached the subject to his boss. "Know how I'm obsessed about stuff going missing on my job sites? I hide surveillance cameras in places the workers won't notice. But I warn them that every nail, scrap of wood, bucket of whatever, piece of construction equipment, and hand tool is counted. And if anything's missing, they're going to pay for it."

"So why the cameras?"

"If something goes wrong on the site, I can find out who did it. Fast! In the past, I've been concerned about sabotage from competitors or criminals with a grudge or looking for items to fence or trade for drugs. Now there's these township guys snooping around, faking an inspection. At this early stage in construction, I knew that was off.

Then this afternoon, that neighbor in the stone house prowled all over the site, taking pictures of everything, including the hole. And he picked up something near the footers and stuffed it into his pocket. He also shot footprints, like CSIs do on the cop shows. No clue why. There's nothing unusual about my guys' feet."

"Glad you called. Thanks for being observant. The surveillance idea is great; should help us avoid false insurance claims. Keep the cameras in place."

"What do you want me to do? Hire security for the down hours? I have some really tough guys who can protect the property. Convincingly."

"Just keep an eye out for anything unusual. Fire any worker who acts suspicious or asks too many questions. And keep watching those cameras."

"You got it."

Chapter 6

Kingsley couldn't figure out what was keeping her awake. Usually she was so sleep deprived that she had to make sure the blankets were perfect before her head hit the pillow, otherwise she'd awaken hours later, freezing or fried. If she tossed one more time, she might waken Todd, his mind overworked by the bank's approaching shareholders meeting and the message he'd deliver to the stakeholders. Of course, he'd agonized that the message must be perfect—increased earnings and profits without any forward-looking statements, the latter a trick that required finesse, lest the regulators call him on it.

Was she concerned about Billy? She reviewed their day. Billy had been so filthy from his romp with the dog that she'd bathed and dressed him in jammies while a comfort food casserole baked. If there was one puddle in the yard, those two found it. She saw him in her mind's eye, so done in by a lovely spring day that he could hardly manage his dinner. Todd had taken mercy on him and fed him bites of mac and cheese. After truncated stories and prayers with drooping eyelids, their son was asleep in record time.

So, what was it? Usually a chatterbox, Billy had been quiet at dinner, in spite of his joyful playtime. Had she and

Todd ignored him, seizing the opportunity to have real adult conversation about new banking regulations that they must digest? Rumors of mergers? To pave or not pave their neglected driveway? Were they missing any family birthdays? No, it was the silence. Billy wasn't himself. Note to Mom—high energy can be confused with exhaustion. And now with a dog to romp with, unlike the child's parents who wore out quickly, both kid and dog might need late-afternoon limits.

She snuggled into her eiderdown pillow and let her mind wander to happy things. The gardens. Soon the budding roses would be flush with leaves. Sunday night— nearly Monday. A new day. She faded.

Until she heard whimpering. O'Malley! Had they forgotten to take him outside? They'd fed him—that she remembered. Okay—one last trip. Why was it that, when she *could* fall asleep, something or someone wouldn't let her? She wriggled her feet into slippers and forced her arms through the tangled sleeves of her inside-out robe. Down the hall, she grabbed the banister, almost tripping over the dog. "What are you doing upstairs?" she hissed. "You know you aren't supposed to be up here." O'Malley ignored her, nose to the crack of Billy's door, refusing to move.

"No. You cannot sleep in Billy's room." He whined, body riveted at the crack while looking over his shoulder at her face. Then he made an imploring noise in his throat that wasn't exactly a bark or a cry. "What is it?" Then he barked—just once at the door, then turned back to her.

She got it! Something was wrong. Throwing the door open, she hurried to Billy's bed. The child appeared lost in his new big-boy bed that his grandfather had crafted for him, his outgrown crib pushed into a corner, just in case he rejected the new piece of furniture. By the moonlight spilling through the window and the glow of the nightlight,

Kingsley could see that her son's face was crimson. She laid her hand on his burning forehead while simultaneously yelling for Todd.

He appeared instantly at the bedside and grasping the crisis, rummaged in the dresser for the fever thermometer. "One hundred three," he pronounced moments later. "Does this thing register one degree more or one degree less than the old ones? I can never remember."

"I'm calling the doctor," she said, rushing for her phone and grabbing her jeans and sweater mid-dash. The answering service quickly dialed the on-calls number, who called back immediately. "Bring him in," the pediatrician said. "I'll meet you there."

"Should we call an ambulance?" Kingsley asked, worried that he might convulse.

"I think we can drive there faster," Todd said. Each threw on clothes, switching off preparing Billy to travel. Todd carried Billy while Kingsley grabbed his go-bag, and then strapped him into his car seat. She slid in beside him, stroking his feverish brow and murmuring softly to him.

Up the driveway, hard left onto the lane, a half-mile and—what? A huge truck, the size of a moving van, was parked across the lane, completely blocking forward progress. Infuriated, Todd blasted his horn without prevailing. Jumping onto the road, he looked for the driver and, as an alternative, a way around the obstruction. He could not go left into a ditch or right where hundred-foot oaks met the road.

"Call 911," he called over his shoulder to Kingsley while sprinting toward the lights that illuminated the worksite. Breathless, he barged into the gathering of workmen. "You've gotta move that truck. We have to get to the hospital!" Nobody moved. "Come on," he yelled. "Please move it!"

Lackadaisically, a guy in a white hat, thumbs in jean

pockets, sauntered toward Todd. "Who you telling what to do?"

"I am! Your truck's blocking the road! It's an emergency. You do not own the road. It's state property. Now get your ass in gear and order your driver to get it the hell out of our way!"

"I think he's out back takin' a leak. I'll tell him when he gets back."

"You'll tell him right now."

"Or else what? What you gonna do about it?"

"If anything happens to my son because you prevented us from taking him to the hospital, I'll make sure you spend the rest of your life in prison. And, in the meantime, you tell your boss—whoever the hell the guy in the Mercedes is—that I'm going after his permits first thing in the morning. Now get that truck out of the street."

As if on cue, sirens pierced the quiet night, approaching quickly. Two patrol cars skidded to a stop, lights flashing, on the far side of the truck. "These assholes refused to move this truck, and we've got to get our son to the hospital. My son's burning up," Todd yelled, pleading for help. He dashed back to collect his family.

"We'll take them. Ma'am, bring your baby. Sir, you stay behind. We'll deal with the truck, then you can follow the officer."

An hour later, Todd tossed the keys to a waiting valet and, after heaping thanks on the attendant, sprinted into emergency reception. As he sped down long broad corridors, flashes of family emergencies flashed through his mind. The rescue that hadn't happened when his little sister drowned in Lake Erie when he was a teen. A sadistic killer who nearly bludgeoned Kingsley to death when she got too close to solving her young husband's murder. A happier time—Billy's birth, as the Valentine blizzard blew drifts across their driveway, Kingsley insisting that first babies didn't just fall out. They barely made it in time.

"William Henning, my son—is he all right? Where did they take him? Where's my wife?" He babbled apologies for being so demanding.

"He's being examined by his pediatrician in bay two on the right. You go; we can catch up with the paperwork later."

Todd imagined his tiny son lost in a sea of white sheets, connected by tubes and surrounded by demonic machines. He skidded to a stop and, forcing composure he didn't feel, stepped into the bay. Billy apparently slept while his mother and doctor spoke in hushed tones. Both looked up at him. "I've just been explaining to Kingsley that she's not a bad mother. You can't stop kids from running around. That's not what this is about. Billy has a virus—and it won't be his last."

"Did we overreact?"

"Not at all. Some children can be desperately ill with a temperature of one hundred, while others are bouncing around at one hundred two. What you could not have known was at what temperature Billy might convulse. We've given him something to bring down his fever, and he's cooler already."

"They want to keep him here in the ER until tomorrow, just to make sure. He doesn't need to be admitted," Kingsley said. "Why don't you go home; grab some sleep. Come back for us in the morning—no, it's already tomorrow. I'm sorry. I can't sort out the logistics."

"Better if I stay. I don't want to risk killing those guys if they're still on the job."

೧೩೮

The dealmaker hung up, then placed a call to a trusted operative. "I may have a job for you, removing an obstacle from one of my projects. I'll try something lowkey first, but if that doesn't work and you're available, we'll make a deal."

"You know how to find me."

He disconnected. This could get expensive, but hell—he'd padded the budget by millions for unexpected contingencies. He knew the timeline intimately and by now, with ground broken, the project had passed the point of no return. He couldn't help smiling. Just when things were getting dull a real challenge he could get his teeth into had presented itself.

ℰᏣℰᏣ

Kingsley instantly recognized Greg's name and voice on her caller ID—the young realtor who had shown them their house when it came on the market. The house was love at first sight, ending their exhaustive search for the perfect historical property. At first, it appeared that they were too late. After showing them the farmhouse, Greg learned that another buyer had made an offer—five percent below the asking price. The prospect also wanted an allowance for new wiring, and the sale was contingent upon mortgage approval.

Todd had been undeterred. "Tell him you've got a cash customer who's willing to pay the asking price and take the property as-is. I'll give him a ten-percent nonrefundable down payment today and the balance in a week if we can sign the agreement *today*. Tomorrow the deal's off the table. Tell him to call you right back." And the seller accepted their offer! Kingsley couldn't tell who had been more excited—Greg for landing his first big sale or them for finding their forever home.

She picked up the phone, and they chatted a few minutes, relishing the major coup they had accomplished together. Greg sounded more confident and mature than when they'd met three years ago. Then a newlywed, the realtor, and his wife now had a baby girl and his business was thriving. "Having sold that property so quickly and for the asking price opened the floodgates for prospective clients, especially high-end buyers. I can't thank you enough."

"You did all the work—getting the listing in the first place, researching qualified buyers, and calling us at dawn on that Sunday morning. What's on your agenda today? Hoping to sell us vacation property?"

"I know what you're going to say before I ask, but I'm obligated to do so. I've been approached by a reputable realtor on behalf of a client whose name must remain anonymous, except to say that the client is a well-known entertainer. Seems his client fell in love with Lancaster County after seeing the movie *Witness*. The client has toured the area repeatedly and fell in love with your house."

"I remember the movie—Harrison Ford and Kelly McGillis—about a little Amish boy who witnessed a murder. That was filmed west of here. Is one of them the prospective buyer? I won't tell. Honest."

Greg chuckled. "No. Afraid not. This person, through the agent, has authorized me to offer you $2 million for your property."

"Two million dollars! That's crazy! They can find any number of suitable properties for half that amount, even considering the cost of renovation. Or build it themselves with the right architect. Tell the client that he or she needs a reality check. And to employ a better researcher."

"Do you want to talk it over with Todd? That's quite a return on a three-year investment."

"Absolutely not. He would tell you, as I will, that our home isn't for sale. You cannot put a value on our experience here."

Snapshots ran through her mind—their painstaking historical research, their hands-on attention to detail, their sweat equity as dream turned into reality. She glanced around their library, its ten-foot cherry bookshelves and refinished plank floors. The fireplace that failed to warm them while they awaited the kidnapper's call that never came. And their joyous entry through that walnut front door, carrying infant Billy safely back home.

"The buyer was afraid you'd say that. Evidently, money is no object. I'm authorized to increase the offer to two-point-five million. And if that doesn't interest you, then please name your price. If you go high enough, you won't need to worry about Ivy League tuition for your son."

"I know you're just doing your job, but our home is not for sale at any price. And please, tell the agent to be emphatic with his client that we must not be bothered. If they try an end-run around you, we will involve our attorney."

"That's what I expected. I'll let them know. By the way, I've learned something new about disclosures that you should have been told, but I was unfamiliar with that rule or with local folklore. It wouldn't have made any difference, since you were willing to buy the property *as is*, but it seems the house is rumored to be haunted."

Kingsley laughed. "You mean we might have our own personal poltergeist? That's hilarious. Where did you hear that?"

"Someone researching paranormal legends found an article in a crime writer's magazine written around the turn of the last century—nineteen hundreds, that is. Seems a double murder, committed in a bedroom in the mid-1800s, is still unsolved, and a ghost prowls the house looking for answers. You can hire a member of the Paranormal Society to examine your house and confirm or deny the existence of ghosts."

"Thanks, but I don't believe in ghosts. And we're

bankrolling enough professionals to deal with normal old-house issues. Word is the exterminator named his firstborn after Todd. But Greg, speaking of mysteries, there is something weird about that multi-million-dollar offer. If you would, please email me about how your next conversation with that agent concludes. And thanks." They exchanged parting pleasantries and disconnected.

∽∾∽

How odd, she thought, to be home on a Tuesday in a quiet house. Even O'Malley wasn't begging for attention. Where was he? Quitting the loan application she had accessed through the bank's mainframe, she closed her laptop and stretched the kinks from her back. Having spent all night in an ER guest chair was catching up with her. A hot shower would feel great, but she feared that Billy would awaken and she wouldn't hear him.

Instead, she closed her eyes and let her mind drift. She loved their library, her *sanctum sanctorum*, their desks abutting in the center of the room. Todd's was a gift from his grandfather when he'd graduated from Harvard, a cherrywood treasure darkened with age. She had chosen a leather-top desk and, realizing its impracticality, had it custom-fitted with a glass top. She had imagined them pouring over banking minutia, face to face, papers overspreading both surfaces. But that rarely happened. They turned out to be kitchen table folks or ensconced in wingchairs by the fireplace.

His was leather, hers upholstered in muted fabric that repeated warm shades of firelight and the ancient pine floor. They'd hoped to retain the floor's ancient charm, but it was beyond repair—chipped paint, grayed, gouged, and splintered in places. Todd had attached it with an industrial sander their first work weekend at the house. She closed her eyes, remembering the day. Todd, dripping in the insufferable humidity, sawdust sticking to bare chest, masked with a respirator, attacking the floors. She'd spent that Memorial Day weekend edging their first garden on the west side of the house and discovering long-forgotten old roses. No way would she consider selling. She grinned, reflecting her little son's wisdom—*Mine!*

Dragging herself from her comfy reflections, she placed her laptop and papers in her briefcase and went searching for O'Malley. When he didn't respond to her call, she glanced around the glass pocket door and looked down the hall. O'Malley was parked at the foot of the stairs, prone but head up, alert. "There you are!"

She stooped to give him some loving, doubting he understood one word of the praise she was heaping upon him for alerting them to Billy's dire situation. What could she give him that he'd understand? "Come on," she coaxed, patting her thigh. "You've earned full membership in this family." He stood, cocking his head left, then right, as if asking for an explanation. Kingsley mounted three steps. "Come on." She didn't need to say it again.

He matched her, step for step, to the top of the flight, around the landing, and up the final six, the first door on the left being Billy's. She'd left it open. "Come. It's okay," she said patting the rug beside Billy's bed. The child slept through the milestone. "Stay," she said, then scurried to her room to fetch fresh clothes. Before heading into the shower, she took one last peek at the tableau. Billy slept and O'Malley was stretched out, head on his forepaws, just as he had under their kitchen table his first evening in their house. "Good little dog," she said. He didn't get up, but his tail thump-thump-thumped on the rug.

When she returned from her fastest shower on record, hair wrapped in a towel, the dog hadn't moved. Billy, however, was curled up beside him on the rug, his arm around the dog's furry body. He grinned at his mother through sleepy eyes, and O'Malley thumped his thanks. She acknowledged the obvious—the pair could not spend their nights on the floor.

Chapter 7

Kingsley spotted the white panel truck with a water company logo that was crunching toward their back door. She jumped from her kitchen stool to meet him. The uniformed driver hopped out, clipboard in hand, and approached the door. Before he could knock, she flung it open, nearly being punched in the eye by his fist. Both jumped back, laughing. He regained his composure. "A delivery for you, Ms. Henning?"

"This way, please." She directed him into the kitchen and pointed to a spot in the corner. "Set it right there." With a dolly, he wheeled the water cooler's base into position and anchored a five-gallon jug on its top.

"If everyone had well water as pure as yours, nobody would need us." He riffled through the papers attached to her order. "According to our analysis, however, you would be wise to install a water softener. Shows here that you have serious levels of dissolved limestone that will narrow your pipes over time. You don't want the expense and inconvenience of ripping them out and replacing them."

"That's what our plumber said when we renovated our home. We took his advice, except for the kitchen cold, which is *hard*. Opinions differ on whether it's all right to drink softened water. I wanted fluoride, which your company carries, for our son's developing teeth."

"Some folks don't believe in that."

"And that's just awful, denying a child a lifetime of perfect teeth when he's too young to make that decision for himself. The American Dental Society spent millions trying to educate people about fluoride, which made the list of the top ten medical discoveries of the twentieth century. Objections have ranged from a communist plot to terrorists poisoning us, to ignorance."

"I remember. A small town out west where people who had lived for generations didn't have cavities. Some smart researchers tested the water supply and da da! Fluoride. Most toothpastes have it now, but that's not the same thing as taking it systemically. Wonder if it makes bones harder too."

He turned toward the back door. "Do you want me to leave extra jugs?"

"That, I hadn't considered. May I see how fast we use this one? And get back to you about delivering more? My husband and I are addicted to our well water, and our teeth are formed."

"Sure. We also can set up a delivery schedule, like we do for our business clients, so you don't have to contend with the weight."

As Kingsley was about to ask if there was paperwork for her to sign, her cell phone, which she'd left in the library, jangled. "Would you excuse me for a minute? I'm expecting a call."

"Sure."

When she returned, clutching the phone to her shoulder, the deliveryman had folded his order form and tucked it into his pocket. She pointed to the pen he held in his hand, but he waved her off mouthing *that's okay*. She fingerwaved to him, pointing to her phone as he pushed the dolly through the back door. After the call finished, she noted Billy's appointment on the oversized family calendar that hung on the wall.

Paperwork? She hurried through the back door to catch the water guy and see if everything was in order or if he needed further information, but he had already climbed into the driver's seat. He must be done for the day—he had swapped his company logo shirt for a tee shirt and denim jacket. He seemed to be fiddling with what looked like sophisticated electronic equipment. She shrugged. Everything was so high-tech these days—even water.

ℯↄℯↄ

"Chrissy! Oh my god, where are you? The last I heard you were planning on working forever in London. You have not stayed in touch as you promised." Kingsley continued scolding her old college roommate.

"I'm home on vacation to see my parents, but K, I'm becoming a real Anglophile. The history, the art, the gracious lifestyle, the king's English, the food—well, maybe not the food, but they do cook a great breakfast, especially poached eggs like my grandma's. You guys doing fine?"

"We are so blessed."

"That's overdue." She didn't need to mention Kingsley's first husband's murder or her good fortune in meeting Todd. Kingsley smiled, appreciating real friends, who bridged time and distance by picking up where they left off, regardless of long separations.

"Speaking of luck, I had a chance meeting with an old friend at a symposium in Boston. She's a history professor, lecturer, and author, and wouldn't you know it? She's researching early-American architecture in your area that goes back to the William Penn Land Grants. Thinking of your wonderful home, I lapsed into my corny Pennsylvania Dutch accent with 'git aught naw.' I hope you don't mind, but I described your house and, well, I sort of gave her your contact information. She'd like to interview you."

"Chris, I never, ever give interviews. I detest the media. When Andy died in that horrible crash, I couldn't even go back to work without them hounding me. They literally drove me from Philadelphia."

"But in the middle of nowhere, you met Todd."

"And when Billy was kidnapped, they printed those horrible lies that we were involved."

"Which they later retracted."

"Too little. Too late. So—no matter how lovely, smart, and interesting your historian-friend is, the answer is no."

"Dr. Suzanne Meade is a history *professor*, not a journalist, whose area of expertise is colonial America. And, she thinks rural central Pennsylvania is more fascinating and under-researched than Philadelphia."

"Chrissy—think to the vanishing point. She writes a best seller, goes on book tours with all that publicity, which puts our home on the tourist maps along with where to buy Amish quilts. Then some hotshot reporter does a little research and, in a flash of brilliance realizes, 'Oh! *That* family!' And sells his editor on 'Revisiting the Hennings,' and it starts all over again. No way. Tell her to try Union County."

"K. She's *not* a reporter. She writes textbooks. Even if she doesn't make specific reference to your house, your names, or location, wouldn't you love to know its provenance going back hundreds of years? She has the education and experience to know where to dig and find all that great detail for you. Free!"

"Why is this friend so important to you if reconnecting with her was a chance occurrence?"

"She enthralled me with ghost stories. Evidently, a lot of your local dwellings are supposed to be haunted."

"She thinks our house might be haunted? That's the second time I've heard that in the past week. Where did she get that idea?"

"I'm saying her research would trace, not only the structure but any folklore, including supernatural events, associated with the property. Or a lack thereof. Come on, K. Think about all the people who've helped us along the way. She isn't the kind of person who would head into the country and knock on strangers' doors. And given the parameters of academic research, she can't just write stories from internet snippets. She needs an introduction to the right people."

"You say you gave her my contact information…"

"Well, um, yes. I didn't think you'd mind, since she's a friend of mine."

Ah, dear Christine, who would befriend the whole world, given the chance. "Ok. I'll talk to her, but please tell her, in advance, that we will require her and any assistants or photographers to sign nondisclosure agreements, or whatever they're called. And they can photograph architectural details only, not the entire, recognizable house. Ditto interior shots, especially those containing recognizable photos or personal effects. And I'll need to sign off on any part of the manuscript that includes any part of our home."

"Done! Now, when can you come to England for a visit? You have a standing invitation. I'll drop everything; cancel whatever and show you the best of London that the tourists can't access."

With a flurry of rash promises, they disconnected. "I'll never hear from that writer with all those strings I attached," she mumbled.

"What strings?" Todd descended the last few steps, carrying jammy-clad Billy, his dark curls damp from his bath. O'Malley lock-stepped beside them.

"That was Christine, my college roomie. You remember her from our wedding. Stunning beauty in a teal flowered dress."

"The only beautiful lady I saw in your parents' garden that day wore cream-colored lace and carried the yellow roses I brought her."

Kingsley blinked a tear at the unexpected sentiment expressed by her practical husband. She grinned at him. "Thank you. But—Chris wants me to meet a friend of hers, a historian who is writing a textbook on colonial architecture." She gave Todd the executive summary of the professor's mission. "Christine wants me to show her our home, but I think not."

Todd shrugged. "It's up to you, hon. I don't feel strongly one way or the other. Unless she's bringing a fleet of reporters."

"Strange—at first I thought Christine was in England. The connection was poor—a bit of static. But she's home visiting her parents. I noticed the static yesterday, too. Call our landline from your cellphone, will you? Intermitted cellphone reception is one thing, but if we're having trouble with hard-wired service, I'll report it to the phone company."

He dialed, and she picked up. "There! Can you hear that? No? Trade me phones."

He did, then shook his head and shrugged. "Can she come visit and bring this academia friend?"

"Unfortunately, no. She's heading back to England tomorrow." They hung up their respective phones.

Todd dropped into his leather wing-back chair, positioning Billy on his lap. Billy thrust a favorite book at his father, nearly clipping his chin. O'Malley wriggled his head between Todd and the chair's other arm, poised to leap onto his lap. "Go. Lie. Down!" Todd uttered. O'Malley slinked to Kingsley's chair and tried the same approach.

"I'll take him outside," she said. At the O word, he leapt

to all fours in one motion and headed toward the front door, pausing momentarily to make sure she was coming. She shook her head. "Guess who's being trained?"

⌘⌘

Professor Suzanne Meade angled her rental car onto the narrow driveway that led to the Conrad Weiser Homestead in Womelsdorf, Pennsylvania. Parking, she joined the Homestead's Charter Day celebration. Costumed 1700s re-enactors representing English and French soldiers, Native American peoples, and craftsmen of the era gave historical talks.

What captured Suzanne's attention, however, was the Homestead's centerpiece two-story home that was built in 1834 that now housed the visitor's center and museum. Its front door faced a small stone structure, believed to be the original *square stone* structure built by Conrad Weiser himself in the early 1700s. Its authentic details included a traditional Germanic floorplan with stylistic 18th-century appointments. Three other stone buildings, constructed of matching fieldstone, graced the thirty-acre park.

Inside the visitor's center, Suzanne lost herself in Conrad Weiser's history. Born in 1696 in Germany, he contributed extensively to early America as a celebrated colonial diplomat who mediated peace between Pennsylvanians and the powerful Iroquois Nation.

Outside, Suzanne drank in the details with a historian's zeal, including the original hardware and shutters. She pressed a volunteer for details, who was happy to share. "Eager to settle the wilderness, Penn enticed prospective landowners and farmers with parcels that were huge by European standards. All the settlers had to do was make their claim, settle, and work the land, which included defending it from unfriendly natives.

"Remember how kids learned the rhyme, 'In fourteen hundred ninety-two, Columbus sailed the ocean blue?' Between 1500 and 1750, natives and Europeans were already doing a lot of trading. So 'Penn's Woods' wasn't totally unknown to venturesome Europeans." The volunteer related how early American surveyors marked the parcels. "Distance was measured by how far a person could walk in a day. Rather than lug heavy pins, the surveyors notched *witness trees* at the corners of properties. Surveys were then filed with the Surveyors Office."

"Where might I see the original land-grant documents?"

He handed her one of the Homestead's brochures, Pennsylvania Trails of History. "Contact this fellow at the Pennsylvania State Archives in Harrisburg," he said, adding a friend's contact information. "I'll give him a heads-up. He'll be happy to help you. And give him my best."

Even though it was late afternoon, internet directions took her to Harrisburg in an hour. As she crossed Third Street, she spotted the beautiful Archive Building on the right. She found a restaurant, grabbed a light dinner, and checked into a hotel nearby.

Once settled, she opened the Pennsylvania State Archives website and learned, to her dismay, that it was closed on Mondays and Tuesdays. What was she going to do for two and a half days? She phoned Kingsley Henning, and before she could finish a detailed apology for delaying her plans, Kingsley picked up.

"I'm here. And yes, of course, Wednesday afternoon will be fine. I hope you won't be too bored filling in the time.

"Not at all. I can use it to visit other museums. By the way, I heard about a fascinating story in an old crime writers' magazine about an unsolved murder mystery in the mid-1800s. While the location of the house was murky, it could even be yours. Did you ever suspect that your house might be haunted?"

Where had she heard that before! "Go on…"

"I'll tell you all about the article when I see you. Is there evidence of structures that might have predated your house? Perhaps an old cemetery? Stone footers or tumbled-down foundations on the property?"

"We do have the remnants of a summer kitchen and spring house downhill by the creek, but that's all." Kingsley wracked her memory for additional details, but she had been looking for old gardens and artifacts like arrowheads.

Kingsley felt her enthusiasm growing at the prospect of expanding her treasure-trove of knowledge about their old house. "I'll be home all afternoon Wednesday, so please take your time. And if your schedule changes, just call or text. And I'd love to hear more about that old article."

Suzanne disconnected, totally out of the mood to answer emails. Instead, she explored the Archive's website and read…

"In 1681 William Penn founded the Commonwealth of Pennsylvania, and the Charter that gave him the legal right to do so lives today in the Pennsylvania State Archives. About 250,000,000 other documents live in the archives alongside Penn's Charter, and though few of them are as dramatic as the Charter, each one has been selected because it has tremendous historical, legal, or financial value to the Commonwealth."

The sheer volume of such a treasure took her breath away, as she digested the home page's details. She also learned that transfer of ownership, beyond the first deeds and the Revolutionary War, would be found in individual county records. Fascinated, she narrowed the topics in preparation for Wednesday. Clicking on *Pennsylvania Architectural Field Guide* she selected *Pennsylvania German 1700 to 1870*, the timeframe within which the

Henning's home would have been built, noting identifiable features.

Christine's photos of the Henning's home reminded Suzanne of the ironmaster's mansion at Hopewell Village, but the Henning home didn't fit all the descriptors. Perhaps she'd found a truly unique example of early American architecture that incorporated European forms.

She wasn't tired, and the Susquehanna Greenway was just a couple blocks to the west. Maybe she'd take a drive, circle the Governor's Residence, and fill her tank. The quiet streets with broad sidewalks beckoned her. With so many fine museums within a short distance, filling two days would be a pleasure. She cursed her indulgence in that glass of red wine which sometimes, coupled with being sleep deprived, triggered a migraine.

Feeling drowsy, she returned to the hotel and parked in the last available place. She decided to grab her puffer jacket from the trunk as the weather was deteriorating as predicted. Unfamiliar with the rental's idiosyncrasies, she fumbled with the fob to pop the trunk and donned the pink coat. Her eyesight became a bit blurry, and she wished she'd looked for a trunk latch on the driver-side floor.

Later, she would recall hearing footsteps on the pavement behind her, which she had chosen to ignore. She grabbed her jacket and prepared to head toward the building. Suddenly a blinding pain split the crown of her head. Her last thought was chiding herself for not following her specialist's advice.

✥✥✥

Robert, an accountant, and water-terrified non-swimmer, met beautiful Juliet, a teacher and Y swimming instructor during a church supper. She'd offered to teach him to swim if he'd help her conquer her greatest fear—Excel spreadsheets. The ultra-introverts bonded, helping each other overcome their shyness. In time, he could power through twenty laps, and she gloried through her first solo spreadsheet that her school required for her expenses.

On an unusually warm March Sunday, although terrified, he accepted her invitation to kayak on the Susquehanna River. Juliet loaded her tandem BKC TX 219 onto her SUV near Duncannon, north of Harrisburg's capitol. A pair of Robert's buddies parked his pickup near their southern destination, just north of Maclay Street.

The water level was high from winter's runoff and Juliet could barely contain her excitement. "I know the river well—its little islands, birds, wildlife, even a private spot downstream for our picnic. If you fish, we can return another time for native brook trout. We'll stay to the left heading south to avoid the most difficult parts of the river. Let's do it!"

"With my truck twelve miles downstream, we'd better quit now or determine to finish." She laughed, as she always did, at his lame jokes.

The elegant craft glided through the calm, smooth waters, Juliet's oars dipping into the water while Robert concentrated on not messing up their trajectory. With the breeze riffling his hair and the beauty and peace of the river, he couldn't help grinning. She was giving the bookish guy the time of his life, and he would do anything to please her.

Halfway, they picnicked on a little island she'd discovered, and lazed away the carefree afternoon, chatting about everything and nothing at all. Abruptly, they realized the sun was setting; they'd lost track of time. Gathering clouds and the river's mist worried Robert, but Juliet seemed unperturbed as they reentered the river. Robert studied the shoreline's irregularity, grisly trees throwing grotesque shadows in the dwindling light. Debris clung to low-hanging vegetation that dragged in the water.

"Should we paddle out a bit farther?" he called over her shoulder. "What if there's underwater roots that could snag us?" He no sooner finished his question when a bright pink object close to the bank grabbed his attention. As they passed, it looked like a swimmer, but the shape wasn't stroking. A discarded bundle of clothing? A mannequin?

"Look! It's a person in trouble! Someone's hung up in the roots."

By the time Juliet processed what he was yelling, they had drifted well beyond the indistinguishable form. Robert extracted himself from the kayak, tore off his jacket, and dived into the water. He swam furiously against the current, angling toward the bank until he could grab dangling vegetation, some of which stripped off in his hands. Half swimming, half hauling himself, he propelled north through the frigid water toward the object. He persevered even as his muscles threatened to cramp.

At length, he found what he had dreaded—a woman, face down in the branches, her auburn hair splayed like a halo, her skin and lips blue. When he snagged her by her jacket, it separated from her body, enabling him to free her and drag her onto the bank. Her skin was ice cold. Although there was no way of telling how long she'd been in the water, he refused to assume she was dead. He checked for a pulse. Feeling none, he checked her mouth—her tongue wasn't obstructing her airway—and began chest compressions while yelling for help.

Juliet approached from the walking trail, having beached the kayak at the first possible opportunity, climbed the bank, and ran north until she could hear Robert's voice. "Call 911," he gasped in between commands to the lifeless form. "Breathe! Breathe!"

Water Rescue, EMTs, and local police descended on the scene. The young couple huddled on the periphery, feeling helpless and disconnected. "She must be alive," Juliet whispered to Robert. "Otherwise, they would have brought her up by now."

"Unless they're waiting for the coroner to arrive and pronounce her. It is Sunday evening. He could be anywhere."

"Maybe we could ask…"

They were about to do so when a policeman approached them. "You the guy who found her?" he asked. As succinctly as possible, they related what little they knew. The cop took down their names and contact information, saying someone would be in touch. Robert was shivering so badly that he thought his teeth might break. He stamped his feet in an attempt to revive his circulation. The cop, noticing his distress, pulled blankets from a nearby ambulance.

It was then that they realized their predicament. Even if they retraced her steps to the kayak, it was too dark and cold to re-enter the river, and they were miles from their destination. She approached the water rescue guy, who by now had figured he wouldn't be needed, and begged his assistance to rescue the kayak and give them a lift. "You the guy that pulled her out of the river?"

"Yeah. Is she…will she be all right?"

"Too soon to tell. If she does survive, it's because of you. Where did you learn to swim like that? The current is treacherous."

He grinned and nodded to Juliet through chattering teeth. "She taught me—at the Y."

"He can do anything. He is so smart. He's an accountant."

"You know who she is?"

"No idea," Robert answered. "But she was wearing a bright pink jacket when I pulled her out of the water. It drifted downstream—maybe it has some ID in the pocket."

Chapter 8

Wednesday afternoon Kingsley filled her favorite China teapot with warm water, set it aside, and turned on the burner to wait for the kettle to whistle. She assembled raspberry rugalachs, mini blueberry muffins, and white seedless grapes on a three-tier silver server along with linen napkins, dessert plates, and silverware. She added two crystal glasses and a pitcher of spring water that she'd chilled in the fridge. With fierce concentration, she carried the heavy tray to the living room as the tall-case clock chimed twice. Dr. Meade would be arriving any minute. She set the tray on the trunk. Returning to the kitchen, she filled the teapot with boiling water and suspended a tea ball.

Ah! Sugar, cream, and lemon! After grabbing the condiments, she placed them on the silver tea tray beside the cups and saucers and hustled to finish the tea. Too late she realized she had overfilled it, and boiling tea sloshed on her wrist. She screamed, but rather than drop the antique teapot, she took precious seconds to set it on the tray before grabbing ice from the freezer. *Clumsy, Clumsy, Clumsy!* She alternated icing her wrist and mopping the spill. She hurried to take the tea tray to the living room, feeling the burn's heat rise incrementally until she could hold more ice in place.

A white Audi inched down their gravel driveway, circumventing the gullies and ruts worn by the winter snow's runoff. *This might be the year to pave it,* Kingsley thought, adding one more joyless challenge to historic homeownership. As the car halted beside the brick walkway, a slender woman uncoiled from its tan bucket seats. She wore champagne-colored boots beneath a black pencil skirt, a white silk blouse, and a matching leather jacket. Kingsley stepped onto the brick entryway, waving to her visitor. The driver, spotting her, waved back, and shut off the engine.

"You must be Suzanne," Kingsley said. She was as lovely as any fashion model with twinkling blue eyes and a winning smile.

"Thank *you* so much for letting me stop for a few minutes." She glanced at her skinny gold watch that sparkled with tiny diamonds when she turned it. "I am *so* sorry to be late. I made the wrong turn," she said, shaking Kingsley's outstretched hand. "Hello again. I feel like we already know each other, after chatting on the phone. I can't thank you enough for meeting me in person and helping me with my research."

She swiveled her head, taking in the magnificent woods. "What a gorgeous setting! It's nearly hidden by what, virgin forest? When Chris described it, I just knew I had to see it in person. I wanted to see what the earliest settlers must have encountered. How relieved they must have felt by—this!"

Suzanne's eyes focused an appreciative sweep of the rhododendrons and wild mountain laurel that obscured the house from the two-lane approach. "It's gorgeous!" she moaned as if drunk with the beauty. "I can't imagine your stumbling onto a place like this and finding it on the market. Just how old is it?"

"The original house was built in 1803," Kingsley said. "You'll notice the date stone above the lintel. The walls are native limestone, 29 inches thick, and the windows are original. See that mortar line?" She pointed to a vertical seam that bisected the house. "Everything to the left of the front door and foyer was added in the 1830s, which doubled the living space."

Stumbled? Kingsley smiled, remembering Todd's exhaustive search before they met, which consumed every weekend after they became a couple. "What you see represents good bones and a lot of sweat equity. I'm afraid, for your purposes, what constitutes *historic* may have been destroyed by previous renovations, repairing old mistakes, or our bringing the house up to code. We joked that insanity must run in the family, but we were determined to preserve its history while making the structure livable."

She turned toward the massive walnut door and motioned for the historian to precede her. "Why don't we chat in the living room? I've made tea, there's ice water, and our favorite little pastries." By the time they were comfortably seated, the ice on her wrist had dribbled a stream to her elbow. "Burned it," she confessed, dabbing errant drips with her napkin. "So clumsy of me. Would you mind pouring?"

"It would be my pleasure. What lovely China!" she said, tracing the floral motif with an elegant finger while having the good manners not to turn her cup upside down to read its hallmark. With the grace of a grand lady from an old English family, Suzanne poured with precision and handed Kingsley her cup. For herself, she declined condiments, but relished a rugalach, expressing awe that they were homemade. Kingsley thanked her, without confessing whose home and at what country market she'd bought them.

"Chris said you were researching pre-Revolutionary Pennsylvania architecture. I'm afraid we don't know much about this property's provenance beyond the datestone and certain elements that haven't been touched. All we needed was a clear title, which an insurance company researched."

"I've read that many of these old homes are haunted. Do you have a resident ghost or two?"

Kingsley shook her head. *Huh! Again with the ghost.* "Nary a murmur, a squeak, or things going bump in the night. Old houses have character, and that includes noises. Why don't we get started?" Kingsley suggested, motioning her guest toward the foyer.

"The original house includes this foyer and staircase, and everything to its right—two rooms downstairs and two bedrooms upstairs. The bathroom, above the foyer, was added in the twentieth century. Former owners included newlyweds who stayed sixty years. The widow spent her last five years in a nursing home while the house stood empty. Her heirs sold it to our previous owner who sold it to us after another five years."

As they paused in the foyer, Kingsley's memory conjured her introduction to her future, as she and then-fiancé Todd had their first peek. She remembered the smell of old wood, well-used fireplaces, dust, and murmuring drafts that occasionally whistled that frigid Sunday morning. North-facing windowpanes had been frosty, it was that cold.

"Foyers got to be twelve feet wide by twenty feet deep," her visitor said, breaking Kingsley's reverie. "What a great space to entertain. And that staircase is amazing. Is it original?"

"That's an unusual detail. Having toured old ironmaster's mansions, such as Charming Forge and Hopewell Furnace, we realized this stairway goes the opposite way. No idea why. Usually, they turn left on the landing before climbing the remaining steps to accommodate the height of the first-floor ceilings." The woman took out her camera. Kingsley held her hand in the stop position. "Please.

No pictures. As Christine should have told you, we're very private people. You can take tight shots of architectural details, but not of whole rooms. I'm sorry."

Suzanne smiled reassuringly, giving Kingsley's shoulder the tiniest pat, dispelling the awkward moment. "Are the windows fair game?"

"Just let me remove a few photographs and family memorabilia—sorry—I didn't know what would interest you. The wavy glass is original. A few were damaged beyond repair, but we connected with a historical renovator who found authentic replacements. Say! Let me give you his card. He has great stories about historical buildings. He salvages items from old structures that are being torn down, rescuing vintage wood, barn boards, mantles, hardware, and so on."

She continued her tour-guide role. "This room, right of the foyer, might have been a formal dining room in the nineteenth century. We thought it would make a great library, using the family's sitting room, which was behind the front parlor—now our living room where we were sitting—as our dining room. The library screamed for glass doors. Hardly historical. We added all the bookshelves and spend many evenings by the fireplace, which is original. Many old homes of this era had fireplaces in the corners. You might make a note of that. We loved that this one's centered on the outside wall."

Kingsley circled her guest throughout the downstairs, explaining where they'd violated the historical integrity like the powder room tucked under the stairs. "Left of the foyer would have been the front parlor and behind it, the family's sitting room. The parlor was used when the minister came calling or to lay out a deceased family member for his wake." She led Suzanne through the dining room and across the back hall. "Beyond the back hall, we enter the kitchen, which would have been the heart of the home."

"Does that door go to a basement?" she asked as they approached the kitchen. "I'd love to see its foundation, especially if it has exposed timbers."

Kingsley laughed. "It's a dungeon. Strictly utilitarian. Borderline clean by a shop vac. Watch your step." They clattered downstairs.

"Is it possible this house was part of the underground railroad for slaves escaping to Canada? Can I look around?"

"Sure," Kingsley said, amused by the woman's circling the foundation as if peering for possible places of concealment. She spotted the bundle of wires that traveled down from the first floor to a breaker box. "New wiring," Kingsley supplied. "No way to fishhook new wire using the old because they were junctured every two studs. The electrician routed new wires through the *raceway*, which looks like part of the molding. Then they were dropped to the basement through that hole in the corner."

"Can I see the second floor too?"

"I can show you the kitchen on our way." As they passed the kitchen doorway, Kingsley pointed to the walk-in fireplace, expecting her guest to gasp with delight. When Suzanne didn't, Kingsley prodded.

"That's original, although we cook with gas. Propane to be exact." But her guest had continued sauntering down the hall toward the foyer. "The hardware dates to the earliest owners who hung their cooking pots," she called after her. "We use them ourselves. The brick, underneath, is original." That feature alone would have sold Kingsley on the house, but the historian didn't seem interested.

Kingsley shrugged and followed her toward the stairway. She guessed Suzanne must be tiring, barely glancing at the fireplaces that were treasured in older houses. Kingsley trailed her, explaining the intricacies of the woodwork and the staircase, and led her upstairs to the bedrooms. "I had been warned," Kingsley said, "not to paint any interior wood until we spent a full year with central heat and air. The former owner never lived in the house during the winter, and his predecessors heated with the fireplaces and a wood stove."

They paused at the landing's window that overlooked the backyard and the farmland beyond. As Kingsley turned right to climb the last six steps, Suzanne hung back, taking a long look at the backyard. "Amazing," she purred. They trooped six more steps into the broad upper hall.

"Before indoor plumbing this hall would have extended to the center front window. Each bedroom has its own fireplace. We added new closets, partitioned between the front and back rooms. Back in the day, people didn't have many clothes, and closets were considered *rooms* for tax purposes. Homeowners used tall chests instead." A quick circle through the bedrooms drew an occasional *hum* until Suzanne spotted the door to the attic. That brought her to life. "May we?" she asked.

The steep, narrow staircase brought them into a cavernous space, its only contents being several boxes marked *Christmas*. Drop cloths and unopened paint cans lined the far wall between two dormer windows. "Here's something worth noting," Kingsley said, pointing to the floorboards. "This floor was a hodge-podge of boards considered rejects, suitable for kids' bedrooms or servant quarters in wealthier households. Be sure to photograph them and compare them to the wide planks in the lower floors, which today's homeowners value. Back then, when they ran out of wood, they used whatever was available. We would have loved to preserve the original floorboards, but they necessitated sanding and refinishing."

"And those boards?" she asked, pointing to an area of newer planks.

"Our expert said we had two choices if we intended to

keep the original first floors—*borrow* some from the third floor or hunt vintage stock. Using some of these was the perfect solution since vintage matches would cost a mint. We swapped some from here for pine replacements."

They descended the narrow stairs single file. "Oh! I hear my son stirring. He's recovering from a virus. I must check on him."

"May I circle through the rooms again to get tight shots of details you recommended? Especially the fireplace in the kitchen. I promise I won't photograph anything personal."

"I'll catch up with you downstairs," Kingsley called over her shoulder, pleased that the awesome kitchen did get her attention. She hurried to Billy's room, realizing she had violated her own rules when agreeing to the interview, but they felt ridiculous now that she'd met her. She was so lovely. And definitely not a reporter. Kingsley gave Suzanne ample time to peruse whatever interested her.

"He's gone back to sleep," Kingsley said, explaining her lengthy absence.

Suzanne was gathering her jacket and looped her Coach bag over her shoulder.

"You said on the phone that a ghost story appeared in a crime magazine. When was it published? I'd like to find a copy for our family records."

Suzanne flipped through her notes. "I'm sorry. I didn't write it down. I believe it was copyrighted decades ago. Something about an unsolved murder. A genuine cold case." She looked up. "An angry lover, a botched robbery, an estranged family member, an unpaid debt, or something like that. According to the story, a ghost still roams the house, possibly one of the bedrooms."

Kingsley laughed. "The only thing that haunted this house before we took residence were raccoons and a fleet of mice that chewed the electrical wiring to death. If any of their descendants remain, our cat, Pandora, would be delighted to catch them. You asked me about an older dwelling on the property?"

Suzanne looked puzzled. "Well, that would be extremely interesting."

"I asked my husband about the research he did when house hunting alone. He said original dwellings were tiny—one room, maybe twelve by twelve, with a sleeping loft for the family. If they still exist, and modern home-owners had been dedicated to preserving them, the old structures would be either free-standing or incorporated into the new houses that dwarfed them by comparison. We even saw a log house in the middle of a huge new living room. But here? No."

Kingsley's curiosity was piqued. It would be fun to walk a grid with fresh eyes in her Wolverines before the weeds in the *north forty* got any higher.

Suzanne tucked her phone and notebook into her bag. "Your house is a treasure. Thank you so much for meeting with me. It's been a lovely afternoon."

"And for me too. And by the way, when you remember the source of that article—if you happen across it again—please let me know." Kingsley did not believe in ghosts but the creative side of her brain hummed with possibilities. And she did love a good murder mystery. But here? She shivered. As Suzanne's convertible turned left onto the lane, Kingsley heard Billy calling for his mom.

෬෩෬

Todd's entrance through the back door was met by six small pounding feet as his son and little dog erupted into his arms. Hugs and head pats bestowed, he disentangled himself from his welcoming committee. "How did the tour go with the historian?" Todd asked, more hugs and kisses bestowed.

"She was lovely and especially complimentary about our home. I gave her the grand tour, and she had no problems about privacy issues."

"What did she think of the walk-in fireplace?"

Kingsley stopped to think, then pinpointed something that had surprised her. "Not only didn't she react initially, but I don't think she photograph it either, and it's the oldest, undisturbed architectural detail in the house. Our fireplaces in the living room and in our office, centered on the side walls probably aren't typical of houses of this era. She thought they were and those she photographed. But she wasn't interested in the floorboards until I pointed out the significance."

"What interested her most?"

"Now that I think of it—how the new wiring was routed to the basement. And she didn't photograph the original ceilings or the floor moldings. Do you know what it would cost in today's market to use one-foot planks instead of pre-cut molding strips?"

Todd shrugged. "She may have seen those details in numerous houses or books. At least you can tell your roommate you were a gracious hostess. Maybe your guest will acknowledge you in her textbook and send us an autographed copy."

Kingsley started to tell Todd about the ghost story but stopped herself in time. In the horrid weeks following their eight-week-old's kidnapping, she'd had a *visit* from her late Grammy and first husband, Andy, who, just twenty-six, had been murdered. In that *visit*, the pair had communicated, "*he isn't with us.*" Whether a wishful dream in her tortured mind or a message that passed the vale, the content had reassured her that Billy was alive and out there—somewhere. But of course, she'd been dreaming.

Returning Billy to Keynote's daycare to reinforce its

safety had taken monumental courage, but many employees needed it for their kids. The facility could have been shuttered, even though the diabolical kidnapping did not involve negligence. Todd had spearheaded the daycare's creation, even before he met Kingsley when the need had surfaced on employee retention surveys and exit interviews. And now Billy thrived in what should have been the safest place in the commonwealth.

Chapter 9

I t's not fair," Kingsley lamented, holding a cold cloth on her fevered brow. "Mothers aren't allowed to get sick. Why now? After making such intricate getaway plans, I have to miss the most important ABA meeting of the year. Everyone who matters will be there. And! With Mom and Dad prepared for Billy's first big-boy mini-vacation with his grandparents? It isn't fair."

She watched Todd add his Dopp kit and a silk tie to his carry-on and zip his suit bag. "I shouldn't let you near those predatory women, wearing that new Italian suit. Pack something old and ugly."

"Look, K. It could have been a lot worse. You could have been sick at home with a rambunctious two-year-old whining for attention. That is the downside of excellent daycare. He hugs his playmates, and we get a petri dish of their germs. You could have become ill in Chicago."

"Huh! Whatever happened to Sesame Street and long naps."

Todd morphed into list-checking mode. "Billy and I will arrive at your folks by noon, have lunch, then I'll leave for the Philadelphia airport, leaving them to spoil him. I'll be home late Friday night."

"And they'll bring Billy home Friday after his nap." She moaned. "I had such plans for meet-ups with colleagues. Thanks to this virus, I had to cancel everything. It's not fair."

"You already said that. And I agree. Now, I've put my itinerary on your desk, the hotel phone number is on your cell—keep it charged—and call me if you need anything."

"And you'll do—what?"

"I'll make some calls."

"I hope you don't catch this. I'm glad I slept in the other room." Although she rarely did, she loved Grammy's four-poster bed in which she'd napped as a child and the wallpaper she'd duplicated from memory. If only Grammy had lived a decade longer. What fun they would have had! She mentally smacked herself, ashamed that it was about her and not about what Grammy was missing.

Todd broke into her reverie. "Better see if our little man is ready for his adventure. He packed his *balese*. His version of *valise*. Who knows what's inside it?"

"Mom will have lots of new toys and oodles of art supplies for him. And Dad says he set up the little table he kept for me in his downtown office so Billy could play banker like I did."

"At two and a half, does your dad think he's ready for spreadsheets? Unless I miss my guess, our little genius will come home knowing his numbers. Imagine, a fourth-generation Henning banker. On the other hand, another artist. You really do look awful, even for you. Can I get you anything before I go?"

"Will you guys let O'Malley out one more time? See that he has water and dry food?" He nodded yes to all. "I'm going to take a pill to make up for last night and try to sleep this thing off. You go. Make lots of new friends." He hesitated. "And have a terrible time without me."

Billy, having no lingering effects from his viral attack, waved to his mom from her bedroom door, a small canvas bag dangling by it strap and his lop-eared rabbit clutched to his chest. She tried not to cry until their footsteps retreated downstairs. She mopped her eyes and blew her nose one more time then gulped two sleep aids with the glass of cold water that Todd had left on her nightstand. Pandora snuggled against Kingsley's knees, stretched, yawned, and purred. Kingsley's last waking thought was *is this what Thursdays are like when no one is home?*

♋♋

A half-mile short of the construction site, the operative turned right off the rural lane and navigated down the dirt path that had been used for decades by farmers to tend their fields. Years of being tortured by heavy equipment, storms, and gully-washers, the potholes had become tank traps. Carefully navigating the Jeep toward the north forty, the operative realized her vehicle would have done better cutting through last year's cornrows. She bounced to a stop a quarter-mile behind the worksite where a bulldozer appeared to be abandoned. With work hours starting at midnight, the site was deserted as promised.

She stood on the seat, binoculars in hand, and swept the exposure between herself and the road, which lay beyond the bulldozer and was completely hidden by the gentle slope of the land. Swiveling, the land to her north showed a panoramic view of sprouting corn. Having seen an aerial photo, she knew that the undulating farms stretched to the vanishing point, broken only by a meandering stream, occasional homes, barns, and the Appalachian Mountains in the distance. She was alone except for circling turkey buzzards in search of their lunch.

The operative swapped her jeans and jacket for camo pants and shirt, a skull cap that hid her blonde hair, and black army boots, then slung a lightweight camo backpack over her shoulder. For the army veteran and experienced tracker, the short hike to the stone house would be a stroll in the park. Still, her guard remained high, especially since time was scarce. Within twenty minutes, she crossed the property line and, as directed, emerged at the rear of an old bank barn. From its lower right corner, she scoped out the back of the house where she was told family and visitors parked. Metal hasps attached to the heavy barn doors on both levels were secured with combination locks. So far, so good. Nobody appeared to be home.

She studied all the windows on the back and side of the house, but no lights illuminated those rooms. Scrutinizing the eaves and windows, she verified, as her intel had promised, no cameras existed. She extracted the tools she would need from her backpack to pick the backdoor lock, electronics to disengage the security system, the tools she'd need, and a canister of nonlethal spray in case she encountered a dog. She crept to the back door and tested the nob with a featherweight touch. Nudged it gently. And it turned. Could somebody be home? Couldn't be—the cars were all gone. But glancing at the security pad, she saw a green light. Might these city bankers be getting sloppy?

Only after she'd stepped into the back hallway did she spot the mutt, which practically danced to meet her with joyful enthusiasm. Spray? Bad idea. The residual effect might raise suspicion, and her orders were to leave no trace of her visit. She dropped to one knee and coaxed the dog with a morsel of steak she'd brought for just such an occasion. He greedily accepted it, licking her glove. What she needed to do wouldn't take very long. The powder room—that would work. She lifted the dog and set him on the fluffy rug between the toilet and sink and closed the powder room door. She paused half a minute; he didn't protest.

She set to work quickly, reprogramming the security system to take it offline, and then slipped through the house to the designated locations, installing devices that she'd committed to memory from a previous visit rather than risk being caught with schematics or a map. Kitchen—checkmark. Then she peeked into the hall, listening with trained ears for the slightest noise coming from anywhere in the house. She heard the dog breathing, but for whatever reason, he refrained from whimpering. Training, she hoped.

She glided to the staircase, stepping close to the banister to avoid squeaks, rounded the landing, and halted. Nothing. Turning right and up the final six steps, she circled the short hallway to the back guestroom. Her last stop was the third floor, through which the heat pump circuitry was threaded to service the second floor. Tracing the wires, she made the desired renovations with expert precision. Her Casio G-Shock military watch confirmed she'd accomplished the mission within the allotted seconds. With stealth, she descended both flights of stairs and crept toward the back door.

As she was about to retreat the way she had come, the dog's whimper behind the powder room door stopped her. She paused, gloved hand on the doorknob. A distant memory flickered—homeless mongrels, starved for food and attention in war-ravaged villages, begging scraps and mercy from soldiers. A flood of compassion caught her off guard. She cracked the powder room door. The dog's eyes locked with hers—trusting eyes that knew no guile. She scooped the dog onto her hip, holding his muzzle shut just in case he might bark, and exited through the back door.

Intent on her surreptitious exit, she inadvertently kicked a glass jug, which teetered, then lost the battle and smashed on the large flat stones that supported a barbeque grill. She froze, listening, and after verifying that nobody had heard, she circled behind the barn, proceeding through the cornfield to her Jeep. "This is your lucky day, little dude," she whispered to the dog as she set him on the passenger seat.

A soft spring breeze riffled the weeds and stirred the leftover leaves from the previous fall. She stood. Breathed. If just for a minute. The perky little dog tilted his head, first left and then right, as if asking what would come next. Business, she thought, extracting the long-distance timer from the depth of her backpack. Before she could press the countdown button, the dog sprang from the passenger seat, vaulted through the open window, and tore in the direction of the road. Oh, well. What would she do with a dog anyway? Always on the move, accepting the assignments as they were presented by trusted sources.

Screech! Even from the operative's distance, the squeal of brakes reached her ears. Maybe the mutt would survive. Better than leaving him in a death trap. She checked her watch. Time to go. She needed to be miles away when the propane exploded.

∽∂∽∂

"Missy, wake up! Please wake up!" She did or thought that she did. The voice was unfamiliar yet heart-warming. A little child's. "Missy, you must wake up. Now! Get up!"

Mmmm. Grammy? No. Couldn't be. She listened intently, transported backward in time, for Grammy calling her to breakfast. She imagined a whiff of Grammy's gas stove. Pancakes? No. She must be dreaming. She could count on one hand the times that she'd heard Grammy's voice in her dreams since her death when Kingsley was a young teen. Or she thought she was dreaming, but she wasn't that sure.

Why was she dreaming about Grammy now? Pandora had roused and was planting little steps on Kingsley's stomach as if she were dancing. The cat alerted as if startled by something Kingsley couldn't hear, and sprang from the bed and tore from the room. Kingsley forced herself further awake—and then the smell registered. Gas!

Instantly awake, she tore barefooted through the house, downstairs to the kitchen that reeked with fumes. Grabbing a tea towel to cover her face, she yanked at the burners' knobs, but that wasn't the issue—they were all off. What? The propane tank? She yanked her phone off its charger and dialed 911 while tearing toward the backdoor, grabbing Pandora, and clamping the cat to her chest.

"Gas leak! Help me!" She backed from the house toward the garden, broken glass and thorns from the rose border slicing her feet. Pandora struggled, but Kingsley hung on for dear life.

It felt like forever, but it must have been only minutes before emergency vehicles sped from the lane. Kingsley stammered, rapid-fire, the probable source of the gas leak. Their security company arrived shortly thereafter, peppering her with questions that she couldn't answer, like why was the security system disarmed? She didn't understand why a fire marshal would come until he explained that, by the grace of God, an explosion and fire had been averted. Police arrived; more questions; no answers.

She shivered, afraid to re-enter the house in search of a jacket and first aid for her bloody feet. "Are you sure you turned off the burner?" somebody asked.

"We didn't cook breakfast this morning. My husband and son ate cereal, and I was too sick to have any."

"Could your son have played with the nob when no one was looking? What about pets?"

"Absolutely not. Billy was never out of our sight, and he's too short," she exploded defensively, trusting Todd's adherence to safety protocols completely, even though she'd been upstairs in bed.

"What about pets? Any gifted animals in your family?"

"Don't be ridiculous." She jerked her head toward Pandora. "Just me and a fifteen-pound dog. No monkey."

The man from the gas company emerged from the kitchen. "Think we'd better call the police. The gas line shows evidence of tampering."

The mention of a dog startled Kingsley. O'Malley. Where was their dog? With all the commotion, he'd no doubt found someplace to hide. She hobbled toward the back door. "Is it safe to go in?"

The security officer approached her, offering to carry her into the house to avoid further damage to her bloody feet. At her direction, he set her on the tiny stool in the powder room where she examined her feet and plucked thorns and glass shards from the soles. Standing first on one foot, then the other, she soaped them in the hand-painted clay vessel. What caught her attention as she dried them was the fur that stuck to her soles. What the hell? When was O'Malley ever in the powder room?

They'd kept the door shut to protect their precocious toddler from drowning. In Parenting 101 they'd been instructed that keeping the lid down wasn't enough. Inquisitive toddlers could still topple in, their little arms too short to push their faces away from the water before someone missed them. "Where were the parents?" someone had asked. "Right there," the instructor had said, reinforcing the point. Henning's childproof doorknob device was still in place. Clumps of long, fluffy fur on the rug were beige, identifying O'Malley. Pandora's coat, except for her tuxedo-white face, was sleek and black.

While the professionals completed their investigation, Kingsley slipped upstairs to dress and bandage her feet. O'Malley—where was her dog? She smiled that she'd thought it—hers. Room by room she called without any luck. Could he possibly think he was in trouble? She searched systematically and finally shook a bag of doggie treats without any luck. As a last resort, she took a new can of dog food from the cupboard and ran the electric opener.

No dog. O'Malley was missing in action. Could he have slipped past her when she bolted outside? No! Absolutely not. She would have seen him. If frightened, he would have velcroed himself to her legs. Something else was at play.

Chapter 10

Her security man wasn't going to let her off without a stern lecture and a remedial lesson on setting the system. Numeric Pad 101. *Got it*. Doors and window locks, coming and going. Guest and Housekeepers' Instruction 101. *Ditto*. Safety with combustibles—gas grill, stove, candles, and matches, and why cook with gas in an all-electric house? *None of your damn business*. Kingsley could feel her heat rising, and not from the virus as her patience tanked. She dismissed him at the earliest opportunity.

The fellow from the gas company who had responded took her aside. "Look, lady, if you have enemies, I'd suspect sabotage. If not, I don't want to call your contractor a crook, but whoever installed the propane connection for your stove should be shot. I can't tell for sure, but either there was extreme negligence or recklessness. Have a certified technician evaluate everything that the contractor touched. Gas installation, of any kind, is not for amateurs!"

"Is it safe to use now?"

"No! The gas is shut off at the tank, so you'll need to make that call now. And don't try to connect it yourself—either of you. I can recommend someone I trust."

After everyone left, Kingsley confirmed her worst suspicion. O'Malley was not in the house or the yard. She dragged her over-extended remains to the guest room and sank into cool, inviting sheets. The dog would come out when he felt it was safe. In moments, she was asleep.

๑๑๑

Kingsley groped for her glasses and noticing darkness through the front guest room windows, groped for the clock. Ten fifteen? The afternoon and evening had evaporated. Startled, she sat up too quickly, causing her head to pound. She dropped to the pillow until the pain eased. She grabbed her cellphone, realizing to her chagrin, that she had silenced the ringer. And she was flooded with messages. The first recording was a giggly greeting from Billy with whispered coaching in the background from her mother. It sounded like they were having a grand time.

She opened subsequent messages in the order received, reading Todd's heightening urgency and concern. He'd missed her entire adventure! As she dialed, she weighed her options—tell him the whole story or wait until he got home. On one hand, he'd be angry that she didn't call him immediately, but then he might have ditched the conference.

No. She'd start by telling him how she'd skillfully handled a minor utility problem. That she'd call the contractor first thing in the morning. And yes, she was recovering. Let the man of the house speed home to help the little woman? Absolutely not. Having ramped her adrenalin, she felt surprisingly better—hungry in fact. Hunger. O'Malley. She had to feed him.

She threw on jeans, a cotton turtleneck, and her old Penn sweatshirt. Gingerly, she tested the wounds on her feet, bathed them again, applied antibiotic cream and fresh bandages. Shoes—no. Her fluffy llama socks would provide excellent cushioning; and if she needed to go outside, she'd appropriate Todd's barn boots. She'd have to be extra careful not to trip on the stairs. Her urgent call to O'Malley produced only the cat, who wrapped her sleek body in figure eights around her legs. Food! The universal aphrodisiac.

For supper—she'd scrounge a leftover, but that could wait. Where could the little dog be? With the early spring temperature dropping through the forties, she shrugged into a winter hooded jacket and the gloves that lived in the pockets. She flipped on the floodlights. By the back door, she snagged a mag light and checked the batteries, which were up to the task. Sweeping the back yard, then the path to the barn, she checked every cranny where a puppy might cower. Nothing.

Up the driveway, toward the front yard and the lane, she arched the light, hoping yet dreading what she might find. The street—the last resort. Powered by urgency, hope, and fear, she trudged, her wounded feet throbbing, open wounds weeping into her socks. The construction site was silent as she approached from the lane. She picked her way through the rubble, letting the light fall on every crevice and indentation while whistling and calling his name. Nothing.

What if he'd escaped in the morning's commotion? Been captured by that evil foreman who killed him and dumped his little body somewhere? Fighting tears she trudged west, down the road past their home toward the Amish farm. Maybe he'd sought refuge at his former haunt, like the coal bin or their summer kitchen. As she passed the white pine fence row that she and Todd had been planting the day Billy found the dog, something caught her peripheral vision. She froze, jerking her gaze to the right.

Under the front entryway's coach lights, she saw a lump that looked like a burlap bag. Instinctively, she covered a gloved scream, imagining the worst—that the dreadful foreman killed her dog and dumped his body on her front doorstep. Hobbled with pain and the clumsiness of the boot-and-sock combination, she limped across the front lawn.

O'Malley lay at the door. At first, she thought the wet muddy lump might be dead and took a strangled breath. "O'Malley," she moaned. At the sound of her voice, the little dog lifted his head, tail thumping on the bricks. She was all over him, laughing and crying while probing his little body for injuries. He struggled to his feet, a mass of mud, brambles, and grease.

Pulling off her gloves with her teeth, she examined his body systematically, assuming he'd yelp if she hurt him, but he tolerated the probing. "Let's clean you up and assess the damage." Once again, another bath in the basement. Besides mud, brambles, and oil, a few blotches of dried blood stuck to his fur. Fearing the worst, she rinsed him gently with tepid water, peering through his sodden fur systematically, not spotting any wounds. Hoping he'd communicate if he were distressed or if the shampoo stung, she proceeded uneventfully. He never growled or threatened to snap. It wouldn't occur to her until much later that she should have called an emergency vet clinic. What if he had internal injuries? She wouldn't make that mistake again.

She cradled him in towels, sitting on the basement floor, gently stroking his disheveled fur. "If we survive this ordeal, little dog, we'll take you to the pretty parlor to get rid of these mats." He gazed into her eyes, then licked her chin, just as he did Billy's. "You're mine too," she said through her tears.

❦❦❦

Friday morning, Kingsley dialed the vet's office that her neighbor had recommended and made an appointment. Although O'Malley had slept uneventfully on Billy's rug, Kingsley still feared internal injuries. Both she and the dog seemed recovered from Thursday's ordeal. Positioning O'Malley's rug on the back seat of her car, she looped his leash as best she could through the lap belts. "Lie down," she said, and he did, his expression doleful. She rubbed his head and scratched behind his ears. "You are a very good dog."

Kingsley filled out as many forms for the vet as she had for Billy's pediatrician. The immaculate waiting room, lined with sturdy vinyl bench seats, was occupied by an assortment of small animal owners and two cats in carriers, a bored-looking Dane, a King Charles Cavalier Spaniel, and a mini lop rabbit. O'Malley seemed somewhat subdued, in spite of the opportunity to make new friends, but Kingsley scooped him onto her lap and kept him as immobile as possible.

In the examining room, the vet entered from a rear corridor and beamed at O'Malley. "Georgie! I'm so glad someone found you!" Kingsley's heart sank. "You've given everyone quite a scare. Wherever have you been?" She turned to Kingsley. "The family went camping, thinking a six-month-old puppy would stay with them, but the puppy must have been spooked by something wild. Georgie bolted, everyone, chasing and calling, but the puppy was long gone. The family scoured the county, shelters, dog finders, placed ads in the papers, tacked photos on telephone poles. Offered a huge reward. But no Georgie. A couple weeks ago they came in with a puppy they'd adopted from the shelter, wearing the most amazing leash and collar system. Guess they learned their lesson."

The vet ran her hands over O'Malley's body, then started to laugh. "You had me fooled for a minute. They look identical, but Georgie's a girl."

Kingsley melted with relief and filled her in on what little she knew about O'Malley's history. "Our neighbors called him Scruffy."

She laughed again. "And is yours his forever family? I knew they were anxious to place him."

"Yes, unless someone else claims him, but my two-year-old would throw a fit."

"Let me get Scruffy's file." She cocked her head. "O'Malley." He looked up, tail thumping. "Great name." Briefly Kingsley told the vet about the altercation, her fear of internal injuries, and residual effects of inhaling gas fumes. She signed for x-rays, blood work, and chipping. "According to our records, he's had his shots, thanks to your neighbor."

"Do you take care of his animals?"

She looked up from the chart. "I'm afraid of cows. Got kicked in vet school. Broke my leg. I'd rather work with these little guys." Happily, the x-rays and lab work were normal, and four hours later they were free to go. Kingsley snapped a picture of O'Malley with his new doctor before leaving the clinic.

Their next stop was Polly's Posh Pooch, where O'Malley suffered the indignity of a full beauty treatment. "What do you think he is?" she asked the groomer after O'Malley emerged looking like a Westminster winner.

She grinned. "He's a dog!" They both laughed. "Seriously, he's a mixed breed. We do not tolerate the term *mutt*. I'd say part Lhasa, cocker, poodle, and something tall and thin, like a miniature greyhound. If your snooty friends question his parentage, tell them he's a Siberian weasel hound. They'll say, 'Ooooh,' like they should have known. And you can say in all honesty that you have no idea where they can find a breeder."

"Will you pose for a picture with him? I need to prepare

my little boy for this transformation."

Their last stop was a pet store where O'Malley was fitted with a dignified collar and leash, dog food recommended by the vet, dishes, and an assortment of toys. She was tempted to buy him a bed, but he was a rug dog. She wondered idly if his next step would be sleeping on Billy's. She sighed. Did they sell car seats for dogs? No, but they sold her a harness that worked with seatbelts. Kingsley headed home with their classy pooch.

❧❦❧

The dealmaker consulted his business plan, which he kept in his mind and nowhere else. It was time to prepare the Holland client for *possible disaster* after an idea his foreman had thrown stuck to his mind. Why not scrap the greenhouse business? A screen between the road and the operation could be faked while saving a ton of money without constructing an elaborate business.

Maybe there was a market for those perfect tomatoes, but what he was planting was far more lucrative and would eliminate the need for employees. And, if all went well, would serve as a prototype for similar projects. All he needed was acres of land removed from prying eyes. Next time, however, he'd be more diligent researching the neighbors. The Hennings were an ultimate challenge whom he needed to mitigate immediately. They were proving extremely troublesome. Not a problem. They weren't unique and could be eliminated as he had done in the past. They were no match for him.

He glanced at his watch—eight o'clock Holland time. Perfect. A new workday had dawned over there. He dialed the phone, surprised that the bulb grower picked up so quickly.

"Good morning," Liam Van Dijk said in perfect

English. "To what do I owe this midnight call?"

The dealmaker affected his smoothest voice. "I thought it best to give you a heads up. We are encountering some challenges with our projected timetable. In spite of our best efforts, some things are beyond our control, like unseasonable weather. If planting is delayed, we may have difficulty with our projected yields and quantities. It's too early to be concerned, but I thought you should know."

"And you've planned for such contingencies?"

Liam had walked right into it. "Of course. That's why we bought insurance to guard against unforeseen loss."

The Dutchman paused so long the dealmaker thought the connection had been severed. "My attorney just arrived for a meeting. I'm going to put him on speaker so that we can discuss this *insurance* together."

"Of course. Good morning, sir. Let's proceed with your questions."

"You forwarded three pages of this insurance policy to my client, but the appendices are missing," the attorney said.

"Just the usual small print," the dealmaker said, keeping his voice neutral, bordering on bored. The actual policy was boilerplate that he had downloaded from the internet and customized.

"We'll need to see that—what do you call it? Legalese? The small print?"

"Of course. I'll fax it to you. I didn't think it would interest you."

"I built a multi-national corporation by reading every word of—what you call—the small print," Liam Van Dijk said. "Businesses are made or broken by that minutia. I, my friend, do not plan on the latter."

"Of course."

"And speaking of small print and your hint that our enterprise might have certain problems—may I refer you to the passage in our contract that prohibits your blaming any failure on our Dutch expertise. The Dutch have been gardening successfully below sea level for centuries. The first windmills appeared in the Netherlands in the 13th century and, from the 17th century onward, the Dutch windmill began marvelous advances. There are 9,000 plus in the Netherlands today. You are responsible for any failure, for which you cannot blame our expertise."

The dealmaker allowed himself a smirk, picturing the windmills, the dikes, tulips, and wooden shoes, and the urgent warnings about rising sea levels caused by global warming. Ignorant prick!

"Now—about my hydroponic greenhouses," the Dutchman continued. "We have a schedule that I expect you will follow to the hour."

"For your comfort zone, I wanted to assure you that, should we have unforeseen losses, your investment is protected with the excellent insurance we've been wise to secure. You cannot lose."

The dealmaker overheard background banter between the Dutchman and his advisor. They chuckled. "Any insurance you have purchased will not compensate for our loss. We expect you to fulfill every tick of our contract. Furthermore, the photos you have emailed about work in progress are insufficient. I expect aerial photos. If you cannot provide them, I will hire private professionals to review your progress and reduce your compensation by that cost." He chuckled. "A good business plan keeps everyone honest. Is that not so?"

"Of course. Please be assured that your business is of the utmost importance to me and my company. We shall proceed as planned. And may I extend my deepest sympathy for any impact that rising sea level may have on your beautiful country."

He ended the call, grinning. He couldn't help that

parting dig, which might prove to be prophetic. But the seed had been planted. However, he'd instruct his foreman to start greenhouse construction, but cover the worksite at six every morning with anti-aircraft camouflage material. Hell, you could buy anything on the internet these days.

He poured two fingers of Glenfiddich and sank into his thinking chair to dissect the next challenge. Under normal circumstances, overtime work could keep the Holland grower placated. Eliminating the major obstacle to his enterprise, however, must be addressed expeditiously.

The next morning the dealmaker phoned his money man, anxious to touch bases and enjoy the thrill of the multiple, fast-moving deals in play while mentally counting his profit.

He dialed the next number, the manufacturing client, whose back was to the wall. That client said, "Our shipment is scheduled for delivery in two weeks. Will your facility be ready to accept it?"

"Absolutely!" the dealmaker said. "Preparations are right on schedule. You can count on my company to accommodate your shipment."

"Have you vetted the foreman we talked about?"

"He's been with me for years. He's reliable, conscientious, and loyal to my company. He has never failed to perform exactly as expected without a hint of divulging confidences. Having such resources is what you expect from someone of my proficiency in safeguarding your investment. Now—turning to practical considerations—the specifications. Please give me a rundown on the containers' composition and their tensile strength."

"The finest steel will endure one thousand years. The seals would hold at the deep-water depth of twenty-thousand leagues. To say they are crush-proof or tamper-proof would be a ridiculous assertion."

"Forgive me. I just have to ask. Liability concerns, you

understand."

"That's what our deal included, correct? An overkill of *insurance* protection."

The dealmaker smiled. "Absolutely. You have my word."

Chapter 11

Saturday morning Barrie popped her head through the back door and yoo-hooed a greeting that brought Billy and O'Malley tumbling into her outstretched arms. "Aunt Bawwie," Billy shrieked, burying his face in her hug. "What's dat?" he said after disentangling himself, pointing to the canvas bag that always held surprises for him. They trooped into the kitchen.

"We're going to make a big, wonderful mess. Doesn't that sound like fun?"

Billy bobbed yes with his upper body and an ear-to-ear grin. Barrie spread a fabric-backed vinyl tablecloth and unloaded supplies that included several repurposed margarine tubs of ingredients, a cardboard container of tiny dye bottles, and a zipper bag of small cookie cutters. Finally, she produced an old short-sleeved dress shirt of Randall's with which she had make-shifted a cobbler's apron, buttoning it down the child's back. It would have dragged on the floor had Barrie not whacked inches off the bottom with fabric shears.

Billy's eyes danced with delight as he dragged a chair to the table. With a monkey's skill and speed, he scrambled onto the seat and reached for the tub closest to him. Barrie was securing her own apron and the tablecloth's ties when Kingsley caught up with them. The friends exchanged hugs. "And what's the project du jour?"

"We're going to make real Play-Doh. And it's eatable."

Kingsley laughed, shaking her head. "This morning, dog food. Now this."

"Maybe Billy will grow a glossy coat."

O'Malley pranced into the room, head high, tail wagging. "You're supposed to make a fuss and tell him he's handsome," Kingsley muttered behind her hand. "The groomer said he'd either be humiliated and hide or think he's hot stuff. He did have a little blue bow on his head, but Billy appropriated that. Said it was 'siwwy!'"

Barrie handed Kingsley the recipe that listed the ingredients, which she approved. "Where's Randall doing with his Saturday morning?"

"He dropped me off, then went to run errands. He'll be back before noon. I swear that man hasn't missed a meal in his life, and look at him! Never gains an ounce. It's not fair." She pulled a small rolling pin from her pack. "Got a bowl we can use? The large stainless one would be perfect. And don't worry—we'll clean up before lunch, won't we buddy?" She took the lids off three tubs, pointed to the bowl, and instructed, "Dump!" And he did.

"Now we're going to squish it all together and make a ball. The best part about borrowing a kid is that I get to be one myself." Kingsley resisted the impulse to say that she and Randall should get on with that wedding and start a family—but the subject of children had never been mentioned by either. And Kingsley had known Barrie since her first day at Keynote National Bank when the bank's controller had taken her under her wing.

She smiled at the pair, heads together, green dye on their masterpiece cookies and smudges on their faces. Kingsley gave thanks every day for Billy—the child she was destined to be denied. She'd failed to conceive and, then when she had, suffered a complicated miscarriage after her young husband Andrew had died. Billy was her and Todd's honeymoon baby. Would she risk another? She'd been spared knowing the gender of her lost angel. She'd always thought *girl*. That she'd carried Billy past his due date—10 pounds 12 ounces—amazed her doctor who cautioned that having another might be dangerous.

"Todd and I are almost finished with our taxes. You'd think a pair of bankers wouldn't wait until the last minute," Kingsley said.

Barrie responded without looking up. "Go! Seize the moment to avoid work without supervision. The gremlin and I will be fine."

As she turned left into the hall toward the library, Kingsley spared Barrie verbalizing what she'd said too many times—*Thank you for being the sister I never had.*

They sat at their desks, just as Kingsley had pictured the scene when the house was an empty cavern. She'd had plenty of *what-have-we-done* moments while the shelves were being made. Would they feel entombed? How could they fill three walls of shelves? Would their baby climb them and fall to his death? When the shelves were installed, the incredible echo was muffled by a thick Persian rug, furniture, and floor-length draperies at the double-hung windows.

The couple passed IRS forms, neatly formatted, back and forth, ready for signatures. She sighed contentedly. Family—exactly as she had dreamed it would be. After her Andrew had died—a newly minted ophthalmology resident and just twenty-six—she had counted on Grammy's sage advice that echoed throughout her childhood. *You've got to stay tuned.* How true that wisdom had proved!

"I hear Randall now," Kingsley said, swiveling to look out a front window. "He's early." What she saw, however, was a black Mercedes navigating their stone driveway. It stopped by the walkway. "Uncle David! Todd, look who's here."

Kingsley flung open the front door, prepared to run across the walkway to hug her beloved godfather. David Wentworth, her father's college roommate, had been her benefactor throughout her life. Through trials, tribulations, and every milestone, from dance and piano recitals to her debutante ball, her wedding, Andy's funeral, her wedding to Todd in her parents' garden, and Billy's baptism, David Wentworth was there. And in his capacity as a renowned attorney, squared off with the detectives who'd tried to blame Billy's kidnapping on them.

She skidded to a stop when she realized that something was wrong. The man emerging from the car, while elegantly dressed in a designer suit, was not Uncle David. Shocked, she dashed back into the house. "Todd! Come here at once! You're not going to believe this."

Striding purposefully toward their front door was the boss from the construction project. She'd never known his name but heard one of the workers refer to him as something that started with a D. Todd stretched beyond his imperial six-foot-two stance which, with the additional elevation of the entryway, dwarfed their uninvited visitor. "What do you want?"

The dealmaker smiled, almost childishly, and began his mission. "I am very sorry that we got off on the wrong foot. I've come to apologize and try to make things right. May I come in for a few minutes?" The Hennings' response was telepathed between Todd's lifted right eyebrow to her and Kingsley's shrug to him.

Todd opened the front door, motioning for Kingsley to proceed him, then ushered their visitor into the living room to a chair opposite their couch. They sat. "Beautiful home," he said although not in the least bit uncomfortable, a fact that surprised Kingsley. This should have been awkward for him, but it wasn't. Out of the corner of her eye, she spotted Barrie, peering around the corner from the hall, retreating, then from a squatting position, pushing something onto the living room floor. As silently as Pandora's little cat feet, she disappeared. Shortly Kingsley heard the distant babble of her son and her friend in the kitchen.

"I must apologize for my foreman, who can be mean as a snake. But the crew respects him, he doesn't cut corners, and brings in my projects on schedule below budget, mainly because he won't tolerate wasted time or materials. Three ex-wives could tell you that combination does not make for a pleasant personality." He glanced from Todd to Kingsley, letting that comment sink in.

"During the day, when he's not here, he's ramrodding another project in an adjoining county. That doesn't leave much time to recharge. No idea when he sleeps, but evidently he gets away with it—has never tested positive in our random drug testing."

"Is there anything you can do about the lights and noise at night? That's what led to our unfortunate confrontations."

He reached into his pocket and withdrew a paper, the creases of which appeared worn from use. With elegant grace, he slid cheaters low on his nose and checked lines of type that Kingsley guessed he probably knew by heart. The page was a prop. "Let me see," he said. "We should have the heavy construction work—bulldozers, cement mixer, power saws, and framers—out of here in a couple of weeks. The indoor work—setting up the greenhouses— will be done during the daytime, but not on weekends. My crews are church-going folk. In other words, you won't even know we're around."

"Well, that is good news. We can live with that short a timeframe."

"And the crew will be installing a fence and a sound-baffling wall." He folded the paper and returned it to his breast pocket. "I appreciate that folks of all ages love to explore construction sites. They're curious, not just about what it will be, but how it's being put together. Kids are the worst, letting their imaginations take flight. They're transformed into pirates and Indians, and alien explorers. Wage battles with tools made from construction scraps.

"But they fall into holes and break bones. Get cut on broken glass and rusty metal. Teens even leave remnants of drug paraphernalia, thinking it's a great place to party. In this rural Amish setting, I didn't think it was necessary to fence the project or post security guards twenty-four seven. Maybe I should have foreseen the problem."

Todd nodded. "I agree that shouldn't have been necessary, given who lives here."

"Anyway, I'd appreciate it if you'd help spread the word that no-trespassing rules will be enforced for everyone's protection. Even mine, from a liability perspective."

Todd extended his hand as a token of goodwill but Kingsley noted his business smile did not reach his eyes. The three rose. Todd proceeded their visitor to open the door through which he strode without looking back until he had stepped off the porch. He smacked his head in an oh-stupid-me gesture. "I almost forgot. One of the guys, who didn't know any better, accepted a parcel for you. If there were outer wrappings, he didn't save them, and there's no return address on this inner envelope. I thought I'd drop it off." He handed Todd a ten-by-twelve bulky manila envelope.

"Thanks," Todd said. He turned the parcel over in his hands and, assuming it was junk mail, dropped it into the incoming mail basket to open later.

Barrie poked her head around the kitchen door, her nose smudged with green dye. "What was that all about?" she asked.

"I think Mr. Make Nice was telling us to keep the hell

off his property," Todd said. Kingsley tapped her ear and motioned to Billy with her head. Todd sighed. "He's pre-occupied with something far more interesting than grown-up conversation."

The child looked up. "Hell." He tried it again, pleased with the sound as it rolled off his tongue.

Barrie clapped her hands with delight. "Hello," she sang to Billy. "He can pronounce the letter L. Can you say 'O'Malley?' That has two Ls."

"O'Mawwey," the child chirped.

"The little prince requested a peanut butter and honey sandwich," Barrie said, nodding at the remaining crusts.

"Thanks. Maybe you can tell me about your stealth mission if I can get Billy down for his N-A-P."

"Noooo. No nap!"

Kingsley sighed. "If you go quietly and promise to go to sleep," she paused, taking a deep breath, "O'Malley can take a nap with you." Boy and dog came to life immedi-ately, Billy erupting from his chair and O'Malley scurry-ing so quickly from under the table that he bumped his head on its trestle bar.

"Hands?" Kingsley commanded, but it was too late as O'Malley was washing the child's hands and face with sloppy licks. Barrie trailed the pair to the stairs, barely keeping up.

Kingsley hurried down the hall and, rounding the cor-ner into the living room, spotted Barrie's cell phone where the floor met the molding. As she picked it up, she noticed the phone's display was still ticking the seconds. Barrie had recorded the interview! She turned it off and carried it into the office where Todd was contemplating IRS rules. Barrie, she told him, had something up her sleeve.

Barrie tiptoed downstairs, turning halfway to peer over her shoulder in case someone was following. Silence pre-vailed. The back door opened and Randall erupted, bellowing his greeting. "Shhhhh! The other three hissed. "We just got him down."

"Sandwiches on the counter," Barrie whispered. "Drinks in the fridge. Bring it into the dining room. You gotta hear this." Kingsley returned Barrie's phone, and the foursome assembled into the back-left quadrant which had once served as the original owners sitting room.

"Play it," Barrie said, switching to business mode. "Just listen without commenting. Then share your thoughts." The recording lasted less than ten minutes before lapsing into muffled background noise. "Well? What's your reaction?"

"Now that I think about it," Kingsley said. "For a guy who makes his living in construction, he didn't even glance around, much less ask construction-type questions about our renovation."

"Who is this guy?" Randall asked.

"He appears to be the owner of the project under construction next door, only we saw him under much different circumstances previously." Briefly, they ticked through their prior encounters.

"By who, I mean, what's his name? And the name of his company?" Randall asked.

Todd and Kingsley exchanged puzzled looks. "Kingsley, you went outside to meet him when you thought he was your godfather. How did he introduce himself? My audio didn't pick up until after the three of you were seated.

"Huh!" Todd said. "He didn't introduce himself by name, did he K?"

She nodded agreement. "Correct. He said, 'I'm very sorry that we got off on such a bad foot. I've come to apologize and try to make things right.' Then he asked if he could come in for a few minutes. We didn't speak again until Barrie sneaked her phone onto the floor."

Randall scowled. "That's not right. Shoulda been the first thing out of his mouth, followed by his business card. Did he leave one with you when he left?"

"No," Todd said. "And I didn't offer him one of ours either. He could learn anything he wanted about us on the internet."

Kingsley snapped her fingers. "Todd, what was in that envelope he delivered, supposedly having been accepted by one of the workmen?"

"I forgot all about it, assuming it was junk mail. I'll get it." Reseated at the table he slit the flap with his penknife and extracted a letter on law firm stationery and a blue jacketed document. The others leaned in to read what it said. Todd skimmed quickly, his face reddening. He looked up at Kingsley in disbelief. "We're being sued."

"By that guy? Or his company?"

After Todd and Kingsley skimmed each page, he passed them, one by one, to the others. "No. By a descendant of the original William Penn Charter claiming ownership of our property. On behalf of his client, the attorney is demanding $75,000 to drop the suit to avoid 'protracted legal proceedings.' Appended to substantiate the claim are pages tracing the lineage that resemble the *begets* in the Old Testament."

"I say ignore it," Randall said with his usual flip attitude. "It's a scam. Someone trying to extort money from you. Besides, didn't your bank require you to buy title insurance?"

Todd was speechless. She guessed that he'd never told Randall that he'd paid cash for the property, not one to give even the slightest impression about his trust-fund wealth. Without a mortgage lender's requirements, Todd had handled the transaction himself.

She diverted the subject for her husband. "I'll sick Uncle David on this attorney and his client. If it's a scam, he'll find out quickly enough."

Todd stroked his jaw. "This bears a striking resemblance to that phone call you took from Greg, the realtor who found us this house. Correct me if I'm wrong, but didn't he tell you that he had a wealthy client willing to pay whatever we asked? And he'd started the offer at two million bucks? Maybe this is round two for that wealthy entertainer."

Randall whooped. "Buddy, when we're ready to buy, we're going to let you pick it. We could flip it in—how long you been here? Four years? and retire."

Barrie rolled her eyes. "You'll never retire—you're a workaholic who's having too much fun flying people with more money than brains and seeing the world."

"Ms. Co-pilot—you love it too and you know it. So, what's the plan, dude?"

"Ask my godfather to check it out, starting with the credentials of this law firm."

"If this is attempted extortion, I feel sorry for real homeowners who don't have someone like David Wentworth," Todd added.

Chapter 12

Weary from an intense weekend catching up, Kingsley couldn't concentrate on the Sunday New York Times and contemplated a nap.

Crash!

She jumped to her feet and followed the sound through the foyer and into the living room. Nothing had fallen off the walls. Pandora met her gaze with a bored blink before returning her gaze to the birdfeeder beyond the front window.

"What have you done!" she demanded, an accusatory note in her voice after rounding the end table that flanked the couch and spotting her earthenware philodendron pot smashed, dirt and tendrils radiating across the pine floor. Pandora, sunning herself in the plant's former spot, yawned and resumed watching the birds as if appropriating her favorite spot for the plant had been unacceptable.

Had that been O'Malley, a simple *what have you done!* would have dissolved him in guilt, slinking away, never to repeat the foul deed for fear of risking her wrath. She sighed. Cats were not dogs. Maybe she was a dog person after all. She rescued Little Philo, draping its vines over her shoulder, and dumped the broken pot and debris in the garbage.

After repotting Little Philo on the basement workbench,

she returned to the living room in search of a Pandora-proof spot. Todd had brought the variegated philodendron to her hospital room after a would-be killer had bludgeoned her. Todd apologized that it was all he could find at that time of night. Little Philo had made every move with them, growing long tendrils that she had rooted for family and friends. After setting it on the west-facing windowsill, she noticed the cat. Pandora had pawed the afghan from the back of the couch and was sleeping as if nothing had happened.

O'Malley, sensing excitement afoot, left napping Billy to investigate the commotion downstairs. He stopped at the living room entry but proceeded no farther. It dawned on Kingsley that O'Malley never followed them into this room. And no wonder. That first day O'Malley was in their house when he'd urinated on the couch, she had reacted with disproportionate anger. He never dared approach it again.

Kill two birds with one stone. Kingsley seized the opportunity to contrive a friendly encounter between the pets. With Pandora curled on the far cushion, Kingsley tucked O on her hip and carried him to the couch. She sat in the middle, anchoring the pup to her left side. He whimpered happy utterances while thumping his plume of a tail. Suddenly, Pandora jerked to attention and glared at O'Malley. He didn't move, just kept wagging his tail while straining to wriggle his head under Kingsley's hand.

She observed the pets, glancing back and forth, neither making a move. Then Kingsley's phone clattered on the coffee-table trunk. All three bolted upright, she for the phone, Pandora for the hall, and O'Malley in hot pursuit. The cat was too fast, leaping onto the kitchen counter while O'Malley tried unsuccessfully to follow, entreating Pandora to come down and play. When Kingsley answered the call, she immediately forgot the animal drama when she recognized her roommate Christine's anguished voice.

"Something awful has happened," Chris stuttered in between gasps for air. Never the drama queen, this must be really bad news. Kingsley's mind raced through their Penn classmates, dreading to hear if someone had died.

"Chrissy, take a breath. I can't understand you. Please start at the beginning." From her own history of catastrophe, Kingsley knew that bad things do happen to good people, sometimes random and sometimes intentional. At first, she'd felt guilty when a day went by that she didn't think about her late husband Andy or remember his burned body in the morgue, but professional therapists convinced her that was nature's way of protecting her mind. "Please. What has happened?"

"It's about my friend Suzanne Meade. She's had a terrible accident."

"The history professor?"

"That's right. She'd texted me that she would be meeting a friend of an archivist she met Sunday at Conrad Weiser's Charter Day. They were to meet for breakfast on Monday since the Pennsylvania State Archives wouldn't be open until Wednesday. He's an expert in what she's researching, and she was so excited about the prospect of meeting him. And that you would accommodate her visiting on Wednesday rather than Monday. I returned to London, but we planned to touch bases after you met."

Kingsley rubbed her temples. "How did you hear that she'd had an accident?"

"Her mother just phoned. Last week an unidentified woman was pulled from the Susquehanna River. The police suspected foul play. The victim was in a coma, unable to tell anyone who she was or what had happened. When nobody reported a missing person, she was fingerprinted. Suzanne's first job after graduation was at the American Embassy in Brussels. For that post, she needed government clearance, which included her prints. The woman turned out to be Suzanne Meade."

Kingsley was stunned, trying to process when the accident could have happened.

"It seemed Suzanne missed Skyping with the family Tuesday night. She had promised her family in Philadelphia that she would participate from her hotel room in Harrisburg. When she didn't, her mother tried phoning, but the call went to voice. Suzanne had left the hotel's name and number, so her mother tried that. The registration form had her rental car's make and model—they require that since parking is limited—and her car was still in the lot. Perhaps she'd gone for a walk, the desk clerk had suggested. Or been picked up by a friend.

"He volunteered to have security check her room in case she'd had an accident. Her travel bag was on the luggage rack and her toiletries were in the bathroom. Everything looked normal; they assumed she would return. Not wanting to meddle in her grown daughter's affairs, her mother waited and worried for her to call and explain.

"On Wednesday morning when her car hadn't moved, and there was no sign of Suzanne, the hotel called the police. They examined her room and her rental car where they found blood on the rear bumper. When they popped the trunk, they found a lot more. Foul play was suspected. Their log showed that an unidentified woman was pulled from the Susquehanna on Sunday evening and transported to Hershey hospital."

"Wait a minute," Kingsley interjected. "That woman couldn't be Suzanne. She was perfectly fine when she arrived at my house on Wednesday. She was driving a late-model import, which looked new. We had a lovely meeting, and everything she said was on point. There must be a reasonable explanation for the mistaken identity. Whatever reason she had for blowing off the meeting…"

"No!

Kingsley grappled to make a connection. "So—does anyone know where she went after leaving our house? Did she return to Harrisburg? Do you think she had any enemies? Or that someone was giving her trouble—a stalker, old boyfriend, jealous colleague? Did she mention anything like that on the phone?"

"She seemed exactly the same as when we got together several years ago."

Kingsley turned that over in her mind. She had dismissed that her visitor was distracted or tired when she toured the house, but not knowing the woman beyond one phone conversation, she'd assumed her demeanor was normal. But given what Chris was saying, was that contradiction worth mentioning to the police who were investigating her apparent attack?

"I assume her parents are there by now. Please give me their contact information. At least I was able to meet her and show her around. And she is a lovely person."

Christine paused. "You met her? That doesn't fit. Sorry—I have enough trouble keeping my dates straight, let alone my friends' calendars. She was so excited about seeing your home. I'd shown her all the pictures I'd taken that I thought might interest her, and she was especially captivated by your walk-in fireplace and that you actually use it."

"When and if her mother lets me come to the hospital, I'll text you an update." Kingsley pictured the lovely Suzanne and wished she'd taken her picture to share. In an attempt to lighten the mood she said, "She's living proof, as you've always insisted, that being tall is attractive. I could have snatched her killer boots right of those long legs."

Chrissy laughed. "You are so deluded. How anyone could call Suzanne tall is so funny. She'd look your pal Barrie in the eye."

Kingsley felt her heart rate take off. "Chris, describe Suzanne to me."

"Well, let me see. A little over five feet, but not by much. Always threatening to lose ten pounds, but she'd never miss twenty. Brown eyes and hair, which she refuses to color. Olive complexion—Greek, Italian, or something else Mediterranean. Why do you ask?"

Kingsley was too shocked to answer immediately and feigned an excuse to hang up. The woman she'd let into her home and given a top-to-bottom royal tour was a stranger. She wandered in a daze into the kitchen, feeling disoriented and uncharacteristically stunned until she saw the mess that the dog-and-cat encounter had made of her kitchen.

"What happened here?" Todd exclaimed, dropping his briefcase in the hall and peering into the kitchen. Kingsley didn't know whether to laugh or cry. Pandora, whose attempts to escape, had been countered by O'Malley's back and forth moves as the cat knocked everything onto the floor, nailing him with the flour canister that popped open. O'Malley had succeeded in dumping a weighted water bowl, which the salesman had assured Kingsley could not be done by a fifteen-pound dog. Billy had canceled his nap prematurely and was gleefully dancing sock-footed in a huge puddle mixture of flour, sugar, and soggy dog food.

"Enough!" Kingsley screamed. O'Malley's quick turn of his head enabled Pandora to leap from the counter and dash through the kitty hole in the basement door. O'Malley streaked after her, trailed by Billy, the pair of latecomers vying for position to try to fit through the hole to follow the cat.

Todd clutched his sides in waves of laughter, tears

running down his face, unable to get himself under control. Kingsley cried. "This is so not funny!" Todd paused for a moment, surveying the damage, then erupted in laughter again.

"Fine!" she said. "You clean it up. Don't forget the dog. He's all over wet flour. Where are you going?"

"Upstairs to change into combat gear."

◌◌◌

Todd lit a fire to ward off the chill of an unusually cold snap. "Look at that," she said, motioning toward opposite ends of the ten-foot stone hearth where their two animals were dozing and warming their fur. "Wore themselves out. Could all three of them have fit through the hole in the door? What if Billy's head got stuck?"

"It's way too small. Nevertheless, if this is our new reality, I'll pick up one of those swinging covers and install it. What are you studying?"

"Look at this," she said, swiveling her laptop toward his desk. "I searched Suzanne Meade. Hadn't thought to do so before her visit. Turns out, she's all over the internet. She even has her own website. A very accomplished researcher with oodles of publications, a leader in her profession, keynote speaker, and here—check out her picture. This is not the woman who I took on a tour."

"Unusual that they'd have the same name. How do you think the mix-up happened?"

"I've been picturing the scene when she arrived on Wednesday. I admit I was a bit awed by her beauty and professional presence, especially since she caught me off guard, preoccupied as I was tending my burned hand. I called her by name and plunged into a spiel about the house and what I hoped she'd find authentic. I admit I was a bit nervous about the renovations the previous owner made, and if our own modifications might have wrecked its historic value."

"Describe her for me."

And she did—from the classy car, her elegant clothes and hair, major but understated jewelry, down to her perfectly knotted printed silk scarf, expertly draped on a white silk blouse.

"Was she carrying anything?"

"A smartphone—the large one—a notebook and pen."

Todd threw back his head and laughed. "My dear, I suspect you gave a tour to a prowling realtor. The kind who visits upscale homeowners in case they 'know of someone'—always with a house like yours—'who might be interested in selling.' You'd be so awed by her aura of success that if you were interested in dumping our property, you'd at least have taken her card."

"Huh! I just swept her inside, rattling on and on about its amazing details. She didn't ask about the fireplaces, but whether our bookshelves were attached to the real estate. Ah! She used the R-word. Mystery solved. I wonder if we'll ever hear from her again."

"If she's legitimate, she'll send you a thank-you note on her professional stationery for her impromptu visit and enclose her company's brochure and a few of her cards—just in case."

Chapter 13

The Henning's landline filled the library's cocoon with its jangle. The weary parents, exhausted but too tired to leave the comfort of the fire, resisted. "Let it go to voice," Todd said. "It takes a lot of nerve for telemarketers to call at this hour." By the time the machine had processed five rings, Kingsley had straightened a bit in her chair. She frowned. Bad news came at odd hours. Her parents? Her friends? The tall-case clock bonged ten times.

When the phone exhausted its attempts, she knew it was too late to spring from her chair and grab the beast off her desk. Someone began leaving a message. "I'm trying to reach Kingsley Henning? This is Alice Meade. I'm Suzanne's mother. It's urgent that I get in touch…"

Kingsley bolted from her chair, the book she'd been reading tumbling to the floor. She snatched the phone. "Hello? Mrs. Meade? It's Kingsley. I'm here. Go ahead."

"Oh, thank goodness. I didn't know if I had the right number and had no other way to get in touch. I'm calling about my daughter, Suzanne." Kingsley took a deep breath, fearing what the mother might say next. "I hope I haven't called at a bad time. It's awfully late."

"No! It's fine. My roommate Christine called and told me about Suzanne's accident. I've been praying that she is recovering. How is she doing? I was so anxious to meet her after we spoke on the phone Sunday evening. And I want to assure her that she can visit any time it's convenient. I'd love to meet her in person."

A dreadful pause made Kingsley slap herself mentally for babbling on and on. What if Suzanne were dead? The caller sniffled, excused herself, and blew gently. "Suzanne has been in a coma for a week, which the doctors said was a mixed blessing, that is, assuming she will wake up. She has a severe concussion from a blow to her head, so her brain has to heal. That means no sensory input—no TV, no music, just remaining perfectly still."

"Oh. How awful. Is she making progress?"

"That's why I'm calling. Suzanne is awakening gradually and keeps asking for you. She was so agitated that the doctor had to sedate her. At first, I had trouble understanding what she was saying, but then I recognized your name. Christine said she was planning to visit you. I took the liberty of insisting that her visit could be postponed, relying on Christine's glowing comments about you and her assurance that you would understand and be willing to reschedule."

"Of course. Absolutely. In fact, when she's well enough, she can stay at our house. We have lots of room, and I could share whatever details she wishes to explore."

"That's not why she's upset. She insists she needs to talk with you now. She keeps mumbling something that sounds like '*Urgent. Danger.* And *killer.*' At first, I thought she was delusional or dreaming, but she kept asking for you. Saying she must tell you something she heard. Of course, I'm piecing fragments together, but regardless of what's on her mind, I would be so grateful if you could find the time to come to the hospital. I know you must have a demanding schedule, what with your job and your family..."

"Of course, I'll come. Just tell me what hospital and her room number, and I'll come first thing in the morning. Are you sure her doctors will permit me to visit?"

"I asked. They thought it might help to calm her. If you give me your cellphone number, I'll text you the details and let you know if…" She paused as if momentarily overcome. "I'll let you know if her condition has changed."

Kingsley dialed Marley's extension at the bank, left her AA a detailed message to postpone her morning appointments and to call if anything urgent occurred. Snagging her calendar, she verified that she did not have a loan closing that day. The compulsory HR training could be rescheduled with another department.

Todd, who had listened with rapt attention said, "If you leave here at eight, you'll miss rush hour traffic heading west and should arrive by nine-fifteen. I'll take care of the little dude. You might want to take your go-bag in case you decide to stay over. That mother might need all the help she can get."

❧❦❧

Kingsley should have enjoyed the drive as the redbuds that lined the highway were loaded with tiny clusters of purple blooms. While too early for native dogwoods and wild cherries, the explosion of tiny new leaves on the bushes held the promise of spring's renewal. The trunks of eighty-foot maples and tulip poplars cast horizontal shadows across the pavement, flickering sun and shade under her car in synchronized rhythm.

She autopiloted from the exit to the secondary highway, and then into the hospital's visitor's lot. At the main entrance, she passed through airport-type security, and having proven that she wasn't carrying concealed weapons, was directed to another security officer. He photocopied her driver's license and printed a large yellow sticker containing her picture and pertinent ID, instructing her to affix it to her jacket. She was tempted to joke that she wasn't a terrorist but assumed they were tired of hearing it.

Her mind riveted to the task at hand as she followed a nurse's directions to the ICU. She gave her name at the nursing station, anticipating lengthy questions and instructions, but instead, they were expecting her. "Is there anything I should know? I don't want to interfere with your routine or upset her. Her mother told me on the phone last night that stimulation might affect her brain's healing process."

"She seems a little more lucid this morning. Just take your lead from her mother. She knows the drill."

Kingsley approached Suzanne's doorway and caught her mother's eye. Alice Meade slid from her bedside chair beside her sleeping daughter and met Kingsley at the door. "Thank you so much for coming," she whispered. "Let's go down the hall to the lounge." Except for a man dozing in a loveseat, they had the room to themselves. Alice perched on the edge of a chair, facing her. That she had slept little in recent days, and probably in the chair beside her daughter's bed, was obvious by her exhausted and rumpled appearance.

"May I take you to their cafeteria for some breakfast? Or get you some coffee?" Kingsley offered.

"No. But thanks. I'll get something later. The days are so long." She blinked, but no tears moistened her red eyes. "She'll be awake soon. We're hoping if she can tell you whatever's troubling her that she'll rest more peacefully."

"I'll do my best, even if it doesn't make sense. I'll tell her whatever she needs to hear." They rose and returned to Suzanne's room. "Is this a good time?" she asked the nurse who was adjusting equipment near her bed. With a nod of encouragement, the nurse left, leaving the door to the hall cracked.

Two chairs flanked the bed. "Sit in this one," Alice said, indicating that her daughter's head was propped in that direction. She smoothed her daughter's hand, which caused Suzanne's eyes to flutter. "You have a visitor," she said in a soothing voice. "Are you up for a little company?" Suzanne gave the tiniest smile. "Kingsley Henning is here. She's sitting in my chair on your left."

Suzanne's eyes flew open. "Hi, Suzanne. It's Kingsley. I am so sorry this happened to you. I wanted to tell you that you can come to my house any time you feel up to it. If you can stay a few days, I'll take you wherever you'd like to go."

Suzanne blinked a few times, and without moving her head, focused her eyes in Kingsley's direction. Kingsley repositioned her head to Suzanne's line of vision. "Had to tell you."

"That's wonderful!" Alice exclaimed. "She's so much more articulate this morning. I'm sorry. Go ahead, dear."

"Danger. Had to tell you. Played dead."

Kingsley looked up at her mother. "Do you know what she's talking about?" Her mother shook her head.

"Go ahead, Suzanne. Tell me what happened."

"Ambushed me. Hit me! Pain. Blackness. I woke up. Heard your name. Pretended to be dead. Two of them, dragging me. Water. Couldn't breathe. Woke up here. Awful. So Sorry!"

Suzanne's heart monitor jumped so erratically that a nurse burst into the room. "Please." The nurse's stern voice left nothing to Kingsley's imagination. She backed into the hall. Teary-eyed, Alice joined her. "Thank you for coming. I'll call you when she's better."

"Be sure to tell Suzanne that I'll be back. And she must not be concerned that we've missed one opportunity. I understand completely."

Chapter 14

Billy noticed before anyone else. From his perch on his long-legged kitchen chair, he craned his neck to look for O'Malley, who usually spent dinnertime under the table. Kingsley suspected the child thought the dog loved him best, but she knew better. O'Malley could pretend to be sleeping, head on his paws, eyes closed but ears perked, waiting for Billy's spilled morsels. When he thought no one was looking, Billy would deliberately jettison a bit of something he hated, like peas. The clever animal could retrieve the treat without moving from his splayed position and without ratting out his co-conspirator.

Tonight, however, something was different. "Where'd he go?" Billy asked after his dinner consumption was deemed sufficient. Hands and mouth wiped, Billy slid to the floor and took off, calling for his dog. Curious herself, Kingsley followed him into the library where boy and dog were standing by the left library window, Billy on tiptoes and O'Malley with his forepaws braced on the sill.

Kingsley had been stern with the child when he'd mastered climbing before safety. Under no circumstances was he to climb onto the deep windowsills. Time and growth would enable a better view of the front yard, but in the meantime, she was standing her ground. A tumble from that height onto the wood floor could break his neck. Little as he was, Billy grasped when his mother could be played and when she meant business.

Approaching the window, she heard O'Malley utter a deep rumble in his chest as he stared beyond the landscape. The only other time she'd heard that growl was the night he had bolted toward the construction project. Tonight, the object of O'Malley's upward gaze appeared to be in the distance. He growled, moving left and then right while remaining balanced on his hind legs. Maybe he'd spotted a raccoon or a skunk. She suspected the former as nocturnal raiders had been emptying their birdfeeders. A particularly clever squirrel had even stolen a whole peanut-chip cylinder in broad daylight. That, however, would have made him bark a plea to go outside and chase the critters.

Leaving the pair by the window, she went into the hall and flipped the floodlight switch by the front door. The scene exploded in light. Affixed high beneath the soffit on opposite corners, the floods projected megawatts in a one-hundred-foot arch without reaching Jacob's farm.

She located binoculars on the adjacent bookshelf, focused, and scanned beyond the lawn and the pair of hundred-foot oaks from which they hung their swing in the summer. Backdropping the lawn, wild rhododendrons, and mountain laurel eased toward the distant highway, which was obscured by a smattering of self-seeded long-needle pines. Wisps of clouds, which had foretold an advancing front earlier that day, now intensified and obliterated the moon as they skittered across the sky in varying degrees of inky intensity.

She was about to turn off the floodlights when something on the hill beyond the lane caught her eye. What was it? Perhaps she could see it better if she killed the floods. "Let's find out if we can see outside better if I turn off the lights," she said in soothing tones to her child, not wishing to alarm Billy. "Just stay put for a moment." She hit the switch that controlled the lamps by their library chairs and killed the floodlights. Returning to the window she raised the binoculars. There! She saw what had captured O'Malley's attention.

On the telephone pole, high on the hill above their lane, something seemed to be caught. Its movement appeared for all the world like an animal that had climbed it and was clinging to the transformer atop the pole. The extent of wildlife in their rural location hadn't occurred to her yet. Perhaps it was an empty black garbage bag snared by the gathering wind? The four-lane highway, from which they exited, ran parallel to their lane a mile above them. Sometimes debris from passing garbage trucks floated downhill onto their land.

"Hey buddy—bath time," Todd called from the hall, a kitchen towel draped over his shoulder. "There's time for bubbles if we hurry." That did it—Billy scampered toward his father, and the pair hustled upstairs.

"By the way," Todd called from the landing to Kingsley. "Remind me to check the light bulb, the wiring, the switch, and the cord in the back bedroom. The bulb is flickering like it's possessed, even though it's turned off at the switch."

Rather than following, O'Malley remained riveted to the spot at the library window. "Let's have a look," she said to the dog, grabbing a mag light and dousing the lights in all the front rooms. Not chancing another harrowing runaway or trusting that O'Malley had learned his lesson, she snapped the leash onto his collar. "In case you're tempted" she apologized to her dog who seemed embarrassed as if he understood every word she just said.

She stepped onto the brick entryway into a night that smelled of spring rain and damp earth, coaxing dormant perennials to life. From the bathroom overhead, a crisp parallelogram of light illuminated a patch of front yard.

"Let's walk," she spoke with more confidence than she felt. As they headed toward the driveway, O'Malley walked forward, his head angled right, his attention riveted beyond the front yard in the direction of the telephone pole on the hill. Again, a growl emanated from deep in his chest.

"What is it? What do you see?" The dog continued to stare into the gathering blackness as they moved toward the driveway beyond the light's illumination. She counted the seconds from the first pulse of lightning to the rumble of thunder in the distance. Ten miles. "We'd better go in," she said to calm her incongruous alarm. The dog must have seen something ominous, which left her spooked.

Once inside, Kingsley unclipped his leash and went upstairs to the bubble bath in progress. It wouldn't be the first time that mopping would be her evening's entertainment. The rumble of thunder seemed closer. Maybe the gathering storm would bypass them. Funny how parental responsibility heightens one's awareness of safety issues she used to dismiss. Could one be struck by lightning while bathing? Not taking any chances, she transitioned the fun with the prospect of milk and cookies for both.

The evening routine proceeded with Todd unconcerned and Billy unaware of the gathering storm. Father and son settled into Todd's library chair to read Billy's favorite book, *Cars and Trucks and Things That Go.* Billy's delight at finding Goldbug never diminished as he giggled with delight, tapping each one with a chubby finger. Watching their nightly routine never got old for Kingsley either, knowing that besides the parental fun, their child was developing a lifelong love of reading books.

This evening, however, O'Malley was noticeably missing from his usual spot by her feet, leaning into her hand for an ear rub. How odd, she thought of the little dog who craved his share of attention. While Billy begged just one more page, she investigated, drawn instinctively to the front window but not seeing him immediately where he had alerted after dinner. Again, he was stretching to reach the sill, his plume of a tail protruding from under the floor-length drapery. As she approached, he whined, looking back and forth from her to something beyond her ability to see. She flipped on the floodlights, but still saw nothing unusual.

Tucking Billy into bed and saying prayers together should have been *it* until morning. Billy, however, wasn't cooperative. "O'Mawwey!" he objected and, overly tired, refused to be placated. He slipped from his carefully tucked blanket, escaping into the hall, and tried his best to holler over the banister for his pet. Momentarily, they heard the jingle of the dog's new license and ID, reminiscent of Morley's ghost. Billy joyfully hugged and kissed his dog, then crawled back into bed.

As they were leaving the bedroom, Kingsley looked back at what had become the picture-perfect scene. Instead of landscaping his rug into a ball, turning his circles, and flopping to sleep, O'Malley stood, following their movements. "Leave the door open a crack, will you Todd? Something's been upsetting O'Malley all evening, and I want to see what he does next." Nightlights in the bedrooms and hall bathed the upstairs in a soft glow. They started downstairs. Kingsley paused at the landing window that overlooked their backyard and flower garden, both coming to life as spring progressed. Peering through the pitch-black night, it took imagination to picture Billy's play gym, the ancient maple under which they picnicked, and the farmland greening in the distance. With their lights extinguished and the dairy farm asleep, the only sound was the quickening wind whistling through the virgin woods.

Had she not stepped outside to rescue her boots lest they fill with rainwater, she would not have realized how quickly the storm had intensified. When the forecast suggested a rumble of thunder, she hardly expected summertime fury unleased this early in the season. She stowed her boots and, bolting the door against the oncoming storm, extinguished the coach lights beside the back door. Turning, she almost tripped on the dog.

"What are you doing downstairs?" she asked, regretting the accusatory note in her voice. She bent to stroke him, scratching behind his ears and smoothing his soft fur from nose to tail tip. Under her hand, she could feel he was trembling. "Ah! You feel the storm coming, don't you?" She picked him up and carried him on her hip to her chair in the library. He settled momentarily, then jerked his head to attention and sprang to his feet, circling behind their chairs to the front windows. She followed him, then couldn't resist taking an unobstructed look by opening the front door. The gathering storm forced her to close it as remnants of fall leaves swirled into the foyer. She bolted the door.

Rain lashed the windows, lightning and thunder crashing simultaneously, the storm settling directly overhead. For the first time, Kingsley doubted the wisdom of leaving the pair of hundred-foot oaks twenty feet from the house. As if reading her thoughts, Todd slipped up behind her, pulling her close to his side. "They're fine," he said. "They've got roots to China, and they're too close to the house to get enough momentum to flatten it. In two hundred years, this house has survived hurricanes, blizzards, a tornado, and countless storms that swept through the valley. We'll be fine."

"Tell that to O'Malley."

"Our black labs were terrified of thunder. I had to comfort them all night long. I think it's their excellent hearing, which must make noise so much worse." At that moment, O'Malley began frantic pacing, back and forth from one front window to another, circling around the couple as if they should follow. Suddenly an explosion shook their windows and rattled the doors as if they were under attack. Running to the window, they saw a giant fireball ignite the trees surrounding the telephone pole and transformer. The house was plunged into darkness.

Feeling her way to the stairway, Kingsley propelled herself toward Billy's bedroom, his battery-operated nightlight casting dim light. She found him sitting bolt-upright, looking dazed, a puzzled look on his face. "Go back to sleep, sweetie. Everything's all right." He was still asleep, she realized, as she eased him back onto his pillow and adjusted his blanket. From the foyer, she heard the tall-case clock bong midnight. Thankfully, they still owned mechanical devices.

As she went downstairs, she wondered how long they'd be without electricity. They did have a small generator they'd bought when they lived at the rental house while renovating two of these rooms. That first Memorial Day weekend, their pioneer spirit drove their decision to move into their dream home. First thing tomorrow, perishable food would need to be hauled to the basement refrigerator that the generator would power. By the time she reached the dark kitchen, she had a plan. For now, she'd round up flashlights, candles, and the camp lantern. Ah! The latter was in the barn.

She was pulling on her barn boots and a slicker, armed with a mag light when Todd came up behind her, motioning her to kill the flashlight, his finger to his lips. "What?"

"Shhh. Someone's outside."

"Who? Our neighbor? The power company?"

He kept shaking his head. "They'd come to the door or in vehicles. Not be skulking outside in the dark."

"Are you sure? What do you think we should do besides keep the doors and windows locked? We don't own a gun, and with the landline dead, we can't call for help." She groped the counters for her cell phone, which she'd last used in the kitchen. "No signal," she whispered.

"Gun—I have an idea," Todd said. Kingsley trailed him to the basement, a concrete-floored, cavernous foundation as large as the house's footprint. His hand tools were grouped on the walls like a tool catalog. An assortment of cabinets held drills and saws. Large power tools—a radial arm saw, joiner and planer, band saw, and a drill press—surrounded a jury-rigged workbench made of metal legs to which Todd had screwed construction-grade two by fours. He yanked open one door after another until he found what he wanted—a hammer drill nail gun that shot nails into concrete, propelled by live Remington ammunition.

"What are you going to do with that thing?" she asked of the device with which he'd nailed plywood to the basement's concrete walls when creating his shop.

"You remember what this thing sounds like?"

"Yeah! We both had to wear ear protection or we would be deaf, and I wasn't even downstairs at the time."

"Keep trying to raise help with your cell phone, and then stay with Billy."

"What will you be doing?"

"Hopefully, scaring the hell out of that guy. Keep the doors locked, no matter what happens. Go!"

She scrambled back upstairs, envisioning her kitchen, now totally dark. The knife box—she'd take it upstairs to Billy's room and wait. She felt her way through darkness as black as a subterranean cave, trying to remember if the chairs were pushed in, the dishwasher or cabinet doors ajar. Then she stumbled on something soft and righted herself. O'Malley owned the expression, *underfoot*. She wondered if he could see in the dark like Pandora. Where was her cat? Momentarily, she felt another soft body, weaving through her legs. "A fine time you guys pick to make friends," she whispered. Risking a penlight, she made two trips upstairs, first closing all the blackout blinds and curtains and then changing into black clothing.

She set the knife box on Billy's chest of drawers, then angled the rocker beside his bed, listening for any suspicious sounds in the house. She knew its very heartbeat. If anyone tried to harm her baby, she'd slit his throat with the carving knife she readied on her lap.

From the pegs in the basement, Todd swapped his street clothes for black sweats, a nylon parka, and a black knit skull cap. His face—what would work? He couldn't bring himself to use paint or varnish that would have to wear off. Greece—or boot polish. That would work. He unlocked the case that held his hammer drill, grabbed it and a strip of ten 22-caliber loads, which he inserted into the gun. From a drawer, he grabbed a handful of concrete nails and dropped them into his jacket pocket. He crept up the steps of the Bilco doors, setting the drill beside him on the top step. As he slid the latch and cracked one heavy metal door, he listened. Rain hammering the doors, accompanied by thunder and lightning, covered any sound he might make. He chanced lifting the heavy door farther to scan the yard at eye-level.

Momentarily disoriented, he remembered he was on the west side of the house, facing Jacob's farm. Todd never came or went to the basement via the Bilco doors, using the barn for mowers and yard tools instead. He grabbed the nail gun and raised the door just enough to crawl into the muddy side yard. As he stood perfectly still in the inky darkness, back pressed against the house, he trusted that he was concealed. He prayed that Kingsley and Billy were safe and that she had been able to raise help.

As he peeked around the backside of the house, he saw a figure, nearly invisible, until the next flash of lightning illuminated his pale complexion. Todd jerked back around the house. How many times he'd loaded and shot the hammer gun during his shop project should now be en-grained in muscle memory as he fingered the concrete nails in his pocket. With dripping hands, he fingered their familiarity. Positioning one at the end of the gun, he crept around the back of the house. He waited until the rhythm of lightning and thunder might give him an interval of darkness.

The skulking figure's back was turned, his right arm ex-tended toward the kitchen door's glass pane with what looked like a rock in his hand. The man lifted his arm above his head as if preparing to smash the glass. Did the security system have a battery backup? Would the alarm sound if the glass had been shattered? It was supposed to, but had the security company tested it after the gas leak episode? He'd had no reason to ask.

Todd's mind narrowed to primitive man. Not knowing how far a nail would travel, Todd pulled back the hammer, adjusted the nail, and taking careful aim, pulled the trigger.

Bang!

The blast split the air with such explosive volume that Todd was momentarily deafened. Was the intruder armed? Might he turn and charge? Todd prayed his deception had worked. He screamed, "Next shot, you're dead!"

He ducked behind the house while cocking the gun and inserting another nail. Only then did he risk glancing. The perpetrator was limping toward the far side of the house. "Gotcha!" he muttered, too surprised to take further action. His sense of urgency returned. He had to make a quick de-cision—fight or flight. He scrambled back through the Bilco door and threw the bolt. He tossed the hammer gun and what remained of the ammo strip aside, which he'd lock up after defending his family. Exchanging his slip-pery muddy clothes for shop overalls, he grabbed a box cutter from his toolbox then tore up the stairs, two at a time, to protect his family.

Chapter 15

Although the Henning house was shrouded in darkness, their land and driveway pulsed in a kaleidoscope of first responders' lights. Beyond their front door with binoculars, Kingsley identified the power company's vehicles high on the hill, hopefully dealing with a blown transformer. Restoring the electricity quickly would be awesome. Through the pines she could distinguish two red oblongs—firetrucks, no doubt, making sure the torrential rain had doused the blaze and prevented a forest fire.

Todd beckoned to her with a nod as he led a township police officer and state patrolman around toward the back. She sighed. If the excitement was over, all she wanted to do was lie down. As Todd entered the back hall, shepherding the cops toward the kitchen table, she darted upstairs to check on Billy. The child, miraculously, had slept through the ordeal. O'Malley was not on his rug but curled beside Billy. He looked up when she entered the bedroom wearing that guilty look he had refined to a science. "It's okay. You can stay." He thumped his tail, lowering his head and curling his balled body against Billy. She closed the door and hurried to join the others.

"...-so, the passerby loads the guy into his car and drives him to the ER. He'd been shot in the leg near an artery and had lost a lot of blood. The ER doc said he'd survive, although we couldn't talk to him until he's in recovery and regains consciousness. The good Samaritan insisted he didn't know the guy or what had happened to him. Just saw him staggering down the road before he collapsed, coming from this direction. At first, he thought he was drunk, but then he saw the blood."

Todd looked at Kingsley, and she back at him, telepathing *should they tell them? Would they believe us? Do we need a lawyer?*

The patrolman produced a photocopy of a PA driver's license. "Ever see this guy before?"

Both squinted at the postage-size picture and shook their heads no. "Who is he?" Todd asked.

"Guy that's been on the most-wanted list for some time in connection with a series of arsons. He's suspected of torching properties, businesses, vehicles et cetera for profit, like a hitman. When it's light enough, the fire inspector's going to take a look at that transformer. Power company says the totality of the damage doesn't look like a lightning strike; more like sabotage."

"Why would anyone blow up a transformer in a thunderstorm?"

"What better timing to conceal a crime?"

Kingsley turned to the state patrolman. "Did you respond because the highway's an interstate and you were in the vicinity?"

"No. Because my barracks got a call from Henry Alderson of St. Davids that his daughter was in danger, her landline was down, and her cell phone connection was breaking up. Said she'd tried phoning and texting for his help, and would we please send someone to this address."

Kingsley smiled. "That would be my dad. The connection was breaking up so badly I had no idea if anyone heard me."

"He'd made out the words 'explosion' and 'fire' and 'intruder.' Did someone break in?" Both said no, a little too emphatically, but the officers, distracted by gathering their things in preparation to leave, missed their mistake.

"I must apologize," Kingsley said. "You came out at three in the morning, and I didn't even offer you something to drink or eat. I'd be happy to make coffee if we had electricity, but there's soft drinks and water. And there's cookies."

"Thank you, ma'am. That's kind of you, but we need to wrap this up."

The minute the pair was out of earshot, Kingsley and Todd exploded with unanswered questions. Somebody had it in for them big time, and they needed to find out fast who it was.

∽∾∽

Weary from a full day of putting out different kinds of fires at their respective jobs, Kingsley and Todd collapsed, finally having a private opportunity to ferret through recent events. "When did our lives get so out of hand?" she asked, curling into an afghan in her chair by the fire. The cold front, ushered in by the monstrous storm, had left their home damp and chilly. Given the past twenty-four hours, her nerves felt raw and the fire, good.

Todd set aside the speech he'd been writing for a banker's symposium. "Thinking back, it began with that call from our realtor, Greg, with an outrageous offer to buy our property, supposedly on behalf of another realtor's celebrity client. And, in that same anonymous vein, a so-called heir to the original William Penn land grant pops up out of nowhere. Of the latter, I would have put money on a scam to extort money from us in exchange for withdrawing the claim, except for that other offer. Somebody tried to force us out, and when we didn't budge, things got ugly."

"No," Kingsley interjected. "Our lives were peaceful until that construction project next door wreaked havoc with our sleep.

Todd shook his head. "That did result in some ugly confrontations, but I think the man in charge is committed to making peace if we'll ignore the inconvenience for a couple more weeks and stay off his site. The owner, whoever he or she is, has no need whatsoever to harm us."

"So that leaves the celebrity and the heir. I'll pick Greg's brain—maybe he could find out a bit more about that wealthy entertainer. And see what Uncle David thinks about that William Penn heir's claim. Surely whoever is behind a scam like that would have been stupid not to realize we have the means to fight them, even if that meant a protracted legal battle."

She rubbed her temples, shaking her head. "Is it possible that whoever's behind this has an ulterior motive that hasn't occurred to us? But what? We aren't a danger to anyone. Maybe it's bank-related. We should pick through our rejected loan applications and people who have been fired or passed over for employment. The only people who've threatened me in recent years are in prison. Our lives have become, well, dull. And our property could be duplicated anywhere within the three adjacent counties. I just don't get it."

"Let's approach this like a business plan to stop whoever is intent on harming us. There's the gas leak, the transformer fire, and the arsonist skulking around and trying to break in."

Kingsley tossed the afghan to the floor and snagged a pencil and pad from her desk. "First thing tomorrow, I'll summon our contractor, the guy from the gas company, and our security tech and find out exactly what caused that leak. And I'm going to ask why the system wasn't armed. We were not careless! If it malfunctioned, they need to fix it, or we'll find someone who will. Would the system have alerted us if an intruder broke the glass? If not, we need an upgrade. We need to be safe in our home."

"And I'll follow up with the fire marshal and whether the transformer was sabotaged. And what the cops know about the guy who tried to break in. Don't say it—I won't let on that I shot him with a shop tool."

Stomp! Stomp! Stomp! Shriek! The parents looked at the ceiling simultaneously. "At least we know where he is and what he's doing," Todd said, a grin overtaking his face, relieved to focus on a happier subject.

"I could strangle Randall for giving him those cowboy boots without discussing it with us. Did you know at daycare he wouldn't take them off for his nap?"

Todd laughed. "I had to bribe him to take them off for his bath."

"I draw the line at sleeping in them."

"Good luck with that."

Having momentarily forgotten the seriousness of the issue at hand Kingsley asked, "What *are* they doing?" It sounded like Billy and O'Malley were running circuits through the upstairs hall and bedrooms. They could follow the footsteps, giggles, and yips from Billy's bedroom, down the hall and, looping into the front guestroom, through their bedroom, then back down the hall to Billy's door. The game seemed to stop by the rear guestroom door.

"Listen," Kingsley said. "Billy's voice diminishes inside the guestroom while O'Malley's whines can be heard in the hall. He's not following Billy into the back room. I wonder why." Kingsley padded sock-footed upstairs to spy on their antics. She arrived on the landing in time to see Billy streak red-faced into the front guestroom. Momentarily, not noticing his mother, he erupted from their room and sprinted down the hall, the dog at his heels. Before he could reach the rear bedroom door again, O'Malley had beaten him to it and stood guard-like at its entrance, legs braced, head lowered, emitting a whine. Billy blew right past him, but the dog didn't follow.

Something clicked—Suzanne Meade's story about the house being haunted. Her nerves were simply too edgy from their harrowing experience and sleep deprivation. "Billy!" she chided in her no-nonsense voice. "Enough!" The child skidded to a stop, face beet red, panting. "It's bedtime." O'Malley, she noticed, had disappeared.

☙❧

Sleep eluded Kingsley. Exhausted, but over-stimulated, she could not stop the mice from running around in her brain. She glanced at the clock, her near-sighted eyes squinting at its oversized numerals. She saw 2:15. Todd turned toward the interior wall, slept like a dead thing. She gave his arm a gentle shake to make sure he was still breathing. Good. He was alive. Slipping out of bed and into her slippers and collecting a penlight from the nightstand, she slipped into the hall and approached Billy's room.

With a finger's light touch, she widened the crack enough to see her son and his dog. O'Malley's head jerked to attention as if to ask what was up. Kingsley opened the door a bit farther and patted her thigh for him to come. He did without hesitation. Gathering him against her hip, she closed Billy's door and crossed the hall. Moonlight cast an eerie glow into the depths of the unoccupied room, throwing silhouettes of an ancient maple's limbs on the interior wall. O'Malley whimpered.

"What is it?" she whispered. "What bothers you about this room?" She lit the penlight, and closing the door behind them, set the pup down. She stooped beside him, and when she pulled him close to her side, felt him trembling. "It's all right. You're safe with me." She sat on the rug, her dog snuggled against her, stroking his fur from nose to tail tip in the calming way he enjoyed. "I wish you could tell me what you know." He cast doleful eyes at hers with a sadness that broke her heart. "If only I knew your history and how you ended up on the highway."

She had an idea. "Come. Let's check it out." When she rose, he stayed close by her side as she circled the perimeter of the room. When they came to the back outside corner, however, he backed up, as if retreating from danger without taking his eyes off the floor.

"What?" she asked, looking first at him, then toward the spot on which he was focused. Or was he listening to something that she couldn't hear? Then she felt a sensation of cold. Not like a draft or the heat pump's circulation, which would have been warm this time of year. Forgetting about O'Malley, she took small steps as if to delineate the cold spot's footprint. What startled her was that she only felt it when she stood utterly still as if it were communicating with her; becoming one with her. She shivered. As soon as she moved, the sensation disappeared.

Stunned, she determined to investigate further. Alone. Tomorrow. And she'd track down the story of the murder. She did not believe in ghosts. Grammy had insisted that one could not be superstitious and Christian at the same time, and Grammy fiercely believed in the latter. How she wished she could have just one more conversation with her grandmother. One never knows when time was running out. She looked at O'Malley with renewed appreciation, having stayed with her where he dreaded to go.

Chapter 16

"Hey Greg. Kingsley Henning. Got a minute? I'm hoping you can do me a favor and save me hours of digging."

"Sure. If I can." The realtor asked with colloquial phrasing. "What can I do you for?"

"I need contact information for a prior owner of our home. I recall he was the heir to the Krick estate. Andrew or Ansel or some other A name. And, if you have it, the name and number of the fellow we outbid. And finally, the most recent owner. The huge favor—would you be comfortable calling them on my behalf and asking if they'd be willing to speak with me? Tell them I have questions about the home's history that they might be able to answer."

In the background, Kingsley could hear keys tapping. "I have numbers for all three. The heir is Amos Krick. You outbid Michael Flannery. And the previous owner, from whom you bought the property, is John Black. I'll give them a call right now." Thirty minutes later, Kingsley had her answers. "Michael is local; he said to call on his cell. John Black, ditto. Amos Krick is a retired, long-time resident of Michigan. He gave me his landline. I'll email the numbers. And good luck with your project. And, if you're thinking about a cabin in the Adirondacks…?"

"You'll be the first to know." Kingsley paced around

the living room, cordless phone in hand, screwing up her courage. When she got no answer at the Krick home in Michigan, she decided to try again later and didn't leave a message. Her mission was too complicated for a few sentence summary.

After taking a few more laps around the living room, she dialed Michael Flannery. When she identified herself, he responded with a jovial laugh. "Ah! My savior. I wanted to thank you and didn't know how."

"I thought you'd be angry with us, practically stealing the house out from under you. My fiancé was determined after years of research and touring with realtors that this house was perfect."

The man chuckled. "You saved my marriage. After I made my bid and did a walk-through with an inspector, I realized I was in way over my head. I attached all kinds of conditions to the sale, hoping I could flip it and break even. Then you came along. Thank you. It was my dream and never my wife's. She'll take a new track house in the suburbs anytime. And that's what we bought."

"Did you know anything about the history of the house? Old stories about a murdered couple? Or it's being haunted?"

"Hell no! If I had, we woulda been outa there."

After they disconnected and feeling less timid, Kingsley dialed John Black, the previous owner, and found him to be a kindred spirit and lover of old homes. "Ever see the movie *The Money Pit*? I had no idea what I was getting into, especially with that slate roof. According to my research, originally it would have wood shingles, but someone replaced it with slate that turned out to be poor quality. Good slate should last 75 years.

"I hired a reputable contractor to replace missing or broken tiles. It got to the point where I dreaded seeing his name on my caller ID. Long story short, most shingles were shot, there was damage to the underlying wood, and matching slate wasn't available. By the time he finished, I'd spent my entire renovation fund without touching the plumbing and wiring. I was up shit creek. But the house has an excellent roof.

"So I put it on the market which, of course, had tanked. One nibbler wanted me to give it away and kept heaping on further demands 'per his inspector.' Months went by. Then this nice guy with an angry wife put in a low bid. I felt so sorry for him. I shudder to think what would have happened to that marriage if I'd taken it. Then on that Sunday morning, your offer came. I gotta tell you, I've never drunk my breakfast before, but I celebrated big time."

"Would you do it again? Renovate an old home?"

"Sure. But I know a hell of a lot more now. I would not make the same mistakes twice. And I'd research it to death."

"So—you don't bear us any animosity?"

"Hell no. You rescued me from the money pit."

"Did you ever sense a cold spot in the upper left bedroom? Or feel the presence of something otherworldly?"

John Black laughed. "Lady, I never actually lived there. The place was uninhabitable. And cold? The entire house was frigid, and the fireplaces unsafe. I had it on good authority I'd burn the place to the ground to say nothing of roasting some critters."

For the next thirty minutes, she answered questions about what they did about this and about that. "You're welcome to visit when you have time. We have a treasure trove of our own horror stories and workarounds." She gave him detailed contact information and they agreed to meet in the future.

Kingsley took a deep breath. A, she concluded, neither had reason to harm them. And B, neither knew anything about a cold spot or ghost stories. She tried Amos Krick's number again. After the outgoing message and beep, she decided to leave her name and number, but before she was halfway through her speech, a man's voice interrupted. "I'm here, Ms. Henning. Go ahead."

After her well-rehearsed preamble, she got to the point. "I'm trying to trace an heir to our property who has served us with legal documents, claiming ownership dating to the William Penn grant. Without sugar-coating it—might a member of your family feel this property is rightfully theirs? We have a clear title, but one never knows."

"Ms. Henning, someone is scamming you. Or trying to. Do you have a few minutes for me to explain?"

"Oh yes, please do. And call me Kingsley."

"The property had been in my family since that William Penn grant. We've secured official copies of the original document. Each generation has copies hanging in their homes."

"Can you tell me about the history of the home's ownership?"

"Let me work backward from what I know personally. My granduncle took possession of the farm in 1920 when his grandparents died. His grandfather—my great great— was just seventeen, the youngest of eight, when he took over the farm. At twenty-five, he married an eighteen-year-old Mennonite girl, joined her church, and won her family's acceptance. They also had eight children. My great-grandfather was their youngest. He married my great-grandmother and they lived on an adjacent farm and died in the eighties. Their son and his wife owned the farm for sixty years. After he died, she stayed on alone for another five, then spent her last five years in a nursing home."

"So you knew your grandparents' generation, and heard the stories of *their* grandparents, and so on."

"I was very lucky. Today's society is so mobile that few

have the kind of roots that we do."

"Why are you so sure that this so-called heir's story is a scam?"

He chuckled. "Before I sold the house to that fellow—what was his name?"

"John Black. And he sold it to us. Evidently, his ambitious restoration project put him in over his head."

"That's it. He's the one. And you're the present owner?"

"That's right. It was my husband Todd's and my dream, and we've renovated it as historically faithfully as possible. Go on—I've digressed."

"I went to the University of Michigan on a football scholarship, then to law school, and was offered a position in my mentor's firm where I met my wife. She has deep roots and extensive family in Michigan. After a decade, as I rose in the firm and made partner, it was obvious I wasn't destined to live in rural Pennsylvania. Besides, my grand aunt was determined to live there forever. We brought our kids home for family reunions to meet their dozens of cousins, but they scattered to the wind to pursue their education and careers. I have fond memories of the rocking chairs and a swing on the front porch."

"I'm afraid the porch is long gone."

"That's all right. I have pictures, and it's locked in my mind."

"You must have hundreds of kin. Are you sure none of them wanted this property?"

"Absolutely. And I'll tell you why. Being the only one of my generation who is in family law, I was appointed to be my great-aunt's guardian and executor. I knew that one day transferring her property would be an issue. She was sharp as a tack to the end and insisted that one day she'd go home with a nurse to take care of her. That never happened. As it turned out, I had five years to query all her living descendants."

"Wow! That must have been quite a job."

"Not really. Thanks to that William Penn connection, everyone was proud of their heritage. Each generation has a historian that kept track of their kids, grands, great-grands et cetera, which by now is kept on Excel spreadsheets. I contacted my siblings, who contacted their families' record keepers and so on, connecting to all living descendants of our great-great-grandparents."

"Nobody wanted a farmette in Pennsylvania?"

"Correct. And no one objected to selling it when the time came. And speaking of which, perhaps you could send me pictures of the place from time to time. I can post them on our family's website."

"It would be my pleasure. We've kept digital records from day one in a series of files. In fact, I can email them to you now."

"That would be grand. I'll give you the address."

"I do have another question, which is personal in nature. I sense a 'cold spot' in the upstairs left rear bedroom, but only if I stand very still near the back corner. It's not a draft. Does that make any sense to you?"

"Actually, it does. You remember I told you my grandfather's grandpa took over the property, just seventeen years old when his parents died?"

"Yes. That must have been awful for someone so young."

"Doubly so. They didn't die accidentally or from illness. They were murdered."

Kingsley was dumbfounded and unable to speak for a moment. Finally, she asked, "Did they ever find out who was responsible?"

"There was a lot of speculation at the time, but the entire family was accounted for, being that it was a Sunday. And way back then, there were no CSIs, blood typing, evidence preservation—modern police methods. Time passed. No suspects were identified, but murder-suicide wasn't ruled out, although the family insisted there was no way. And they were very protective of their reputation, so idle speculation was squelched."

"Thank you. That's fascinating history. May I call you again sometime? I have lists of little questions about the house."

"Of course. And thanks again for offering your photos. I'll be sure to share them with the extended Krick family."

Chapter 17

Glorious sun streamed from the east windows that should have dispelled yesterday's gloom. Determined to resolve their gnawing questions and her sense of impending doom, Kingsley sent Todd and Billy off to the bank, freeing her to deal with the contractors herself. Without an audience, she could be as blunt as she wished. In response to her take-no-prisoners no-delay demands, a line of service trucks arrived simultaneously, the men crowding into her back hall. She decided to deal with her contractor first and led him and the gas company technician into the kitchen.

"You hired the subs who ordered and installed the equipment," she reminded her contractor, policing herself to stifle the anger she felt might escape in her voice now that she'd had time to digest the near-fatal catastrophe. "The guy who shut off the gas tried to suggest one of my family was at fault. We're not having that conversation again. Also, he suggested that substandard equipment or an inexperienced installer screwed up. That our house and us in it could have been blown to bits. I've never found any fault with your work. The stove functioned perfectly the previous night, and nobody used it the following morning."

Her contractor straightened, glaring at her. "You know

very well that we never scrimp on materials, and all my subcontractors are the best. I assure you when this job was completed, I checked every last detail personally. I understand how upset you must be, but I assure you, my crew was not responsible."

"I apologize. I had to repeat what was suggested to me, even though we have every confidence in you." She turned to call over her shoulder. "Mort? Would you please join us in the kitchen for a minute?"

The guy from the security company, who Todd had employed for several of his former residences, popped his head into the kitchen. "I have a list for you, but first, would you find out why our alarm didn't sound when the house was filling with gas? And we absolutely did arm the system, but when I discovered the gas emergency, it wasn't activated. If our equipment isn't that sophisticated—which I thought it was—then we need to talk about a serious upgrade."

After the grilling she'd received that night as if they had been careless, she was prepared to get ugly if confronted again. Mort, however, was a *yes'm* kind of guy and returned to his van to grab tools. By the time she returned to the kitchen, the contractor and the mechanic were shaking their heads. "Looks fine in here," the mechanic said. "Let's check outside."

Kingsley frowned. "That doesn't make any sense. If the leak was outside, why would the house fill with fumes? I distinctly remember the first responder from the gas company say they could only smell gas outside when the back door opened, which I did to escape."

"Just the same..." Fifteen minutes later the pair returned to the kitchen from outside, resuming their checking of the line. From his truck, the mechanic retrieved a 200-watt trouble light and a magnifying glass. He repeated his inspection of every millimeter while the contractor frowned at the spot that now drew his attention.

Kingsley said, "I need to speak with my security man, but if you need me, just yell." She left the pair who by then were crouched in front of the stove exchanging whispered comments. Not knowing anything about electronics beyond which buttons to push, Kingsley approached Mort who was inspecting the circuit board that normally was hidden behind its cover. "Ain't right," he said, shaking his head. "Who else ya got in here working on our equipment?"

"Nobody. Your company's the only one we've ever employed. Todd hired you for our rental house before we moved in here, and before that, for his bachelor condo. That goes back years."

"Yeah, I remember. You had us here for what you called a *work in progress*. Barely livable. Electricity, plumbing—no, you were using that generator. We set up the security system about the same time the electrician was running the wires. Hottest summer on record. That I remember."

"Why did you ask about another security company? No one touches our equipment but you. We have no reason to switch—you guys are the best." She remembered how they'd responded when the kidnappers' operative had broken into their house while they were flying cross-country trying to locate baby Billy. Not only had they responded instantly but they'd had the presence of mind to sweep the house for listening devices.

"Someone's hacked my stuff then. Replaced the circuit board. Looks the same if you don't know what you're doing. This, this thing!" he growled, stabbing the air in its direction with a screwdriver. "It allows remote access to shut off the alarm without a code. I'll replace it with the real deal. Go to the basement, will ya? And hit the breaker marked *security*. I labeled it in red. Yell when it's off."

From his toolbox, he chose a different screwdriver.

"Wait! Don't finger that circuit board with your bare hands. I'll get gloves and a baggie to save it for the police."

"First the breaker. Then the baggie."

After handing Mort a gallon zipper freezer bag and a pair of Todd's XXL latex gloves from the workshop, she went to check on the men in the kitchen and found them in deep conversation, gesturing to something behind the stove. They looked worried, and at that moment, she was afraid to ask why.

Since they didn't seem to need her, she excused herself and went to the library to call Margaret. She smiled, picturing her friend and co-conspirator, her smile that lit up her sapphire blue eyes. On Kingsley's first day at Keynote National Bank, her new boss had told her that the vice president in charge of residential real estate lending could be trusted with anything. Whatever Kingsley needed, Margaret could get it, find it, or know who could. And she never betrayed a confidence. How Kingsley loved that woman who had helped her when she was drawn into three different crimes. She speed-dialed her friend.

"Congratulations!" Kingsley gushed. "That promotion to senior VP was long overdue. And, speaking of your promotion, does it come with a corner office?"

"Kingsley, hey kiddo. Thank you, and yes. Can't wait to move in. And I'm counting on you to help me arrange the beautiful bookshelves that come with the territory. Say, are you at home? Any luck with that awful project next door with the murky provenance?"

"I think we have a truce at the moment. Mr. Thousand-dollar Suit stopped by with a *mea culpa* and sort of a promise things will quiet down in a couple of weeks. The reason I'm calling…"

"You need a reason? Uh oh. There's trouble in your voice."

"I've got a mystery to solve, and I'm hoping you could help me track someone down." As succinctly as possible, she summarized mixing up Dr. Suzanne Meade, the history professor, with a complete stranger, whom Todd thought might be a realtor looking for business. "I'm hoping, if I describe her, she sounds familiar."

"I'll try."

"While we chatted, Suzanne number one told me a fascinating story about a nineteenth-century murder that might have taken place in this house. And supposedly, it's haunted. She said she'd read an article about it that was published decades ago in a true crime magazine. She said she'd get in touch if she remembered the source, but I don't have her contact information."

"You didn't catch her name or her agency? And no card or sales pitch? That's odd if she really is a realtor."

"I called her by the wrong name, and she didn't correct me."

"Huh! Describe her for me, and I'll make a few calls. If she's a realtor, she'd be licensed and probably a member of the Board of Realtors. Being a residential real estate lender, there's not many agencies in the tri-county area that I haven't done business with or met through professional organizations and seminars."

"She's about five-ten, size two, three-foil highlights on light brown hair, designer wardrobe, killer boots that wouldn't stop at $500. Drives a white late-model midsize coupe with tan interior."

Margaret laughed. "The kind most women would hate on sight."

"Oh! Magnificent blue eyes with tiny black lines that sparkle like tinsel. A mega-watt smile. Perfect orthodontia. Stunning little gold and diamond watch that looked 14k.

"Warts? Moles? Scars?"

"Don't be ridiculous."

"I'll ask around. And I'll check with those who have a history of buying or selling so-called haunted properties. Believe it or not, they're not that uncommon. And I have a contact in the Paranormal Society."

"Margaret? I know this sounds silly, but there's a cold spot in that back bedroom, and it's not mechanical. The room spooks our little dog. O'Malley won't venture in by himself. I'd love to meet your Society's contact."

"I'll reach out to her."

"Thanks! Lunch by the fountain first warm day we get? Or at the diner next week?"

"You're on."

"Ms. Henning?" Their contractor waited in the hall outside the library until she hung up.

"I'm sorry. I didn't see you." She got up and followed him into the kitchen. "Did you pinpoint the source of the problem?"

"Yes, Ma'am, we did, but we'd better not fix it." Kingsley noticed he was fidgeting with his cap. Had they screwed up when installing the gas line and the stove? Were the materials wrong or did he find shoddy workmanship? Maybe the stove needed a part, which was either obsolete or no longer available, meaning they'd have to replace the stove.

She sighed. "What is it? What did you find? Tell me— I can take it, even if it means no more cooking with gas."

He was shaking his head. "That's not it." He glanced at the technician, who looked equally worried. "There's signs of tampering. I think you should call the police."

"What kind of signs? Like cuts or scrapes?"

"The shutoff valve has been replaced with one that looks for all the world like the original, except that it has a remote switch that can open or close the gas line."

"What? Why would anyone do that?" The reason dawned on her by the time she'd uttered the words.

Tampering was intentional! The house could have blown up and her with it had she not wakened in time. Why would anyone hate them that much? She was too stunned to say anything except to ask what came first to her addled mind. "Is the house safe now?"

"Yes. The gas company correctly shut off the gas at the source. We won't touch it until you let us know what the cops have to say. You might want to tear out the line altogether." After she thanked them, they gathered their tools and beat a hasty retreat.

Kingsley felt paralyzed, the word *remote* ricocheting in her brain, having just heard it twice. This couldn't be a coincidence. She approached Mort, not knowing where to begin. "Is there any way of telling how long ago our security system was hijacked?"

"Afraid not. I'll check our records for the date of your last inspection. Everything was fine then."

"And, using that replacement panel, could someone re-arm the system remotely so we wouldn't notice?"

"Yep."

Kingsley felt her skin prickle and rubbed her arms to squelch the sensation. If someone in recent months could have entered their house while they were at work without triggering the alarm, what else might they have done or taken? "When you finish there, could you sweep the house for listening devices?"

"I'll let the office know that you want to schedule the technician."

"No. Wait. I'll call when I'm ready. If we have to involve the police, it's best to let them investigate first." In the meantime, she remembered the HVAC technician was due in an hour for their spring inspection, which had been scheduled for months. Why had she thought that efficiency was a good plan? Each appointment had expanded exponentially into a much bigger problem.

⁊෴⁊෴

Kingsley paced while the HVAC technician inspected the two outside units, then went to the basement to check the unit that powered the first floor of the house. She followed him upstairs when he headed to the third floor where the unit that serviced their bedrooms and baths was installed. As he was replacing the cover on the unit while giving her a verbal report on their system, he asked if the plastic shields that directed the airflow needed adjusting. That gave her an idea.

"I have a concern with the left rear guest room. Would you mind checking it out?"

"Be glad to. By the way, whoever suggested two zones was spot on. With a house this size, you couldn't have uniform temperature with one huge unit. The downstairs would be cold, the upstairs hot, with individual rooms all over the place."

"In here." Kingsley directed the technician without mentioning the cold spot, watching him circle the space with expert eyes. If he noticed anything peculiar, he didn't react.

"Side window faces west? That would make the back facing north. You're extremely fortunate to have the thermostat in the hall where it wouldn't be affected by sunlight. Put that device in a room that gets direct sun and it will be tricked into thinking it doesn't need to call for heat. Other rooms could be freezing—or roasting, depending upon the time of year. May I?" he asked, pointing toward the other bedroom doors.

"Sure. But we're not having problems with them."

Checking anyway and returning quickly, he nodded with appreciation. "Yep, someone knew what they were doing. Now about that draft."

"It's not moving air. It's just a cold spot. Stand right over there, facing the corner, about four feet back from both walls—there. Stop. Just stand still for a minute, like you're thinking about something. Try closing your eyes." They stood, unmoving, for several minutes. "There. Did you feel the cold?"

"No, but I remembered I was supposed to pick up ice cream on the way home. Thanks. Let me reposition that plastic shield. Ceiling vents should be great in the summer, being high on the wall. Cold air falls. But in the winter, you need to force the air up. Just flip it around. A ceiling fan might help."

As he was preparing to leave, the technician tripped on the edge of the area rug, wind-milling to retain his balance. He looked, puzzled, for what caused him to stumble. "Here," he said. "This wire came loose." He apologized for his clumsiness. When he gave it a tug, Kingsley recognized speaker wire. She shoved it under the edge of the rug, this being Barrie and Randall's home away from home when the four of them were flying before daybreak, or when they'd partied too much to drive. Must have been Randall's customization.

Chapter 18

Ms. Henning? Hi. I'm from the Ultrapure Water Company. I apologize for taking so long to get back to you. When an employee departs, well, unexpectantly without advance notice, sometimes it takes us longer than we'd like to give our customers the service they've requested. I just came across your order from a few weeks ago. And again, I apologize.

"That's all right. I understand. Actually, we won't be needing additional jugs for a while."

"Additional? Oh, I'm sorry if you had to find another water company to deliver fluoridated water to your residence. Or worse, I hope you didn't buy an inferior product from the grocery because of our tardiness. We are the only local company that bottles our own naturally perfect spring water, which meets the state's most stringent testing requirements while having the added benefit of fluoride for parents who value a lifetime of perfect teeth for their children."

Kingsley rolled her eyes, anxious to hustle the salesman off the phone without being rude. She eyeballed the bottle, nevertheless, verifying that they hadn't used any of it, as she still had a stockpile from the grocery. And the new bottle's spigot had sprayed water all over the floor when she tested it. Billy drank milk and juice and insisted on daddy's well water. She didn't want to admit her tardiness with her child's care. "Sir, your company didn't inconvenience us in the slightest. In fact, your delivery man was prompt, courteous, and knowledgeable."

A protracted silence confused her. Maybe he had hung up. "Sir? Are you still there?"

"Um, yes, but I'm just a bit troubled. Our delivery man didn't have a chance to finish his reports, and I can't find your visit in our records. Would you mind verifying, as exactly as possible, when he was at your house? If you can't remember, that's okay."

Kingsley snagged her large-block calendar from the kitchen counter where she had been transcribing family appointments onto the master that hung on the wall. "Let's see. I remember. When he arrived, he installed one of those wooden bases and then brought in the water bottle. We chatted briefly about whether or not he should bring in additional jugs; that we could set up a schedule at our convenience; and we shared our enthusiasm about fluoride for my child's teeth.

"We were wrapping it up when my phone rang. I was expecting an important call and excused myself to answer it. By the time I returned to the kitchen, your man had climbed into his van and was preparing to leave—his engine was running. I started to go to his window to say goodbye, thank him for coming, and verify that I'd call once we knew how much water we'd use, but I saw he was changing his shirt. I assumed he was done for the day or had personal business elsewhere. You know, like taking someone to lunch and wanting to wear personal clothing. So I made a U-turn."

"Do you know what time that was?"

"It was early. I needed to get to work but had waited until nine when my doctor's office would be open. If it's important, the time would still be on my iPhone."

Again, a long pause. She waited.

"Ms. Henning, I know this will sound very strange, but could you describe our technician for me?"

"Sure. About my height in heels—that would make him five-nine or ten. Slender. Fit. Carried that jug on his shoulder like it was weightless."

"Did you notice his hair or eye color?"

"Not really. He wore aviator shades and your company's baseball cap. No, wait. It had a hardware store logo. He had on a gray shirt with a name embroidered in a white circle, which I didn't catch. The sleeves were rolled to the elbow. I noticed he had tanned arms. If he drove a truck around all day with his elbow on the window frame like guys do, why did his arms match? Both my husband and my father think it's a big deal to wear sunscreen on their arms so they match when they get their golfer's tans. Guess it's a guy thing."

"Would you recognize the delivery man if you saw him again?"

"I might, but probably not. Say, what's this about?"

"Do me a favor. Take a look at the water bottle. What does the logo look like?"

She squatted beside it and looked carefully at all sides. "It doesn't have a logo. It's plain glass."

"And the vehicle?"

"It was a panel truck. White."

"Did you notice its logo?"

"It had something to do with water, but I wasn't looking and can't recall. Why? What's this about?"

"I don't know who delivered your water, but don't drink any of it. And call the police right away. Our regular delivery man was found dead in his apartment that same day. And the police said he'd been dead for twenty-four hours."

She gasped. "You mean..."

"I'll give you the name of the detective in charge of the investigation. Please call him right away."

Kingsley grappled to digest the implication. A total stranger had invaded their home. With shaky hands, she dialed the cop's number.

An hour later the detective from the murder scene arrived and launched into an exhaustive interview, for which she gave excruciating details about her brief interaction with the stranger. The Q and A took three times longer than the imposter's actual visit. Shortly, a crime scene investigator showed up and scoured her kitchen for evidence.

"Did you move it? Or touch it?" the CSI asked, referring to the stand and bottle. He dusted every surface the man might have touched with black powder. "If you did, we'll need your fingerprints for elimination purposes." She stifled a groan at the mess he was making and cringed, dreading how hard it would be to remove the black powder that was clinging to everything. Was it poisonous to people and pets?

"It's exactly where the guy placed it," she said. "And my prints and my husband's are on file with the state and the Fed for our employer's security clearance."

The CSI removed the jug and hauled it to his vehicle, returning for the stand. "Did he leave anything behind? Paperwork, brochures, cards?"

"Actually, he didn't. In fact, that was why I followed him out to his truck to see if I needed to sign something. But, as I said, he was preparing to leave and I wasn't comfortable interrupting him since he was changing his clothes." She remembered not knowing if he had already pulled off his slacks and she hadn't wanted to find out.

"And you're very sure nobody drank any of the water? We'll test it immediately, even if you did…"

"No. I couldn't get the spigot to work. I thought I'd ask my husband who's handy what I was doing wrong, but forgot all about it until the water company's manager called this morning."

"Regardless, we'll let you know what we find. In the meantime, if you think of anything else about that technician, please call me." He handed her his card onto which he inked his cellphone number.

✑✐✑

Todd spent the morning mitigating bank business, returning calls and emails to department heads, key shareholders, and the corporate secretary all of whom had a role in the upcoming shareholders meeting. How he enjoyed working with such consummate professionals, compared to the agony being thrown at his family. This should have been a peaceful year, enjoying their family and working in obscurity. Why so much trouble? And why now?

He shook it off, reflecting on how much he admired Kingsley's response to tragedy, having been raised for a life that no longer existed. She managed to make good things happen. In spite of her husband's murder and sheltered upbringing, she'd shed her cocoon and flown undaunted into unchartered sky. He smiled, picturing his fearless lightweight, mixing it up with construction thugs, threatening to shoot them.

Enough. He dialed the fire chief instead of the detective, thinking he'd leave the latter a message, thus giving the detective the option to ignore him. The fire chief picked up on the first ring.

"I appreciate that you must be overwhelmed by nonstop calls from citizens and the press," Todd said after introducing himself. "But I'm hoping you'd be willing to tell what you learned about the transformer explosion and fire. Since we live right below it, we can't help but feel threatened. I'll understand if you can't tell me anything."

The fire chief's response surprised and delighted him. "Todd Henning—the bank's president, right? I'm so glad you called. Keynote's generous donation to our capital campaign paid for our new fire truck, which we badly needed. The old one belonged in a museum. It's been such a pleasure to have Ms. Granger on our board. Did you know her father had been a fire chief in another city years ago? She said it's in her blood."

Todd pictured his senior vice president in charge of HR and branch administration, who had started her career while still in high school as a part-time teller, spending years working her way through college, and becoming a valuable member of the executive echelon. Few knew she had waged war with an abusive, dead-beat ex while raising two great kids and serving the community. As chair of the bank's corporate contribution program, she lobbied that its budget be properly funded.

Todd eased the subject back to the fire. "What did the arson inspector find? Does he think we were the target? Had it not been for that torrential rain, those old-growth trees could have fueled a forest fire and turned our home into an inferno. In the confusion, fire, and storm, we spotted a stalker carrying what looked like a rifle or crowbar. Fortunately, my wife's father was able to summon help."

"Here's the deal," the fire chief said, his tone sobering. "You cannot discuss this with anyone other than your wife. That includes family and friends. Law enforcement needs to apprehend whoever is responsible and can't risk polluting a jury when the time comes."

"I may have information to share if the police haven't been in touch," Todd said. As succinctly as possible, he reiterated what the officers had told them about their would-be intruder the night of the fire. That, in what appeared to be an unrelated incident, the stalker had been shot and later identified as an arsonist-for-hire for whom a

BOLO had been circulating for some time. "I'm hoping you can tell me if there was, in fact, evidence that the transformer had been sabotaged."

"The BOLO originated with our inspector. Not only was the transformer rigged, but an accelerant was doused on the slope above your lane. A hazmat crew has been on site to neutralize the remaining contaminant. I've got the card of the detective in charge in my desk here somewhere. I suggest you talk to him." Sounds of rummaging proceeded. "Got it. He's a young guy, but sharp. I think you'll find him easy to talk with. I'll give you his contact information."

"Our experience with detectives was with an older man and a woman."

"Yeah. I followed the kidnapping story. We all did."

"Had we not located our baby, I have no doubt that those two would have tried charging us, body or not. You understand why I'm not anxious to deal with those detectives again. In the end, they looked foolish, their incompetence publicized. I wonder how they're coping with the fallout."

"He retired and left the area. She 'took a job in the private sector.' Probably a mall cop somewhere. Civilians outperforming detectives is a career-ender."

"There must have been hell to pay in the department."

He lowered his voice to a whisper. "The captain's no longer there either. That case grew legs. I'm surprised you didn't hear about it."

"Nobody told us, and we didn't notice any media updates. Our family left town for an extended vacation, and by the time we returned, the uproar was over. As far as legal action involving the kidnappers, the last I heard the Feds were dealing with jurisdictional issues, the players implicated in the kidnapping ring having operated across state lines.

"If you'd prefer not to contact the detective immediately, I'll let you know as details unfold."

"And I will honor our deal to keep my mouth shut."

ಿೀಿೀ

"Hon? Are you still at home?"

"I was about to leave for the bank. Why?" Kingsley asked. "Did you forget something or need me to pick something up? How about meeting me for a quick bite at the diner?"

"The detective in charge of the arson fire and explosion called. He wants to talk with us. Together. I thought it would be best if we met him at home. Billy understands, or misunderstands, far more than we may realize. He's a bright little boy whose passive vocabulary is immense. One of us could pick him up at the regular time."

"I hope this guy is nicer than the last two."

"That wouldn't take much doing."

The detective arrived fifteen minutes later, parked on the lane, and hiked down their driveway to Henning's front walk. Kingsley watched from the library window as he halted every few steps as if to gain perspective on the top of the hill that had been the site of the transformer explosion and fire. The hazmat crew, whom Kingsley had seen poking, scraping, bagging, and spraying the ground with an unidentifiable substance, had packed up and left. By the time the detective neared the front door, Todd's SUV was exiting the lane and crunching down the driveway. The men converged on the brick porch. She opened the door.

Deja vu, Kingsley thought, as a flashback swamped her mind—the strike on the pineapple knocker announcing those two vile detectives, armed with a fresh round of accusations. This detective couldn't be more than late twenties, but looks, she acknowledged, can be deceiving.

"Come in," she said, motioning him into the living room and the pre-ordained spot for police—one of two chairs facing the couch. Everyone sat. Kingsley took a moment and couldn't help making a quick analysis. Nondescript still face. Close-cropped hair, like a Marine. Hazel eyes. Calm demeanor. Still, no-fidget hands. No visible tells about his reaction to them or his surroundings.

"May I?" he asked before setting a folder on the trunk between them. "I'm investigating a homicide that involves an employee of Purewater Company. I was told you used them to deliver a jug of spring water with added fluoride. Is that the only water you purchased from that company?"

"It is. We had just initiated contact with them a few weeks earlier and arranged for a trial. I didn't know if it was a good idea or not, being especially worried about the stand's stability and whether a two-year-old could climb it or topple it over on himself. And whether we liked the taste of the water. I also wanted to ask my dentist's experience with that company." She sighed, self-consciously. "First-time mother, you understand."

The detective nodded politely with an unreadable face. "So, was that jug the only one the company ever delivered to your house?" Both parents nodded. Kingsley began to feel slightly nervous, her heart rate rising. This questioning seemed odd since their knowledge of the delivery man had been a fleeting, one-time encounter.

The detective said, "The officer who was here this morning put a rush on the water bottle that the CSI collected from your kitchen. What they found leads us to believe there's more involved than meets the eye." He opened the folder that contained a half dozen sheets of paper. He chose the top one. "Analysis of the water showed a toxic concentration of ethylene glycol."

"Antifreeze? That couldn't be right," Todd said. "Antifreeze is green. You know, K, that greenish-yellow stuff you sometimes see on garage floors that people are cautioned to keep pets from licking. It tastes sweet. And it's poisonous. The water in our jug was colorless and looked pure."

The detective was nodding his head. "Antifreeze is dyed green so that consumers can see it and protect children and pets because it does taste sweet."

"How did antifreeze in its colorless form get into our water jug? Did someone mix up ethylene glycol with fluoride? If so, every jug they made should be pulled off the market immediately and consumers warned."

The detective raised his eyebrows and sighed. "Sir, the bottle that was delivered to you did not come from Purewater Company. Their jugs have a distinctive blue and green leaf and waterfall logo. Given that their employee was murdered and that an imposter was substituted, we have to assume that your family was targeted for some unknown reason. Do you have any idea who would do that?"

Shocked, Kingsley jumped to her feet. "No! We have no idea who. Or why." She sank back onto the couch, hyperventilating. "My God! Our baby could have been poisoned—and died! Who would do such a despicable thing?"

Todd encircled her shoulder and pressed her against him while looking over her head to the detective. "My wife's too upset to continue this interview. This has been quite a shock. You'll have to go. We have no relationship with anyone, business or personal, at Purewater Company. And my wife never saw the dead man before." He stood. "If you can think of any relevant questions to ask us, get in touch. Otherwise, leave us alone." He handed the detective his card and accepted his.

"If you know something and are holding it back…"

"Get out! Now!" Kingsley sobbed.

The detective rose slowly. "I understand how uncomfortable you must be, after your experience with my predecessors."

"You. Have. No. Idea!" Kingsley spluttered.

"I'll show you out," Todd said, motioning toward the foyer and following him out the front door.

The detective faced Todd on the front porch. "Look—I read the police report about the stalker, the explosion and fire, and have spoken to the arson investigator. And now we have a murder and someone posing as the dead man trying to poison your family. I don't like coincidences. If you have any idea who's behind this, someone holding a grudge, or has threatened you for any reason, talk to me. Don't try to get even yourself. You could make it so much worse and end up in a whole lot of legal trouble yourself."

"That sounds like a threat. We don't know anything. Believe me, we've thought about little else. But legal trouble? Us? You do not want to go there again."

Chapter 19

The familiar tap-tap-tap-tap-tap followed by the backdoor being flung open brought Billy and O'Malley bolting for the visitors while Pandora streaked upstairs to the landing. As soon as the cat heard Sarah Alderson's voice, however, she poked her head around the balustrade and changed her mind. Shortly, she was weaving figure eights through Kingsley's mother's legs and purring for her share of grandmotherly loving.

Sarah plunked her traveling cooler of comfort food on the kitchen floor before Kingsley could catch up with her. "Dad's got the chocolate group covered," she said, motioning to Henry Alderson with her chin. Billy threw himself into his grandma's arms before she could stand up.

"That husband of yours tattled. Said you were that close to the edge, so naturally we had to come. Your grandmother used to say, 'Two heads are better than one, even if one is a cabbage,' so four might double the odds. And since you never ask for help, we thought we'd just surprise you. If the microwave isn't out of commission as well as the oven, dinner will be ready at six."

Kingsley gave her mom a protracted hug. "You are the best! Really, I'm fine. And it's not all that complicated. We've acquired an enemy who's trying to kill us or drive us out of our home. And we seem to have acquired a ghost—or it acquired us."

"I'm so glad to see you haven't lost your sense of humor and can make light of what Todd describes as a dreadful situation." The three adults simultaneously looked at the child who was far more interested in his grandpa's containers and the word *chocolate* than the grownup's conversation. Henry sneaked him a cookie.

Henry set his stash on the counter, shaking his head. "Didn't I tell you it was a terrible mistake to leave Philadelphia?" Kingsley laughed for the first time in days at her father's hackneyed joke about luring her home as if she were a runaway teen.

"Todd said you're considering loan applicants that you rejected. Of course, you can't bring every file home," Henry continued. "We thought we'd spoil you-know-who so you could do your research without watching the clock. Then maybe you and Todd can go out for a nice dinner. Be alone for a change. We can stay as long as you wish."

"Dat's O'Mawwee," Billy proclaimed to his grandpa of the little dog that was begging for his share of attention. "He's mine!"

Henry frowned at the pet. "What kind of dog is he?"

"A Siberian Weasel Hound."

"Really! I haven't seen one of them yet, and I watch Westminster every year. Must be some new breeds or a re-established ancient one. I wonder what the breeder charges for one?" Sarah raised one eyebrow and turned her back to her husband to hide her bemused expression.

With motherly efficiency, Sarah took over the kitchen while Henry tended bar in the living room, treating Billy to a sippy cup of ginger ale, a double treat since food and beverage were never allowed beyond the kitchen. Kingsley sighed and sipped a chilled Riesling, which Sarah had withdrawn from a chest and uncorked. First the dog in the bedroom and now wandering refreshments. What battle would she lose next? Sighing in resignation, she extended her flute for a refill.

Hours later, with Billy in bed and the men debating new banking regulations in the library over brandy, Kingsley took her mother into the back guestroom. "Stand here," she said, positioning her mother on the imaginary X that marked the cold spot without telling her why. "Now close your eyes and clear your mind. What do you feel?" Several minutes passed, then Sarah opened her eyes. "Well? Did you notice anything?"

"There's a draft in here, and it's coming from up there," Sarah said, pointing to the vent. "You might want to pivot that deflector toward the outside wall."

"That's it? You didn't feel the cold spot? Try again, but stand very still." Her mother went along with the game until her smile turned into a giggle then a full-blown laugh. Kingsley couldn't help herself as the contagion enveloped her too. They laughed until tears drenched their cheeks.

"What on earth are you two doing up here?" Henry asked Todd, trailing him upstairs. Sarah started to reply but dissolved in laughter again. Henry batted his hand. "Women. Dear, I'm going to bed. Good night, Kingsley. Todd. You coming, Sarah?" he asked as he headed toward the front guest room. Mother and daughter surveyed the perplexed pair, then convulsed again.

After the men settled into their respective rooms and the ladies into their jammies, Kingsley and Sarah slipped downstairs for sherry and crackers. Incident by incident, Kingsley ticked through the series of threats to her family. Sarah listened attentively, finally echoing her own mother's philosophy. "Make a list, in chronological order, then set it aside on the nightstand. Let the list do the worrying overnight. Let your sleeping mind sort what you know and propose answers, which may surprise you."

ᏭᏬᏭ

From the minute she awoke, Kingsley knew what she must do. She left her mother sipping coffee with her dad while Billy, exhausted from the late-night of hanging with the grownups, slept. Todd was long gone. The morning had dawned crystal clear, and the drive beneath a periwinkle sky freshened her spirits. She enjoyed the forty-minute drive, which gave her time to switch from mom to banker mode. She parked her old Lexus in her assigned space and enjoyed greeting her professional friends on her way to corporate lending on the fourth floor. It never got old.

As she passed through the new security enclosure, she marveled at how much had changed since Todd took the reins. So many upgrades, not only security but to technology and flexible hours without sacrificing the small-town bank aura.

"I heard what happened the other evening. Are you all right?" Marlee, Kingsley's trusted AA asked, trailing Kingsley into her private office. Worry etched her lovely face.

"I'm fine. Really." She knew she hadn't looked fine that morning and had taken a few extra minutes with her makeup. That, she decided, didn't make her look less exhausted, just painted. The antidote would be finding some answers. "How are classes going? Finals must be coming up soon. Remember, you have days of compensatory time coming. Stay home and study. Or take a bunch of half days. You're nearly halfway through your sophomore year, right?"

Marlee beamed, her corn-row beads jingling as she bobbed her head. "I upgraded the associate degree courses in favor of ones that transfer to the baccalaureate program. The bank will reimburse me 100% for each of my A's. I'm grateful you pushed me. I'll be the first college graduate in my family, and I won't have student loans to repay."

"You've worked hard and done it all by yourself. I am so proud of you." A day didn't go by that Kingsley didn't thank her lucky stars for inheriting this spunky gal when Kingsley arrived at the bank. Smart, clever, ultra-professional, a warrior who did not believe in making mistakes. Problems, she refused to call challenges and could apply the minutia of banking regulations and placate the testiest customer.

"So—what's on the agenda?"

"I need to pull the files for every loan I've turned down in the last four years. I want to see the physical paperwork. Summary sheets would be computerized, but I want to look for hand-written notes and unusual circumstances."

"Are you looking for anything specific?"

"Applicants who might hold a grudge." She toyed with the idea of calling the few that she still felt guilty about—those she wasn't able to help for reasons beyond her control. Banking regulations were complicated and might seem unfair to the uninitiated, even to experienced bankers sometimes. "This may be tedious…"

"Got just the thing. Hang on a sec." Marlee returned to her desk and returned carrying a red file folder. "Here. It's my death list. I thought it might come in handy one day." In Marlee's neat printing, listed chronologically, were the applicants' names and the loan number, its landing and declination dates. "It's just a list. No comments or details, other than they were turned down. I'll make you a copy."

"You are an angel."

An ordinary day flickered by without complications. Between four-thirty and five, the loan department's staff began trickling out, and the fourth floor's corporate area became quiet. Kingsley's dear friend Margaret popped in from real estate lending, followed by Barrie, who looked every bit the ultra-professional controller in a gray sharkskin pantsuit, black shell, and chunky silver jewelry. "Got your message. We're here to help," Margaret said. "Put us to work. What are we looking for?"

"Someone who wants to kill us."

Barrie laughed. "They're all in jail or dead."

Margaret scowled. "That is in terrible taste."

Barrie shrugged. "But it's true."

Kingsley said, "I've sorted a list of loans I rejected, eliminating the ones that aren't possibilities."

"Such as?" Barrie asked.

"They're deceased or found a better deal elsewhere. Or succeeded in a different line of work. One even thanked me for saving them from making a terrible mistake. I'm looking for likely suspects—prospects who were particularly bitter or threatened or scared me—a gut reaction I put in my notes."

Armed with Marlee's list, the trio trooped to Central File where rolling bookshelves aligned perpendicularly in a twenty-foot alcove. The bookshelves, when not being searched, were slid to the far end of the huge open closet, pressing the shelves into a fraction of the space. The clever design left room for growing the bank's lending portfolio. Kingsley separated a particular pair of bookshelves that exposed her department, leaving room for the trio to hunt.

"Here's the list. We'll pull the files, set them on the conference table, then I'll go through them. That I'll have to do by myself. Todd's working late. He said to call when I'm done, and he'll help put them back."

"Is there a prize for who finds the most files?" Barrie asked.

"You bet. I just don't know what that will be. I'm open for suggestions."

An oversized industrial clock with a sweep second hand jerked the seconds into minutes until an hour later the conference table was covered with folders, bumper to bumper, like cars on a train. Twice, bulging folders buckled, spilling the contents onto the floor, requiring chronological re-sorting. "You go. I'll stay," Margaret said to Barrie. "I know you have a meeting, and there's some bank business I need to discuss with Kingsley."

"You just want to gossip about me and our wedding plans, which I'm not divulging. You two be okay?"

"Go!" they said in unison. Barrie hustled toward the door.

"What's on your mind," Kingsley asked as she opened the oldest file and riffled through its contents for her lined yellow legal-size paper.

"I've been thinking. Every bizarre thing that's happened to you is overkill. Someone wants you out of there badly. Is it something about your land? Or you personally? Have you considered multiple people? Someone with a motive who has enlisted others through blackmail or their own ulterior motives?"

Kingsley looked up from the folder she'd been searching. "Like who?"

"L. J. Zaun could be a co-conspirator. That junior officer you've been placating since the day you arrived. Everyone knew she wasn't qualified to head commercial lending. She had the old CEO's attitude about hiring from within, regardless of whether an outsider was more qualified. You didn't steal her job like she complained to anyone who'd listen. It was posted internally first, and when nobody qualified, they ran the ad that attracted you. She's not smart like your AA Marlee, who rocks."

"Okay—I'll keep her in mind."

"She was pea green when you married the boss and then had Billy."

Kingsley sighed, remembering the woman, fifteen years her senior, looking daggers. "You go ahead—I'll be fine. Much as I love and appreciate your company, I need to concentrate on what these files might reveal."

"You must want to make me cook dinner for Pete. But I'll take you at your word." With a quick hug, she snagged her bag and left, leaving Kingsley to contemplate her suggestions.

Laboriously, she scrutinized four years of dashing applicants' dreams. She liked to think of hers as a helping profession, but sometimes the gray area between *qualified* and *risky* made her second-guess her decisions. In every file she found hand-written notes, detailing multiple phone conversations. No applicant was clueless as to her reasons, of that she had made sure. At least she didn't have to worry about large declinations—Loan Committee made those final decisions.

The first candidate was easy. The under-capitalized applicant moved out of state before the formal rejection was made. Still, she looked through each document for what went beyond numbers in boxes. She set it aside and picked up the next file. Loan by loan Kingsley realized the decisions were pretty straightforward. The bank did not make start-up loans without a qualified co-signer. Loan applications to existing businesses were rejected if the business wasn't generating enough income to make the payments. Some applicants were saddled with too much debt to other creditors. If the loan was too large for a bank of their size, she either got a second bank to participate or recommended a big-bank competitor. By sheer volume, she realized she'd made a significant percentage of requests that reached her desk.

Could she have been blamed for a junior officer's work? Not likely. Customers dealt with their personal relationship manager, not her. Even though junior officers reported to her, and she advised them as requested or was necessary, she did not hover or micromanage. She wanted them to grow in their profession and confidence. Even if that meant accepting positions with competitors or making a lateral move from corporate lending, she understood that commercial lending wasn't a good fit for everyone.

What jolted her attention was the last rejection. She'd almost missed two scraps of paper with notes from Connie, the branch/ cluster manager, and Bruce, the VP of small business lending. The name of the applicant was Miles Soriano, to which Connie had added *a.k.a. Emilio*. That sounded familiar. Where had she heard it before? A finger of dread prickled her spine.

Chapter 20

Kingsley scrutinized the application, pretending to see it for the first time. Miles was a thirty-year-old who did day labor for building contractors. He described himself as a sole proprietor, specializing in an itemized list of skills for local companies. He wanted a loan to incorporate his business, buy equipment, and hire part-time office help. His well-thought-out business plan, which was appended, detailed the need for a physical office, employees, legal, accounting, and bookkeeping services, et cetera.

She understood. The eager, hard-working blue-collar fellow had capitalized on his vo-tech education and on-the-job experience. He should do well. However, as she had told him in a follow-up conversation, Keynote did not make start-up loans. Once his business generated sufficient income to make loan payments, they could talk again. But being his own contractor, he had argued, would triple his income, even after expenses. While that might be true, he still didn't have those clients signed up at that time.

Another issue that she didn't mention was that his contractor-bosses paid him in cash. The copies of his tax returns seemed in order, but who knew what he wasn't declaring? She wasn't questioning his honesty—that wasn't her job—but it was a red flag. Poor guy, she'd realized—

as a self-employed person, he was paying double social security—as his own employee and as his own employer. Surely a pro bono accountant could fix that.

He had explained that workers like him were expected to provide their own tools and insurance against theft, which made saving money nearly impossible. When she suggested he look into savings opportunities through their branch, he sounded angry, saying "Thanks, but no thanks," and hung up on her.

The note from Connie that had gone unnoticed was added to the file after the fact. It said *gloves* and *to SBL* with Connie's initials and the date. Small Business Lending had forwarded it to Kingsley with a note that said, *not for us*. That note, also, had been added later. She wondered if both managers had waited until her decision was final. But why?

She glanced at her watch. Nearly seven. She should wait until morning to ask Connie about *gloves*, shorthand for *handle with kid gloves*. Since they had a solid relationship, however, she decided to risk being rude rather than stewing overnight. She caught Connie in between doing the dishes and starting a movie with her kids. "I was surprised you didn't ask me privately at the time," Connie said."

"I just found your note and wondered what was the deal." She was relieved that Connie didn't ask why she was reviewing the file again now.

"You probably didn't recognize his name, which I did. It's all-American vanilla ice cream unless you knew the association with his extended family. His mother had married some low life who took off for parts unknown when Miles a.k.a. Mikey was little, and her uncle, who is her godfather, took an active role in the kid's life. His name wouldn't mean anything to you since you're not local, but it's understood he's a small-time mob boss. Teflon.

Nothing sticks. Rumor has it that he has an editor-friend in the media, so you'll never see articles about him."

"Why on earth did this young man want a start-up loan from our bank? Surely his mother's uncle would underwrite or co-sign his business, especially if it's legitimate."

"Can't answer that, and it wasn't my business to ask since he never mentioned his family nor that he had substantial backing. I told him that I was referring him to small business lending, which I did without comment. In writing, that is. I did, however, alert the fraud department so they could keep an eye out for unusual activity if you made the loan."

"Like money laundering."

"Precisely. But when you turned him down, it was moot, at least at that time."

ℝ

After returning all the loan folders to the bookshelves and having a bite at a favorite Thai restaurant, Kingsley and Todd returned home to a quiet, sleeping house. "Guess their grandson wore them out," Kingsley said, smiling at the thought. Although they lived a couple hours away, Billy would have cherished memories of them as she did of Grammy. If only she'd known her grandfather, but after spending years listening to family stories about him, she felt like she did.

As Kingsley was reaching for O'Malley's leash, her cell phone rang. Simultaneously, the tall-case clock in the foyer chimed ten times. Who, she wondered, would be calling at this hour? She dreaded answering it, checking the caller ID. The number was familiar. "Hello?"

"Kingsley. This is Suzanne Meade. I'm sorry to be calling so late, but it's important."

She sighed with relief. "I'm so glad to hear your voice!

You sound so much better. How are you feeling?"

"Better every day. They say my brain is healing. But I couldn't wait any longer." The caller's voice acquired a note of urgency. "I couldn't sleep without warning you, and I don't want to take any more pills."

"Warn me about what? What are you talking about?" For the life of her, Kingsley couldn't remember any way their lives intersected, except through their mutual friend, Christine.

"Perhaps I should start at the beginning. I had originally intended to visit you Monday or Tuesday until I learned that the Pennsylvania State Archives wasn't open until Wednesday. Fortunately, the man I'd hoped to interview agreed to meet me Monday morning over breakfast. He said that, after a bite, he'd introduce me to other museums and historic sites that would be open. I was so excited."

"And you called me Sunday evening to tell me your good news, and we agreed that you'd be heading to my house sometime Wednesday afternoon."

"Correct. I went for a drive to get my bearings so I wouldn't get lost Monday morning. I'd taken my things to my room before dinner, but the weather was changing dramatically. I'd left my warm leather coat in the trunk not wanting to leave it on the back seat where someone might break in and steal it. It's my favorite—a birthday present from my family."

Kingsley's mind had begun to wander until Todd entered the front door with O'Malley. As soon as he unclipped the dog and hung up the leash, Kingsley motioned for him to join her. With barely a glance toward her, O'Malley bound up the stairs and, by the widening crack of light reflected off the upstairs wall, she knew the dog had nosed his way into Billy's room. She turned her thoughts back to Suzanne.

"Todd, my husband is here. May I put you on speaker?"

"Go ahead. This concerns him too. At the time of the attack, I thought I was having a stroke or an aneurysm. The pain was excruciating. Now I've remembered some details. Two men came to my rescue, lifting me by the elbows from behind. Momentarily, I was grateful, thinking they'd call 911. But when they carried me toward a car, I assumed they'd drive me to an ER themselves. It was strange that they said nothing to me. I mean, wouldn't anyone who'd found an injured person and wanted to help? But they popped the trunk and bundled me inside. I was being abducted!"

"Did you get a look at them or hear what they wanted?"

"My instincts kicked in the minute they popped the trunk. I played dead. It was horribly hard since my head was exploding. I passed out from the pain, I realize now, because of the bleeding in my brain. My next awareness was a blast of cold air, the sound of the river, and those two men talking. The one guy called to the other, 'Mike, this pays your debt. I'll tell the old man.' And the other guy, who sounded young said, 'What about the Hennings?' And the first guy said, 'Not your problem. Geraldine's on it.'

"Then I felt myself being lifted out of the trunk. I was drifting, in and out, thinking if I could just play dead long enough, maybe I could escape. I was terrified they'd hit me again. The icy water shocked me, but then—nothing."

"What happened next?"

"I regained consciousness in the hospital. Pain, blinding lights, lots of people. Then darkness. They told me days later that I'd been in a coma and coded twice, but now my vitals are improving."

Kingsley forgot she was sitting by the fire. "Did you see the tunnel? The lights?"

"No. I guess it wasn't my time. I was told I had a severe concussion. To keep my head perfectly still. But what my attackers said dribbled back to me. I had to warn you, especially if it makes sense to you. Regardless, please be careful."

"That name—Mike—was it a first or last name? Did you tell the police?"

"I told them everything I could remember, except I didn't recall names until after you came to the hospital. My memory's been fuzzy. The doctor told me that the cold river water protected my brain, but I would have succumbed to hypothermia if somebody hadn't found me so quickly."

"Please get better. And thank you so much for the warning. We will be careful. And when you're able to travel, please come and stay as long as you can. I'd promised you a tour and I'll make it worth your while."

Kingsley disconnected, feeling dazed and confused and unable to sort what she had just heard. "The timeline. I don't understand. Whoever attached Dr. Meade must have known she was coming to our house the following Wednesday after I had just spoken to her Sunday evening. That predates everything that's happened to us since. How would a complete stranger know our plans?"

"Did you tell anyone?"

"No. When would I? Suzanne and I spoke in person for the first time on Sunday after she'd checked into a hotel. She was attacked after we spoke. It's as if someone was eavesdropping on our conversation." She dredged her memory for an explanation. "When Christine first called— you know, the day the water guy delivered the water—I thought she was in England because the connection was breaking up. That's when she asked me to give Suzanne a tour."

"Did she call on your cell phone?"

"No. The landline. That's the only number my old friends have had for years."

"What about between Sunday and when Christine called with the bad news. What day was that?"

"Let me think—oh, yes. Christine called Saturday."

"And the other Suzanne showed up the previous Wednesday instead of Dr. Meade. The person we've been thinking was an opportunistic realtor."

"Todd, Margaret scoured the databases in multiple counties, realtors, and her counterparts in real estate lending, including credit unions. She knows absolutely everyone. The woman who toured our home is a ghost."

"Then if she's not a realtor or a historian, who the hell is she? And why was she here?"

"Margaret suggested she might be a thief, casing the place for a partner."

"We'd better find out."

"But how? Where do we begin? With a police sketch artist?"

"We have a name—Geraldine. Maybe it isn't that common." Todd strode to the front door, double checking the lock and bolt, then circled throughout the downstairs. "Tomorrow let's get our security company in here. Whoever has it in for us might be back."

Kingsley could not say it again, but the thought tormented her. *Who is doing this to us? What have we done?*

⁇

Randall and Barrie gathered with the Hennings at their dining room table, enjoying Sarah Alderson's delicious beef burgundy, salad, and a dry red wine. Kingsley had unleashed her mother's hospitality genie, and she knocked herself out, setting the table with Kingsley's Castleton wedding China and the Gorham's Chantilly flatware. Barrie brought fresh flowers from the market, which spilled from Grammy's cut glass pitcher. Usually a picky eater,

Billy delighted his grandmother by asking for seconds of everything, including the carrots.

When the child began to squirm, Sarah murmured to him, "ask 'may I be excused please?' then your mom will say, 'you may,' and then you can go watch that new video Papa brought you."

Billy frowned in thought. "Scooze? Peeeese?" Everyone except Kingsley smothered a grin, while his mother said, in her most dignified voice, "You may." With a grin to his grandmother, Billy slid from his long-legged chair and dashed for the library, the dog at his heels. While the adults finished their dinner and sipped more wine, the real conversation began.

Henry Alderson began with an authoritative note in his fatherly voice. "I had a call from your godfather. He will be sending you a letter confirming, as you suspected, that this so-called William Penn heir business is a scam. The attorney doesn't exist, nor does the law firm on the letterhead. His investigator wished you had the outside envelope, as there were no fingerprints or identifiers on the paperwork. With your permission, he said he would turn it over to the state attorney general's office in case it's a new scam or part of an ongoing investigation. He added, 'Don't get your hopes up.'"

"Did he know what the scam was supposed to accomplish?"

"Hold you up for money if you were really, really stupid. I cannot believe people fall for these things, but if the perp can isolate some uneducated or misinformed individuals, they will try."

"Then it could be unrelated to everything else that's happened. The gas leak. The poisoned water. The transformer explosion and fire. That guy who tried to break in."

Todd said, "I think the last two were related."

Randall, who had been unusually quiet, spoke up.

"Maybe it's not about you guys at all. Maybe it's the land that someone is after. Like what's buried beneath it. Ah! Treasure. Gold coins. Artifacts. Don't laugh, Barrie. I'm serious. Have you guys dug under the old summer kitchen down by the creek? Why I keep asking myself, would there be a summer kitchen without a house? Maybe it's long gone, but…"

"Sarah, did you mention pie?" Henry asked his wife.

"The minute I open the freezer door for the ice cream, Billy will be part of this conversation. Now, where were we?" Randall held up his hands in surrender.

To Todd's pensive expression, Kingsley asked *what*. "You said something last evening that's been lurking in my subconscious. You described a timeline. Think back. When did the trouble begin? Or better stated, when was there no trouble? Just living our ordinary lives? What changed?"

"How about the day O'Malley bolted for the construction site and you threatened that guy with…"

"Don't say it again, Barrie. Will you ever let me live that down?"

"What I meant to say was," Barrie continued, "if you're considering a timeline, you were already mid-crisis. When we chatted over lunch, you mentioned you were exhausted, your sleep being interrupted by a construction project in the neighborhood. When did *that* start?"

Todd and Kingsley exchanged glances. "Todd and I were planting the white-pine snow fence on a Saturday, and I'd heard it three nights in a row. That would have been Friday, Thursday, Wednesday night." She counted back the dates on her fingers. "That is unless I hadn't noticed it before, but that is unlikely."

"Saturday was when I asked you if you'd heard it again," Todd added.

Kingsley nodded her head in agreement. "Saturday was

the day Billy found O'Malley. Then Sunday we tried to teach him to come when we called. He ran off Monday night, and I had the altercation with that horrible worker who tried to murder my dog."

Todd laughed. "*Your* dog. Right."

She brushed it off. "Let me grab a sheet of paper, the kitchen calendar, and a pencil. I want to construct a time-line, leaving gaps between each day."

"You think that will help?" Barrie asked.

"Maybe not. But at least I'll feel like I'm doing some-thing. Maybe pinpoint something we're missing that we can research." She snapped her fingers. "Like the speaker wire. Randall, I've been meaning to ask you. In the guest room where you guys sometimes stay, did you notice a length of speaker wire sticking out from under the rug? I found it the other day and didn't remember seeing it before or what its purpose might be."

"No. I'm a wireless man. Completely." Barrie nodded in agreement. "The first night we slept there—remember, we were flying the next morning at four—the mattress and box springs were on the unfinished floor. Clean bare pine. No rug, or anything else except for a lamp on a U-Haul carton."

"That's right. We started renovations in earnest Memo-rial Day weekend and moved our bedroom furniture into our room on the Fourth of July, so that would have been mid-summer three years ago, the year before Billy was born."

"I'll cut the pie, scoop ice cream, and start coffee if you want to check out that wire," Sarah said. "Papa, if you'll see what our grandson is doing, I'll call when dessert's ready."

"Great idea," Henry said, rising slowly. "I need to stretch my bones anyway."

The friends trooped upstairs and entered the guest

room. "Over there," Kingsley said, pointing to the far side of the room. "I pushed it back under the rug after the HVAC technician found it."

"On it." Randall knelt and rolled the edge of the braided rug, exposing a foot of bare wood. No wire. He followed the curve of the rug and continued where the rug protruded beyond the foot of the bed, then along the side facing the door to the hall. "Whatever it was, it's gone now." Todd shrugged, and Kingsley scowled. "Maybe the technician gathered it up?"

"He couldn't have. He proceeded me from the room and didn't return."

"The ghost took it," Barrie said, grinning.

"What ghost?" Randall asked.

Todd sighed. "Kingsley is convinced there's a cold spot that can't be explained," he said, pointing toward the back corner. "Go ahead, K. Tell them where to stand."

"One at a time," she said, motioning to Barrie. "You guys move into the hall." Kingsley positioned Barrie on the invisible X and stepped back. "Clear your mind and be very still for a few minutes." It didn't take two minutes before Barrie started giggling.

"It's the wine," Randall called from the hall. "Let me try." Kingsley directed him, but the experiment went south as fast as a party game.

"Nobody felt anything?" Kingsley asked, disappointed.

"Just my intense desire for your mom's apple pie a la mode."

Hours later, after Randall and Barrie had left and the family retired, Kingsley couldn't sleep. Sock footed, she padded down the hall toward the guest room. As she approached the door and flicked on the lamp, she felt a presence. Turning, she found O'Malley at her side, looking straight toward the corner. "Come on, buddy. Keep me company."

Sweeping a tiny penlight beam left and right, she illuminated every inch of the rug, the exposed floors, and the spaces beneath the pair of bedside tables' legs. On the rug, near her imaginary X, she spotted something—a tightly coiled length of opaque speaker wire. If the guys were playing a joke on her, she'd make them pay. But when she stood on the spot to retrieve it, a dreadful cold enveloped her. When she turned, O'Malley was gone.

Chapter 21

I do not believe in ghosts," Kingsley told herself, over and over, before dialing their security company's office from work. "I'd like to schedule a follow-up inspection for our home and property," she explained, realizing she shouldn't exclude the bank barn they used for their cars and lawn equipment.

"Yes, Ms. Henning. Our records confirm our technician was there a few days ago to investigate evidence of a break-in and tampering with your system. He recommended a follow-up visit. Has everything been functioning correctly since then?"

Break-in? Understatement! "He indicated that a specialist would be needed to do a full sweep for any electronic breaches."

"Yes. That's what he noted on this report. When would you like her to come?"

"As soon as possible."

"Would this afternoon be too soon? We've had a cancellation."

"If you could make it after four, that would be fine," They agreed on five o'clock.

The timing was perfect, she thought. Her parents had taken Billy home to St. Davids for a big-boy overnight. She hadn't thought about how much more time her son might have with his grandparents until she noticed subtle changes in her dad—a hitch in his gait. A little more salt in his shock of thick hair. And, in a few short years, she couldn't snatch Billy out of school on a whim like she could now from daycare.

Todd had seized the opportunity to participate in a dinner meeting with one of the nonprofit boards on which he served. Did he need to know she'd scheduled a security sweep? He might say she was over-reacting or, worse, paranoid. She would not lie if he asked her, but if the visit proved to be a routine non-event, she saw no reason to mention it. Kingsley barely beat the specialist to the house, having wrapped up a loan closing precisely at four. The familiar panel truck pulled up behind her. A tiny woman in brown coveralls, her company's baseball cap, and black lace-up boots jumped from the vehicle, looking for all the world like a USPS driver. She extended her hand, and after a firm shake, followed Kingsley into the house.

"I'd like to start with the boxes," she said, gesturing toward the master panel inside the back door and pointing to its duplicate in the foyer by the front door. "After I finish, why don't we chat about your concerns? I understand you had a break-in that was perpetrated by someone circumventing our equipment. Did the police apprehend anyone yet?"

Kingsley frowned. "We didn't call the police." She chose not to mention the bad blood stemming from their handling of Billy's kidnapping. If the technician read the Henning's security file or the newspapers, she'd know all about it anyway. "The security breach was discovered in relation to a gas leak which, at the time, everyone thought was a malfunction associated with the propane tank or its installation. I didn't want to insult your company by suggesting your equipment was obsolete or incorrectly installed. He swapped out the faulty circuit board and that was that.”

“I suggest you rethink any prior problems with the police. We can safeguard your home and possessions, but we can’t catch bad guys or stop them from targeting you.”

Before Kingsley could be goaded into revealing too much, she caught herself. “I’ll be in the library. When you’re finished, we need to talk about our ghost.” That brought the technician’s head up abruptly from scrutinizing the panel. “There’s a cold spot. A presence, if you will, in one of our guest rooms. I’d like to know if it’s caused electronically. We’ve been calling it ‘*the ghost.*’”

The technician looked at her watch. “I’ll start with the barn before it gets dark if you’ll give me the combination to the locks. We do have better suggestions for that.”

By seven o’clock, the technician had swept every square inch of the Hennings’ house and barn. She passed Kingsley a piece of notepaper and a pen while putting her finger to her lips. She wrote, *show me your ghost.*

Kingsley rolled her eyes and scribbled, *you can’t see it. You have to <u>feel</u> it. Follow me.* Once inside the guest room, she gestured where the technician should stand, as she had the others, on the X. The technician closed her eyes as if meditating for a good five minutes. Opening them, she shrugged.

The technician added another message to the paper. *Follow me outside.*

On the front porch, Kingsley said, “Well, what was that all about?”

“I didn’t feel a presence. A ghost or anything supernatural, but I can recommend a paranormal expert who might be able to help you.” She brushed lint off her pants. “Now. I’ve gotta tell you. You do have bugs.”

Kingsley sighed. “Oh, terrific. One more professional service to bankroll. Guess it’s to be expected, here in the woods. A bit too much nature if you ask…”

"No. Wrong kind of bugs. Listening devices."

"What? Where? How? We're being spied on? Can you yank then out?"

"One in the kitchen under the table. One under the windowsill on the upstairs landing overlooking the backyard. How? When your security system was rigged to bypass your codes, whoever's responsible could come and go at will—like when you were at work. Or when any other person can amble about the house unsupervised."

"And they're listening to every word we're saying? That's horrible!"

"The range might not be that good. This is a big house with thick walls, but they could still hone in on your plans, especially if you discuss things at dinner."

"Show me—then let's yank 'em."

"No! You don't want to let them know they've been found. I have a better idea. I can install an electronic scrambler near the bugs with a remote you can turn on and off. Have your private conversations, then engage it from time to time to confirm it has intermitted malfunction or poor reception. Run a vacuum upstairs; the dishwasher in the kitchen, and so on. And, I strongly recommend, that you get the police involved. They can set up a sting operation."

Kingsley couldn't help but laugh, picturing the detectives they'd dealt with in the past being remotely interested in their *little problem.* "Just go ahead with the scrambler. My husband and I will decide how to deal." She finished the thought, *with assorted enemies,* but kept that to herself.

⁋⁋⁋

The following morning, Kingsley glided to a stop in front of the deserted construction project. The chain-link fence that surrounded the area that the bulldozer had excavated now was enclosed by a ten-foot wood fence that wrapped all four sides of the rectangular area. Glancing around, she exited the car but kept the motor running. From the trunk, she grabbed the grubby sneakers she kept handy for touring clients' muddy projects. With practiced hops, she swapped her pumps for the sneaks, threw her leather shoes into the trunk, and double-folded the hems of her linen trousers.

Checking for oncoming vehicles and seeing or hearing nothing, she picked her way around the new fence's perimeter. There—at the northwest corner, she found a vertical seam in through which she could spy through its slats. Centered, beyond the spot where O'Malley had nearly met his maker, was what looked like a smaller interior building, thrown together like a shack. If it had windows, they would face north toward the cornfields. Refocusing and tilting her head to see the back-left corner, she spotted the juncture where the wire fence sections came together and studied the locks that were secured with multiple chains. Barrie! Her dear buddy, the bank's investment genius, jet pilot, and consummate lockpick—yeah, this had Barrie's name all over it. She would love helping Kingsley recon what was inside!

Once at work, Kingsley took deep breaths, screwed up her courage, and overrode her distaste for calling the detective who had been to the house about the Clearwater murder. She would ask for a meeting.

"What's up?" he asked, then deflected her request by citing a preponderance of cases and an impossible calendar.

"It's important," she insisted. "You said to call if I thought of anything."

He sighed, not bothering to hide his annoyance. "There's a coffee shop a quarter mile from your bank on the highway. I can give you fifteen minutes if you hurry."

"This was your mission, remember? You're the one with the dead body. You told me to call if I thought of anything. And that fake delivery guy may have done more than deliver poisonous water."

"Oh all right. Twenty minutes max."

"Back in thirty," she flung at Marlee as she bolted for the stairwell and managed to beat the detective to the diner. She slid into the booth in the back corner, then remembering cop-show scenes, relocated to the opposite side to let him face the door.

Striding toward the booth with an economy of steps, he sat and motioned to the waitress for coffee. Same still face, no-nonsense demeanor. She realized as a stream of sunlight illuminated his face that he was older than he looked in her living room. His light brown hair showed a faint line of white against his face. Huh! He dyes his hair. Forties? Definitely not a kid who had lucked into promotions.

As succinctly as possible she started with the timeline. The guy who delivered the water jug could have tampered with the security system and left the listening devices since he'd been alone in the kitchen. She wasn't with him every minute. Tampering with their security system enabled an intruder to rig the gas leak. When that didn't blow up their house, the explosion/ fire/ stalker incident might have killed them. The overkill was horrific; they were lucky to still be alive. And now, the bugs. They'd found the listening devices, which were still fully operational.

Her instincts cautioned her not to mention Suzanne Meade or her warning, especially the names she'd overheard. "Is it possible for you to trace whoever's doing this by setting a trap using those listening devices?" She paused for a breath.

He stared at her in disbelief. "Either you have really ticked somebody off, or none of these situations have anything to do with you or can be explained. I'm guessing the latter."

"So—can you take this seriously for one minute and assume the worst? It all started with that construction project next door."

"Not exactly next door. It's a mile from your house. And yes, all your complaints are well known by now. You've angered some very important people who have a vested interest in that project. We've had an earful. Consider yourself lucky to have avoided arrest for trespassing and other offenses. If you've caused the project's delay in any way, you may still be in for a lawsuit."

"Our complaints are legitimate. He tried to kill my dog and prevent us from taking our son to the hospital. That occurred on a public road, which taxpayers like us maintain. Can you at least look into everything that has happened? I'm sure it's connected."

He narrowed his eyes and glared at her. "We're understaffed and overworked. We lost three fine detectives, one of which was my captain, because of you playing Nancy Drew. No way will I get involved in your little dramas."

"You're talking about our son's kidnapping? If they'd done their jobs…"

"No way, lady. You can't pin that on our officers. They were played by big-time sophisticated criminals but would have solved the kidnapping faster if you had turned over the evidence you withheld." He made finger quotes when he said *withheld*.

"The detectives falsely accused us from the very day Billy was abducted. They didn't want to hear the truth. *'It's the parents. It's always someone they know. It's the husband. It's the boyfriend'*" she sing-songed to him, her face heating. "Those so-called detectives would have us in prison and Billy would be dead if we hadn't traced him ourselves."

"And if you'd turned over the evidence you found—albeit through crimes of your own, like breaking and entering and grand theft for starters—your son would have been home in days, not weeks."

He shook his index finger at her. "And that grandfather of yours rattling every connection he has, calling in every favor from the governor down to make sure two fine detectives and my captain were fired. Do you have any idea how hard it is to get officers of their caliber to serve in the middle of nowhere?"

"My grandfather has been dead since I was five years old. Whoever was out to avenge our mistreatment was not…"

"David Wentworth?"

"He's not my grandfather, nor is he related to me. He's our attorney."

Kingsley jumped to her feet, sloshing the detective's coffee. "Good luck with that water guy's murder, since you don't want my help."

"Yeah, yeah, yeah. Why don't you trust-fund types go back to the Mainline, Miss Philly Society, and leave the real work to the professionals? We belong here; you don't, and I don't give a rat's ass who your family is."

She bent, her voice quiet and resolute. "Okay. So you're jealous of us. If you'd read my *vitae*, you know my credentials were earned, not inherited nor bought. You want to join those who thought they could best me? Go ahead. Try. But unless you do it with honesty and integrity for which citizens like me pay you, you'll be on your way out the door too." She grinned.

"And if I learn you had *anything* to do with the attempts on my family's lives or enabled the perpetrators in any way, I'll nail you. As for your fine buddies who lost their jobs, they were incompetent and lazy, taking cheap shortcuts only to be shown up by amateurs."

By the time she reached the door, she felt downright giddy. The meeting exceeded her wildest expectations, the disconnected pieces gelling in her mind. He'd tipped his hand. The construction project was the epicenter, had been from day one. She'd angered some *very important people who have a vested interest in that project*? That meant big money, but whose? And for what end? To grow field corn and a bunch of vegetables? She had enough experience in agricultural lending to know that didn't add up.

She thought about bank deadlines—the shareholders meeting, quarterly and annual reports, the FDIC, OCC, and SEC requirements, for which they were pushed hard every day. Deadlines, deadlines, deadlines. What messed up these criminals' timeframe? Risked a catastrophe with their *investors*? As Margaret had researched, the business was privately owned by an obscure alphabet-soup corporate entity. Since they weren't publicly traded, it wouldn't be easy to trace the players, but she intended to get to the bottom of their *business*.

For now, she'd follow another thread and track down Mike, a.k.a. Miles or Ermilio. And find the woman named Geraldine, whom Kingsley suspected posed as Suzanne Meade to get into the house and do—what? Plant the bugs that enabled co-conspirators free access to their house? She had ample opportunity to do so as did the Pure Water imposter. Kingsley needed to have an adult conversation with her godfather, David Wentworth, to learn if his involvement in the detectives' firing was true.

Chapter 22

Barrie grinned with delight as Kingsley described the construction building, the perimeter fences with chains and locks, and her brainstorm to investigate the motive for such overkill. "Picking and entering—I love it. Count me in."

Kingsley reflected back to her first day at Keynote National Bank four years earlier, discovering in a casual conversation over lunch that Barrie had a talent that should have barred her from working at any financial institution that required a security clearance. If her superiors knew, they had dismissed it as a joke because she had unerring judgment when it came to investing the bank's money. All the same, she never met a lock she couldn't pick and loved expanding her skill set.

"What do you think we're going to find?" Barrie asked.

"Something highly illegal that demanded our removal from our property next door."

"Maybe their vendetta became necessary after you refused to sell out."

"No. It's gotta be the other way around—something we saw or they think we saw that we shouldn't have. Doesn't really matter whether or not we grasped the meaning—just the chance that we did."

"Something they can't risk, now that you're on high

alert and have brought it to others' attention. They could have saved themselves a whole lot of trouble if they'd just played nice. Sent you some chocolates. Or a fruit basket. A David Austin rose bush would have been nice."

Kingsley laughed at her crazy friend. "Well?"

"I'm in. Let's do it! Just tell me when." Barrie grinned, slapping her best friend with a high five. "Besides, I'm curious as hell to know their plans for that hole. From its location, it might be ground zero for their enterprise." She rubbed her hands together with fiendish delight. "What are you going to do about Todd? And Billy? We can't tell them we're going shopping. One—we don't shop, and two—they'd see us."

"Billy is staying a second night with my parents and Todd has a rescheduled meeting that was canceled because of that freak ice storm in February. About our timeframe— it gets dark around six. The construction crew starts straggling in any time after ten. Unless the large-animal vet needs to make an emergency visit next door, our neighborhood will be quiet once Jacob finishes milking around six. Wear something black but bring spare clothes to leave in your trunk in case Todd gets home early. It's an easy hike from behind our barn to the back corner of the fence."

"We need better weapons than your garden clippers,"

"Will you stop?"

Barrie laughed. "I'll bring my handgun. The little one I carry in my opera bag."

"You know you can't do that anymore. They have airport-type security at the theater."

"Which they won't see through my little bag."

"What's it made of—lead?"

"You don't want to know. So—what are we looking for?" Barrie asked, turning serious.

"Evidence of their purpose that explains their need to kill us and install security as tight as a maximum-security prison. I mean, they've stopped just short of razor wire. They're up to no good. I feel it. That land was rented for crop farming long before we arrived, and we've seen corn planted, then harvested six months later uneventfully. Large equipment came in the spring, disappeared, followed by harvesters in the fall. But nothing like this. Agribusiness? Like hell!"

"And the nursery business? Hydroponic, I believe Margaret learned," Barrie said.

"Something about a grower whose family has been in the tulip business for generations in Holland. I've had greenhouse loan customers before. They need concrete flooring, frames for the glass, liners, and supports for raised beds. Pipes for irrigation. They should be drilling a well and installing a septic system by now. And they aren't."

"All the more reason to take a peek and crosscheck if the reality corresponds with the building permits. Did Todd get a copy?"

"He did, but I don't know where he put it. I'm guessing they're in his office at the bank. After the township inspector called on the foreman, things got ugly. I didn't pay attention after that."

Barrie snapped her fingers. "Triggers. The dog incident, Billy's emergency, the truck blocking the road, and the township inspector showing up, all of which led to your threats against them. They paid way too much attention to what they could have dealt with quietly. You couldn't find a quieter neighborhood. You're the only threat for miles. But then, bang! Their over-reaction. Maybe that's key. Privacy. Operating in obscurity. No witnesses. Quiet bankers. Cornfields. The Amish and their cows. They could smuggle an army of aliens and who'd know the difference unless someone—meaning you—took too much interest."

Kingsley nodded in agreement. "That means outside

intrusion wasn't factored into their game plan, which threatened their operation; without the option to change their plans or relocate."

"Bodies! How about graves for their enemies?"

Kingsley laughed at the silly notion, batting her hand. "Let's just have a look. I've seen enough construction projects in their early stages to know it isn't always obvious what they'll become unless you've seen the drawings."

"Six? Your place? I'll drive around back and park in the barn."

ဆဆ

As Kingsley drifted downhill toward the bank barn, it never failed to awe her. Built of native limestone, it bore the matching date stone as their house, which meant both were built at the same time by the same mason. Identical repetitive patterns in the barn's end walls repeated the pattern on their home. The barn's street level, a great open space, once was used as the threshing floor and for hay bins.

Kingsley envisioned inviting family and friends for parties—children's birthdays, square dances, wedding receptions, graduation, or anniversary parties and reunions. She imagined the smell of fresh hay, the glow of lanterns, and the strains of local musicians. That evening, her car hugged the left side of the barn, zipped downhill, and looped around to the huge lower doors.

She flipped a switch to illuminate the barn's lower level, which could not be seen from the house or the street. Once used for animals, it now garaged their cars, riding mower and garden tractor, and an array of gardening implements. The doors to this ground-level entry faced north, away from street view, which hid the contents from nosey people. Most days, when the weather was fair and they didn't want to trek to the barn, they used the driveway's gravel loop to the back door where they parallel parked. Neither dreamed of adding a detached garage or breezeway, which wasn't historic and would not *look*, as the local Pennsylvania Dutch would say.

She didn't have long to wait for Barrie's vintage Mustang to crunch down the drive and circle into her personal spot, the wheels so expertly positioned that she needed no steering adjustment. She hopped from her convertible and grabbed Kingsley into a hug. Stepping back, she frowned at Kingsley's coal-black stretch pants, old bomber jacket, skull cap, and barn boots.

"Nice for a goth party if you add makeup and nails, but not for this gig. I've got something better." She popped the trunk and withdrew a large black furry bundle. "Ta da!" She singsonged. "In case they've installed cameras, we're going to take a walk on the wild side." A serious shake revealed two black bear costumes.

"What the hell..." Kingsley gaped in amazement as Barrie fluffed their fur. "Specialty costume shop that deals in, well, wild things. Here—try one on. You'll probably want to strip since they've gotta be warm."

Kingsley took one, too surprised to question Barrie's bizarre idea. "Since I have no idea about camera range, we'll have to bend over and lope a bit."

"I refuse to crawl a mile in a bear suit. What were you thinking?"

"Camouflage comes in all forms. And no, we don't have to crawl. Now come on. Time's a-wastin', girlfriend. And here—blacken your face with this stuff. And before you object, I brought cream and sponges to remove it." Both removed their outer clothes and pitched them into Barrie's trunk. They struggled into the furry suits.

"I am not wearing the head until I absolutely have to."

"Not that way," Barrie said, watching Kingsley

struggle. "It zips up the side. You ever see a black bear with a zipper down his back? There. Now hustle. And hands—these dark latex gloves should help with mobility. The costume came with mitts and claws, but no way I could pick locks."

"They're purple! How many bears have you seen with purple paws?"

"How many have you seen picking locks?"

"What if we get caught?"

"I'll think of something. Just let me do the talking."

As Kingsley adjusted her suit, she couldn't help grinning, remembering the night she and Barrie had sneaked into the bank's executive inner sanctum, searching for missing files that would identify a killer. That might have been easier to explain since they both worked at the bank, but not at midnight in the executive bastion with picks and flashlights. The ends had justified the means without their being caught.

"Ready?" Barrie whispered for effect. Kingsley nodded. "Follow me. And kill the light."

"Got your picks?"

"Yeah, in the pocket. I'm unarmed, although I do have a switchblade, mace, a cell phone—the usual stuff. And you?"

"I've left the guard dog at home sleeping off a very big dinner."

"Let's do it."

"Penlights!" Kingsley grabbed two from her car, handed one to Barrie, and took a deep breath. "Go!"

༄༅༅

Randall Shannon flew low, lazy circles over his client's target of interest. His companion, a night photographer and long-time associate said nothing, focusing in deep concentration about the mission at hand and what lay beneath them. The fellow had joined Randall at the airstrip on short notice after Randall had agreed to his client's specifications and parameters. The work had to be done that night with the photographer's digital file emailed immediately to the client. As soon as Randall'd connected with the photographer, both accepted the assignment.

Randall was accustomed to quirky clients—corporate executives and multi-millionaires with the good sense to know when owning jets was not a good investment, as long as they could get Randall to fly them and their entourage expeditiously. Like tonight. Randall lived for the adrenalin rush of unexpected assignments that might take him anywhere in the world on an hour's notice. His best clients knew, however, that if they waited intentionally, he might not be available. So they didn't play games, knowing if they had a real emergency, Randall would accommodate them.

On this particular evening, the new client had referenced a mutual friend in Columbus, Ohio, an industrial designer with whom Randall had both a business and a personal relationship. Randall could not place the client's accent, which seemed to wander around western Europe, as with many people who had lived, studied, and had homes in multiple countries. Ordinarily, he would have given his friend Dan Griffith a call, but the client, anticipating the need, had authorized his bank officer to expedite a wire transfer as soon as he asked for it. And the prospective client had emailed proof of that correspondence for the big bucks.

"The site should be right below us in a minute according to the coordinates," Randall said. But as soon as he said it, he had the stunning realization that this looked awfully familiar. And it was! The very construction site he and Barrie had taken shots for the Hennings, which had been *the source of the Henning's discontent.*

"The client wants a general overview from all angles, and then individual close-up shots in a grid. Can you do that?"

"I can shoot until you run out of fuel."

"How long will it take to see if you captured good shots?"

The photographer gave Randall an insulted smirk. "Trust me. They will be good, or you don't have to pay me. And your client won't either."

How many times had he heard that and never once had to take him up on it? The guy did great work. "Take it up a little higher, then circle the site in close circles. Then let's go north to south, then east to west. If there's one ant on the ground, your client will see the surprise on its face." In half an hour the job would be completed and the pair heading back to the airstrip.

Randall said, "One other thing, as per our usual agreements, the nondisclosure agreement applies, no matter what, unless both the client and I sign off, or if your pictures are subpoenaed."

∾∾∾

Kingsley followed Barrie as she emerged from the eastern corner of the barn and approached the exposed open farmland. How many times had their north forty felt benign and beautiful, carpeted with wildflowers from years of nobody cultivating it? In the dark, every indistinguishable object appeared sinister. "Slow down! You're going too fast." Barrie braked momentarily, then picked up her speed. Kingsley wished she'd worn her hiking shoes instead of boots, but her only consideration had been *black*.

She tripped, righted herself while reminding herself that she'd sucked Barrie into this misadventure that had nothing to do with her and everything to do with a possible altercation with law enforcement. Barrie had tucked her blond curls under a black skull cap and was carrying her bear's head under one arm like a football while swinging her right arm for balance, penlight at the ready.

As they came within a quarter-mile of the construction fence, they donned their bear heads, somewhat relieved that the eye holes were large enough to enable them to see adequately. "Gloves," Barrie whispered as if the whole world might be listening. Cautiously they closed on the fence, mindful of the snapping corn stubble beneath their feet. A dark cloud scuttled over the moon, plunging the area in inky darkness. Kingsley had never been more aware of how extremely dark rural farmland could be without industry, buildings, highways, or houses to illuminate the countryside. The only light she could see was the distant glow of her library's lamp thrown on the garden beyond her front walk.

"Stop!" Barrie held up her hand like a drill sergeant. They did. "Listen—what's that?" A hum reached their ears. "Electronic surveillance?" They crouched, motionless, inside a trench that must have been dug and abandoned by the bulldozer which was nowhere in sight.

"There. I hear it too. What do you suppose?"

Barrie giggled. "It's just a plane. A small commuter, probably on route to Reading, Harrisburg, or Philadelphia. Or a crop duster. Something small."

"You sure it's not the police checking for trespassers?"

"Even if there were escaped prisoners, they'd be using helicopters, not prop jobs."

Before they could speculate further, the plane made a nosedive in their direction. "Into the ditch! Now! Ball up, face down, like a big rock. Freeze! Maybe they won't see us." The sound of a plane's engine rattled above them, changing direction, and by the sound, climbing and soaring, then swooping toward them again. Kingsley pressed her face into muddy stones, praying no spot of skin reflected the plane's headlights, revealing her face or the purple gloves that were clenching the bear's head in place.

Pinging—a new sound reached her ears. Straining, Kingsley identified droplets of rain, falling on her makeshift grave. "Come on. It's gone," Barrie hissed.

"What if they're calling in the troops?"

"Kiddo, I'd be much more afraid of bear hunters. Now, pull yourself together. Task at hand."

Kingsley struggled out of the bear's head and gulped fresh air. "No! Barrie hissed. "We're within range of video surveillance. Come on. Be a good bear and let's get this done."

Kingsley followed Barrie's swaying rear to the corner of the fence where within minutes she disengaged the locks and reconfigured the chains to convince any remote surveillance equipment that might be sweeping the area. Trailing Barrie toward the building, she crouched, peering in every direction, ears prickled for anything beyond the spattering rain, which was picking up. At least the moon would be hidden.

What surprised them was the amount of work that had been done since Kingsley had rescued O'Malley and when Randall and Barrie had shot pictures of the hole. Now a surrounding structure had been built. Hardly a shed, the interior structure was huge with a crude window facing north that was covered with sheeting. A lock secured a windowless door, which Barrie lost no time in picking. Everything inside was pitch black. Kingsley crept into the interior while Barrie fished for her camera.

"Aaaah!" Kingsley yelped, slipping over the edge of a chasm, her feet dangling in thin air. Barrie, having just turned on her phone, saw disaster unfolding as if in slow motion. Dumping the phone, she lunged for any part of

Kingsley's body she could grab.

Chapter 23

Randall Shannon and his photographer taxied to a stop on a nearby private airfield. As soon as the wheels stopped bouncing over the ruts, the photographer previewed hundreds of shots, considering their relative merits. "Let's do this," Randall suggested. "Send the entire batch to our client and let him delete what's irrelevant. Regardless of their quality, or lack thereof, I don't know what's important to him."

"Let's go for it. I'll phone and let him know that they're coming. If he wants something else, we'll do another flyover and finetune what we missed."

Randall looked at his watch. Now knowing exactly what they were photographing, his mind buzzed with suspicion. What was a Holland bulb farmer's interest in a cornfield in central Pennsylvania? Was he an investor? The grower? As usual, part of his business dealings was assuring his client that he be told only what he needed to know. Anything he learned on assignment would be held in strictest confidence.

Liam Van Dijk flipped from digital photo to photo, gasping in disbelief at what he saw, or rather, what he didn't see. A cornfield with last year's stubble, this year's new sprouts poking through the soil, a flat rectangular area, and a huge wooden fence that surrounded a warehouse-type building. And something that looked like black bears. He zoomed in and out, clicking the next shot and the next, his surprise turning to shock and then rage.

"Randall—correct me if I'm wrong, but there's nothing there except a huge construction shed with one window in the back? Sprouting corn and last year's stalks, piles of dirt, and a bulldozed area like a dirt parking lot? No other construction in progress?"

"That's about it."

"What about my building materials—lumber, rebar, block, framing of any kind?"

"Nothing. You're looking at what we shot in real-time. Nothing else, and no way to see inside."

A big sigh. "I'd better come and see for myself."

Liam Van Dijk disconnected and ran his hands through his hair. He'd been had—he just knew it! Returning to his computer, he opened his financial folder and double-clicked his experimental hydroponic project's spreadsheet. It should have been nearly completed, the aerial shots he'd been sent looking through the glass and the equipment ready for plants. His first thought was to scream for his lawyers, but he hated looking foolish, even in their eyes, after their skepticism at his accepting the dealmaker's pro-posal. Worse, he dreaded facing his adult children, his heirs, who trusted his business decisions. He had to see for himself and pray there was an explanation.

Should he call ahead? No. At this point, he didn't trust the dealmaker not to take him to an alternate location that had no connection to his investment. Of course, the dealmaker's photos had been shot somewhere else.

He summoned his executive assistant from his office at the bulb grower's headquarters. "Please clear my calendar for the next several days with my apologies. I have to per-sonally check our American project." His assistant looked at him quizzically but held his tongue. "I know you're curious, but confidentially is crucial. In my absence, will you please interface with our distributors and key outlets? I'll call my sons and daughter from the airport to explain."

He phoned his travel agent and booked a nonstop flight from Amsterdam to Philadelphia, a connecting flight to Harrisburg International in Middletown, and requested a Ford Focus rental in any color other than red. If he hurried, he could be on-site by dark, eastern time.

He withdrew a do-and-take list from his wallet and ticked through its reminders. His emergency go-bag lived in the corner closet. From his safe, he withdrew his Holland passport, driver's license, international driving permit, and sufficient US currency to avoid a trip to the bank. He dropped crucial copies of all legal documents germane to HPC Inc. into his carry-on, which had a built-in battery charger. By the time he exited the building, a cab waited at the curb.

❧❦❧

Barrie lunged for Kingsley's flailing arm and came up with her right one. She grasped the slippery fur and yanked with both hands, pulling her by the sleeve that thank God stayed intact. With a burst of energy, she pulled Kingsley from the abyss, who dug backward with her heels into the side of the cave until she tumbled onto the dirt floor, gasping. "What was that?" she stammered when she was able to speak and hazarded a peek into the darkness.

Barrie flicked on her penlight and swept the entire area to comprehend what they had found. "That's the biggest damn hole to China I've ever seen. It's gotta be the size of an Olympic-size pool. You could have broken your neck."

Kingsley started to laugh, verging on hysteria, and couldn't stop. "You. With the phone. Calling 911. First responders running. To get your friend in a bear suit out of that hole…"

"Don't be silly. I'm sure there's a length of rope around here somewhere. I could drop one of those chains for you to send up the bear suit."

"You said it would be hot. You said to strip to my undies. You said…"

"Well, I assume you wore clean ones. The newer the better. If you're recovered from your near-fatal accident, let's make this near disaster worthwhile and grab some pictures. But do NOT get near the edge of that hole again. It's not reinforced and could cave in."

Regaining her equilibrium, Kingsley cast her penlight around. "Do you think it's a foundation for a big building?"

"Hardly since it's *inside* a building."

They edged, backs to the wall, allowing ample space between themselves and the edge of the chasm until they reached its eastern border and an interior room the size of a construction shack. Kingsley willed her heart to stop pounding and settle. Barrie's spirit of adventure redoubled at the sight of an unusual lock, which she proceeded to pick to gain entrance.

Inside, an old door, supported by cinder blocks on one side and a rusty filing cabinet on the other, appeared to serve as a desk. "Any paperwork must be in the files," Kingsley said, dropping her bear's head on the desktop and yanking the file's handle which, of course, didn't budge. Barrie rolled her eyes at the owner's stupidity and had it open in one twist.

Kingsley pulled the first file and began to read. "No time," Barrie said. "Pass it here, and I'll shoot it." Page by page and file by file, they developed a rhythm.

"Here," Kingsley said, wasting precious moments to scan something that looked vital. "Shoot all of this. Make sure you get the drawings, too. You'll have to unfold it and do it one section at a time."

"Think they'd miss it?"

"Well, duh!"

"Had to try. On it." The entire procedure took entirely too long, but even Barrie grasped its importance—probably worth more than anything else in the cabinet. "Put it back. We'll sort the photos later. See anything else that looks promising?"

"The rest of my life if we get the hell out of here alive." With precision and speed, Barrie relocked their way out of the shed and the makeshift facility's building, securing the locks on the chains. Donning their masks, they began to feel giddy, wagging their rears to the site, crouching and loping northwest toward the cover of the woods.

Suddenly a brilliant light blanketed the site, sweeping the area. Cops? Or hunters spotting deer? The beam hit them directly. "Wait! We need to get our bearings."

Barrie laughed. "Go, go, go!" They bolted upright toward the tree line.

"I can't wait to see what you shot," Kingsley gasped as they finally were able to duck into the barn.

"Let's change and go have a peek. I'll leave my car in the barn because, oh darn, it's raining and I left the top down. I'll have to stay over. Got any wine?"

"A Riesling I think you'll love."

જીજી

"I used to be a lady," Kingsley slurred as they polished off the bottle and set it on the trunk with a *thunk*. It teetered for a moment, then righted itself. She set her wineglass beside it.

"And what did that get ya?" Barrie asked, her eyes closed.

"Too many men who wanted to fight my battles for me.

Poor Todd. When he finds out what I've been up to, he's gonna freak."

"You gonna tell him?"

"If he asks. I never lie to my husband. I selectively omit—stuff." The pair dissolved in giggles. Kingsley straightened, trying to be serious for a moment, which was a struggle. "I have no idea what those tiny drawings mean. Since you're going to stay over, let's sort them out in the morning. If you download your photos to my computer, we can blow up the images. That might tell us a lot."

Barrie stifled a jaw-splitting yawn. "Can I have the front guestroom? I don't want to sleep with the ghost."

The following morning Kingsley was dead to the world when Todd gave her butt a playful slap. Opening the eye that wasn't buried in her pillow, sunshine stabbed it. "What time is it anyway?"

"Seven fifteen. And there's no signs of life from the guestroom. If you don't want to get fired, you might think about getting up. I'll put on a fresh pot of coffee." He started to leave the bedroom. "By the way, I had a text from your parents—they'll bring Billy home after he wakes up from the nap he's supposed to take. I should warn you—your mom says he rarely agrees to take one anymore. That's shaping up to be our next battle."

Kingsley slid out of bed with her eyes barely open and crossed the hall to knock on Barrie's door. "I'm up," Barrie said, opening the door fully dressed, having showered in the guest bath, and looking fresh-faced. "I need coffee. Meet you downstairs."

Todd glanced in Kingsley's full-length mirror to adjust her favorite blue silk tie that matched his eyes perfectly. "You girls have fun last night?"

"A perfect opportunity for a girls' night out. We had lots to talk about. How was your meeting?"

"Great dedicated people; same rubber chicken. And speaking of food, I'll pick up something to grill for your parents. I'm thinking pork tenderloin, which is fast and hard for me to ruin."

"I have a client call at ten, twenty miles in the opposite direction from the bank. Thought I'd do some work here on my computer instead of having to double back." Don't say *it sounds like a plan,* she thought. He didn't.

She didn't bother re-washing her hair, necessitated last evening by her faceplant in the muddy ditch. In twenty minutes she was ready to tour her dairy client's barn in dress jeans, boots, a cashmere turtle neck, and her favorite black leather jacket. She smiled, remembering four years ago when her parents bought it for her birthday, trying too hard to make up for her husband Andy's tragic death. In retrospect, every day layered new adventures. She'd worn the jacket on her first date with Todd, new memories drifting over old tragedies, soothing as fog.

Barrie was sipping coffee and munching an English muffin slathered with peanut butter while watching the weather report when Kingsley joined her. The newsman switched to a local story, the kind meant to segue into a moral lesson. A frightened yet relieved-looking mother was describing their harrowing experience and a close call in a suburban community.

"This adorable bear cub approached our patio while my husband was grilling steaks. Then its momma came barreling out of the woods. We ran for the house and slammed the door. I was so scared she'd batter our door, but all she wanted was our food."

The reporter, facing the camera, reinforced the point of his story. "Pennsylvanians should remember there are approximately 20,000 bears living in the Commonwealth. At this time of year, sows and their cubs will be looking for easy meals. A 200-pound male can run 35 miles an hour, climb trees, and swim. Homeowners must make accommodations to co-exist peacefully with these large animals. Don't encourage them. Hungry bears will eat anything. Once bears find an easy food source, they'll keep coming back, becoming more aggressive as they lose their fear of people."

The reporter ticked through a list of ways people could protect themselves and safeguard their homes then switched to another testimonial. A woman said, "We took a wrong exit onto a country lane. We saw two black bears crossing a farmer's field. I swear, those critters can run on their hind legs. They must have been six feet tall!"

Kingsley and Barrie gasped. "What about our costumes? They're a mess."

Barrie shrugged. "I'll tell him they were stolen right out of my car and I'll pay for them."

Kingsley shook her head. "My mission; my expense."

As soon as she put their plates in the dishwasher, Kingsley booted up her computer.

"Delete the ones of our feet. I'll start a new photo album on my computer and call it *Bears*. While I do that, email your photos to me." When her email box pinged, she opened each, dragged the individual pictures to *photos*, which her computer installed.

After Barrie had finished sending batches five at a time, they huddled over Kingsley's computer screen. At first, she scrolled fast to grasp the overall content, then returned to the beginning for detailed scrutiny. One by one, they enlarged each photo, deleting duplicates and those that were undecipherable.

"That hole is big enough for a swimming pool," Barrie said. "Look beyond the far edge. We couldn't fathom its width in the dark, but it's a long way from one side to the other. Holy cow. It's cavernous! And you almost found out just how deep."

As they continued the tedious process of sorting the shots Barrie asked, "When you cased the place yesterday morning, did you see any construction materials in front of the building? Two by fours, rebar, cardboard packaging, blocks, bricks, siding, anything?"

"No. I assumed those materials would either be inside, lying outback or be delivered at a later date."

"And there's nothing inside except the pit, the shack, and a lot of empty space."

"Huh! Well, maybe it's too soon for construction to begin. One of my client's projects was on hold for a year because he ran out of money. He'd paid cash for the land and the start-up but couldn't continue until he secured a loan. When Margaret researched this company, you remember, she didn't find any liens. The owners, whom she couldn't trace, must be financing it themselves. So—maybe that explains what's happening here."

"Ah, here's the good stuff," Barry said, squinting at a photo. "Man, do I wish we could have borrowed those blueprints."

Kingsley frowned. "But they weren't *blue*. They looked computer-generated."

"Hurry up. Let's print out the drawings and piece them together. With a little luck, there will be enough overlap so we didn't miss anything."

While the printer spit out the copies, Kingsley opened a document that seemed to contain one complete drawing in miniature. She saved it as a jpg, hoping she could blow it up later to make out the components. Its tiny scale appeared to be an overview of the entire project. Rotating the image, as if she were facing the street, was a greenhouse, complete with a birds-eye view of plants on tables. The area would encompass a seventy-five-foot by thirty-five-foot area. The back of the greenhouse was separated by a wall, behind which would be housed an equipment area, office, and mechanical shed. The gigantic hole was not on the drawings.

"Looks like they're going to grow vegetables after all. Or flowers. Or herbs. Hey—bedding plants. Check these out," Barrie said, double-clicking another photo's image.

Again, Kingsley repeated the process, enlarging the drawing. "This one's an elevation. An artist's rendering of the front interior of the building. See, it's flattened in two dimensions as if you're standing with your back against the opposite wall. Looks like—raised beds, irrigation lines, glass windows and ceiling, floor, even a tiny worker in a lab coat. The artist had a sense of humor. Let's do the others. There should be four elevations, then all the HVAC specifications and the mechanicals."

"Look. Itty bitty in the corner of each drawing is the client's name. It says HPC Inc."

"Okay. Now we know it looks like they're going to do something legitimate."

"You disappointed?" Barrie asked.

"Not convinced. This could be window dressing. What we saw doesn't fit the dimensions of the drawings. Let's have a look at those business documents you copied. We did it so fast that nothing I saw registered. I didn't even notice if they were in English. At least the pages are on business-size letterhead. Let's print them."

"Go!" Barrie prodded.

As Kingsley was opening the first business document, the back door slammed. They jumped. "Anyone here?" Todd called.

"Oh, shit. What's he doing home?" Kingsley muttered, quickly saving and quitting the documents open on her screen and stashing the printouts in a desk drawer.

Chapter 24

Todd called again. "You still here?"

Kingsley cultivated a calm voice and responded. "In here. We're checking out wedding planners." Barrie scowled at her. "Well," she whispered. "It was the first plausible thing that popped into my head." To Todd, who had poked his head into the library she added, "Top secret."

Barrie grinned and whispered, "Liar."

"We'll be leaving shortly. Barrie's coming with me to check out my client's dairy farm. Seems he has an airstrip that she and Randall might be able to use for the hedge-hopper and a helicopter that he's thinking of buying."

Todd frowned. "He never mentioned he was considering a helicopter."

"Oh, Todd, don't let on," Barrie pleaded in her sweetest voice. "He wants to surprise you. You won't rat me out, will you?"

Todd glanced at the grandfather clock as it bonged nine-thirty. "You better get going if you're expected at ten. And I'm heading for Conshohocken, then after my meeting I'll swing down the Blue Route and invite your parents for dinner. Goodbye, ladies."

As soon as Kingsley heard Todd's SUV crunch up the driveway, she peeked around the library's drapery and watched until his taillights disappeared. While Barrie scrolled through the photos to their hastily closed documents, Kingsley phoned her farmer-customer. "I'm terribly sorry, but I'm running a little bit late. Would you be inconvenienced if I came closer to eleven? I could juggle some things. One o'clock? Are you sure? That would be even better. Thank you so much."

"Let's hope Todd didn't forget anything else," Barrie said before turning her undivided attention to the screen. "Can you put some legal-size paper in the printer? We have some spreadsheets here. Some may still need to be pieced together."

One by one, Kingsley collected the documents while Barrie squinted at the images. "Here—rotate them," Kingsley suggested, taping the edit mode and clicking the circular arrow.

Barrie, impatient for the printer to finish, tipped her head to grasp the headings. Hovering the curser, she indicated the titles of several documents. "Looks like multiple projects to me. HPC, Inc, the greenhouse project, and a lease agreement with a farmer to plant field corn.

"Whoa—this is interesting. A third project's description is hand-written. Something cryptic. See the name's a third entity? And look at this—a drawing of a sphere with its dimensions that looks like…"

"The hole! Does it say what it's for?" Kingsley asked.

Barrie shook her head, clicking through a sequence of photos taken at the same time. "That's all, folks. A hole to China for—what?"

"Can't be good. I'd bet on it."

"What are we going to do about it?"

"Not us. Me. You've done enough. I'm going to keep a hawk-eye on that construction site. Sooner or later, something's going into that hole."

Kingsley set the printer to copy, made two of each

document, then handed Barrie her set of papers. Barrie stated, "You better keep me informed."

"I may need to speak to Uncle David confidentially in his capacity as my lawyer for some advice."

"What if he asks how you obtained the documents?"

"Not going to show him unless it becomes absolutely necessary. I deal with a lot of confidential information on the job and he knows that."

"And Todd?"

She sighed. "I've given that a lot of thought. It's inevitable that we need to renegotiate our roles. You don't tell Randall everything, do you?"

"No. In the first place, we're not married. I've spent my entire life on my own and value my independence. I don't need a man to complete me, much less to report to. I didn't even meet Randall until your wedding day, remember? Now we can't imagine life without each other, which happened pretty quickly, but that doesn't change who we are."

Barrie sobered, then continued. "Confidentially is part of our jobs and our DNA. I have insider information long before the bank's financials are disclosed to the public. One word to *anyone* and I would be fired or sent to prison. And, in Randall's business when I am the co-pilot, no matter how we insulate the clients, I overhear conversations. Even *who* we're flying *where* is confidential and could be a deal-breaker. So, it's our way of life to repeat nothing."

"Not even juicy gossip?"

"That can ruin lives."

"We'd better get going. If you're going to meet Elsie and Bessie and Flora and a couple hundred of her bovine friends, you'll need a pair of my barn boots." Kingsley rummaged in her desk drawer for a couple of blank thumb drives and made two copies of *Bears*. "When we get a chance, let's take a look at those spreadsheets, then compare notes when we can."

❦

As a gorgeous spring day enveloped historic Lancaster County, Kingsley's evening adventure receded further into her mind. Driving west, the Appalachian foothills that anchored Berks and Lancaster Counties smoothed into the flatter, fertile valleys, prized for its deep, rich limestone soil. Kingsley's west-coast friends, who lived near the Cascades, joked that her eastern mountains were *hills*. At least she didn't have six months of rain.

As she exited Route 222 and headed south, the farmland stretched in a vast checkerboard of varying greens as the land repeated its age-old ritual of renewal. They began a gradual decline into a valley that seemed to expand forever toward distant mountains that were studded with pine, deciduous hardwoods, redbuds, and flowering wild cherries that looked snowy in the distance. Cumulous clouds in a cerulean sky threw scalloped shadows on the valley floor. From their elevation, Kingsley could almost imagine she was flying.

"There—down there!" Barrie exclaimed with delight. "See that strip of bare clay? That must be the airstrip Randall's been talking about. I asked him if planes would frighten the cows, but he said the barns and their pastures are on the opposite side of the runway. Let's go have a look."

As they descended a country lane toward a large frame farmhouse and barn, a tiny speck in the western horizon grew larger. "Oh my god; it's Randall," Barrie chirped as the tiny craft grew larger as it rolled toward them. Pilot and friend hopped to the ground and hurried to greet them.

"I'll leave you guys here," Kingsley said, spotting her client striding toward them. Everyone shook hands.

"What do you think?" the dairyman asked Randall.

"Will it do for your purpose?"

"It's perfect." They shook hands again, then the pair started toward the plane. "Barrie, you want to fly back with us?" Randall called over his shoulder.

"Sorry. I have a date to meet some ladies, and my car's at K's."

"What's going on?" Kingsley asked Barrie."

"You're going to love our next adventure. But for now, it's a secret."

❦

Kingsley met her godfather at her favorite historic luncheon venue located off Route 30 in Lancaster County. The Inn epitomized old-world charm and quieter times, perfect for anniversary dinners or lunch with her girlfriends. David Wentworth rose from an antique chair in the vestibule to greet her, having already requested a table somewhat removed from lingering groups.

"It's a lovely dining room, especially during the holidays," Kingsley said as an apology to the hostess for their requesting the lower level. To her godfather, she murmured, "I agree it's best to opt for privacy."

"And right you are, especially considering the conversation you began on the phone. I thought we should continue in person." They descended the steep stairway to a pair of elegant private rooms on either side of the landing. David ducked his head to miss the ceiling above the last step, build in the days of much shorter men.

"Come on. Admit it. You wanted to see if my expression matches my words," she teased as they settled into upholstered chairs and spread linen napkins on their laps.

"Occupational hazard, my dear," the attorney admitted. The waitress approached. "How about a glass of wine?" her godfather suggested. "Just one, diluted with a meal and their outstanding coffee and dessert." The waitress jotted Kingsley's preference and left to bring her iced tea.

"If I start at the beginning, we'll be here until breakfast."

"Pick up with the part where you said you needed legal advice. And you insisted that anything you said was confidential and protected by client/ attorney privilege. That got my attention. And yes, to both, although I'm almost afraid to ask what you're gotten yourself into this time."

Having told the story so many times and endured countless mental replays, Kingsley skipped through the terrifying episodes in staccato summaries, the worst of which wasn't the gas leak, transformer explosion and fire, the attempted break-in, or security breach, but how close Billy had come to being poisoned.

"I had to find out more about that construction project next door. Perhaps I should have been more like the Amish next door and ignored the project, regardless of the annoyance. Respected their need to conduct their business and be left alone. But from the beginning, they wanted us off the land. I mean, two million dollars or name-our-price to buy us out? Seriously?"

"Kingsley, what did you do?"

She paused while the waitress placed their drinks and waited while they chose their meal. "Kingsley, you know I cannot lie for you, nor could I allow you lie under oath. Be careful what you tell me."

She laughed, dissolving his frown. "It's not about what I did as much as what I didn't find. And I don't know how to go about exposing what looks like major crime and fraud. The drawings on the building permit show a commercial enterprise that doesn't match the work being done. And there's no reason for an Olympic-size hole to China.

"How did you come by the permits? And how do you know what's behind the fence you described on the phone?"

"Todd got the permits from the township office. We were concerned about zoning and the proximity to our land. They're a matter of public record. And I, well, had a tour of the construction site."

"Um—who took you on the tour?"

"Someone who insists on being anonymous."

"If that person is a worried insider, I suggest that you advise him or her to seek legal representation. But be sure that person asks about whistleblower protection. That person needs to think seriously about personal peril. It might be wiser to seek employment elsewhere. Or leave the area entirely."

"Okay. Next. Do you know of anyone who could help me identify the person who masqueraded as Dr. Suzanne Meade? Someone overheard her called 'Geraldine.' I can picture her clearly from her visit to our home. Margaret exhausted her contacts thinking she might be a realtor. I think she's the person who planted the listening devices in our house which enabled others to know our schedules and tamper with our security system at will. Considering the timeframe, she's the only one who had access."

"I know a retired police sketch artist whom I can ask, then get our PI involved in tracing her. I know how you feel about the police, but really, they should get on top of this, especially after the overkill of criminal acts that have been perpetrated against your family and home."

"Not going to happen. I contacted the detective who questioned me after the murder of the water company employee. He was dreadful." She summarized the detective's scorn of her background. "I will not apologize for my parents nor our not being poor or uneducated. For generations, my family has earned everything they had and gave back to the community many-fold over."

"And this new detective, like his predecessors, blames

you for showing up the police in Billy's kidnapping?"

"That's the next point I must ask you. And I desperately hope you won't be angry at me for asking. Did you, through your connections or in any other way, have anything to do with those two detectives and the captain being fired?"

David laughed, covering his mouth with his napkin. "My dear, regardless of the high esteem with which you and your family hold me, I do not have that kind of clout, especially beyond Philadelphia County. Your detective either made that up or someone lied to him. Why don't we pay him a visit, on your behalf, about the threats to your family? And I, as your family attorney, will represent you."

"Unless you think that would make me look guilty."

"Of what? Dear, that is fiction."

"All right. As long as my confidentiality applies. And that extends to my parents. I cannot trust them not to insert themselves into the drama. I want to protect them, not the other way around."

"You have my word. And, when the time comes, it will be up to you to tell your family as much as you wish, with or without mentioning my name. And you decide whether you want to include Todd in that discussion."

Todd—she couldn't decide. "I'll have to think about that."

"Does he know about your *tour*?

"No. While I didn't need his permission, I knew he wouldn't approve and would try to stop me."

David patted her hand. "I understand your wanting to avoid an unnecessary quarrel, especially since you didn't know what you would find."

"Thank you. And you're hired. But just for the record— you were not, in any way responsible for getting those three detectives fired? I need to hear you say it."

"I admit only that I did complain, most vociferously to them *personally*, about their accusing you and Todd and for not pursuing appropriate leads. But I never crusaded to have them fired for their ineptitude. I did, however, hear from a confidential source that the captain's dismissal stemmed from an entirely unrelated situation."

ⱷⱷⱷ

The dealmaker stormed around his opulent office while his operative watched in quiet amusement. "You think this is funny? That banker couple—they're ruining everything with their snooping around, which my foreman *thinks* he caught on surveillance! Millions down the drain."

Geraldine laughed. "Calm down. You're forgetting your moneyman, the entrepreneur, knows nothing about your side deals. As long as you cover his investment, you have nothing to fear. Just make sure you don't expose him. He'll seize your offshore accounts, find every hideout, and expose the identity of everyone you count on who owes you favors."

The dealmaker stopped pacing, an idea fomenting in his id. He stilled, easing the volume. "You're right." The key, he realized, was to prevent the manufacturer from making a deal of his own. Get that job done—immediately—even if the timing was off. Damn those bankers. He'll make them pay later.

"And," she continued, pausing to force his undivided attention. "Remember, your name is on nothing. Thanks to your exceptional mind, there's no paper trail and no computer records." She tapped her temple. "You don't exist, except on some numbered accounts, which cannot be traced to you."

He nodded. "Thanks. I'll let you know what I decide and when I'll need you."

"After we've tied up loose ends, I'm disappearing for an indefinite vacation."

He was momentarily distracted by Geraldine's gorgeous legs as she uncrossed them and slid with a ballerina's grace toward the door, flipping her luxurious hair over her shoulder as she turned to wink at him and exit his office.

Settling into his chair, he swiveled, deep in thought, mentally reviewing each spreadsheet. She was correct. His name was on nothing. Nothing! *Alan Deal* did not exist. He'd never been fingerprinted, served in the military, nor been subjected to a security clearance. His blessed father had groomed him in the art of amassing wealth from under the radar.

The field corn was sprouting nicely, the good ol' boy farmer pleased to do business on a handshake, as he had done for decades with the previous owner. Check. No need to worry about the crop cover until harvest, by which time everything else would be finished.

Second, if the Dutchman was unhappy, he'd buy him off from his personal reserves, a magnanimous gesture the moneyman would appreciate as long as he made his percentage. He too believed in life under the radar. It might even work to his advantage, proving to the entrepreneur that he delivered on his promises. A second checkmark.

But that manufacturer—he must finish that job immediately before the district attorney got edgy and offered the manufacturer a deal that might risk his own anonymity. If it hadn't been so damned lucrative, he would have passed on that deal, but he'd been unable to stop himself.

Nothing, however, would quell his rage until he dealt with those intruders who just would not leave his business alone. First, he'd finish the manufacturer's job—immediately. Then he'd eliminate the bankers. He dialed the foreman's number and gave the instructions to fast-forward the date of the merchandise's delivery. Then, the minute the delivery was completed, recall the excavator to finish the burial.

Chapter 25

U m, buddy? I hate to throw you and Kingsley into the middle of a situation, but a client of mine needs some Yankee hospitality." Randall sweetened his pitch. "That construction project next door to you? Well, my friend has a vested interest in it and is making an emergency, unannounced inspection tour from Holland to check on a grisly problem."

"Of course—invite him to stay with us. Tell him we insist. If he's never been here before, he wouldn't know where to find accommodations. And give him the GPS coordinates so he can find us. When is he coming?"

"Well, um, as close as I can figure, he'll be landing in Harrisburg right about now. He's gained time flying trans-Atlantic and has been up over twenty-four hours. Nevertheless, he's apoplectic about something going terribly wrong with his business."

"We'll put on the floods and watch for his car. I assume he picked up a rental. If not, I'll make an airport run."

"He said he'd asked for a Ford Escort, any color other than red."

"How much can I tell Kingsley? Your business dealings are confidential."

"I'll leave that up to him. And to make it easier for you, I said that I didn't tell you anything, except that he had a business interest in the construction project down the lane.”

Kingsley slipped down the stairs in her soft-soled moccasins, hoping that their third round of goodnights had stopped Billy from fighting sleep. Of late, he wanted to miss nothing and thought he should stay up as late as the grownups. The lines were drawn, no matter how many times they had to return him to bed. She kept an ultimatum up her sleeve—to forbid O’Malley in his room unless he cooperated five nights in a row. That would get his attention since he could count to five.

“Was that Randall on the phone? What’s up at this hour?”

“We’re about to have an international guest. One of his clients is coming from Holland to check up on some business—you’ll never guess where—next door.”

“Really! You gotta be kidding. I am so on it!” She looked down at her flannel jammies and made a U-turn, then whispered over her shoulder. “He’ll have to sleep with the ghost. I haven’t changed Barrie’s sheets yet.”

“I’ll do it. Bottom drawer in the big chest?”

“The flowered ones that look like tulips would be nice. And turn on the floods.”

An hour later a blue Ford edged down the driveway, stopping at the brick walk. O’Malley tore down the stairs and danced at the front door. “Down! Quiet!” Todd hissed, and the little dog obeyed. Kingsley grabbed him and anchored him on her hip while Todd opened the door to a rumpled traveler. Hands and paws were shaken.

“Randall told me all about his best friend and wouldn’t hear of my making other arrangements. He insisted you wouldn’t mind.”

“He was correct. You must be exhausted. And starving. Why don’t I show you to your room while Kingsley fixes us something to eat? Come to the kitchen when you're ready."

Kingsley called after him. "Is there anything you cannot or prefer not to eat? So many of our friends have allergies and intolerances that I always ask. Todd will fix whatever you'd like to drink."

He smiled. "Anything but rattlesnake would hit the spot."

Kingsley magicked a light supper, nuking frozen home-made quiche, home-canned peaches, cookies, and decaf, which they nibbled while chatting at the kitchen table. "That," Liam Van Dijk said with a broad smile, "was won-derful. Thank you. I literally dropped everything and grabbed the first available flight in a panic over something that has gone terribly wrong with my business."

Todd said, "Why don't we settle in the library, have a nightcap, and give you a chance to unwind. Brandy, sherry, wine, beer, a little more coffee or tea—pick your poison."

Liam reached into his pocket and extracted a thumb drive. "If your computer is compatible, I'd like to show you what Randall's photographer shot and I can tell you what prompted my visit. And, yes, if you please. A swal-low of brandy would be lovely."

While Kingsley tidied the kitchen, Todd settled Liam at his desk and pulled up a second chair to view the pictures together. By the time the exposures were scrolling, Kings-ley had slipped behind them, knowing far more than he did and couldn't let on. But then Liam unrolled professional blueprints and renderings that exceeded hers and Barrie's feeble attempts.

"Right now. Today. The hydroponic greenhouses should be nearly finished and ready for plants. My Amer-ican gardeners are on call to receive their materials. In four weeks, seedlings planted in soil should be sprouting and nearly ready for shipment to retail garden centers, with subsequent waves of plantings on schedule for each rotation. But look! No greenhouses. Photos I've been sent must have been taken at another facility—not mine."

"Are you sure you have the right address? Perhaps the property next door isn't yours."

"I have the coordinates. This is the place."

"Tomorrow is Saturday," Todd said. "Their workers aren't around on the weekends."

"Excellent. I'll inspect the facility without them. I might need to locate a locksmith…"

"I know one," Kingsley said. "She's never met a lock she couldn't outwit."

Todd scowled at Kingsley and rolled his eyes.

"Why don't I give her a call and see if she's available first thing tomorrow?" Without waiting for an answer, she located her cell phone and dialed Barrie from the living room."

"Am I available! Girlfriend, just tell me when and I will drop everything. Oh! Please mention to Mr. Van Dijk that I'll be driving my personal car. Wouldn't want him looking for a van with a logo."

"What about Randall?"

"Maybe he could join us for dinner? As in *much later*? I'd prefer that he not see my *tools*. He never asked if I had any sidelines and this wouldn't be the best time to tell him."

"I told Liam Van Dijk I knew someone who was licensed. Todd just gave me *the look*, but didn't pursue it."

"You wouldn't have any reason to know what a locksmith's credentials entail. And I doubt your Mr. Van Dijk will ask."

She returned to the library as Liam was wrapping up his story. He sighed. Exiting the file, he pocketed the thumb drive. "I have half a notion to stroll down the lane. Have a quick look if you have a torch I can borrow."

"I don't recommend it," Kingsley responded, almost too quickly. "Black bears have been spotted at night in the vicinity, and they're very protective of their young and their territory." The clock dutifully chimed eleven times. "Why don't you get some rest. Tomorrow's another day."

❧❧

Kingsley snuggled into Todd's embrace, drained from their unexpected entertaining and their *Friday night special*, their bonus for surviving another work week and finally alone. Todd slept, but she lingered, enjoying the touch of his skin and the joy of having him all to herself in the sanctuary they'd created with love. Sleep. She must. Exhausted, she tried to say the Lord's Prayer but slipped into dreams by *our daily bread* as peace enveloped her—until.

Something nudged her mind, bringing her to near-consciousness. An innocent voice, whispering that something crucial needed her intervention. Enveloped in darkness, she slipped from their bed, tiptoed down the hall to the back-corner guestroom. When no light reached her, she realized she must be dreaming. She seemed to float toward the invisible X. She shivered.

"Who are you? What happened to you? What do you want me to do?" She thought that she'd spoken out loud but knew that she hadn't. Icy tendrils enveloped her.

Jolted awake, she realized she was sleepwalking. By the hall's nightlight, she verified that she was alone. Even O'Malley hadn't joined her. She retreated down the hall toward their bedroom, but something caused her to stop by the front guestroom door. Strange; it was ajar. With one finger, she nudged it. Then a little more, not wanting to invade their guest's privacy. The bedroom was empty.

Immediately she startled fully awake, grasping why she had been summoned. She must have heard him get up, but the guest bathroom door was wide open too.

A quick circuit through the downstairs verified what Kingsley suspected. Liam was gone. And she knew where.

She slipped into their bedroom, locating jeans, socks, a long-sleeved tee, and a wool sweater. She padded quietly downstairs, throwing on her hooded jacket against the night's chill, and pulled on her wellies. How familiar this routine! She grabbed a powerful mag light, her cellphone, and a box cutter, just in case. Instead of taking the driveway and the lane, she chose the same route she and Barrie had taken on their recent reconnaissance. If she followed Liam down the lane, she'd feel like a stalker if he was merely out for a stroll. From behind the construction site, she would be hidden and, after ascertaining the situation, could decide how to proceed or retreat unobserved.

When she reached the back corner of the fence where Barrie had picked the lock, she found the chains disengaged and unguarded. And, as she puzzled what to do next, she heard men's angry voices. Drawn, as if by a magnet, she crept through the gate toward the enclosure and that terrible void where she nearly tumbled to her death. Hidden in the shadows, as her eyes adjusted and focused on an implausible scene, she plastered herself against the inside wall, praying to remain undetected.

Near the edge of the pit, burly men in gray coveralls were offloading barrels from a truck, rolling them down a makeshift ramp where they landed with a thud at the bottom. Clipped instructions demanded *faster*, like a drill sergeant commanding his men. As Kingsley hid, shrouded in darkness, the hole began filling with its strange-looking cargo. This couldn't possibly be legal, her brain screamed, but who should she call?

Frozen, unable to react, she remembered her mission—

Liam Van Dijk. He must have been unable to sleep and preempted their Saturday visit to investigate by himself. But where was he? From her path that paralleled the lane, she should have spotted him. How long ago had he ventured from their house? Did these hostile operatives discover and detained him? Kill him? Was he lying crumpled in the bottom of the pit, covered by those black barrels? Perhaps inside one of them?

Against her better judgment, Kingsley inched, her back to the wall, toward the small shed that she and Barrie had breached. A dim light spilled from the cracked door. Two angry men loomed over Liam, peppering him with accusations, none of his answers satisfying them or producing the desired effect.

"Throw him in the hole!" An angry man, who had been hidden from her view, jeered instructions over Liam's protests that he, Liam Van Dijk, was the owner and this was his job.

Kingsley retreated halfway down the wall, stopping short of the men who were rolling the barrels. She muffled her cellphone's beeps while dialing 911, praying that one bar was sufficient. She stole another look, then scrunched against the wall when the operator answered. Burying her face in her sleeve, lips pressed to the phone, she gave her coordinates, twice, and begged for assistance. Again, she risked exposure, terrified of what might be happening to Liam.

Wait for help? Hope that Liam could convince those detaining him that he had a legitimate reason to inspect his operation? Coward, she scolded herself, momentarily pushing self-preservation and her responsibilities to her family from her mind. Back against the wall, she planted her left foot far from her body and brought her right beside it, inching fifteen feet in a matter of seconds. Simultaneously, Liam glanced toward her, his mouth forming an O, shaking his head, just as one of his captors lunged for him.

Kingsley screamed, kicking the door so hard that it rebounded on its hinges against the interior wall while holding her mag light high above her head and a box cutter in the other. "Let him go! I've called 911. If anything happens to him, I'll slash you to death!" Too stunned to react, the pair relaxed their grip on Liam's arms, who seized the opportunity to wriggle backward, knocking the chair on which he'd been sitting between them and his assailants. His captors stared as she screamed threats, momentarily dumbfounded.

"Liam! Come!" she yelled. Too surprised to do anything but comply, he stumbled toward her. One of the three took a step, reaching to grab her, but she slashed at his arm with the box cutter. He recoiled, yelping in pain. Indistinguishable in the darkness and blinded by her mag light in their faces, the others froze. "I have a gun," she screamed. "Take one step more and you're dead." They hesitated, too stunned to risk it.

Chapter 26

Distant sirens grew louder until the cacophony reached deafening proportions. Responders swarmed the scene, digesting the emergency, barking orders, and separating people into groups. Kingsley, gripping Liam's arm, peppered the nearest officer with more information than he could assimilate. The three who had held Liam prisoner demanded their release, and when that didn't happen, their attorney.

Kingsley assumed she and Liam would be escorted from the premises but given law enforcement's focus on the angry men hurtling threats at the police, they were overlooked. To help matters, Liam Van Dijk articulated his business interest to their officer, producing abundant identification and his displeasure at being mistreated by these animals. He convinced the officer, at least for the moment, that they had hijacked his business for illegal purposes. He then insisted that he be permitted to view the hole that was receiving the barrels, as long as he kept a safe distance.

As Kingsley focused her torch into the hole, one of the officers, recognizing the hazmat logo, radioed for backup and ordered everyone out of the enclosure. Kingsley, taking Liam by his elbow, located the officer in charge, explaining as briefly as possible why both were on the premises, and could they please talk at her house down the lane.

After exhaustive questions and negotiations with his peers, the officer agreed to escort them home where he would take their preliminary statements.

☙❧☙

As dawn threaded the horizon, Liam explained over coffee when they were finally alone. "I couldn't sleep. I heard noises down the street and decided to investigate. And they grabbed me. I thought they were accusing me of trespassing, not knowing who I was. But then the truck arrived. I saw the barrels and recognized the hazmat identification on the first barrel that someone had tried to cover with paint. They knew that I saw it. And, unfortunately, I blurted that I knew the purpose of their business. They knew I was trouble. But how did you know I had come? That I was in trouble? I was extremely quiet."

"It seems we have a very protective ghost."

☙❧☙

"What about Billy?" Kingsley asked later that morning after they had consumed waffles, bacon, fruit, and coffee." Liam had followed Billy upstairs when the child insisted on giving him a tour of his special room and favorite toys. "If he knows Aunt Barrie's involved, he'll insist on coming, and a construction site is no place for a two-year-old child."

"I'll stay here with him. You introduce Liam to Barrie, and she can give him whatever help he needs to gain access to his project. Don't be surprised if the site is taped off as a crime scene."

"Did you find out how much of the enterprise Liam owns? Judging by how upset he is, it seems that his business is ruined."

Todd raised his eyebrows and shrugged. "Liam said he's insured. That he signed an agreement with the property manager named Alan Deal who owns the land and leased a portion of it to Liam. Liam owns his business. His equipment and supplies will be ordered and paid for as needed. Deal's foreman and crew were hired to build the facility. That made sense to Liam since his people couldn't supervise the construction from Holland and they were sending him photos of the work in progress.

"But it's a scam—a cover for the illegal and extremely lucrative enterprise. Camouflage that was intended to fail, for which Deal would reimburse Liam after the project failed. But Liam was intent on his project's success and his deadlines met, having researched exhaustively. You sure you're okay staying home with Billy?"

"I would rather not watch Barrie in action." Todd chuckled. "She's something else."

"Why don't you take Billy to the grocery and pick up something to grill? Anything other than rattlesnake. Oh! And by the way, I rescued a paper from your jeans pocket when doing the wash. I put it in your kitchen basket."

"I'd forgotten about it. I found it wedged beneath a scrap of wood at the construction site." He retrieved it, smoothing the rumpled paper. "I don't know what the symbols mean."

"I do," Liam said. "It's a universal symbol for a particular kind of hazardous waste. I saw it on the barrels."

 espen

Kingsley met Barrie at the site while Liam dealt with his business disaster. As Todd had predicted, the entire area was cordoned off with yellow tape. Workers in protective jumpsuits, boots, goggles, and gloves swarmed the site's footprint. Vans lettered with governmental insignia parked perpendicular to the makeshift building, which had been intended to hide the pit where Liam Van Dijk's greenhouses should have risen.

"Don't suppose we could sneak in through the back," Barrie suggested. "I'd love to see how it's being handled. Hey! Let's ask that guy over there. He looks friendly enough. We can tell him we're concerned citizens and neighbors, which happens to be true."

The friendly-looking guy, upon spotting the women, lost his approachable demeanor. "You can't be here." Flat. No civility.

"I certainly should be," Kingsley retorted. "I'm the one who intervened, rescued the business's owner from those thugs, and called 911. I have complained about this suspicious operation from day one. The least you can do is answer a few questions for us."

"Afraid not. Our job's to remove the hazardous material."

"What's it called? And where are you taking it?"

"Sorry. Can't discuss that."

"Well, can you tell our friend, whose business was hijacked for an illegal dumping ground? He's right over there," she said, jabbing a finger in Liam's direction.

"Look, lady. This is going to get very complicated. The police will investigate the illegal enterprise, and it will grow legs through environmental entities." He nodded toward the structure that was cordoned off with different colored tape and logos.

Kingsley's impatience grew exponentially. "I live right next door. Down the lane with my husband, small child, and our pets. The least you can tell me is whether any of those drums *I reported* being dumped have spilled into our water supply. We do have wells out here in the country."

He thought a minute. "That seems fair enough. Let me

get someone with the authority to answer." Shortly a man with a different uniform and logo approached then."

"All I want to know…"

"Stop. Nobody's trying to stonewall you. It just isn't that simple. The seal of every drum must be tested and soil samples taken to specified depths, all per government regulations. Their point of origin, and throughout any area where they were transported, offloaded, transferred, dropped, then removed, and by whom. The complexity is mind-boggling. It's way too soon to give you an answer.

"What about our friend? His business is ruined. He'll need to know how soon he can resume."

"He'll need to coordinate with the authorities and hire an attorney to manage the fallout.

In the meantime, safety barriers will be installed. You seem like a responsible woman—keep your family at a safe distance. In time, this will be resolved. Until then, I suggest you buy bottled water."

That! She couldn't suppress a laugh.

"Sir?" The first man interrupted the recitation. "Up there. By the road. News van and reporters at twelve o'clock." Kingsley's Q and A was over.

∽∾∽∾

The dealmaker waited in the tiny luncheonette that was snuggled into a corner of the department store's anchor. He almost didn't recognize Geraldine as she sauntered in and scanned the dozen tables and booths. Then, with a smile, she broke into a fake-braces grin and approached him. He stood and gave her a fatherly peck on the cheek.

The transformation was amazing. In ripped jeans, a Penn State sweatshirt, and Nittany Lion baseball cap with a ponytail looped through the back, she could have been anyone's student daughter. Even with aviator shades and age-altering makeup, her sparkling eyes and fine bones betrayed her beauty. He motioned for her to sit. Both did.

"Happy birthday, Dad," she said, just loud enough for the elderly couple nearby to hear. Both smiled back as they collected their shopping bags and prepared to depart. Geraldine handed the dealmaker a small paper bag bearing the distinctive Boscov's logo and repeated her birthday message loud enough for the benefit of anyone within earshot.

He took the bag by the handles and peered inside at the colorful wrappings and fluffy bow. "May I open it now?"

"Not until Monday evening at the *party*. I wanted to make sure you got it since I can't attend. I'll be flying to Europe to begin my foreign exchange program." She winked.

"Yes of course. Your tuition and living expenses have been deposited as usual. Let me know if you need more for books or incidentals."

By two in the afternoon, the luncheonette had emptied. They ordered coffee and coke, respectively, and without looking around suspiciously, started their meeting, being sure to make appropriate gestures and smiles in sharp contrast to the harsh business at hand. "Do we have a date?" he asked.

"The listening devices the water guy installed in the kitchen and the one I installed when playing Doctor Historian worked decently enough to hear their inane chatter. The grandparents will pick up the kid around two-thirty, at which time the parents will go to the daycare, meet her parents, and make sure the boy understands the drill. First-time parents. You get the idea. Then they'll go to their offices to collect their stuff for the 3 p.m. meeting. Both attend department head meetings on Mondays in the bank's board room. That wraps up around five."

"So, by 6 p.m. all kids are off the premises. And the daycare is located...

"Extreme opposite end of the complex from where he parks his SUV.

"Wouldn't want another Oklahoma City bombing daycare catastrophe."

"On Monday, the Hennings will share the ride, then go to a restaurant, so her Lexus won't be in the lot. In fact, it will be in the shop for routine maintenance. You'll get two with one *present*. Unlikely to cause collateral damage, since this operation involves just one vehicle. And you'll have complete control over the situation."

"Sounds good. Continue."

"Should anyone still be parked near the SUV or be in the vicinity, you can abort and postpone. From what I've learned, however, that's unlikely to be necessary. He's a creature of habit. Staff begins leaving at 4:30, and officers who work later are gone by six. He prides himself on being the last one out."

"So—how does my *present* work?"

"What I've given you is a remote detonator. You'll park high on the hill in the adjacent building's parking lot that overlooks his assigned spot. Give the targets time to get into the SUV, then push the button. Glide leisurely down the hill, turn right onto route 10, and proceed south. The coordinates where you'll swap cars is in the gift bag. Memorize and destroy it."

"Wait a minute. Won't you be noticed attaching the device? There's bound to be people coming and going on bank business."

She grinned, flashing her fake braces. "It's already in place."

His eyes widened. "When? What if…"

"Can't happen. Not without you pressing the button within range. I've test-driven the parameters and am leaving wiggle room so the timing you need is precise in case several other cars happen to be occupying prime space, although I don't know why they would be there. The parking lot next door is empty. The new owner's work crews would either be parked by the service entrance or be long gone for the day."

He frowned. "I can't sit there overlooking the bank for long stretches of time."

"You'll get a call from a friendly insider, who will say 'incoming.' That means they've exited the elevator. I considered having you signaled when they started down the corridor to the parking lot, but they wouldn't necessarily meet until they approached the car. I also considered anything that could impede your travel to or from the building. Better you be parked nearby, but with enough time to get into position."

"When did you place the device? And how"

"Dude does lots of evening meetings, usually in hotel dining rooms not packed family restaurants. Doesn't park by the door. Avoids getting his vehicle dinged. Once you gave me my orders, I stuck a GPS tracker underneath his SUV where even a carwash wouldn't dislodge it. I studied his habits and bided my time, not wanting to install the *present* too soon—just in case he had a reason for it to be up on a lift where an eagle-eyed mechanic might spot it."

"It sounds like you've thought of everything."

"That's why you pay my exorbitant fees, baby. And speaking of which…"

"I'll wire fifty percent, divided among your designated accounts—today—and dribble the other fifty when the job is completed."

She grinned. "Make that one hundred percent. Today. I can't work around your getting, um, delayed."

"All right. Done."

"And I need to know what to tell my accountant I'm 'building' this time?"

"A business complex in Malaysia. We'll both file with the IRS, so they can't charge us with tax evasion."

Chapter 27

Kingsley thrilled at the view from her eastern window of a spectacular June dawn, picture-perfect for Barrie and Randall's wedding. Gray wisps were surrendering to streaks of pinks and blues, as lovely as an unfurled silk scarf. Kingsley threw on her robe and hustled downstairs, losing herself in her hostess checklist. She didn't hear Todd's tiptoeing feet on the stairs as she ticked through her bullet list, touching each point while imagining the scene as she entered each room. *West end of the living room rearranged, tables with cloths aligned for the bar. Dad will tend. He knows what to do. Check.*

She entered the dining room behind it, analyzing traffic flow. *Table set with Grammy's lace cloth. Flowers from the garden—two vases. Silver flatware arranged. Check.* Chairs—oops—they should be pushed to the wall for buffet traffic. She moved them. Eyeballing the vases, she repositioned them before proceeding into the kitchen.

Although it was large, she'd moved every unnecessary countertop appliance to the basement to give the caterer as much working room as possible. *Assign breakfast and lunch clean-up to Todd.* She grinned, penciling an arrow beside his name.

"Kingsley, I…"

She jumped, clutching her chest. "How long have you

been following me?"

He laughed. "Sorry—I couldn't help myself. Your routine is so cute."

"I want everything to be perfect, whether it ends up being a brief reception or a party that goes until midnight."

"How many are we expecting?"

"I'll tell you tomorrow. Why are you up so early? It's not even six."

"I need coffee before you stash the pot. What's the agenda?"

Kingsley flipped to page two. "Band's arriving around ten to arrange the haybales in the barn. They had the grand tour yesterday, will set up their equipment while we're at the wedding. Our parents are caravanning from St. Davids, bringing your sister and her family. Mom texted that your family flew into Philly last night uneventfully. They're having a grand time gossiping about us. They'll arrive here about eleven. I have sandwiches, cookies, and beverages in the basement fridge. We just need to bring them upstairs. Wedding guests who don't trust their GPS will meet us here, but I've warned them—no later than two o'clock sharp if they intend to follow us to the farm."

"What time's the wedding?"

"Sometime in the vicinity of two-thirty; maybe as late as three. The hands of the clock must be rising—for luck."

"I hope Billy remembers his role. Being a ring bearer is a big responsibility for a two-year-old."

"Going on five. Don't worry. We've practiced and practiced. He knows there's a special present in it for him. Besides, I think he'd do anything for his Aunt Barrie and his godfather." Kingsley flipped back to page one. "The caterer will be here at two and set up while we're at the wedding. Besides heavy hors d'oeuvres for the cocktail hour, they're bringing coolers for beer, soft drinks, and water, and will put them in the barn for later. The straw's on the floor, the bales around the walls covered with picnic blankets, and the lanterns look super cool."

"Musicians—what about our Amish neighbors? The noise. The traffic. Disturbing the cows…"

She gave him a smug smile. "One always invites the neighbors when one is having a noisy party. I did. And they'll join us for supper around six. And the musicians will finish by nine."

"Guess there's not a whole lot we can do until people arrive."

Thud! Thud! Thud! "The door—get that for me, will you?" Kingsley asked, sprinting toward the stairs. "I'd better throw on some clothes."

"Are we expecting anyone this early?"

"I don't think so. Randall or Barrie might have given out-of-town friends our address in case they get to town early."

Todd opened the door and accepted a package. As the delivery van pulled away, Todd pulled the string that secured the padded mailer. Inside, a silvery envelope, similar to wedding stationery, bore their names in calligraphy. He pulled his penknife from his pocket and slit the flap. Enclosed was a piece of matching folded stationery on which was scribed in black ink—*You just don't learn. Now it's too late.*

Todd's head jerked toward their driveway and the lane, but the van was long gone. What coward was out to get them on this day in particular? Without waiting for Kingsley to return, he dialed 911 and repeated the threat.

∽∾∽

"What are we going to do?" Kingsley whispered to Todd, as police swarmed their property. "We can't cancel the reception, and we can't risk people's lives." As they were watching the drama unfold from the relative safety of their front lawn, an officer and his canine partner approached the open front door. The beautiful Belgian Malinois, given a command, went to work and disappeared into the house. Billy was delighted and wanted to follow, but his startled parents commanded him to stay. O'Malley, leashed, watched from behind Kingsley's legs. Pandora was missing in action.

Shortly technicians from their security company arrived, conferenced briefly with the police, then addressed potential security breaches. Even the barn and their vehicles were searched, including boxes left by the band. That, they realized, would have been an excellent place to conceal a bomb. Like a Trojan horse. And the Hennings didn't know the musicians personally, who had been vetted by their caterer.

Todd, Kingsley, and the officer in charge spoke quietly beyond Billy's earshot. Todd said, "The obvious person with a vendetta against us is behind the toxic-waste crime. Find the mastermind and you'll find our enemy. If this were my investigation, I'd start with those workmen—the truckers who showed up with the barrels and the foreman on the construction job. I'd bet on the latter. Then follow the food chain."

The officer didn't react but changed the subject. "Have you received any other threats? Angered someone on the job? Been blamed for clients' poor business decisions?"

Kingsley slammed her palm on the table. "No! We've been over and over this since the trouble began. Ask the detective who's investigating the murder of the Clearwater guy. It all leads back to that project next door. Maybe if he had taken my suggestion and used the planted listening device that our security company found and followed where that lead…"

The officer stopped writing. And stared at them. He set

down his pen. "What listening devices?"

Kingsley glowered at him. "Just ask that detective. There's a record of everything."

Hours later, having found nothing potentially lethal, the police departed. Their security chief approached them with similar news. The listening devices, while still in place, were inoperable. "About your party—how can we help?"

Kingsley and Todd exchanged glances that underscored how conflicted they felt. Todd said, "If both you and the police believe there's no danger from explosives or intruders, then we'd like you to provide around-the-clock security on the premises, especially while we're off-site this afternoon. Bring in as many people as you need."

"What about your guests? Can you verify the identity of each?"

"I asked my dear friend, Margaret Stiles and her husband, Pete, to make sure everyone signs the guest book. She'll know many of them by sight." Kingsley pulled a favorite photo from her purse. "You'll recognize her if I don't introduce her first. She has the most amazing blue eyes. In case she's delayed, you can cross-check guests' names against our invitation list. If there's any doubt about anyone, ask."

☙❧

By one o'clock, a line of vehicles bordered their lane, guests having made three-point turns to return to the highway. The Hennings led the caravan to the Lancaster farm and were met by a man in jeans, boots, a plaid shirt, and a ten-gallon hat who directed guests to parking spots in a field. Everyone gathered beside a runway where Kingsley and Barrie had watched Randall exchange a cryptic conversation with the farm's owner. "Will it do for your purpose?" the dairyman had asked Randall. And Randall had responded, "It's perfect."

As everyone waited watching the runway, the guests mingled and chatting, introducing themselves and learning where their lives intersected with the bridal couple. A woman whom Kingsley recognized from photographs introduced herself and her husband as Barrie's parents. "She was our wild child. Planes, not horses, captured her imagination. After high school, she tried to enlist in the military to fly with any branch that would have her, but her near-sightedness squelched that dream. So she went to college and excelled in business and math."

"She ended up flying with Randall anyway."

"I don't suppose she talks much about me. We had a falling out that never healed until Randall played 'match-maker.'" She encompassed the view with a sweep of her hand. "This is so different from the last time."

Kingsley nodded. "She told me what happened."

Mrs. Brown stiffened. "We didn't know. The church, the reception, her gown, their wedding trip—we'd pulled out all the stops for our only child. Then, two weeks before the wedding, she called it off and wouldn't say why. I begged her to patch things up with her young doctor; that couples can have pre-wedding jitters. She exploded, packed up her apartment, and left town."

Kingsley knew why, but it wasn't her business to explain. Fortunately, the mother picked up the story. "Eventually a friend, who felt sorry for me—I mean, I'd done far too much bragging about my daughter. Her beauty, her grades, her popularity, scholarship offers, and now to be Mrs. Doctor whoever. He dumped her for the Chief of Staff's daughter where he was a resident."

"And you didn't know."

"Seems he'd been cheating on her for some time to advance his career. Well, that came back to bite him. The chief ran their marriage, his career, every aspect of his life until he'd had enough and quit. No idea what he's doing now. My source from church passed away. It's just as well."

"Randall's quite the opposite."

She elbowed Kingsley for the third time. "Yeah. A crazy, loving man for my wild child." She dabbed a tear with a tissue."

"Where's the minister? Todd, we should introduce ourselves, but I don't see him anywhere." Kingsley introduced the Browns to her parents, then added as they departed, "Promise you'll come to the house for the reception." Once out of earshot, she nodded toward Billy and said to Todd, "This might be a good time to *empty his tank*. Privately."

ⓔⓢⓔⓢ

Billy noticed before anyone else, his rapt attention focused on the sky. "Look!" He exclaimed, pointing a chubby finger at a tiny black dot which, as it circled lower, turned into an airplane. As the speck got a little bit closer someone exclaimed, "It's a Cessna."

"That's odd," Todd said to Kingsley. "Randall doesn't have one in his fleet. And I've never known him to mention any interest in acquiring one."

"Maybe someone's giving them a lift. They could have been waylaid and didn't have time to drive." All eyes fixated on the craft as it flew lazy circles overhead, reminding Kingsley of a red-tailed hawk.

Todd pulled a pair of binoculars from his bag, as did many others in the gathering. "He emailed me to bring them—evidently others got the same message." He focused. "The plane's side has a large opening where doors should be. And…"

As four bodies tumbled out of the plane, a muddle of

gasps and cheers emanated from the guests as the meaning became clear. "A sky-diving wedding!" The foursome appeared to be drifting lazily, but in reality, they must be descending at a great rate. Barrie, in a white jumpsuit, sneakers, and helmet with a long, trailing veil, reached Randall's outstretched arms. They locked wrists. Iridescent blue and gold stripes, his jets' colors, identified his shiny black jumpsuit.

A third party, who descended in tandem, was filming the event, while the fourth person appeared to be speaking to them. From high above the Pennsylvania farmland, they kissed. What seemed like an eternity later, the foursome separated sufficiently to pull their ripcords and begin the lazy descent to earth. With near-perfect accuracy, Barrie and Randall landed on the clay runway near the gathering.

After untangling themselves from their gear, the four approached the crowd. The minister picked up a portable mike and called to the guests, "Who gives this man and this woman?" Everyone roared in unison, "We do."

"May I have the rings?"

"Now," Kingsley whispered to her son, handing him a stuffed black bear with white ribbons tied around its neck. She held her breath, but Billy trotted forward with determination toward his beloved people. When he tripped, everyone gasped, but he righted himself and continued, unconcerned. Together Randall and Barrie pulled the bows that secured each ring and handed them to the minister. Each bent and gave Billy a hug.

In a shrill voice that needed no magnification, Billy asked, "Can I keep the bear now?"

Chapter 28

The Henning's eleven-year-old neighbor, wearing a crisp gray dress, white apron, and sneakers with her blonde hair secured under her *capp*, was sitting on the front step when the Hennings pulled into the driveway. She jumped to her feet, grinning and obviously up to the job. Kingsley was elated to see her and gushed her appreciation for the little girl's help.

"You don't have to play with him all the time—just know where he is every minute. The creek fascinates Billy. With all this activity, he'd never be missed and could drown."

The girl nodded, her face solemn with understanding. "My first job, when I was too young to gather eggs, was to watch Ben. Mam said it was very important because he could climb anything. And he could."

"Put this in your pocket," Kingsley said, handing her an envelope.

"Oh no." She waved her hand. "That's all right. We're neighbors."

"I insist. It's a real job, and it's very important." Hesitantly, the child pushed the envelope deep into her pocket. Billy ran toward the girl, chirping his delight at seeing her while ignoring his mother. "If you'll take him upstairs, he thinks he knows how to use the potty, but I'm not so sure.

His play clothes are on his bed if you don't mind. He'll insist on wearing the boots." The girl reached for Billy's hand. He proceeded to drag her toward the stairs, the wedding bear clutched to his hip while chattering nonstop and flanked by O'Malley.

Just as Kingsley had pictured, people spilled onto the property. Some lingered in the garden where floral scents lured them to wander the grounds while others drifted into the house. *Be calm. Give them time. Don't rush things. Let it evolve.* She forced herself to relax.

Security posted a woman to check ID and direct parking along the lane, leaving access for the bridal party. Time passed in a blur as Kingsley greeted their guests and circulated. Old corporate training kicked in as she remembered it took guests an hour to find the buffet unless the hors d'oeuvres were passed. As if reading her mind, a server with a silver tray began mingling with goodies and napkins.

As drinks were consumed the decibel level rose. Beautiful Margaret, flanked by her husband Pete, graciously captured signatures while Pete directed guests to the library to leave their gifts. That, Kingsley realized, had not crossed her mind, but leave it to Margaret to think of everything. As usual.

Backgrounded by horns and shouts, Barrie and Randall erupted through the front door to cheers and a cacophony of greetings and congratulations. They'd changed from their jumpsuits to party clothes, pumped to enjoy every second of their day.

From all directions, guests crowded to watch them cut their flower-trimmed cake. Kingsley held her breath when the antique table wobbled under its weight, but Barrie deftly flipped a piece onto the plate that he held and proceeded with the traditional bites.

"Where are you taking your bride for your honeymoon?" Randall's New England cousin and Air Force Academy roommate shouted.

"Texas!" He quipped.

"What's in Texas?" another friend called.

"Flight school. We're giving ourselves advanced lessons."

The party unspooled, as the happy couple visited with family and friends who had traveled hundreds of miles to share their milestone. From the barn, the band's first notes echoed across the grounds. Randall grabbed Barrie's hand. "Come on, everybody! Let's go dance." They led the way across the freshly mowed grass to the barn.

Kingsley hung back, surveying what she might have missed doing, and spotted her neighbors. "Why don't you round up your family? It's supper time, and there's lots of food in the barn. That is if you're permitted."

The woman grinned. "Ja. We asked the bishop. He said it was good to be neighborly."

As Kingsley was supervising the caterers preparing goodie bags for the guests to take home, Margaret's friend Victoria approached her. "Margaret tells me that you have a ghost story. I assumed she was kidding—old house and all—but she mentioned that you'd had some 'odd experiences' that you couldn't explain. I hope that was all right—that she told me, I mean. Margaret knows about my special gift."

Kingsley studied the woman whose demeanor betrayed nothing *off*. "What is your gift?"

"I belong to the Paranormal Society. My talent lies in being able to sense spirits, but only in certain circumstances."

"You can see ghosts?"

"No. Nothing like that. Sometimes I can detect a presence when others can't. One time, I attended a historic property tour that included a 'haunted' house. We were invited to stand in a particular bedroom to experience a cold spot. Some in our group weren't interested. One couple scoffed that it was sacrilegious. Another woman concentrated as if putting herself into a trance, but confessed she felt nothing; that it was a hoax.

"We needed to move on because the next group was becoming impatient. Before I left, I stood on the spot. The vibe was so strong that I was terrified. Later, I tried to find out what had happened in that bedroom, but nobody knew. That's when I began researching the paranormal."

Kingsley said, "My cold spot comes with a disclaimer. Whenever we need the room for overnight guests, I ask them if they'd mind spending the night with our ghost. That brings mixed reactions, but most think that's hilarious."

"Are you experiencing footsteps? Slamming doors that you knew were closed? Voices? Missing objects reappearing in strange places?"

Kingsley said no but thought of the speaker wire. "My experiences are limited to those two things—a cold spot in a bedroom and a dreamlike message—a forewarning that something is terribly wrong, and that I must prevent it."

"And does it happen anyway?"

"No—the warning awakens me. If you'd be willing, I'd be happy to show you. No. Wrong choice of words. There's nothing to see—just experience."

"My flight doesn't leave until tomorrow evening. I could come back in the morning around ten if that's convenient."

Kingsley grinned. "That would be wonderful. Stay as long as you can, and I'll make sure you don't miss your flight."

☙❧☙

Before Victoria arrived, Kingsley called Amos Krick, the founding family's descendent and patriarch, to ask his blessing to share the murder story. Not that it was necessary—it just seemed polite, since digging up old family skeletons might attract unwelcome publicity.

After initial chitchat about the renovation photos she'd sent, Kingsley got to the point. "We've met a person who claims to have unusual powers. I'd love to have her look at that bedroom room with the unexplained cold spot. I don't want to intrude on your family's privacy, but I'd like to ask you a few more questions about the murders. That is, if I'm not intruding."

"Ask away. I'd be interested to hear what she thinks. Is she a ghost hunter?"

"Not exactly. Her expertise involves paranormal phenomena. Unlike many of her investigations into hauntings, we know something extraordinary happened in that room and to whom."

"It was so long ago. I'm not sure I know anything other than what I've already told you. But the idea of a cold spot and your dog's reaction intrigues me."

"Are there any stories in your families' memoirs about the murders? Old records? Newspaper accounts?"

"Nothing comes to mind. But what always intrigued the family was the lack of a motive, especially since the entire family was accounted for that Sunday morning. Why weren't they in church since they weren't ill? Back then, there were no phones or easy transportation, so welfare checks weren't done without a reason.

"Everything my generation knows was passed down by word of mouth. We children were told by the teenagers that the room was haunted. My father and my grandfather said the door to *that room* had always been locked; that our ancestors were savagely murdered in that room. Granddad said his grandfather spoke about 'all that blood they couldn't wash off the floor.' No one was allowed to enter. The door was nailed shut. To this day, nail holes might still exist. It was as if that part of the house didn't exist.

"Generations of cousins, coming for reunions, slept in the barn, but nobody did. Macabre stories of brutal murders were embellished over the years, scaring the daylights out of the little ones. Older cousins dared each other to breach the locks and confront the ghosts. And teenagers faked ghostly sounds in the woods and howled at the moon.

"In the old days, families didn't 'air their dirty linen in public.' Had there been any impropriety, it would have been hushed up. After their death, their eldest son joined the army and his wife went home to her family. The young adults scattered. That left the youngest—just seventeen—to run the farm, which he did until the turn of the century."

"And the case was never solved?"

"That's right. Even without today's CSIs, the police weren't dumb people. As the story goes, a thorough investigation was conducted, which led nowhere."

"Our HVAC technician found no reason for the cold spot, drafts, or irregular construction abnormalities. And I have no explanation for what warned and lured me from sleep to avert danger. Even my dog appears to sense something frightening."

"Well, thanks for asking. Do as you wish. And do let me know if you learn anything interesting. But frankly, I don't believe in ghosts."

"I never did either, but something is calling me to confront these inexplicable experiences and I've exhausted structural explanations."

ಐಐ

Victoria arrived promptly at ten. "Not knowing I'd have this opportunity, I didn't bring any equipment with me, like special lights or recording devices. One of the first things we do in a home is research its history, the real estate records, family legends, newspaper accounts, even church records."

"Would it help if I told you what I know about the property and the room in question?"

"First, may I experience it? I don't want to be influenced by preconceived notions."

Kingsley led her upstairs and pointed the way to the back-corner guest room. "There. I made an X with two pieces of ribbon to show you where I feel a cold spot. Would you like to go in alone, or should I come with you?"

"I'd like to approach the X by myself."

"Is there anything I should know? Might you get a shock? Do you wear a pacemaker?" Immediately Kingsley regretted the intrusion, but the woman laughed, her good nature undoubtedly a product of numerous such questions.

"No. And I've never been harmed by a ghost either." She proceeded into the room and stood, soundlessly, staring at the back corner of the wall. Slowly, she stepped back, lowering her gaze to the center of the X, then wandering in concentric circles, sometimes stepping back and retracing where she had been. Over the next ten minutes, she stepped deliberately on every exposed foot of the floor, absorbed in her thoughts.

"Hmm," she muttered. "I don't feel a cold *spot*. It's more like an aura that fans out from the epicenter." She took a cleansing breath and closing her eyes, lifted her face toward the ceiling. "Something tragic happened here. I sense that a *being* wants your attention. A troubled spirit that's tortured with unbearable knowledge." She appeared to relax as if the intensity of the moment had passed.

Kingsley stood transfixed in the hall, momentarily worried that Todd and Billy might return from walking O'Malley, Todd having promised to keep them occupied during Victoria's inspection.

"Are you sure you didn't know anything about this house that might have subconsciously colored your impression?"

"No. I'm Randall's cousin from Connecticut. I moved to Columbus after college graduation, and have never been to Pennsylvania. Your friend Margaret made me so welcome. We found many common interests, segueing from one topic to another. But this specific room wasn't mentioned—only that you were having otherworldly experiences you couldn't explain. Then I mentioned my gift. Given your house's age, she thought you might enjoy hearing my stories that date to New England in the 1600s."

"Are you beyond being unduly influenced?"

She grinned. "Tell me the history."

Kingsley summarized, including her conversation with Amos Krick about his family's history dating to the William Penn grant. "Here, in this room, there was a double murder around 1850. It was never solved. Police at that time, while having no modern forensics, exhausted dozens of leads. No suspects, no motive, no clues, no weapon were ever recovered. It remains a cold case."

Victoria was quiet for a minute, reflecting. "Margaret told me about your renovation that included replacing damaged floorboards in the first floor with some from the attic. So you're no stranger to pulling up floors, correct? If this were my house, I'd want to know what lies beneath."

"Surely you're not suggesting that the murderer committed the crime, pried up a board, and hid evidence. Or that by removing the boards over the cold spot that we can release a spirit."

"Not at all. I would have no idea what I was looking for

until I found it. But my curiosity would kill me until I did."

Kingsley led Victoria to the kitchen where she poked through party platters covered with plastic wrap. "Let's have some lunch. Then I'd love to have your opinion about what worries me the most."

An hour later and settled in the library, Kingsley joked about refinishing the floorboards, only to cover them with an area rug. And she detailed the experiences from which her strange dreams had saved her, especially the gas leak when a small child's voice awakened her in time. "I'm torn about what might happen if we disturb that floor. Might the boards be trapping a malevolent spirit? An angry ghost or whatever name you give it?"

"In all the *warnings* you have experienced, did you ever feel threatened or endangered by the *messenger*?"

"No. Never. It was a call to action. To prevent something awful. The messenger itself? Never. We even invite guests to experience the cold spot if they can, but no one feels it except me. I had become resigned to co-existing with it."

Chapter 29

"You want to do *what*?"

"Find what lies beneath."

"The floorboards? That's crazy. What are you hoping to find?"

She smiled and manufactured a response that sounded reasonable; not crazy. "Evidence. We have an ancient cold case, and I want to solve it. Todd, think of it as an adventure. Come on—it'll be fun. Besides, I've put that last room on the 'ugly stepchild' list long enough. It's overdue for restoration."

He sighed and flopped onto his back. And then grinned. "If you'll make it worth my while…"

"Not so fast. You have to agree to help me first. I've studied the room. We need to remove the end tables, mattress, and box springs—and find a safe place to stash them. I thought about standing them against the wall in the hall, but pictured Billy toppling them over on himself. But—we're not expecting guests anytime soon, so we could park them in the front bedroom."

"The mattress could lie flat in the hall outside the door. Billy would have a ball jumping on it," he said, warming to the practical side of not hauling heavy objects. "We dragged it upstairs that first Memorial Day weekend."

"That was just the mattress and we didn't have Billy.

Yet. We can roll up the rug and stash it under the front guest bed. That's available since we took the dining room table boards downstairs for the reception."

"But you just finished wallpapering that room. Have you considered the damage?"

She grinned at him. "Yep. Your brilliant wife ran the paper *to* the baseboards, not behind them. But speaking of which, if you don't want to ruin the floorboards when prying them up, we'll need to pry them in the order they were installed."

He groaned. "At least the ones downstairs were shorter than the width of the room. Remember, back in the day when this house was built, there was no particle board. What we'll find underneath the beams is the lath and plaster from the backside of the dining room ceiling. Drop something, and there goes your elegant table."

She shook her head. "On it. I'll tarp it, just in case. Or better yet, move it to the living room. Besides, we measured, remember?" The dining room has a drop ceiling installed by the previous owners. We chose to keep it that way to A, conserve heat, but B, leave room for the tall clock, which ended up in the foyer anyway. And, if we wreck the dining room ceiling, we can raise it to its original height. With the heat pump's registers on the floor, I'm not concerned about the room being cold."

She snuggled a little bit closer, giving his neck a playful lick, to which he wrapped her up in his arms, laughing and rolling her a complete three-sixty. "So, you'll help me?" she gasped.

"Help? Sure. If you sweeten the offer, starting right now."

෴

"Here honey, you can hold this," Kingsley said,

handing Billy the retractable metal tape measure. On closer inspection she noticed a bit of grass and mud, a remnant of the day she and Todd were planting the white pine snow fence and O'Malley joined the family. She counted backward. Had four months slipped away? Billy pulled and snapped it, pulled and snapped until he decided his father needed help moving a table lamp. Vaulting the mattress that lay in the hall, he grabbed the cord, trailing his dad as if he were walking a dog.

"I need a lamp," Billy complained as Todd set it on the front guest room's dresser.

"Thanks for your help. Let's shop for a big boy lamp for your room." Billy brightened immediately and ran to his bedroom to check for a suitable spot.

"There really wasn't much stuff in that room," Kingsley lamented. "I had every intention on decorating it beyond new wallpaper, which was necessary to cover layers of water-stained damage that predated the new roof." She sighed. "Our orphaned ghost room."

"Baseboards, genius. They're on your list," Todd said, handing her a sheetrock knife. "Careful—I put in a new blade."

Kingsley bent to the task, swallowing her sadness at ruining her perfect calk bead with which she had sealed the quarter-inch gap where the bottom of the wallpaper met the top of the baseboard. Remarkably, it separated cleanly without trashing her elegant fabric-backed vinyl. In the meantime, Todd studied the boards' integrity and remarked about how perfect they were. "Amazing how they cut and planed such long pieces before they had power tools." He sat back on his heels. "How many floorboards do you intent to remove to satisfy your curiosity?"

"Don't know yet." Carefully she enlarged the space between the baseboard and the wall, which revealed a half-inch of old paper and, below that, bare plaster. "First, we need to take out the last baseboard installed, since they aren't angled at the corners. Looks like we have to start— over there! On the north wall. The fourth is the board behind the bed."

❧❧

"Gently! Gently! You don't want to shatter the wood," Todd instructed, hovering over Kingsley's shoulder to supervise her technique. "A little to the left. You want to be right over the nail, not beside it."

Weary after a full week of work at the bank, she stopped and glared at him. "You want to do this?"

He held up his hands in surrender. "No. You're doing fine. Keep going."

Kingsley poised the flat pry bar between the baseboard and the wall, giving it a tap with her hammer, then applying gentle pressure to separate the nail from the wall. It worked. Eye against the wall and glancing to the right behind the baseboard, she spotted the next buried nail. She repeated her technique, which rewarded her efforts by revealing additional nails, lined up like little soldiers up to the job. She scooted another foot toward the northeast corner and loosened more nails, then glanced around the perimeter of the room. "At this rate, it'll take me all night.

"Are you very sure…"

"Yes!" she snapped. "And I intend to make every second of our childless weekend as productive as possible. If you want to be helpful, please order us a large pizza with the works and extra cheese."

"Did you tell your folks what you're planning to do?"

"Didn't have to. I mentioned a work weekend on the house, and they bit. Seized the opportunity, delighted to have him. Mom keeps telling me he's a perfect angel and has the makings of a gifted artist. Intelligent and advanced beyond his years. Here, it would have been hard to keep him safe and occupied. I have nightmares, envisioning him spread eagle on the dining room floor." She gave the prybar another whack. "Why did they have to use so many nails? Were they afraid it would fall off?"

"Dear, the nails ensure that the boards conform to the irregular bow of the wall. In case you haven't noticed, plaster isn't as forgiving as drywall. And they never anticipated you'd be pulling it off."

She sighed. "I'm glad we decided to preserve the plaster. Installing drywall over it would have made the room smaller, considering its added thickness in addition to the one-by-three furring strips. It's not that big to begin with, considering that we stole space for a closet and a guest bath that opens off the hall."

"I was happy the contractor knew how to re-route the plumbing after adding the powder room downstairs like a Harry Potter closet. Wouldn't the original owners have loved it?"

"I'm not so sure. Long ago, indoor toilets were considered disgusting."

"K, if you're determined to lift the floorboards, let's start at the western wall and work our way out. Maybe we'll find what you're seeking before we reach the hall."

"We? Oh, I love it when you talk dirty to me." She blew him a kiss, cocking her head in a suggestive way.

Two hours later, while digesting pizza and swigs of red wine, they abandoned the tools and examined the baseboards piled on the floor. Two walls down, two to go. At least she hadn't destroyed them, although the inevitable little gouges would need to be patched and sanded. Stain or paint before re-installation? Lost in thought she imagined colors that would complement her lovely country French toile wallpaper. That decision would need additional research and her artist mother's insight. Saturday's another day, she thought, about to drag her cramped body to a hot shower. But then the phone rang.

"Kingsley? It's Amos Krick. Something occurred to me while I was admiring your garden photos. I remembered my aunt prized her roses and assumed they'd be long gone. I wonder if they'd grow in Michigan."

Kingsley plopped on the top step, stretching her legs and rotating her ankles. Brushing dust from her bib overalls, she stifled a sneeze. "You must drive to Pennsylvania. I'll dig you some of their children for you to take home. Old roses are such a treasure. New hybrid teas, while gorgeous, simply don't smell like their ancestors and aren't as hardy."

"Thanks for the invitation. Maybe I'll take you up on it. I thought of something you might find interesting. Those Bilco doors are new. During the five years when my aunt lingered, I had her power of attorney. And knowing that eventually, I'd be selling the house to settle her estate, I had an inspector evaluate the property and recommend contractors in my absence. It was impractical for me to fly back and forth to supervise what needed to be done.

"A realtor calculated the fair market value in two ways—renovated to move-in condition or as a fixer-upper. Of the latter, he listed code violations and disclosures for prospective buyers. I did a walk-through with a contractor and chose projects where the smallest investment would yield the greatest return. Don't forget, I had the cost of my aunt's welfare to consider and wanted to maximize her holdings.

"I decided the tile roof, HVAC, wiring, and so on could be the buyer's problem which, of course, they would know in advance. But one major violation that could cause injury or death to prospects and workers was the lack of egress from the basement. People would be trapped in case of a fire. I'd never been allowed down there as a child and didn't know what to expect. I found a lumpy dirt floor, decades of junk, and walls cobbled together for workrooms—but definitely not living quarters.

"Buried beneath piles of debris were old, rotted steps. At first, I'd assumed they'd gone to the first floor, but those were solid original timbers. On closer inspection, halfway across the western wall, was a one-foot irregularity in the foundation, clean-cut, as if the mason had worked toward the middle from opposite corners. The break included the space above the foundation's wall.

"Recessed, filling the gap, were bricks. The foundation, as you know, is stone, but outside we found mismatched stone, which by then was crumbling. And behind that were the bricks. We concluded that the old steps, about the right height and width of a ladder, served as a way out. When I was young, a big old holly tree hid those exterior stones.

"I authorized the contractor to tear out the old brickwork, widen the space, and install Bilco doors. But first, the dirt floor was leveled. Rebar, concrete, and a sump pump were installed. Being that close to the creek, and after Hurricane Agnes's flooding, I didn't trust the downhill grade, thus the pump. I have 35mm pictures—before and after—that I'll send you."

"That would be wonderful! Thank you."

"Another thing—the old family cemetery is down by the creek which has meandered over the years. The old graves may be underwater by now. If you'll shoot me pictures, including the house and the barn, about fifty feet west and north of the summer kitchen ruins, I'll triangulate. Headstones would be worn smooth, some shaped like footstones in today's cemeteries."

"What became of your aunt's furnishings? If she owned the house for sixty years and hoped to go home, your family must have a treasure trove."

"Toward the end she summoned me, having made a

plan for her heirs. She left nobody out, letting her kids and the grands know that she loved them equally. We picked a date when everyone could come, visit with her, then meet at the house. The goal was for each to choose something special and cart it away. Everyone did a walk-through, then pulled a number from my hat, then listed in order what they wanted most. Funny! Nobody wanted the same stuff.

"Young families with vegetable gardens divvied up mason jars. One of the gals rejoiced over a butt-ugly lamp. One guy, a photographer, volunteered to take the old family album home—said he'd send 'thumbnails' for everyone's choices, then he'd make copies of what they wanted. One of the wives loved the claw-foot tub, but the husband vehemently rejected it. A rusty gate stashed in the barn went home as 'yard art.' And so it went." We made repeated rounds until everyone was satisfied and nothing of value was left."

"Did anyone want a souvenir from the murder room?"

"It was empty. A few took a peek, but nobody lingered. A Mennonite friend introduced me to the *mud sale*, which takes place when the ground thaws in early spring—you guessed it—in the mud. You can buy anything from a used buggy, yard tools, tractors, furniture, household stuff, and miscellaneous junk. He brought a wagon and collected what was left. I told him to donate the proceeds to his church."

"Were there any old portraits?"

"I'd moved them to the living room—just old people in 1800s Sunday clothes. There's duplicates in the albums. And a sampler—the little girl who *wrought it* was eleven years old. I took it home. An artist replaced the damaged frame and used museum-quality glass. The backside of the artwork is amazing, where the unfaded colors of the original floss had been protected from light."

Kingsley had an idea. "Let's coordinate a reunion for

your family. Maybe Labor Day weekend. There are motels nearby, and we can round up sleeping bags for the kids or anyone else who wants the barn experience."

Amos chuckled with delight. "I think everyone would love that. You're on. And thank you." After Kingsley disconnected, she went to the basement and studied its western wall, eager to see Amos's promised photos and wondering who used the ladder back in the day.

☙❧❦

Saturday morning she secured the phone in her overall's pocket and focused on her task, wishing its execution were as easy as she'd imagined. She positioned a thick bathmat by the western wall and, taking a deep breath, flicked the button on her sheetrock knife. Its shiny new blade caught the reflection of a gorgeous morning, reminding her that she could have been in her garden, or the three could have gone to the park. But no. She had to pursue this insane project. At least Todd didn't get ugly about it—his personality didn't have that trigger, bless his indulgent heart. When a good buddy invited him to play golf, she had practically pushed him out the door to salve her conscience.

Job at hand. This time, removing the fourth and last piece of calk would not be a smooth *slice and pull*. When she had finished wallpapering the western wall, she'd been delighted by how easily she smoothed the paper behind a serious gap. But she'd paid, big time when the gap defied sealing. Losing her patience, she had stuffed globs of putty into the gap, which only sucked farther and farther—to where? To the dining room ceiling? She'd finally saturated shredded paper with white glue, stuffed the gap, and let it dry. Then she applied a perfect bead of caulk and smoothed it with her finger, albeit an inch wide, and toasted her ingenuity with a chilled chardonnay.

Today she made the first slices and grasped that she needed serious tools. A skinny spatula, narrow screwdriver, long-bladed tweezers—screw it. She needed the whole damn toolbox. Once in the basement, her calming angel suggested that she did not need wrenches and pliers. Forget the toolbox and grab anything that looked promising off the pegboard. She dumped her selection into a bucket and stuffed smaller tools into her pockets.

Her first vicious slice yielded more than expected. A hunk of skin off her left index finger. Sucking madly to staunch the blood, she wrapped the injured digit with gauze and heavy-duty adhesive. She returned to the task, determined to apply more brain and less brawn. After a few awkward starts, she developed a rhythm—a foot-long slash that did not involve fingers, pry the putty with a screwdriver and lift what cooperated. Repeat, repeat, repeat, and tug the nasty stuff with pliers and six-inch industrial tweezers.

By the time she conquered the corner, she'd excavated a volleyball-sized wad of gunk that defied naming. Rather than making a sticky spot on the floor, she gathered it up, trying to deposit it in a plastic grocery bag without tearing the bandage from her finger. It stuck to her skin, her clothes, and the outer side of the bag before she realized she should have wrapped the ball in paper towels first. She squinted at the offensive object as if she could force its cooperation. And almost missed the tiny, incongruous scrap of paper, stuck to the ball, which had no business being there. She looked closer at a yellowed triangle, which looked like Grammy's World War II airmail stationery. What was buried beneath the floor?

Chapter 30

Relaxing her fanatical goal of historic preservation, Kingsley grabbed the pry bar and gave the fourth baseboard by the western wall serious yanks every few inches. With a groan and a shriek, the old nails separated from the wall. Kingsley found herself looking at the backside of the twelve-foot length, its vicious nails aimed at her feet. She scrutinized every inch, taking care to avoid being cut by rusty metal while looking for additional pieces of the odd paper.

If more had been attached to the putty-and-caulk debris, surely she would have seen it. She grabbed a penlight and magnifying glass and approached the gap that had been hidden by the baseboard. Scrunching her cheek against the wall for the best possible view, she saw what appeared to be a folded piece of paper protruding from beneath the first floorboard and the joist.

Kingsley's first thought was to wrench the floorboard free. That, she realized, was a two-person job. She attempted to squeeze her fingers into the one-inch gap, and with a feather-light touch feel the smidgen that protruded, its torn edge looking like a missing puzzle piece. A tiny crumb disintegrated and fluttered toward the ceiling below. She'd have to wait for reinforcements.

Kingsley busied herself, throwing steaks into marinade,

mixing a green salad, and husking corn for the grill. From time to time she ran upstairs to peek into the recess as if expecting something would change. But it hadn't. By the time Todd returned from golf, relaxed and happy after an exceptional round and a near hole-in-one, Kingsley was ready to explode with anticipation. Had he expected a cold beer, refreshing shower, and a rare date night with his wife, he was not disappointed.

Hours later, Todd rigged a trouble light to supplement a lamp that sat on the floor. They crouched by the far western wall and began the laborious job of extracting flat-head nails that anchored the floorboards to the joists. Tap the screwdriver's blade under the nail's most promising edge. Rig a fulcrum, raise the nail enough to clamp it with plyers. Twist and tug. Repeat. As her fingers cramped, she lamented another job that was never meant to be undone. *Tink. Tink. Tink.* The redundant nails filled a repurposed tomato soup can.

"It's after ten. You had enough for this evening?"

"Nope," she muttered. "I am determined to free whatever's trapped under this board."

"Let's give it a yank with the prybar. If we can raise the far edge a little, you might be able to snag it."

"After all these years it's gotta be fragile. I don't want to risk it disintegrating in my fingers."

"Subsequent boards will be easier—drive a wedge closest to us, pry it loose, then bonk it toward the gap we're creating."

"Bonk. No one taught that technical term in my MBA classes at Penn."

They positioned themselves two feet from opposite walls, grabbed the far edge of the board, and yanked with prybars. Rip! Just like the baseboards, the first floorboard relented with a grudging squawk. The old pine floorboard surrendered, practically toppling them backward. With caution, they extracted their legs and balanced the board on its side. In quick order, they tapped the underside of the remaining nails free and pull them through the top side. Stowing the board out of the way, they crawled to the breach.

They squinted toward what was buried beneath, Todd sweeping the one-by-twelve expanse with a penlight. Under the floor joists, they could see the backside of the lath that formed the original dining room ceiling. Gray plaster, which had oozed during the plaster's application, had fused the breaks in the lath. "There!" Kingsley edged on her belly toward the spot where Todd's light played. "The paper. It fell to the lath when we pulled up the floorboard. What's the best way to snag it? My arm's too short."

"Use the twelve-inch tweezers like forceps. Slide the bottom side underneath, close, and lift. Gently."

"First, let me get something clean to set it on." She sprinted downstairs to her desk and returned with several sheets of duplicator paper that she'd stapled to a thin piece of cardboard. She set it on floorboard number two, perpendicular to the hole. Sprawled on her stomach while Todd held the light, she reached an arm's depth and followed his instructions for grasping the paper. She held her breath, guessing how much pressure to apply without damaging or dropping it. She remembered Grammy's voice when she'd been trusted to handle her first raw egg. *Gently, Gently.*

With a huge sigh of relief, she practically dropped the folded object onto the duplicator paper. "Gloves. I still have a pair of Grammy's white cotton ones I used when playing dress-up when I was little." She didn't add that she'd saved them for the little daughter that she'd never have. "I'll get them."

"Let's take this to the kitchen table where there's better light." Todd lifted the precious cargo by the duplicator paper's corners and slipped his hand underneath for support.

Once seated opposite each other with the dimmer switch cranked to the max, they began their examination.

The paper was as thin as the old-fashioned onion skin that typists used to make duplicates back in the day. It had been folded multiple times. And, judging by the depth of the creases, it had been opened and closed repeatedly. The first two folds created a packet, one-third the width of the paper. Opened, the paper was then folded in thirds again, starting at the bottom, its opened dimensions approximated six by eight inches. Thankfully, it proved sturdier than expected. Yellowed with age, the beautiful script had faded to brown yet remained legible.

"What's it say?" Todd asked. "I can't read the fancy script upside down.

"It's a list of dates. It says…

"*1850 Fugitive Slave Law. Warning. Take care.*

"*1860 Let us have faith that right makes might, and in that faith let us to the end dare to do our duty as we understand it.* "

Kingsley said, "That's Abraham Lincoln. We learned that quote in school.

"*1863 Emancipation Proclamation signed. We must persevere.*

"What do you think it means?" she asked. "That the writer was an abolitionist? At the very least a supporter of the president?"

"Is there anything else on the paper?"

"It seems like the start of a prayer that begins with '*Teach Us Good Lord To Serve Thee As Thou Deservest. To give and not to count the cost…*' Whatever comes next is rubbed off, as if someone fingered it repeatedly."

"I wonder how we can preserve it until we know its provenance." She snapped her fingers. "I have two pieces of framing glass that I was going to use for Billy's new portraits. Let's sandwich it between them for now. It has UV protection and is acid-free."

That accomplished, they needed the best place to keep it. Kingsley's triple dresser, with its wide, deep drawers, seemed perfect. She removed a layer of bulky winter sweaters and placed their treasure on the bottom. "The hole in the floor," Todd said, motioning down the hall. "In our days before Billy, we could walk away from projects. Why put things away only to drag them back out? Saving time was of paramount importance back then. But with an inquisitive, fearless two-year-old, everything changed the day he learned to roll over. And over. Even before he could crawl."

"Rather than keep the door closed and invite his curiosity, why don't we muscle that first board back into position. Can we lower it without damaging the dining room ceiling?"

"Long as we don't get careless, overlook a tool, and kick it into the hole. Let's do it. No way our son can manage what takes two adults to handle."

"Speaking of handles, let's stretch a rope under each end so we have something to lower and lift it."

Kingsley smiled her appreciation. "Times like this I wish we could complete what we start. Have I thanked you enough for supporting my ridiculous project?"

He grinned back at her. "*Dessert* was delicious."

❧❧❧

Kingsley dreamed she was scribing messages in fluent cursive, reminiscent of earlier times when ladies prided themselves on their perfect penmanship and eloquent poetry. She dipped her pen in the ink bottle, letting the excess drip before committing her inspiration to paper. Kingsley couldn't remember her dreamer's prayer and so inserted something familiar. *Our Father, Who art in heaven...*

Something awakened her, and she felt drawn from her bed. Trancelike, she eased the familiar route toward the room dimly lit by moonlight that cascaded through the western window, throwing ghostly silhouettes of the ancient maple tree's branches on the southern wall. She felt drawn into the empty space by a presence. She obeyed. Step by step she approached the X but sensed that it had moved. She was coaxed, instead, toward the northern wall and halted three feet short of the edge by something other than her own will. She paused. Waited. And the cold enveloped and rattled her. She looked down and saw—something. But the image was blurred.

"Kingsley? Where are you? Are you all right?'

Instantly awake, she realized she must have been sleepwalking. "Just restless. Needed to check on—everything," she attempted, with no plausible reason for what she was doing, prowling the house as the clock in the foyer bonged twice. She made a brief stop in the bathroom, as if that had been the reason, then crawled back into bed.

"You okay?" he asked in a sleepy murmur.

"Yes." Answer enough. She tried to reconstruct her strange dream, but as with all dreams, its essence evaporated like mist. Something about the X having moved, with an increased message of urgency. Her last image as sleep overcame her was of a little girl in a white muslin dress, sitting on the floor of the murder room.

ℲℲℲ

Kingsley's eyes flew open, an image clear in her mind. She had dreamed or noticed something. She grabbed her glasses and, shoving them onto her face, eyed the clock. Four-thirty. Not even dawn. Even the robins hadn't sounded their first chirp, which signaled every other bird to erupt in a competitive chorus. Todd, lying on his right side, slept like a log. If she hadn't seen his body rise and fall, he would have looked dead.

Wide awake, she slipped from the room, knotting her ratty old robe against the drafts, the floors chilly under her bare feet. She glanced through Billy's open bedroom door. Empty. She shuttered, experiencing a trigger of that terrible timeframe when Billy was their lost angel. How long had it taken to brave his room, dreading he'd never return?

She smiled. Billy was with his grammy and papa in the special room where her mother had let him paint his own mural. He'd still be asleep with a pile of stuffed animals, his worn lop-eared bunny and black wedding bear tucked in his arms. Pesto, the family's cat, might be curled at the end of his bed. Task at hand, she scolded herself.

Entering the murder room, she groped for the light and flicked the switch. A lamp, set on a box, blazed with 100 unshaded watts. First, she scanned the floor and then, armed with the penlight Todd'd left on the sill, studied every inch of the floorboards. There! Why hadn't either of them noticed the irregularity? What should have been the sixth board spanning the southern to the northern wall had been installed in two pieces. The juncture was so perfect, so smudged with age and wear, that it seemed to disappear and would have been under the bed, abutting the northern wall.

On hands and knees, she slid her fingers around the edges. Just like the other boards, the little gap along its length was a sixteenth of an inch wide. Maybe, when installed, the wood had been green and had shrunk over the years? She shined a light in the crack, but all she could see was accumulated dirt. That board, she rejoiced, simply did not belong.

She slipped into the bathroom and from the hamper retrieved her dirty coveralls and yesterday's socks. She dressed. On tiptoe, she closed their bedroom door and shut herself into the murder room. The incongruous board couldn't be more than four feet in length. She fell upon it, compelling her newfound skills to wrench it from its moorings and expose what secrets lay beneath.

So intent was she on her work that she didn't hear Todd enter the room until he was bending over her. She jumped. "I'm sorry," she said. "I just couldn't wait. I think I found the ghost's secret." As she wiggled and pulled the nail closest to the wall, it lifted as if it hadn't been anchored at all. Todd repositioned the lamp beside her on the floor. Both gazed at what had lain hidden—a number of papers, some folded like the original, and some in packets that formed makeshift envelopes.

"Let me get a gift box from our Christmas supplies on the third floor," Todd offered.

"Why don't I make coffee, you get dressed, then we'll examine these artifacts downstairs."

Chapter 31

Kingsley took a cleansing breath, internalizing the gravity of what they'd discovered. Arrayed on the kitchen table were several tri-folded pages, just like the one they'd previously found. She opened the first one with gloved hands and trepidation.

"Read it to me," Todd said, although he was bent over her shoulder. "I can't read that tiny script."

"This one is a list of women's names followed by numbers. Maybe their ages?

"*Abigail 34. Barbury 13. Betsy 18. Catherine 17. Ceceiliax 20. Charlotte 28. Coffey 45. Hany 17.* The second paper includes—*Lucy 17. M.A. 16. Mitilde 17. Patty 4. Phibe 16. Rebecca 5.*

"Two were just little girls. It goes on,

"*Ruth 60. Susan 9 months.* Just an infant! *Venus 19. Ruth 40.*"

"All women and little girls," Todd said. "Do you suppose they were runaway slaves on the underground railroad?"

"The next page looks like men's names—Except for Scipio 8 months, they're all Anglicized. If they were slaves, they've been stripped of their African names. I wonder what's in the little parcels?"

With tremendous care, Kingsley unfolded the first one

and gasped at its contents. "Hair. Little snippets of curly black hair, tied together with what looks like embroidery floss—the kind young ladies used for samplers that were part of their finishing school curriculum. Each has a scrap of paper with initials."

"Do they correspond with the lists of women and men?"

"There weren't any last names—just firsts—and they probably aren't even theirs. But the floss might be color-coded—navy for men, pale blue for boys, red for women, and pink for little girls. Maybe we can match them up."

"Kingsley, wait. We'd better contact Amos. This is his family's history. We should tell him what we've found, ask him to come at his earliest convenience, and turn it over to him."

"I'll take a leap of faith that his Krick ancestors sheltered runaway slaves on their journey to freedom. They came and went through that sliver of a break in the cellar wall. Amos mentioned the remains of decrepit partitions, like rooms, but unfit for human habitation."

"Unless you were a fugitive family on the run needing shelter. The family could sneak them the food and clothing they needed."

"That was dangerous, considering that bounty hunters, who would kidnap any black person for ransom claiming they were runaway slaves, tracked someone to this house, and murdered the couple who sheltered them. Let's call Amos. Right now. And ask him to book a flight to Harrisburg and we'll pick him up."

Kingsley held up her finger in a hold-the-phone motion. "There's two more papers." She opened it. "It's just a torn scrap with a childlike scrawl. It says—'*Jesus luvs*'. Whoever wrote this was a believer. And the other is a crude line drawing that looks like a map, an X in the middle beside what must be a creek.

⋐⋑

Amos Krick and his friend Cecilia took the first flight that connected in Pittsburgh to Harrisburg. He said to her, "The Hennings insist that of course you are welcome, and they'll be disappointed if you don't stay with them. There's lots of room—her parents are keeping their son."

"This could be the end of a very long journey," Cecilia said. "Ancestry websites can take you only so far, and of course I know my family was kidnapped in Africa in the early 1800s. But whatever became of them can't be calculated forward. I've thought about a DNA database, but…" She trailed off, then added. "I'm determined to learn what happened to my family."

Amos threw their overnight bags into the rental car and plugged the coordinates into the GPS. Within an hour they arrived at the old Krick family farm, which was blazing with floodlights and lamps in the windows. For a minute he gazed at the beautiful structure, overwhelmed with memories. Kingsley's photos hardly did it justice. "Come on," he urged. "You've come nearly two hundred years to find answers."

⋐⋑

"I don't know where we should begin," Kingsley said, sweeping the pair into the house. Amos, she'd recognize anywhere from the photos he'd shared through his earliest childhood. The woman, his dear family friend, had a link to the house as evidenced by her dark complexion and the story she had begun by email and was anxious to continue. After a quick tour, they settled into the living room where Kingsley laid out their find on the trunk with gloved hands. She let them draw their own conclusions. "Amos, I think you should take all of this home. They're your family's history and an important clue to the murder."

She turned to Cecelia. "The passage of these people through this house would have happened in the 1800s before the murder. If the people listed on these pages made it to freedom, their descendants may be alive. I doubt that DNA evidence survives that long, but if you look at the hair samples with a magnifying glass, you'll see it was pulled, not cut. Maybe, even if the family had scissors, they hoped attached skin had special significance. They might have feared their existence might never be discovered, but they did not want to be forgotten."

Cecilia stared at the array of hair samples, tears in her eyes. "I don't know if Amos told you. I'm a genetic scientist. Humans of all races are 99.9% genetically identical. That tiny extra sub-percentage is cosmetic. Cosmetic! Consider the atrocities that still persist based on people's appearance. But I'm not going to dwell on that. If you'll trust me with this treasure, I'll research all the names on that list and the corresponding samples. It might produce a glorious reunion, if not for me, for others."

"Amos, did you bring the pieces of the embroidery snippets from the backside of your old family sampler?"

"I did." With great care, they compared Amos's samples with the hair bindings.

"Maybe Cecilia can match the initials with the hair samples and the names." Kingsley added, "and the last paper—the list of ships' names and the dates of their passages. That might provide their ports of origin and final destination."

After carefully re-packaging the documents and samples for transport, Kingsley showed them to their rooms, Cecilia being the best fit for Billy's bed, and Amos happy to sleep in his grandparents' old room. While circling through the upstairs, Kingsley raised the question. "Would you like to see the murder room? We've used it as a guest room, but we're the first to do so since the murders. It's empty now. We set the floorboards aside where we found the papers." They agreed.

"Then why don't I leave you alone to explore. Take your time, and then join us in the kitchen for something to eat."

☙☙

With Billy at his grandparents and Cecilia still sleeping, Kingsley and Amos shared pre-dawn coffee while swapping tales so important to both. "I'd like to find the old family cemetery."

"Do you remember its location? We never had a surveyor set pins. We assumed our land ended where the cornfields begin. I'm afraid I haven't noticed any markers or stones in logical alignment, but I wasn't looking."

"Why don't we take the path to the right of the barn? Back in the day, the farm was several hundred acres, but the family sold sections when they needed money. Your Amish neighbor, to your west, owns part of it now, and an investor bought the land to your east, which changed hands again recently. Guess the new owner lets the crop farmer continue as he had for decades."

Amos, choosing to drive, took the dirt road beyond the barn, which crossed a one-lane bridge that bisected the farmers' crops. "That lane and this part of the cornfield belongs to your property."

Kingsley jerked to attention. "Are you sure? We didn't know that. As long as we had a clear title, and knowing it was seven acres more or less, we didn't hire a surveyor to place pins. Guess we should do that."

"Correct. Because, without your permission—which was a gentleman's handshake years ago—the crop farmer can't access his parcel. It's landlocked. And I'm guessing the cemetery is unintentionally buried in his cornfield." He squinted in all directions, ultimately focusing on the roof of the barn above them high on the hill.

"Creek's a lot closer to your house than in the old days. I never came back here while settling the estate and wasn't doing any of the labor myself. There wasn't time—my practice, my family, the distance—seems odd that I didn't."

"Is your aunt buried here?"

"No. She was cremated and buried beside her husband in their family's church columbarium in Michigan. To the best of my recollection, nobody's been buried in the old cemetery for a century and a half. Kids grew, went away to school, married, and scattered where their work or the military took them." He studied the terrain, then the position of the early morning sun. "That way. Over there."

Kingsley stubbed her toe on the edge of a rock that was nearly buried in silt. "Got something," she called, as Amos peered at the soil and began darting through the rows, laughing with delight.

Pulling his phone from his pocket he called to her. "Stand right there. I think that's the corner of the cemetery." He began snapping photos, using her as a marker, and stones that, while worn with age and exposure, were similar in dimensions. He bent to one, lovingly removing the dirt.

"Amos? Remember we spoke of your family coming here for a family reunion? Let's do it this Labor Day weekend. Have your folks arrive Saturday, then Sunday afternoon we'll have a treasure hunt for the old markers. Between now and then, you can email your families' historians for their support."

"I don't know, Kingsley. That's awfully nice of you, but it sounds like an imposition and a lot of work for you."

"Nonsense. Growing up, my father's extended family had just such events. Kids—small through teens—slept under a big tent. We grilled, had bonfires, smores, sang camp songs, the whole bit, and even distant cousins made lifetime friendships. We don't need a tent—we have the barn. Go home and talk it up, and I'll sketch out the details."

"It sounds—wonderful. And maybe we could tell family stories around the campfire."

"Even about *the room*?"

"The timeframe will give us the incentive to finish our research over the summer."

Kingsley and Amos took a last look around, then returned to the kitchen where Cecilia sipped coffee in her bathrobe. "What are your travel plans?"

Cecilia said, "I'm seizing the opportunity to attend a two-day conference in Pittsburgh, Amos will visit old friends, then we'll fly back to Michigan together."

Later, as their visitors' rental car eased down the lane on route to Harrisburg's Middleburg Airport, Kingsley waved and uttered an exhausted sigh. In the blink of an eye, they'd be home in Michigan, half a country away. Kingsley couldn't explain what she felt but it bordered on bereavement. She wandered aimlessly from room to room, ending up in the library. Todd removed his reading glasses and smiled. "You done good, kid. Come here." He pushed back his chair and patted his lap. She snuggled into his embrace.

Still, she felt something was missing. If there had been a lingering spirit—trapped in between one world and the next—it needed to be released. A benediction.

After all these years, even if luminal proved positive for human blood, it was decades too degraded for DNA testing. Some stains would belong to the murdered couple, but might another person have died in that room? His or her body buried in secret to hide this stop on the underground railroad? She'd ask her priest if he'd ever conducted such a blessing, even though she did not believe in ghosts.

⌇

"Why did the surveyors set up their equipment over there?" Kingsley asked Todd as they watched the professionals working beyond their driveway.

"Amos was right. We do need to know our physical boundaries, which was not the responsibility of the title insurance company. I'd assumed our land was bordered by everyone's cornfields. Guess it's just like the suburbs where people set up their swing sets in undeveloped lots until one day the builder shows up with a bulldozer. I've asked the men to set pins every one hundred feet. We can tie fluorescent tape around them and cement them into the ground."

"You don't suppose we own part of our neighbor's barn, do you?"

Todd laughed. "If that's the case, we'll need to deed that portion over to him. God knows we don't need it for cows."

"Cows? No. Maybe alpacas. I could knit beautiful sweaters and scarves with their luxurious fleece."

Todd rolled his eyes, shaking his head. "As if you'd have time…"

The surveyor in charge approached them, documents in hand. "We're finished. If you'll walk with me, I'll show you the markers. Some are a bit hard to spot. You'll need to clear some vegetation if you're planning to secure them, which I recommend. You do not want to pay us again when some fool pulls the pins to make mowing easier."

"Mud boots," Kingsley said. "I'll meet you by the road." They trooped after the surveyor, noting their bearings. August, she noticed, smelled different. The corn was drying down, birds were subdued, the summer relenting. "Bigger than I thought," she muttered to Todd. "And the access lane that the crop farmer has used all these years is ours. What are we going to do about that?"

Todd's generous smile warmed her. "Give him permission for as long as he's farming. We'll deal with whoever comes next when it happens."

They continued, stopping at every pin and looking around. "The little bridge over the creek is ours, as is the creek, and, halleluiah, the area Amos thinks contains the old cemetery." They continued, stomping waist-high weeds and the nubs of a prior year's corn stubble, rounding the northwest corner that bordered the dairy farm, pleased that the surveyors found no more surprises.

As the surveyor headed back toward the road, Kingsley spotted their neighbor returning from the barn. He waved Jacob over, pointing to the pin by her feet. "Yep," he said, mopping his florid face. "About what I thought. What ya thinks goin ta happen to that land yonder?"

Kingsley and Todd followed his gaze to the east, exchanged glances, and shrugged. "Hadn't given it any thought. It's shut down for now. Guess the lawyers will be fighting it out for years to come."

"Sure would like that farmland for my son and his bride. If you hear anything…"

"I'll make a point of following it."

"Bishop has a phone. I'll give you his number." Kingsley was tempted to ask why they couldn't just run next door with any news but realized she didn't know Amish protocol and kept quiet.

As they strolled across their front lawn to wrap up business with the surveyor, they gazed beyond their eastern border to the abandoned construction site. "I'm worried about someone requesting a zoning variance. We could still end up living next to a rendering plant."

Kingsley elbowed him. "With me protecting us with my clippers? Silly man."

Chapter 32

onday's department head meeting dumped a dose of reality on Kingsley after her journey into an ancient murder. She was always relieved when her turn at reporting was finished. The nods and smiles around the board table confirmed that her ship of commercial lending was headed for safe harbor. The numbers proved it, but explaining the minutia in intelligent, non-condescending terms, was always a challenge. Returning to her real-world was surprisingly soothing as she settled into her responsibilities.

As Shirley Granger finished reporting on HR and Branch administration, someone asked at what level the bank should be funding its corporate giving program. Was it enough to make them a business of choice? Shirley replied, "The formula we've used for years is 0.9% of pretax net income averaged over three years." A lively discussion followed over the newly updated contributions guidelines and the difference between philanthropy and goodwill advertising. *Huh,* Kingsley thought. *That never occurred to me.*

Shirley explained. "*Charity* involves contributions. In our case, 80% cash and 20% for in-kind gifts, products, loaned executives, use of our facilities, and surplus. We have a separate budget for goodwill advertising, which is included in marketing's budget. Those ads in the symphony booklets and logo pencils branch managers donate for community events' goodie bags. In the end, the goal is to be a good corporate citizen."

After two hours, Todd concluded the meeting with what he called *housekeeping*. Recommendations and items of interest from the rank and file that were then discussed and routed to the appropriate department heads if approved. From down the table, Shirley mouthed to Kingsley, *got a minute?* And when Kingsley nodded, Shirley waited in the outer office for her to emerge. She took Kingsley aside.

"There's something I thought you should know. It's confidential but involves a *challenge* you've had since you joined us four years ago. L. J. Zaun, who thought she was a shoo-in for your original job as head of commercial lending, and then lost out, again, when you were promoted to overall lending head—she just gave notice. I know you worked very hard to position her for promotions and salary increases without making her feel like you were tossing her crumbs."

Kingsley nodded. "She was dreadfully disappointed, both times, even though she wasn't the best qualified applicant. Time-in-grade doesn't guarantee promotions in today's banking culture. How she resisted software upgrades and ignored new regulations! Still, I tried to make sure no stumbling blocks stalled her advancement."

Kingsley had tried to ignore the woman's catty comments, dour looks, and suspicion that she had fed vicious misinformation and lies to the detectives when her baby was kidnapped, even though Kingsley knew she helped turn the detectives against them. Kingsley made sure the bank paid for her latest computer classes, lobbied for her promotion to junior officer, and to be given a vacated officer's position. Then she didn't get it. Again. For which, according to gossip, she blamed Kingsley, supposedly for stabbing her in the back.

Kingsley shook her head and momentarily forgot a professional response. "What's she done this time? Was she finally undone by her dreadful attitude? I'd feel hypocritical, rallying the troops to give her an exit party and a gift."

"No need. She had accrued enough personal time off for her two weeks' notice. She'll stop by at her convenience to pick up her stuff. Seems a rich relative died and left her a sufficient inheritance to retire well."

"Retiring at what? Fifty? I'd say I was happy for her, but in truth, I won't miss the attitude. One of my biggest challenges has been her poisoning new staff."

"Which should not have been your problem. As long as you don't violate anyone's civil rights—which I can't begin to imagine—newcomers need to respect you and your office. Period."

"Thanks, Shirley. I'll be sure to act surprised when I get the news."

ↄ∽ↄ∽

L. J. waited in a corridor alcove near the elevator bank in the lobby. She watched, transfixed, on the elevators' lights as the cars descended. Ding! She jumped, even though she'd anticipated it down to the second. The doors swooshed open, disgorging weary bankers who quickly untangled themselves and fled toward their respective exits to freedom and their real lives. L. J. had parked a rental car in a visitor's spot for her own hasty escape but for a different reason.

She stood in a blind spot missed by the cameras, but still wore a slouchy new hat, and clothes that nobody would recognize. She focused on the express elevator, dedicated to the fourth and fifth-floor executives who deserved special treatment. Underlings, like herself, understood from day one that they should wait their turn with the general population or take the stairs. That wasn't covered during orientation, but non-officers *knew*.

Sometimes, for spite, she took the executive ride the way college freshmen strolled senior walk. As long as you look like you belonged, nobody questioned you. Still, it angered her. She'd learned it the hard way when a senior officer, seeing her struggling with a huge stack of files, whispered conspiratorially, "Come on. I won't tell," and ushered her into the express. The interior was fitted with polished brass rails, carpeted walls, acoustical ceiling tiles, and classical music.

Today she watched the numbers zoom from five while the other elevators stopped at every floor. Ding! Todd Henning emerged first, followed by other suits. He paused, chatting with them briefly—a gathering of the fraternity elite. Hands were shaken, shoulders clapped, manly waves exchanged as the executive officers disbursed. Henning lingered. If what she'd been told to expect was happening, he'd be waiting for—ding! And there she was.

They grinned at each other and exchanged a few words. The beautiful people, far too correct to share a touch or quick kiss. She read his lips—you ready? And they entered the corridor that led to the rear parking lot. L. J. dialed, and to a man's "*yes?*" she responded, "Incoming." Clicking off without waiting for a reply, she strode through the front door to her rental.

L. J. was vaguely aware of a thumping noise, and as it grew louder recognized the source—a helicopter that must belong to Channel 8 News or the weather channel. Maybe the soldiers from Fort Indiantown Gap were out on maneuvers. She chirped her key fob, slid into the rental, and glided from the parking lot for the last time into the life she deserved.

As Kingsley and Todd traversed the corridor that led to the rear lot, his cell phone rang. "Dude!" Randall's voice erupted so loudly that Todd didn't need to put him on speaker. "Barrie and I have a big surprise for you. Meet us in the front parking lot."

"We're parked out back. We were just about to leave for dinner. Why don't we swing around front and pick you guys up?"

Kingsley shouted, "We want to hear all about your trip."

"Leave your car; just cut back through the building. We have a surprise for you." Todd and Kingsley exchanged puzzled looks and shrugged.

"Okay. Just give us a few minutes to ditch our stuff and we'll be right there."

"A new car?" Kingsley guessed. "Hey! You know something, don't you? Or you guessed."

Todd held up his hand. "I cannot tell a lie, so I'll just keep quiet."

The dealmaker maneuvered into the perfect position to aim the remote through his front windshield. Arriving with fifteen minutes to spare, his presence went unnoticed, his only observers being a pair of mourning doves pecking the asphalt for morsels to eat. Suddenly his quarry emerged from the building.

Todd Henning held the door by the crash bar to enable her to precede him. Which she did. He was carrying a briefcase in his left hand, hers in her right, while he guided her by her right shoulder. They would pass, from left to right, through his field of vision, one hundred fifty feet below him, in exactly the number of seconds he could now count with the stopwatch in his head.

As the pair stepped off a third of the distance across the hundred-foot lot, a large white van pulled up beside the dealmaker, blocking the view of his target. Aw, shit! He was entirely too pumped to abort. The van's driver opened, boots hitting the pavement without him killing the engine. The dealmaker stole a peek through the van's right-side window. No passenger and the side-view mirror wasn't angled toward him.

He counted the footsteps his target must be making and listened—hard—through his cracked windows. Another thirty seconds…

Todd's phone rang again. "Forget dumping your stuff. Come now or I'll be in big trouble. There's a cop turning into the lot, and I'm giving illegally parking a new name."

"You double parked?"

"Worse. Now! Double time it, dudes."

Todd threw his head back and laughed. "I get it. About face! Go! Go! Go!" Grabbing her elbow he hustled her toward the back door.

Five, four, three, two, one, ignition. The dealmaker eased down the button, but nothing happened. "Aw, shit!" he exploded, squeezing his thumb hard on the button.

Todd's SUV exploded in a fireball—metal, glass, and debris raining on a fifty-foot radius, rocking and burning two other cars in the vicinity. Kingsley and Todd, who had just stepped into the corridor, gaped in horror at the inferno that had been Todd's SUV. Randall barked orders into Todd's ear. "Get out here! Now!"

They ran through the corridor, into the lobby, and through the front door toward a shiny silver Airbus. "Someone's shooting at us!" Randall screamed as shots splintered holes in the asphalt, narrowly missing the chopper. He frantically beckoned, engine thrumming, while Todd and Kingsley lunged for the opening and vaulted inside.

Barrie tumbled into the co-pilot seat, commanding that they buckle up, as Randall lifted off. He angled low, hidden by the boomerang-shaped building, heading south, and didn't gain altitude until he was out of range. The four peered down at the scene, the bank complex growing smaller in perspective. Randall's sharp, ex-military eye spotted muzzle flashes and the shooter, rifle in hand, lunging for an old station wagon high on the hill.

"Barrie. Call it in!"

"Which? How? I'm blanking that lesson from school," she screamed, frantically scanning the instrument panel.

"Try nine-one-one on your cell phone. Tell the dispatcher that an old navy station wagon with a terrorist-shooter on board is heading south toward Route 10. Now he's on Route 176 heading toward Morgantown or the turnpike." In a matter of minutes from their vantage points, they could see multiple responders' red, white, and blue lights pulsing through the trees. Fire engines tore into Keynote's parking lot and circled the bank.

Randall started to laugh. "What's so funny?" Todd called from the back seat."

"Barrie, cover your mike. We've been ordered to go directly to the Reading Municipal Airport, land, shut down, and wait for the police and further instructions."

"We're going to do that?"

"Not on your life. Keep talking, Barrie, as if we can't hear. Just keep reporting what you see. And tell me they're not responding. We're not letting that shooter get away."

Todd and Kingsley slid to opposite windows of the four tawny leather seats and buckled their seatbelts. "Todd, watch out for the cellphone towers and power lines that we can see from the office windows," Kingsley shouted.

"On it."

Looking down, they had a bird's eye view of route 176, the turnpike, and secondary routes that they took every day. From multiple directions, responders' vehicles, lights pulsing, looked like toys on the highways below them. Soon, another helicopter paralleled their course. Even

Kingsley could see a uniformed person gesturing orders at Randall. Some sort of universal signals, she guessed.

Randall returned a smart military salute and banked toward Keynote's parking lot where police cars intercepted them upon touchdown. "Uh oh. They look like business," Barrie giggled, betraying her glee over their first adventure with their new toy.

"I'll do the talking," Randall said, hopping to the pavement where a crowd of exiting bankers kept a safe distance from the two helicopters and patrol cars. By the time Kingsley had extricated herself from the complicated seatbelt, Randall and Todd were trading emphatic statements and gestures toward the hill and the pavement for the cops who were scribbling notes. A cloud of putrid gray smoke drifted from the rear parking lot where firemen were quelling the inferno.

As the dealmaker fled south, he was too rattled to remember where he should swap cars, and instead of taking the last exit to avoid the turnpike, he found himself approaching its entrance. He'd be prime meat, whether he chose I-76 east toward Philly or west toward Pittsburgh. He braked hard, his only recourse being a U-turn short of the toll booth to find that Morgantown exit. Used as he was to driving luxury vehicles, the balky old wagon fought his attempts to navigate the curve.

The dealmaker stomped on the accelerator and yanked the wheel, attempting to correct his miscalculations. Failing to check for oncoming traffic, he never saw the northbound tractor-trailer that was hidden by the toll booth, having taken the Morgantown exit at forty miles per hour. Thanks to E-Z Pass, the trucker had cleared the booth without slowing, counting on his forward momentum to conquer the steep uphill grade onto 176 north.

In that horrifying split second, the dealmaker grasped his mistake. He yanked the wheel while standing on the brake pedal, but it was too late. His trajectory hurtled him between the truck's cab and its trailer, which tipped onto its right side. Truck, trailer, and, station wagon toppled and smashed into the guardrail and slid down the embankment. Miraculously, the dazed trucker crawled through his shattered window and, smelling diesel fuel, scrambled to safety. What hit him appeared to the first responders to be an indistinguishable hunk of crushed metal.

ↄ◌ↄ

L. J. Zaun drove to the out-of-town community credit union with all her necessary documentation. Sometimes it paid to work at a bank, which enabled her to create a foolproof financial work-around. Okay, she was paranoid. She'd done nothing wrong. Her benefactor, on behalf of his client, had deposited her *inheritance* at the institution she chose and would continue to do so for future installments. The initial deposit, shown on her statement, was for more than she made in a year. All she'd had to do was phone an unknown number and utter one word—*incoming*. She had no idea what that meant, although the word smacked of military jargon.

She chose to ignore that the call had anything to do with her antagonists. A coincidence, no doubt. That bank and its big shots were no longer her problem. Her benefactor had supplied her with a new phone, instructing her to smash and drop her personal one in a McDonald's trash can after making that one call. But when she saw how many minutes remained, she couldn't resist calling her friends, sharing her retirement news, and arranging a little celebration party at their favorite bar. So many minutes still remained! No way was she wasting this additional benefit. She dropped it into her purse.

The next day, slightly hungover yet giddy over her

incomparable luck, she hit the road, arriving two hours later in Johnstown, Pennsylvania. Maybe after she bought that Rav4 and packed what little of her old stuff she'd keep, she'd head west. Or south. Or wherever the wind beckoned. She was free! She could imagine the breeze in her hair; the sun on her face.

For the second time in two weeks, she pulled into a customer slot at the credit union. Feeling every inch the beautiful, rich, important customer, she slid on her new sunglasses, fluffed her expertly styled and colored hair, and added a dab of lip gloss. She smoothed her lovely new outfit as she stepped from the car, balancing on shoes that cost a month's salary. She hoped every man within eyesight was drooling. L. J. lifted her chin and strode into the lobby.

Instead of approaching the teller line, she swung directly toward the assistant manager's office. The poor woman, whose fingers flew on the numeric pad while glancing back and forth to a spreadsheet, muttered to herself, frowning. L. J. cleared her throat. The woman's head jerked up, obviously startled.

"I'm so sorry. I didn't hear you. Is there something I can do for you?"

L. J. stifled a smirk as she remembered the HR mantra—*Always be gracious. Always be helpful. Always "no trouble at all," no matter how obnoxious the customer.* Well, not from L. J., ever again.

"I want to close my account and want some privacy." Not a request. A command.

"I'll be happy to help you with that, although we'll be sorry to lose your business. If there's anything we can do…"

"No. I'm leaving the country for an extended vacation after which I'll be residing out of state."

"Very well. I'd be happy to expedite your request. May I have your documents please?"

Odd. She hadn't given any thought to what denominations she'd need. Cash, of course. The balance in a cashier's check, but was that safe? Did they still make traveler's checks? The woman returned directly. "Our manager, Mr. Smith, would like a moment if you please. Just follow me."

L. J. followed the woman into a corner office, which was all right as offices go, but not like the ones her former Keynote managers occupied. Introductions made, he motioned her to a chair. "Ms. Zaun, I'm sure you know yours is an '*or*' account, meaning either of the account signatories can add or withdraw funds. The original deposit of two weeks ago was made by the other person."

"That's correct. I have my copies as well as deposit and withdrawal slips. At this time, if everything's in order, I want to withdraw the funds and close the account."

"Well, I'm sorry that you weren't informed by the other person. Yesterday he withdrew the balance and closed the account."

"What? That's impossible! He wouldn't—he couldn't! There must be some mistake. Please check again." L. J. shook so violently that the manager jumped and called for someone to bring her some water.

"I'm sorry. This must be quite a shock. Why don't you give him a call? Perhaps he transferred the funds to another bank and didn't have time to get in touch with you on short notice. Is it possible that you came to the wrong institution?" He settled his cheaters low on his nose and studied her paperwork again. "Please. Try to relax for a moment while I trace the actual transaction." He escaped.

In her gut, L. J. knew she'd been screwed.

Chapter 33

Todd and Kingsley, represented by her godfather, David Wentworth, conferenced with two detectives at their turf's polished table. Perched in the corner was a woman who was introduced as an assistant district attorney although she hadn't called the meeting. The atmosphere hovered around civil. At first, the Hennings had resisted the meeting, begging exhaustion from their harrowing experience, but the investigators kept notching up their implications until the Hennings decided to confront them.

David Wentworth hijacked the meeting the moment everyone had been introduced. "First, since my clients are under no obligation to be here, I am declining on their behalf that any portion of this meeting to be recorded." He smiled as their inquisitors nodded. "Your verbal response, if you please." This time, their agreement was audible. "Good. Go ahead with your questions. But I'll stop the proceedings if you stray into inappropriate areas." *Like accusing us of a crime, for instance,* Kingsley thought.

Kingsley studied the pair. The detective who had investigated the Purewater murder and met her at the diner was flanked by his superior. When she'd asked him to investigate the listening devices and trace their enemy's identity, his denial had been rude. Now his spiral notebook lay open, a pencil poised, but he avoided eye contact.

The lead detective spoke. "I'd like you to take a look at some photos and identify them if you can." Kingsley expected mug shots, but instead, the woman slid three 5 by 7 professional-quality color photographs across the table.

"Go ahead," Todd said to his wife.

She gasped. And tapped the first photo "That's the woman who posed as Dr. Suzanne Meade! We now believe she was part of a complicated conspiracy to force us out of our home. That man," she said, pointing to the other detective, "must have a fat file on our case, beginning with the construction project next door through the poisoning of bottled water delivered to our house. That conversation included this woman."

"And you never saw her before or since that visit to your home and you don't know who she is?"

Kingsley said, "My realtor friend…"

David Wentworth cleared his throat, frowning at her.

"I tried to find out who she was, but no. I'd never seen her before and haven't since. But I'd know her anywhere."

"And this person?" The detective tapped the other woman's picture.

"That's L. J. Zaun. She worked in my department until she resigned recently. If you want to know anything about her, I suggest you contact Shirley Granger, who is senior VP at Keynote National Bank under whom HR falls. She's had extensive dealings with this woman."

"And you?"

Huh. How much to tell her? "She reported to one of my subordinates, not directly to me, but she resented that I held a position to which she thought she was entitled. Shirley can explain the bank's hiring procedures, in which I wasn't involved."

"Did she ever express any animosity toward you?"

"I don't know how to answer that, except that I felt sorry for her and encouraged her professionally whenever possible."

Todd spoke up, pointing to the picture. "Everyone knew she was a disparately unhappy woman who cast blame on anyone whom she perceived got breaks she thought she deserved, including my wife's job. Twice."

"Why wasn't she fired?"

Kingsley said, "You need a better reason than a bad attitude. And when under pressure, she did satisfactory work. Not at the level that would have led to promotions, however."

"Were you ever concerned that she might harm you?"

Kingsley smiled. Sticks and stones. "Physically? No. Never."

"All right. Now this third photo. The man."

Kingsley nodded to Todd. "He's the one who came to our house. He's the boss of the construction job next door. I think he may own the business and/or the land. Maybe both. Even though he stopped by our house once, we never knew his real name, did we Kingsley?"

"Right. We only heard his crew refer to him as 'the boss.' And he didn't introduce himself to us by name."

"What did you learn about his project next door?"

"I think you should ask the man who leases the land to grow field corn. And also, a Dutchman—Holland, not Pennsylvania—named Liam Van Dijk. He has a greenhouse business called Hydroponic Products. We've met him and can give you his contact information."

"Are either of you familiar with a manufacturing company based in New York state? It's called…"

"No," Todd and Kingsley said in unison, then laughed. "We heard third hand that a manufacturer had an interest in the construction project, but haven't heard the company referenced by name, what they make, or anything about them."

"One more thing," the detective who had been silent asked. "Did the woman who posed as Dr. Meade leave anything with you that might have her prints?"

"No. Even dusting our house at this time would be unproductive since we just entertained a couple hundred people for a wedding reception." She thought a minute, then snapped her fingers. "Wait a minute! Our security company installed a nanny cam in our baby's bedroom that incorporates the hall around his nursery. Ever since the kidnapping, we've told them to keep all footage—forever. It requires motion activation. I know that sounds paranoid, but that imposter passed in front of our child's door on our tour. The camera might have seen her. I'll call them if you like."

"Dear, would the camera capture any private moments of you and Todd that you wouldn't want reviewed?" her godfather asked.

"I thought of that when I was nursing. And since we know the camera's line of vision, we can avoid it, even in the hall."

Todd asked, "But if you already have this excellent picture, what more do you need to identify her?"

"Her name. And, other than requesting a tour of your home and finding her photo among a person-of-interest's effects, without identification we can't tie her to a criminal conspiracy. Can you? Other than misrepresenting herself to get a peek inside your house?"

"Stupid me. I welcomed her by her supposed name. We even thought, afterward, that she was a realtor drumming up business."

Kingsley mugged at Todd, her expression conveying *told ya.*

The meeting appeared to be ending. Kingsley said,

"We've been trying to unravel why anyone would try to harm us or force us out of our house when there must be dozens of similar properties on the market. I kept thinking about my grandmother's potato sack theory. Pull the wrong thread, and you need to unravel the stitches, one loop at a time. But pull the right thread, and the whole chain unravels. This case always came back to that construction project next door. That's the right loop. Maybe we saw—or they thought that we saw—something that threatened their business."

The assistant DA, who had been silent, grinned. "Potato sack theory. Great metaphor." With a glance at an incoming message, she jumped to her feet, nearly toppling her chair. "Nice meeting you. Good luck." With a brief nod to the detectives, she swept from the room, her footsteps clattering toward the elevator. The detectives, who had risen as if to stop her, stepped into the corridor. Kingsley seized the opportunity and, focusing her phone directly over the photos, captured them. By the time the detectives returned, she had resumed her seat, affecting a bored expression.

Kingsley was gathering her purse when something hit her. "I almost forgot. There's an important connection, and my brain just pulled the right thread. The real Dr. Suzanne Meade was attacked to enabled the imposter to take her place and do *whatever* inside our house. The Harrisburg police have the details, and I have Dr. Meade's contact information.

"Around the same time as her attack, I'd been reviewing every loan application I had turned down, looking for anyone who might want to hurt us. That seemed unrelated at the time. Or so I thought. But when the real Suzanne's brain began healing and her memory came back, she called to warn me. She'd remembered details of her abduction—the frigid air, the sound of the river, and her attackers talking. The older guy had said, 'Miles, this pays your debt.

I'll tell the old man.' And the younger guy said, 'What about the Hennings?' And the first guy said, 'Not your problem. Geraldine's on it.'"

"Geraldine. That name, your photo, and your security tapes might help identify her. Who was this Mike?" the detective asked.

"Ermilio Soriano, a.k.a. Miles and sometimes Mike. According to a fellow officer at the bank, his mother's godfather is an alleged 'Teflon don.' He owns a manufacturing business. Chemicals, I think. I turned Mike down for a business loan. Does that help?"

David Wentworth interrupted. "You'll need a search warrant for their security tapes. Kingsley, please provide them with the exact date and time of that woman's visit."

"Security technicians! Of course!" Kingsley laughed with delight. "Don't worry about dusting for prints on surfaces. Get that bogus circuit board that gave someone unhampered access to our house. Our security technician found it in the console and replaced it. His hands were gloved. I had him drop the fake device into a sandwich bag and told him to hang onto it for the police. Since we never involved the police, I bet the security company still has it. Add that to your warrant. And the plumber—he replaced a part that enabled the gas leak. I'll give you his contact information too."

"Anything else, Ms. Drew?"

Kingsley ignored his sarcasm. "I'm thinking. No. Not at the moment, unless you know something about ghosts or a mid-1800s double murder."

The detective sighed. "You have ticked off some dangerous people."

"They tried to murder my family and my dog. This is war."

ℰℐℰℐ

Kingsley recognized the detective's name with whom she'd now had three unpleasant encounters. When he introduced himself, she laughed. "You again! What is it this time?"

"Ms. Henning, I thought I'd get back to you about all your potential fingerprint sources—the gas valve, the security circuit board, the listening devices. I followed up with all of your professionals. I'm afraid your perpetrator was exceptionally careful. Can you think of anything else she might have touched?"

"The entire time she was touring the house, she had her hands full—a Coach shoulder bag, a small spiral notebook in her left hand, and a pen taking notes with her right. She didn't handle anything—not even for enjoyment. You know how some people can't resist touching stuff—in stores, in people's homes, in museums, even if they shouldn't. Think of all the fingerprints on jewelers' cases and the constant need to spray and wipe them."

"Did you hand her anything to look at? Like a book, a magazine, or a business card that she didn't take?"

"I'm thinking. I'm thinking. No. I don't think so. But I let her take photographs of details she was interested in while I checked on my son, so I wasn't with her every minute. I wish I'd been a slovenly housekeeper. We had tea." She sighed. "What a pity—we had such a lovely visit." She felt sad and defrauded. "I used my best China and silverware and she drank from a teacup that she balanced on a saucer, like ladies will do. And of course I washed everything after she left."

"Tea. My grandmother had one of those fancy silver tea sets. It had a tray. Might she have touched yours?"

"No. I used two trays and put everything on that chest in the living room. She never touched either—there was no reason. I thought entertaining her in that room was a good place for her to get a sense of the house, you know, as it might have been in the old days." Kingsley smiled to herself. *Not in that room—there would be a preacher or a dead body.*

"So you washed everything. Any chance you missed something? Like a fork or spoon?"

"No. She didn't take cream or sugar, so no need for a spoon. And the rugalachs and mini blueberry muffins are finger food, so no forks. Even if she had touched it, my grandmother taught me to wash every piece of sterling that had been on the table, in case even a single grain of salt or sugar remained. That can pit the silver. Every piece was washed, and it never goes in the dishwasher."

"Sounds like a lot of trouble."

"As she always said, 'No use having something if you aren't going to enjoy it.' She did not tolerate careless handling, however."

"Did she touch the doorknob when she left?"

"No. I opened it for her. As did a couple hundred other people at our recent party."

A long pause followed. "I wish I could think of something. Anything. If only I hadn't washed the China, but after all this time, that would be silly." Another long pause. "Wait a minute—she poured for me! I'd burned my wrist. Pouring requires two hands since the teapot is heavy. One to hold the handle and one to support it. No, that's not right. She did it perfectly with one hand."

Kingsley replayed the scene in her mind. How focused she had been to be a gracious hostess to a world traveler and famous professor. And then she burned her damned hand. In her memory, she watched a re-enactment of lovely Suzanne's perfect fingers, lifting the pot, pouring, setting it down and…she fingered the flowers!

"I've got something for you. Can you come over with

your fingerprint powder? She fingered the motif."

"But you washed the dishes."

"Not dishes. China. Antique bone China. I washed the cups and saucers in warm water and mild soap, then let them air dry." She felt her excitement rise. "I did not expose the outside of the teapot to soap. I washed the inside only with a soft cloth, rinsed it, then set it on a terry towel to dry, holding it by its handle. I remember placing it upside down on the dining room table, the lid beside it. When both were dry, I put them in the China cabinet. The teapot hasn't been touched since she fingered the flowers!"

"It's a long shot…"

"Come this evening after eight. And bring some luminol with you."

♋♋

Fascinated, Kingsley watched as the technician twirled a soft brush with dark powder over the teapot's flowers. "Hey! Do the lid, too. I didn't notice, but she had to make sure it was secure before tipping the pot. If not inserted and aligned correctly, it can fall out and—disaster!" The technician did as she asked.

"Got something," he said, looking up at the detective and smiling.

"And you don't need my prints for exclusion because they're on file with the Fed and the state."

"And no one else touched it?" She grinned her response, exchanging high-fives with him.

Kingsley motioned the detective into the hall. "I've been thinking it's time we mend our adversarial relationship. How would you like to take partial credit in solving a really cold case? Like mid-1800s. If you've remembered your luminol, I'd like your CSI to inspect what may be human blood, even after all these years."

He scowled, then started to laugh. "You just can't quit, can you?"

"Come on. I'll explain as we go." The pair trooped upstairs, trailed by the technician who was game for her drama. She led him into the guest room where she and Todd had removed half the floorboards nearest the western wall. "We've inspected all sides of every board, but only the ones we've set aside have visible marks. Krick family lore says this is the murder room where a husband and wife were slashed to death. No motive, no weapon, no witnesses, no clues. If the crime took place in this room, there should have been lots of blood."

The technician stepped forward, studying the half-dozen boards leaning against the wall, then glanced into the depths above the dining room ceiling. "Hey, looks different from this angle," he joked, then squinted in concentration. "Huh—let's have a look."

Todd appeared in the doorway, loosening his tie and shedding his jacket. "I'll get the trouble light." He disappeared and returned with the cushion from a patio chez. "Here. Your bones will thank you for this."

The technician sprawled above the hole to investigate what lay beneath. "Kill the lights. The hall too." He spritzed luminol onto the lath. "I'd read that luminol was used as far back as the Lizzie Borden case in the late nineteenth century, but—when did you say this murder took place? Mid-century?" He repositioned the mat to the center of the room, repeated the procedure, then moved to the right. "Yep. The stains are blood."

"How about the boards?" Kingsley asked. "The edges, where blood would have seeped."

"If this murder were recent, no amount of scrubbing would have removed every trace from boards' surfaces. But…"

The four watched as the test proceeded. The technician

moved from board to board, finally standing and shaking his head. "What lies beneath has been protected the entire time. These boards, I'm guessing, have been exposed for too many years. Heat, cold, light, products of any and every kind. Or, it's possible that the boards were replaced."

Todd shrugged. "Maybe. The installation technique and the old wood and nails are similar to what we found downstairs, but not identical." He turned to the detective and the technician. "Then, based on the papers we found beneath the boards and the fact that a lot of blood was shed in this room, is it safe to conclude that family lore is correct—that this is a murder scene? Documents were recovered…"

"Please say you'll look into it," Kingsley said. "For the Krick family's sake. And all the former slaves who hid in this house. Please?"

The detective sighed, shaking his head. "Oh, why not. Give me the contact information, and I'll talk with the Kricks. Maybe old police files still exist. Perhaps this cold case can still be solved, although the perpetrator and the witnesses are deceased."

"Prosecuting them isn't the goal. Wonderful people buried evidence for someone to find, trusted others to reveal the truth, and carry on their mission."

The detective smiled. "A worthy undertaking if ever I've heard. I'll see what I can find."

Kingsley couldn't help herself, giving the detective an impulsive hug. "Thank you! I knew we could count on you."

Chapter 34

We got her. And her name's not Geraldine. It's Brooks Cavindish, a former US Army intelligence officer who was released from the military five years ago. Her file and the details of her separation are classified. Since then, however, confidential sources have linked her to entities that needed her special skills. She's a soldier for hire. Someone who operates under the radar for big compensation, enabling her employers to achieve otherwise *unattainable* goals."

The detective smiled, shaking his head. *A determined mother/banker, her teapot, and her outrage at some lame-ass foreman who threatened her dog? Oh why not!*

"Cavindish's movements have been followed from her visits to various banks. She'll be arrested as soon as a warrant can be secured. She just visited a travel agent. Things may move quickly if she tries to flee."

"Do you think someone gave her a heads up?"

"If she knows her employer, Albert Deal, is dead she'd would know that his records could implicate her. If I were her, I'd collect any funds that aren't secured overseas and book a flight beyond extradition. Vanish for a protracted vacation."

The following evening at seven, the flight to Zurich was called in the Philadelphia international terminal. A thin woman, once tall but now bowed by osteoarthritis, approached an airport employee for assistance. He arranged for an escort and cart to wheel her through security and check-in. That accomplished, she arrived at her gate to await her international night flight. She gave the employee a generous tip and waited near the desk where disabled fliers would receive priority boarding. First class, all the way. This bit of deception, while probably unnecessary, still gave her a thrill.

As the minutes ticked down, she longed for a top-shelf drink. There would be plenty of time for such indulgences when she arrived at her new life and whatever that held. She glanced, again, at her little gold watch and replayed favorite memories of her latest deception. Kingsley Henning's lovely tea and herself pretending to be high society. She'd pulled it off but couldn't help feeling envious of the real deal. She would have loved to linger and learned about Kingsley's background, and how people like her were created.

Another hour. She permitted herself to doze. "Brooks Cavendish?" Her name jolted her awake, but as her years of intensive training kicked into gear, she ignored the summons. Two men in gray suits, flanked by police officers, surrounded her. "Ms. Cavendish, will you come with us please." A command, not a question.

She blinked through fake tinted bifocals and continued to be unresponsive. She stared at the one who was talking as if she didn't understand English.

"Ms. Cavendish, you'll have to come with us. We're placing you under arrest."

She continued to blink, perpetuating her supposed confusion. In a time-weary croak she said, "Young man, are you talking to me? I see your lips moving, but I am quite deaf."

The arresting officer laughed. "Nice try. We've got

you."

"Help!" She warbled in an eighty-year-old voice. "These men are threatening me. Help!"

Airport security mobilized from every direction, surrounding the surprised officers who were fumbling for identification. Passengers awaiting their flights jumped to her defense and surrounded the officers and security agents. "I saw it!" A young man, who appeared to be a student, injected himself into the fray. A young couple with a baby sprang into action, separating the woman from the officers with their stroller. "These guys were threatening to harm that dear old woman."

In short order, the area became dense with travelers, anxious to dispel the monotony of their protracted delays by joining the drama. Dozens of passengers, airline personnel, and even an off-duty pilot pressed in, blocking the officers from their prey. By the time the heads of security and airport police had sorted it out, the poor old woman had disappeared.

☙❧

Two days later, Kingsley and Todd could hear background terminal noises. From the speaker, they realized Amos was in Pittsburgh with Cecelia, awaiting their flight to Detroit Metro Wayne County Airport. "Did you see the article in this morning's New York Times about your next-door neighbor?" Amos was practically bubbling with exciting news.

"Not beyond the financials. Why?"

"Big arrest. Huge! Seems those barrels of toxic waste you guys found were traced to a manufacturer named Soriano who was trying to make them disappear rather than pay the outrageous fees to dispose of them legally. A source 'close to the investigation' also linked the crime to the death of one Albert Deal, and other unidentified associates. Soriano is pleading not guilty to all charges. It goes on to mention his million-dollar bail, and that 'the crime was discovered by a rural Lancaster County homeowner whose name is being withheld by police.'"

Kingsley gasped. "That's all we need."

"Gotta go," Amos said. "They're calling our flight—finally. There's been multiple delays. Something about the weather in Atlanta causing a ripple effect."

Kingsley resumed breathing. "Amos, speaking of that crime, I'm texting you a BOLO—a picture of the woman who posed as a history professor to access our home. I sneaked the shot when the detectives interviewing us got called away momentarily."

"And if I see her hanging in Michigan?"

Kingsley laughed. "Why, you just phone our pain-in-the-ass detective who calls me Ms. Drew. I'm sending her photo and his contact information—just for fun."

Amos and Cecilia checked their roller bags at the plane for the overbooked flight. He followed her down the pathetically narrow aisle to their seats in the belly of the jet. Thank god for small mercies, he'd snagged an aisle seat, which would give his long legs room to stretch. Tiny Cecilia fit the center seat with room to spare, and a petite grandmother by the window reinforced their luck. They sat. And they waited.

Finally, the pilot's voice came over the intercom expressing apologies—again—for the unavoidable delay. "That's one lucky dude," a fellow passenger muttered, as a breathless passenger was granted last-minute entry. Amos glanced at the newcomer who appeared to be negotiating unsuccessfully for a first-class seat. Tall and thin, Amos recognized the US Army uniform and overheard the attendant address him as *major*.

Amos opened his emails, and having exhausted them,

turned his attention to text messages. His wife sent him a goofy photo, asking if he'd remembered to bring an S— surprise—for their daughter. "And for you, and no clues," he texted back. He scrolled through birthday reminders and read answers to texts he had sent. Finally, he opened Kingsley's promised photo. The woman was gorgeous. Pretty as any he could recall seeing. He would remember. It was the eyes. They seemed to sparkle like old-fashioned tinsel.

He looked up at the exact moment the major scanned the seats for the crumb of a seat he had been tossed. Two things hit Amos simultaneously. The hat. Wasn't he supposed to remove it indoors and tuck it under his arm? And those eyes! They were unforgettable. Imagine two people having those magnificent orbs, and these being wasted on a man. At that moment, as the guy was still eight rows ahead of him, his sleeve caught on a lady's armrest, lurching him backward. "Sorry," he muttered in the highest-pitched voice Amos had ever heard from a man.

"Please take your seats quickly and fasten your seatbelts. And turn off your electronic devices. We are cleared for takeoff."

Something forced Amos to disregard her directive and take another look at Kingsley's photo. It was her! The major turned as if to head toward the front of the plane. Amos stabbed the detective's number into his phone and babbled Kingsley's message. When asked a third time to repeat, he forced himself to enunciate. "Responding to BOLO. Geraldine is on Delta flight leaving Pittsburgh International for Detroit Metro Wayne County Airport *now!* Repeating…Geraldine on board, dressed as a male army major."

An eternity passed. The major continued to argue with the attendant, apparently not taking no for an answer. He pointed toward the cockpit, which was locked for security purposes. The attendant raised her voice, enabling Amos to hear her say something about the door being locked; that returning to the terminal at this point was not permitted. Amos scrutinized the face. There was no doubt about it.

The attendant said, "Excuse me a minute," then took a few steps toward the cockpit door. The major attempted to follow until a male attendant erupted from his jump seat and extended his arm with a clear message. *An Air Marshall*, Amos guessed. "Please take your seat. We're cleared to taxi to the runway." The jet's engines roared as the plane began backing from the gate. Amos glanced out the window where a ground crewman, his demeanor calm, communicated to the pilot with long orange wands.

Another attendant, who had been stationed near the rear of the plane, appeared at Amos's side, giving him a stern nod toward his cellphone. "You can use it in airplane mode after we're airborne," she said and stood over him until he shut it down. *Please, just get underway and let someone else deal with her when we land in Michigan.*

Just as quickly as the roar had begun, the engines cut back, halting the jet's forward momentum. Something was happening, and Amos suddenly felt cold. From his vantage point beyond Cecelia's window, he could see stairs being rolled into position and personnel in various uniforms jogging up the steps. In a flash, the door was opened, and security poured into the aisle.

The major, startled, pulled a weapon from out of nowhere and took aim. "Stop right there or I'll shoot!" she screamed, aiming at the men, backing up incrementally until she came abreast of the seat in front of Amos. Without lifting his foot, he slid his smooth leather-soled shoe into the aisle. As she backed up, he jerked his leg upward, tripping her, which sent the gun flying as she tumbled onto her back. Several passengers in aisle seats behind Amos jumped up and pounced on the major while others scrambled to safeguard the weapon.

ოელი

Kingsley vented her anger at the detective. "Who told the press about our location? If you ever, EVER, bring the press to my doorstep again, I'll make your life miserable."

The detective couldn't help laughing. "You are something else. I have no control over the press, but I promise, they didn't hear it from me—and they won't. I'll keep your secret. Now—about the arrest of Brooks Cavindish. Would you care to enlighten me how I'm supposed to explain my exceptional coup?"

"Simple. You 'received an anonymous tip'—which is true—that 'an armed female terrorist posing as a US Army major infiltrated a commercial airline for clandestine purposes.' And, 'thanks to sharing the tip, a national emergency was averted within minutes.' How does that sound? You did not, if you recall, ignore the stranger's tip as a hoax, but instead brought security running. Just take a bow and some credit. You did the right thing when timing was crucial."

"And what do I owe you in return?"

"Just do your job. Keep the crazies at bay. And never, ever, mention us to the press."

"You're that sensitive…"

"I could tell you the stories of my life under a microscope, starting when I was a child, but all I want now is peace for my family and loved ones. Period."

"Ms. Kingsley—it's a deal. And thank you for trusting me. You could have told your friend to call 911 or anyone else that you know, but you trusted me instead."

"I detect a decent guy under all that bluster."

ოელი

"What's bothering you, K?" She'd been so engrossed flipping through her prayer book, Bartlett's Familiar Quotations, and small volumes of poetry that she didn't hear him enter their bedroom. She took in his handsome face, day-end and responsibilities weary, after hours of fine-tuning his keynote speech for a bankers' symposium. She patted her side of the bed. He sat.

"I've been stalling about putting the guestroom back together. We need to decide what to do about the floorboards, like how to preserve them. Even after everything we've learned and after following the story to its rightful conclusion, something still feels unfinished. That it's too soon."

"Are you uneasy about the bloodstains on the lath? We'd spoken about raising the dining room ceiling to its original height. We could…"

"No. The joists would have to be cleaned as well, and that would involve major surgery. I'm troubled about the cold spot that encouraged—even lured me—to probe. I still don't believe we have a ghost, but I sense the presence of a benign spirit. A *being* that's compelled to linger, trapped by the horrific events that took place, waiting for someone to expose the truth, and a need to protect us."

She glanced at the array of books on the quilt. "I'm looking for something that says, 'It's all right to go now.' And, 'Your work here is finished.' Or simply, 'Thank you and God bless you.' I'm drawn to passages from our Book of Common Prayer's burial service, but that should be read by a priest or lay minister at the time of death. A chant I sang as a child in our choir had a phrase about 'let thy servant depart in peace.' That turned out to be the wrong context."

"Have you considered writing something yourself to say, think, pray, even sing when you feel drawn to this presence?"

"I suppose I could close myself in the room, light a candle, sit on the rug, and let my thoughts flow." She smiled at the séance-like image. When he didn't object, she let the idea flower. "Sometimes Grammy's words came to me unbidden when I was in crisis, but I don't believe she speaks from beyond the grave. Rather, that I had internalized what she might have said. That love passes the vale. As long as someone remembers and cares, they still exist."

"And Amos Krick's family and his friend Cecilia will try their best to ensure that happens for those whose ancestors passed through here. I've been thinking about the old cemetery and your invitation for the Krick family to have a reunion here in the fall. The descendants could have an adventure locating the markers. Then later, once we're sure of the boundaries, we could install one of those quaint wrought-iron fences and a gate around it. What do you think?"

"I think they'd love it. I'd hate to have an abandoned cemetery on our property and not honor it. Let's propose it. You do realize we won't find marked graves of any freedom-seekers. That would have been dangerous. This stop had to be kept a secret."

"Let's pray they all made it and lived to tell their stories to their descendants who had remarkable lives."

Todd gestured to the books and writing materials that encircled her. "Maybe what you're reading is meant to inspire you, rather than something to read to someone else. You might ask our priest. Maybe there are prayers for old souls and dedicating old cemeteries."

She chuckled. "We Episcopalians aren't very good at making up prayers. I always felt it didn't count unless it was in the BCP. Or something supplemental that priests kept on their bookshelves."

"Give it some time. There's no rush putting the room

back together." He rose from the end of the bed. "Why don't I leave you to it? I'll be in the library touching up my speech, but you can join me if you'd like to be my audience." He paused at the door and turned. "Just don't expect a rubber chicken dinner."

Chapter 35

Todd drew the line over Billy's head, who jumped back to admire the mark. Kingsley and her parents applauded the occasion, even though Labor Day was weeks beyond his turning two and a half. "Our Valentine baby is growing up," Kingsley lamented, torn between celebrating the milestone and relinquishing his babyhood.

"How many Kricks are you expecting?" her mother asked.

Kingsley laughed, hands raised in supplication. "Somewhere between one hundred fifty and two hundred. You would not believe how excited and organized the Krick tribe has been. Forty second cousins took responsibility for organizing their branches of the family and have coordinated everything from travel to historical records to contact information. Some are extending the trip to visit the other side of their families or historical venues like Gettysburg."

"What about accommodations?"

"The families reserved blocks in nearby motels but loved the idea of the kids camping in the barn."

"You're copying our Alderson family reunions…"

"Exactly, Dad. We don't need that big white tent since we have the barn. I did rent a portable restroom. A bit fancy for the country, with two stalls and a vanity, but I'd worried about having only two and a half baths. Todd rigged the outdoor shower—you know the kids will get filthy, digging for salamanders and crayfish in the creek."

"And here comes the first caravan," Todd said, heading outside to direct traffic as an RV, two vans, and several cars pulled into a makeshift extension east of the driveway. A teenage cousin hopped out to shepherd young arrivals toward the barn with their bedrolls, guitar cases, and duffels.

"What's on the agenda?" Sarah asked

"Welcoming and touring as folks arrive. A picnic and bonfire this evening. Amos encouraged anyone with kids to let them experience a sleep-over in the barn, which was his family's tradition. Sunday noon, potluck meal, which the family is providing, after which the cemetery dedication. Then we'll barbeque, have a bonfire with smores and roasting marshmallows for kids of all ages. By late Sunday evening, everyone will be leaving."

If Kingsley had fretted about whether this reunion would be successful, her fears dissolved quickly. Older kids took younger cousins under their wings, and games materialized on the lawn. Families who met in person for the first time threw themselves into sharing family stories. Coolers of food and goodies were stashed in the basement freezer and fridge, and teens toted snacks and drinks to the barn.

By Sunday noon, nearly two hundred people streamed through the Henning's foyer where the meal was arranged on adjoining card tables. They piled food on paper plates and exited to lawn chairs and blankets on the back lawn. The kids gobbled their food, then were off to chase butterflies, play ball and tag, hunt crayfish, and see if they could swim in the creek before somebody yelled.

"Where's O'Malley?" Kingsley asked Todd.

"In the middle of that group of kids, having the time of

his young doggie life."

"You don't think he'll take off…"

"Not with all that attention, to say nothing of food."

Amos, who had brought a portable mike and amplifier, called for attention. His first business was *housekeeping*. Did everyone sign the register? Were bio sheets completed? Was someone assigned to know where the kids were at all times? Nods of compliance repeated throughout the gathering.

"Now, family news." He read a list of births, weddings, and deaths from recent years. "And for the best news of all." He waited until he had everyone's undivided attention. "Officially, there is no ghost." Everyone laughed, sighed, or booed. "But seriously, you do know we kids were barred from *that room*, enjoyed scaring the little ones, and dared the teens to breach the lock. I'm honored to announce that the murder has been solved. And no, it wasn't by one of our family."

Silence. Then murmurs and speculation.

"A detective friend did some exhaustive research for old police records, media, and crime sprees of that period. Evidently, bounty hunters tracked and killed runaway slaves, even targeting freed slaves who had papers, just for the money. In this house, your ancestors maintained a stop on the underground railroad.

"Evidently, they were discovered and for that, they were murdered one Sunday morning when everyone else was at church. Important documents have been discovered under the floorboards telling the slaves' stories, which we'll share as they are compiled. By the way, folks, make very, very sure we have your current contact information if you want the details."

That brought murmurs of surprise and appreciation.

"And now, the Right Reverend Michael Krick, our retired bishop from Michigan, will ask the blessing. Bishop

Mike, if you will…"

The family grew instantly quiet. "The Lord be with us…" he intoned.

"…And also with you…" they responded.

"Let us pray." The bishop then blessed their reunion and the food they were enjoying.

Amos Krick took the mike "While you enjoy this magnificent feast, I'll describe this afternoon's labor of love. Since the earliest Kricks settled this land in the 1700s, your ancestors have been buried in a long-forgotten family cemetery. Nobody has been interred there for at least one hundred fifty years, the creek has meandered, the land has been farmed, and the graves forgotten.

"If you glance north, beyond the creek, you'll see four tall metal poles with flapping white ribbons that delineate the boundary that appears to be fifty feet square. We're asking our youth, and anyone else who wants to participate, to locate as many graves as you can. You might find toppled or broken headstones or half-buried footstones. Most will be worn smoothed by exposure, their names illegible. If you find stones beyond the poles, please let us know that too.

"When you find one, call out. We'll mark it with a rod and flag. I had worried that this might be viewed as a treasure hunt—a lark. But we must respect that this is your ancestors' final resting place."

"If I may?" The bishop asked, reaching for the mike. He cleared his throat. "Your archdiocese reports that no records survive as to whether the original cemetery was consecrated, or if subsequent burials were attended by clergy. That's understandable, given the travel restrictions of the era. I shall therefore consecrate our cemetery as if it were never done.

"I'll coordinate with your diocese—there's more paperwork today than in William Penn's time." That brought a chuckle. "Our service today will be more informal than if we were in a churchyard, but consecrating this ground is just as important. One of the ladies—yes, there she is flapping some papers—duplicated service leaflets for your participation. In place of acolytes, vestry, priests, and a choir, Amos and the family elders will lead the procession down the dirt path to the site."

With their meal completed, the family proceeded across the bridge and gathered at the edge of the cornfield. The bishop positioned himself near the cemetery's center where a circle of waist-high weeds had been cleared. As he opened his *1914 Book of Offices*, a hush settled over the congregation. Even the children stopped chattering. A gentle breeze rattled the drying cornstalks, and redwing blackbirds circled the fields.

"Let us pray." The Bishop's baritone carried with grace and emotion, turning their setting into a big green cathedral. Prayer by prayer, and with enthusiastic responses, the touching service continued. The Bishop concluded with a benediction suitable for graves in unconsecrated ground—

"O merciful God, with whom the death of Thy Saints is precious, and who hast taught us in Thy Holy Word that the bodies of the faithful are members of Christ and temples of the Holy Ghost, and that having been sown in weakness, they will be raised in power; We humbly beseech Thee to sanctify these Graves to be a peaceful resting-place for the mortal remains of our dear brothers and sisters here departed; and grant, O Lord, that they, with all those that are departed this life in Thy true faith and fear, and are fallen asleep in Christ, may attain to the resurrection of the just, and may have the full fruition of perfect bliss and everlasting glory, both in body and soul, in Thy heavenly kingdom, through Him who is the Resurrection and the Life, who died, and was buried, and rose again for us, and who now liveth and reigneth with Thee and the

Holy Ghost, One God, world without end. Amen."

ⲉⲟⲉⲟ

Elders meandered back to the yard while the kids tore into the headstone hunt. "Over here!" a young voice shrilled from the far reaches of the plot. "Got one!" another kid called. In a remarkably short time, dozens of rods were inserted, their streamers fluttering in the breeze. Much to Kingsley's delight, the elder teens and young adults snagged hoes, shovels, rakes, claws, and wheelbarrows from the barn and began attacking the overgrown weeds and leveling the ruts left by years of farming.

Todd distributed heavy-duty elbow-length gloves, describing poison ivy in intricate detail. Cleared circles emerged in orderly rows around ancient stones. Among the weeds, toppled headstones were unearthed, some face down for so long that their inscriptions were protected.

"We need brushes. And brooms," one of the teens declared, assuming the job of stone cleaning supervisor. Soon the site resembled an archeological dig as they worked with painstaking care. Thousands of photos were shot. The official matriarch, flush with excitement, braved the site, flapping a sepia-colored cemetery photograph encased in plastic that she had brought from her family's album. Two grandsons carried her over the ruts while she scrutinized the layout and finally pointed. "There's my great-grandpa!"

With that point of reference, Kricks who had visited as children began narrowing their personal searches. Kingsley and Todd slipped away, leaving them to their personal journeys. When the photo op ended, the young workers gave a celebratory whoop, stripped to their underwear, and jumped into the creek.

"Hot day like this? All that hard work? Had to happen,"

Todd said, laughing and shaking his head.

"Should we get them towels or something?"

"They'll sort themselves out. Besides, it's just family."

"Speaking of which, where is our son?"

"Your dad set up the sprinkler for the little kids, and it's being well supervised. You have, I might add, one very wet dog."

A perfect evening carried a subtle reminder that summer's days were numbered. Sunset came early, and the fire felt good. The kids, hoping to find fireflies, were disappointed until someone substituted flashlight tag and a watermelon-seed spitting contest. For the youngest, one sleepover in the barn was enough. It was whispered that the teens had smuggled in beer for later, but no one was confirming or denying.

"Thank you so much for giving us a memorable experience." Amos's words brought the group to attention as the kids toasted marshmallows. "We are declaring you official members of the Krick family. And we want to give you something special to commemorate the occasion." He handed each a heavy package. "Go ahead. Open them, but don't drop them on your feet."

A beautiful plaque, suitable for mounting on stone, read—*House of Henning.* Underneath the word *Established* was the date they were married and bought their forever home. The second gift held a framed copy of the original land grant certificate that all Kricks had in their homes.

Kingsley choked, staring at the beautiful gifts, and stuttered a reply. "Thank you for sharing your family and legacy. I hope this is just a beginning. You're welcome any time."

"Well, someone needs to come weed the cemetery," one of the teens quipped.

"We plan to erect a fence and gate around the

perimeter," Todd said.

"Todd, the family discussed your idea, and we insist on covering the expense, including a fellow who cleans gravestones for cemeteries. And, you might consider, if we can provide the provenance, putting your home on the historic registry."

"I have a question about what you learned from the tombstones," Amos said, addressing the kids. "What surprised you? Did you feel an emotional attachment to any of them?"

A little girl, about nine, flapped her hand as if she were in school. "I expected to find lots of old dudes. But the babies! One little marker that's broken in three said 'unborn daughter.' And a matching pair had parents' names with 'infant son' and 'infant daughter.' But they died three years apart. That made me cry."

"The contest! Who won the contest?" a little cousin shouted.

Amos laughed, holding up a list. "Well, all of you did. Great work, folks. The object of the contest was to find the clearest, oldest family marker. And the winner is—drum roll please—Mary Elizabeth Krick from Pittsburgh, Pennsylvania. Mary, tell us what you found."

The little girl jumped to her feet. "I didn't find any old ancestors, but I did find this really great stone. It has an angel and a name carved into it, but it had mud ground into the name. So I got water from the creek and a brush and cleaned it up. And it's so beautiful. But there's no last name or a date."

"What does it say?" Amos asked.

"'Rebecca 5.' That's all. Like she's an angel who was five years old."

"I have a question then," one of the teen girls asked her tentative voice mingling with the crackling fire. "Does anyone have a Rebecca on their family's list?" There was silence.

Finally Amos said, "We'll check the records and let you know."

Kingsley said nothing but remembered *Rebecca 5* among the names on the papers they'd found beneath the floorboards. A very little girl, found in their cemetery, without a last name. Well, she's ours now. Might she be the spirit? Kingsley considered making that leap and might if only she could believe.

Chapter 36

She sat cross-legged on the cushion that remained on the murder room floor. Dozens of curious Kricks had oohed, aahed, or immersed themselves in the room's aura. Nobody mentioned a cold spot or imagined a presence. But this Sunday evening with everyone gone, Kingsley absorbed its wonder alone. It was time. She lit a lantern, trying to duplicate the 1850s ambiance. Had a little five-year-old named Rebecca died in this room? If so, why wasn't her last name and date on her marker?

What would this caring, committed family do if one of the fleeing children was desperately ill, perhaps with no parents? They'd hide her and tend to her lovingly as well as they could with the primitive home remedies of that era. And, when she passed, they'd continue to hide her existence among their own family members.

Whether she said it or thought it, Kingsley uttered the Lord's prayer, the twenty-third psalm, and then cleared her mind, waiting for a heart-felt message to surface. "Rebecca? Are you there? I hope you know, somehow, that what you have shared will be a blessing to so many people. But your work is done here. Thank you for saving my family. It's all right to leave. I promise. Everyone will be fine."

She wasn't a minister, and didn't know the boundaries of sacrilege, but added, nevertheless—"Go in peace."

Momentarily, she sensed a shift in the air.

That night, Kingsley slept soundly until the alarm beeped. The birds were rejoicing mid-chorus, and sunshine splashed a path across her quilt. No dreams, no ghosts, no calls to action. Yawning and stretching, she paddled to the guest room, peered in, and was surprised by how normal it looked. Just another old room in serious need of decorative touches. She entered, her bare feet touching every floorboard, now set temporarily in place. She paused where the cold spot had radiated and waited. It was gone. Completely. In fact, the room emitted a welcoming warmth.

જીજી

Kingsley couldn't stop reviewing the snippets of conversation with the Krick family. "Imagine, having so much family. I'm the only child of an only. If it weren't for Billy, I would have been *it*; the end of the line. Now that you know the rigors of forty-year-old fatherhood, do you feel young enough to enlarge our family?"

Todd grinned. "I'm game if you are, but I'm not willing to sacrifice you by trying. Your doctor said you were lucky after the miscarriage you suffered when Andy was killed. He said…"

"Billy was a miracle. A blessed fluke. We've counted our blessings every day. But my doctor says there's nothing to prevent me from having more healthy babies.

Todd grinned. "Okay. Sounds like you've already made up your mind. Just how many more do you propose?"

She held up two fingers. "Around April."

Todd dropped the lawn chairs he'd been toting from the yard en route to the basement and swept her into a hug. "How long have you known? And why didn't you say something?"

"Since Friday. But this weekend was theirs, and I didn't

want to divert their attention. Or have anyone hovering or feeling they were putting me out. Now—how do you feel about repurposing the murder room?"

"Regardless of how we divvy up bedrooms, we need to banish that name. After that, one thing at a time."

﮼

Todd, Kingsley, and Billy accepted their Amish neighbor Jacob's invitation to their son and daughter-in-law's housewarming and barn-raising picnic. The renter's old frame house wore a fresh coat of white paint, and green blinds half-covering the windows. Pots of geraniums adorned the steps where one day little children would play. Old corn stubbled had been plowed under to plant winter wheat. Picnic benches, set under hundred-year-old oaks, groaned with delectable food placed by women who beamed welcoming smiles to the Hennings. Beyond the house, horses with buggies tied to rails flicked their tails, oblivious to the festivities.

Billy spotted their neighbors' kids and ran off to play with them. Jacob hurried to greet them. "Welcome," he said, pumping their hands. "Thank you for making this happen. Land is so dear, and this location? It is a blessing. Thank you for influencing the bank to accept our offer."

Todd demurred. "I did nothing except bring a qualified buyer to their attention. I'm so glad it worked out."

Shortly, the young couple approached them. "Danka," the husband said as his diminutive bride blushed.

"I have a wedding present for you," Todd said, handing them an envelope. "Go ahead. Open it." They scanned the document with puzzled expressions. "Our present to you, our new neighbors, is the deed to what we call Dogleg Lane, the little bit of acreage that connects your property to the road. This means you won't be land-locked or indebted to some future owner's goodwill."

The husband was so taken aback, he didn't know quite what to say except stumble his thanks. She ushered Kingsley to the picnic benches to join the ladies who bubbled over the exciting news. Across the meadow, dozens of men and boys in suspendered pants, work shirts, and straw hats hammered feverishly to raise their new barn. Someone rang the bell mounted in the yard, and workers spilled from the scaffolding to join the feast. Once seated at his and her tables, all bowed their heads in silent prayer. Nothing in Kingsley's experience equaled family tradition.

Epilogue

Civil cases settled faster than anyone expected. A bank foreclosed on the two tracts of land east of the Hennings. The crop farmer, anxious to retire to Florida, had no interest in buying it. He harvested his last crop, packed up his camper, and split, enabling Jacob to purchase the land cheap.

Once the DER certified the soil toxin-free, thanks ironically to the impregnable construction of the drums, all trace of the former enterprise vanished. The eleven acres fronting the lane were sold to a Mennonite farmer to expand his nursery business. Todd and Kingsley joyfully anticipated that they would be surrounded by farms for the foreseeable future.

As the criminal cases trundled through the courts, Kingsley and Todd lost interest except for occasional calls to testify, which rarely materialized. They read media accounts about little guys, like the foreman and the arsonist, either ratting out their bosses or taking pleas for reduced sentences. The chemical manufacturer, while out on bail, filed for bankruptcy and left his subordinates and shareholders to deal with the fallout, then fled the jurisdiction. A brief note in an obscure publication noted his death by unidentified perpetrators.

Liam Van Dijk had quite enough of the Yanks and focused his resources on computerized windmill technology.

Insurance covered his ill-fated investment in hydroponic gardening.

Randall Shannon and his bride, Barrie Brown, are thrilled with their new baby, an airbus helicopter, for their private and business aviation clients. In gratitude for their success, the pair are adding pro bono opportunities for emergency medical transport and search-and-rescue missions. As for babies of the human variety, neither was saying nor was anyone asking. Barrie is committed to remain as Keynote National Bank's controller, to ensure that her best friend Kingsley's life doesn't become too dull. She continues to hone her lock-picking skills.

O'Malley maintains the upper paw in ways dog lovers would appreciate. Pandora is weighing her options, having been placated with a new carpeted tree. A truce of sorts is holding for now.

The End

ACKNOWLEDGMENTS

A resounding thank you for your encouragement as I slogged through the Covid isolation at my Mac. You've bolstered and humbled me. I hope the latest Trust adventure inspires, amuses, and mystifies.

I cannot adequately thank all the people who patiently answered my questions, corrected my misconceptions, and provided details, color, and technical information. Even in writing fiction, one cannot just make it all up. I am grateful to everyone who double-checked details to ensure my work's accuracy.

I'm specifically indebted to the following professionals for sharing their time, expertise and saving me from making egregious errors: Angel Cabrera, Criminal Investigator, retired, Reading, PA Police Department; Stephen A. Hoare, Sr., Capt. USAF and Civilian Airline Transport Pilot; Daniel W. Hughes, NCIDQ, Senior Technical Design Coordinator; Elaine D. Hughes, DVM; The volunteers and staff of the Conrad Weiser Homestead, Womelsdorf, PA; Antique Auto Expert Jeff Lesher, and Tracy Lesher, *HCCA Gazette* and *Dodge Brothers Club News* Editor. Director Mark Duffy and Christopher Ann Paton, C.A., Archivist for Institutional, Research and Public Service, The Archives of the Episcopal Church; Master Gardener Priscilla Pluchinsky; *The Herbalist's Kitchen* by Pat Crocker; P D Halt; Saralyn Richard; and Sheila J. Levine, Esq.

In spite of the pandemic, the following fearlessly tackled the daunting task of converting in-person crime-writer events to Zoom conferences and webinars. I am indebted to MWA's New York Chapter; ITW; SinC; and Penn Writers. And my readers, book club buddies, friends and fellow writers who navigated the challenges to simulate normalcy. Thank you!

My publisher, Black Opal Books, deserves my enduring gratitude for their confidence in publishing my novels. I am particularly indebted to Susan Humphreys for her dedication to detail, tolerating my idiosyncrasies and myriad phone calls, and for capturing my trademark clue in her cover design. Behind the scenes, Black Opal's staff handled details and challenges with speed, grace, and humor. Bless you all.

And as always, my hero, love, and rock, Bill Hughes, who waded through early drafts and provided technical details about farming in the Pennsylvania Dutch country. Thank you for having my back every step of the way.

About the Author

Nancy A. Hughes, a native of Key West who grew up in Pittsburgh, lives with her husband in south-central Pennsylvania. Following graduation from Penn State where she studied journalism, she spent years as a business writer, specializing in media, community, and public relations for small to midsize businesses.

In recent years, Nancy turned her attention to murdering people—on paper, that is. Her focus is character-driven crime-solving mysteries, her subgenre being amateur sleuth. Her debut mystery novel, The Dying Hour, was released in 2016 by Black Opal Books. A Matter of Trust, the first in her Trust trilogy, followed in 2017, Redeeming Trust, also in 2017, and Vanished in 2018. Her latest book, The Innocent Hour was published by Black Opal in 2020.

When she isn't writing, she is devoted to shade gardening, volunteering at the VA, and spending time with family and friends.

Visit her on her website at hughescribe.com.

And, if you enjoy this book please "like" it or write a review and post it. Thank you.